DEAD END:
C I T Y   L I M I T S

DEAD END:

CITY LIMITS

AN ANTHOLOGY
OF URBAN FEAR

EDITED BY:

**PAUL F. OLSON AND
DAVID B. SILVA**

ST. MARTIN'S PRESS   NEW YORK

Production Editor: David Stanford Burr

Design by Judith A. Stagnitto

Library of Congress Cataloging-in-Publication Data

Dead end : city limits / Paul F. Olson and David B. Silva, eds.;
    foreword by F. Paul Wilson.
        p. cm.
     ISBN 0-312-06328-8
      1. Horror tales, American. 2. City and town life—Fiction.
I. Olson, Paul F. II. Silva, David B., 1950–
PS648.H6D39 1991
813'.0873808—dc20   91-20578
                                           CIP

First Edition: November 1991

10 9 8 7 6 5 4 3 2 1

CONTENTS

Don't make eye contact.

At least not in The City. In most suburbs, and especially in rural areas, it's rude *not* to make eye contact. That and a little nod comprise a validation of another person's presence. It's part of a proper greeting.

Not in The City. Eye contact is a challenge, usually met with, "Whatchoo lookin at, fukkuh?" And sometimes you're lucky if that's the limit of the response.

That's not the way it was supposed to be.

The City. It started out as a place of commerce, often growing up around a convenient natural harbor. Traders came, seeking business; workers came, seeking jobs. And either they brought their families along or they started new ones. The resultant crowding called to those whose tastes and behavior were out of step with the norms of the provinces, and so the outcasts came, seeking anonymity and others of their kind.

And the predators came, seeking victims.

The City doesn't have a lock on predators. They're everywhere. You find them in rural towns and suburban malls, and at all levels in The City, from financial district boardrooms to the subways. But predators tend to concentrate in The City. It's only logical. All predators follow herds of prey. Used to be they skulked along the periphery. Nowadays it seems they're running the herd.

As a result, The City has become a sprawling nightmare.

It wasn't always like that.

I remember my adopted city, Manhattan, in the early to mid sixties. I met it as a callow fourteen-year-old busing in from the Jersey suburbs to attend a Jesuit high school in the Chelsea district. In the morning I'd breeze through the Port Authority, grab the A train down to West 4th, where I'd transfer to the Sixth Avenue line and ride the D train up to West 16th Street, where Xavier was located. I'd come home a different route, taking the express D train up to 125th or 145th Street—the heart of Harlem—where I'd wait for an Eighth Avenue train to whisk me up to 168th Street. I'd hang out at the White Castle in Washington Heights until my bus was ready to leave for Jersey.

Was I ever hassled? Occasionally, sure. But no more than I got hassled back home in Hackensack.

Would I want to ride those routes again today, especially the one home?

No way. Not even with a fully loaded Uzi. I mean, have you seen the PA lately? Heard what's going down in Harlem?

But people do run those routes, every day. They just don't make eye contact.

The City's not all bad. Really. The arts are perhaps most alive in the city. It's where everybody who's too far out or too original or too brilliant for small-town America winds up. Plus, there's the feeling that this is where it's at, no matter what particular "it" you're referring to. This is where things are happening, where the action is, where fortunes are being made and lost, where everybody's got a chance at the brass ring if you just know where to stand when it swings by.

And then there's the excitement, the rhythm, the incessant up-tempo beat of city life. Each city has its own, with New York's undoubtedly the most frenetic. But no matter what the city, the pace is heavier and headier than that in the environs.

Some people can't handle it for more than a minute, some can't go a day without it. Some can't take it as a steady diet but do crave a fix now and again.

You've simply got to learn to watch your back. You've always had to watch your back in The City. I learned that. I came of age in my city. I learned where I could get served underage on the Bowery (and the drinking age then was only eighteen) and knew who was selling illegal fireworks in the Village or Chinatown. I learned to spot trouble coming and make a detour, to sense when a situation might be deteriorating. I became streetwise. That's always been necessary for survival.

But what I sense now is different. There's a siege mentality in The City these days. The unspoken sentiment is that it's become ungovernable. The people who can afford to are leaving; those who can't are adding extra locks to their doors and are huddling all their belongings and loved ones close around them. You don't lay anything down, you don't leave anything—or any*one*—you care about unguarded, even for a moment. At night you drag whatever you can inside your fortress—your car radio, your bike—and you chain down whatever you can't, including the trees and small shrubs in your yard. You do it because you've learned that nothing is too big or too small to steal. No crime is too low to be committed. And nothing is too trivial to kill for.

You can be killed for a fad.

Perfect example: As I sit down to write this, a news story from my city says another kid was killed last night for his 8-ball jacket. One of the local DJs has a running gag about buying 8-ball jackets as gifts for people he doesn't like. They're hot, those jackets—multicolored leather affairs with big black 8-balls centered on the back and the elbows. Wear one in the wrong neighborhood on the wrong day and you could be confronted with a demand to hand it over. Refuse, resist, you wind up dead like that kid last night. Next year, when it's passé, you'll be able to wear your 8-ball anywhere you damn well please and no one will give you a second look. But now it's like putting your life on the line.

Death by fad.

Only in The City.

Which is the only place the stories in this volume could happen. In The City. They may claim to be set in NY or Big D or LA or Chi or Frisco or Deeetroit. But that's just a cover for their *real* setting.

The City.

It embraces the best and worst of all cities. If you have your own favorite or most-loathed part of any city, you'll probably find it here. It ain't pretty, but you'll soon discover there's one thing all these stories have in common, one thing each one of them forces you to do with its city:

Make eye contact.

F. Paul Wilson
February 2, 1991

INTRODUCTION

1

An introduction can be a tricky thing. Tradition suggests that
you might find something on the meaning of horror in this
part of the book. Or perhaps something of an explanation as
to what it was the editors envisioned—in the lateness of the
night, after too many beers or Diet Cokes—as the theme of
this particular collection of original short stories. We don't
mean to disappoint you; however, we thought we'd like to do
something a little different here. Instead of tradition, we
thought we'd like to share with you some of our experiences
in putting this book together, and maybe along the way,
throw in an occasional personal observation about the status
of today's horror anthology market.

We hope you find your time here well spent.

2

It was after dark. We had gone out to a little pizza shop
around the corner, had a nice dinner, and then returned to
Paul's apartment. The World Fantasy Convention was still a
couple of days away. St. Martin's had already received the final
manuscript of our first anthology, *Post Mortem,* and seemed
genuinely enthusiastic about the book. So we sat down at
Paul's computer to brainstorm some ideas for our next one.

What we needed was a catchy "theme"—something St. Martin's would find both timely and intriguing.

(A slight digression here. How exactly the trend came about, neither of us is qualified to say. But back in 1987—and we believe it holds largely true even today—if you hoped to have one chance in a hundred of catching the interest of a publisher, you had to package an anthology in the guise of a "theme" book. This meant the stories were required to address a common issue of some sort, usually established by the compiler(s) of the anthology and agreed upon by the publisher.

There were exceptions, of course. In fact, some of the best anthologies ever produced have been exceptions. Most notably Charles L. Grant's *Shadows* and Kirby McCauley's monumental *Dark Forces*. More recently, Douglas E. Winter's *Prime Evil*, Dennis Etchison's *Cutting Edge,* and the *Masques* and *Borderlands* series. Still, these were exceptions. More commonly, if you hoped to sell an anthology to a publisher, you needed to package it in some sort of quasi-contemporary theme that would—according to the theory—make the book easier to market.

So a whole lot of folks in the horror field—the two of us included—set out to come up with ever more clever ideas for theme anthologies. In hindsight, some of these books proved to be quite successful (at least in terms of sales): *Book of the Dead* (zombies), *Blood Is Not Enough* (vampires), *Hot Blood* (sex), *Silver Scream* (movies), *Women of Darkness* (women writing horror), *14 Vicious Valentines* (Valentine's Day horror), *Hunger for Horror* (killer foods), *Stalkers* (stalkers), and on and on. Others of these anthologies . . . well, others turned out to be concepts that never quite made it to a publisher or died early deaths or in some cases are still floating around: *Square Meals* (cannibalism), *Deaders* (another zombie book, we believe), *H²Orrors* (water-oriented horror), *Road Kill* (road kill), and so many others that it might turn your stomach if we listed them all.

We mention this only because it's our humble belief that the horror field is close to going off the deep end with this non-sense. In fact, it may already be plunging headfirst into the empty swimming pool of overindulgence. In our own list of theme ideas, we came up with such significant ripples as computer horror, assassination stories, video/audio horror, and stories involving magic and witchcraft.

Enough is enough, for God's sake.

We have promised ourselves that this will be our last theme anthology—though as you'll see a little later, we still hope we might be able to do one additional book that may be miscon-strued as a theme book, though we intend it to be much more than that.

We've come to believe that what the horror genre needs most right now are short-fiction markets that leave the cre-ative process entirely to the authors. The best work in any field comes when writers are permitted to explore their own personal themes. Leave the editors to their editing, the pub-lishers to their publishing.)

3

It took nearly three years before St. Martin's finally committed to doing *Dead End: City Limits,* the book you now hold in your hands. To this day we remain uncertain why it took so long. They were enthusiastic about the reviews of *Post Mortem* and hinted that they were interested in doing another. But if the wheels of the deal didn't halt altogether, they certainly came dangerously close to a complete standstill.

Part of the problem was certainly our own. Neither of us is the type to hound an agent or a publisher. We tend to trust that the system is working the way it's supposed to work and that as long as we're patient, everything will come together in the end. We've come to wonder, however, if perhaps it isn't wiser to be the squeaky wheel in this quirky business. Publish-

ers, we've been told by more than one successful writer,
behave in ways which anthropologists will someday find
quite puzzling. We're beginning to understand that it never
hurts to give them a whack on the side of the head every once
in a while.

And perhaps we could use a little whack of our own now
and then.

Dead End: City Limits was not our first choice for this book.
We originally wanted to do a book (and still someday might)
called *Disciples.* The concept was simple enough: we'd go to
the fifteen or twenty top names in the field and ask each one
to select—and write an introduction for—an up-and-coming
writer whom he or she admires. The up-and-coming writer
would then contribute a story to the book. St. Martin's liked
the idea. But they had qualms about putting the names of
well-known authors on the cover. They were worried about
reader reaction when it was discovered that the best-known
authors had contributed only introductions. We never actually
got around to asking them why they couldn't simply leave the
big names off the cover. Besides, we knew what they would
have said: "Big names sell books!"

(Another digression, if we may: big names *do* help sell
books. There's no question about that. The problem is, there
aren't that many big names in the horror field. Certainly there
aren't that many whose names will actually sell more books.
Stephen King. Dean R. Koontz. Robert R. McCammon. Anne
Rice. Peter Straub. Clive Barker. Ray Bradbury. These are the
writers who, for the most part, have been able to attract huge
numbers of mainstream readers to their work.

When a publisher says you need big names on the cover,
what he really means is you need the names of those writers
who have the largest mainstream followings. Horror readers
will naturally find their way to a new horror anthology. They
hunger for almost anything related to horror, as long as it's
good, and they'll be familiar with the genre stars like Ramsey
Campbell or Charles L. Grant or Nancy A. Collins. But the

mainstream reader? He's a harder fish to reel in. His interests more often lie elsewhere. So the bait needs to be familiar. The publishers know this. Hence the quest for big-name authors.

So whenever we editors are putting together an anthology we go hunting for these six or seven big names. Unfortunately, these guys get offers every damn day of the week. Not for a couple of cents a word, either. We're talking one or two thousand dollars a story. And they deserve it. They've worked hard to get where they are. They're all quite nice when they say, "Sorry but I haven't got the time," or, "I just can't seem to come up with anything for you right now." But niceness aside, the bottom line is this: these writers are hard to attract, and there just aren't enough of them to go around.)

4

St. Martin's, straight and simple, felt more comfortable with the *Dead End: City Limits* concept than anything else we had to offer. Originally we had envisioned it as the first of a three-book series, the other two volumes to cover rural and suburban themes. But somewhere along the line that got lost, and now, looking back, we suspect that that was a good thing. It would have been difficult to float the remaining two themes of the series. Even attempting all three in the same book would have been tough. In all honesty, there just wasn't enough substance there—a dead end of another sort.

Finally, though, the contracts were signed and it was time to get down to business.

We wanted to open *Dead End* to over-the-transom submissions, something we hadn't done the first time. For *Post Mortem* we'd gone out and begged for nearly all the material that finally made it into the book. We had made a list of the writers we felt would be perfect, then hounded them mercilessly until they finally said, "Okay, here're your damn stories! Now leave us alone!"

For *Dead End* we wanted to try things a little differently. There was a slight altruistic reasoning behind our decision. For years now, there's been a tendency in this field for anthology editors to do what we did with *Post Mortem*—invite participation from a small, select group of writers. They're called "invitation only" anthologies, and they happen more often than not. In the early years of our careers as writers, we both had times when we scratched our heads and wondered how the authors in that new anthology in all the bookstores had found out about the book without us ever hearing a thing.

Invitation only.

We remembered how frustrating that had been.

Where are talented young horror writers expected to find encouragement and room to grow? When so many other avenues seem more promising for newcomers, how are any of them going to be convinced that horror fiction is worth pursuing? Isn't "invitation only" a form of snobbery, and doesn't snobbery limit growth? Doesn't it serve to keep horror fiction in the gutter by keeping away fresh blood, new voices?

So we decided the only fair thing to do was to open up *Dead End* to anyone and everyone who wanted to send us a story. And that's what we ended up doing. (Though we did hedge our bets. We sent invitations to ten or twelve authors we thought were likely to provide strong stories. As expected, not all of them said yes. But we figured we might catch five or six, and that turned out to be fairly close to the mark.)

Notices went out to *Scavenger's Newsletter* and *The Gila Queen's Guide to Markets,* two monthly market reports that reach a total of several thousand writers. More so than others, those newsletters tend to reach mostly horror, fantasy, and science fiction writers.

Still, responses were surprisingly sparse.

We talked about it often, over the phone . . .

"Anything come in this week?"

"A science fiction story about creatures from another planet taking over city government. How about you?"

"Nothing. Not a single submission. This is weird. I don't understand why we aren't hearing from anyone."

"Maybe they're all working on novels?"

"Or maybe they all have the flu?"

What we finally decided was this: the field was choking on anthologies, many of which were failing to live up to their promise. Yes, there were those half a dozen or so annual successes, but for each triumph there were two or three others that never made it to publication. And still others disappeared altogether, without any word at all from their editors.

And who was getting burned?

Why, the writers, of course. They were the ones spending precious time writing on spec. They were the ones left holding their otherwise unmarketable theme stories after the latest anthology fell apart. They were the ones who most often got turned away from the invitation-onlys.

Now, we reasoned, they had finally grown gun-shy.

Or else . . . they found the concept behind *Dead End: City Limits* uninspiring.

Or maybe, just maybe, they too needed a whack on the side of the head.

5

Paul wrote the concept behind this book.

As we envisioned it, there were a million stories in the naked city. We wanted the ones that were both horrific and germane to the contemporary city experience. If it was just a rural story with alleys and garbage tossed in, if a story could stand on its own without using an element of the urban experience, then it wasn't right for the book. As simple as that.

Except it turned out not to be simple at all.

Almost immediately, we realized that most of the submissions were lacking that sense of place. In many you could have crossed out "parking lot" or "gutter" and substituted "pasture" or "backyard barbecue" and not lost a thing. And even in those submissions that were real, genuine city stories, we became aware of an unsettling trend.

Nearly eight out of ten were set somewhere in the future. It was as if these writers were struggling with their personal beliefs about today's urban environment and were choosing to distance themselves from its harsh reality. There was a safety net of sorts in carrying their stories into a time which did not yet exist. The drugs, the gangs, the alienation were less painful there.

This was not an unparalleled trend in the horror genre. We often disguise issues behind metaphor, giving them the mask of a monster or some other equally menacing supernatural force. That approach can be both powerful and effective, and it was certainly acceptable for this book. However, we were eager to address the concerns of *today's* cities, not some futuristic projection of what they might be like ten or twenty or a hundred years from now. We felt strongly that there was enough horror right here, right now.

6

This was our original premise, as outlined by Paul:

Imagine a nameless city, a city of millions.

The climate is devastating. In the summer, the heat and humidity are crippling; ozone levels climb; each day brings new air quality alerts. In the winter, high winds and freezing rains make it difficult to get from place to place. Occasionally, massive blizzards bring *everything* to a standstill.

The city is corrupt, from the highest offices of government to the lowliest police officer pounding his brutal beat. Machine politics lingers. Reformers try to alter the system and fail, or worse, become tainted and take on the very qualities they attempted to change. Racists of all colors inflame audiences, using hatred and fear for political or financial gain.

The city is polarized. In the gentrified neighborhoods of the north, young people hide behind walls of new money. In the decaying ethnic neighborhoods (German, Polish, Hungarian, Bulgarian) to the west, desperate people cling to a way of life that vanishes more each day. In the city center, expensive retailers sell their wares along "Platinum Row" and traders play games with the economy in the financial district—while across the steaming, polluted river that divides the city, blacks and Hispanics huddle in the projects where drugs are the only escape and where senseless assaults, drive-by shootings, and murder in the name of football warm-up jackets are a daily reality.

The city is in trouble. Schools are huge, ancient dungeons where unteachable students are watched over by terrified teachers. The health-care network, from free clinics for the poor to emergency trauma care for everyone, is on the verge of bankruptcy. The infrastructure of roads, bridges, sewers, and water lines is old and crumbling. The city's sports teams receive lavish new stadiums while thousands of people go homeless for lack of housing funds. Fire and ambulance protection is unreliable. Mass transit is inadequate and unsafe.

If the residents of this city have one thing in common, it is this: they are trapped, mired in their situations either by choice or fate. Helpless to change or move on or move away, they drift through their lives, alone among millions of others.

New York? Chicago? Some other eastern metropolis? No. And yes. And no.

Dead End: City Limits sought stories set in this environment, stories imbued with the overall sense conveyed above. We didn't want standard stalker/slasher stories, nor did we want tales of subway maniacs. We were looking for the supernatural and psychological horror that springs from human suffering, from loneliness and alienation, from despair. We wanted the horror of facelessness and anonymity, the terror of large crowds or that single man standing beneath the streetlight on the corner. We were searching for the fear of large buildings and dark alleys, vast warehouses and tiny shops. We wanted the horror of fast-paced lives out of control, of urban technology, of jobs and of *joblessness.*

But be warned, we told those who wished to submit stories. We are partial to tales that allow in a ray of hope, that discover a way to reach beyond the misery and come out whole on the other side. Realism—even in supernatural themes. Human dignity and determination—even in the face of overpowering fear.

This was the city of our proposal.

Welcome, we told our writers. Welcome, and enjoy your stay.

7

It wasn't always easy, but the best writers came through for us when we needed them most, and for the most part that summary above describes exactly what you, the reader, will find in this anthology. Stories about isolation, about becoming comfortable with the violence around us, about becoming *part* of the violence, about the insanity of the streets against the tenuousness of threatened lives.

It's all here.

We hope you like it. And maybe in the process, something here will touch you, make you think about things that are often too unpleasant to think about, make you do something a little differently today that will make a difference tomorrow. For you see, in the end we realized what all those folks who wrote about the future were trying to do. They were looking ahead because that's where the hope was. But as many of the stories you're about to encounter will show you, there's hope out there today as well. Sometimes it's thin; sometimes it's hidden; sometimes the path to get there is dark and scary. But it's there if you know where to look.

8

One final point: one of the few forms of urban terror *not* in this book is the horror of modern corporate conglomerate publishing. It's a brave new world for books and editors and writers, but the fact that you're reading this introduction, having a chance to step momentarily behind the scenes and think about some of the things (both flattering and unflattering) we've suggested . . . well, that just might be the most hopeful thing of all.

—PAUL F. OLSON and DAVID B. SILVA

PARADE

LAWRENCE WATT-EVANS

Lawrence Watt-Evans says: "I was lost in Boston as a child, when my sister put me on the wrong car on the green line. I've walked through the NYU campus at one in the morning and lived. I got frostbite walking the streets of Pittsburgh when I couldn't get a bus. I once slept in Thirtieth Street Station in Philadelphia, after missing a train. (Since I had a suitcase, the cops rousting drunks left me alone.) My wife and I took a wrong turn in Baltimore and got to watch the cops raid a bar. I was nearly attacked by a mob in Berlin—for crossing against the light. But I love cities. Really."

Watt-Evans, of Gaithersburg, Maryland, was born in 1954 and has the distinction of being a Princeton dropout. He is the author of numerous columns, twenty-six short stories, and fourteen novels, among them The Nightmare People *and* Nightside City. *He won the Best Short Story Hugo Award in 1988 and is the editor of the recent anthology* Newer York. *He is married, and he and his wife have two children.*

As usual, Jack Handley was the first out of the elevator, striding quickly across the lobby.

Megan Fausel was next, chatting quietly with Amy Drinkwater. Claude Charette followed them, listening, while Tom Petilli held the DOOR OPEN button and studied the elevator's control panel.

Tom wondered why the buttons for the different floors were arranged in two rows, rather than three or four. One would obviously have been too long, but why settle for two? A child might have trouble reaching the top few, as it was; why hadn't they made it three rows?

"Tom!" Megan called, "Are you coming?"

"Sure!" he said. He forgot about the buttons and hurried after his office mates.

Jack was already at the street door, waiting impatiently.

"Come *on,* dammit," he said.

"What's your hurry, Jack?" Megan answered. "I mean, we're just going to lunch, and then coming back here, so what's the rush?"

"The *rush,* Megan, is that I'm hungry and I want to eat, and I've got a shitload of work on my desk that I want to get back to." Jack turned and shoved the door open; the roar of the street spilled into the lobby, washing over the five of them.

Amy sighed; Claude glanced at her, then turned quickly away. Tom noticed, and wondered why—he saw nothing repulsive about Amy, nothing that would make a man look away like that.

Jack was out the door already, Megan close behind him.

Tom heard Jack's voice clearly, despite the noise, as it said, "Damn!"

"What is it?" he asked, stepping forward; Claude moved aside to let him through, but he bumped against Amy.

Jack didn't answer. Tom made his way out onto the sidewalk, Amy beside him, Claude close behind.

The sidewalk was jammed with people—not hurrying along, as they usually did, nor standing and talking as groups might sometimes, but lined up in rows, staring out at the street.

"What is it?" Tom called. "What's going on?" He rose up on his toes, trying to see.

A wave of cheering swept over him, coming from up the street, and he craned his neck, trying to spot the reason.

Jack was more direct; he had shoved his way through the crowd to the curb. Megan was close behind, peering over his shoulder.

Amy stood in the entry to the building, looking about in bewilderment, and Claude pressed himself flat against the gray stone wall, staying back where no one would step on his feet.

The cheering was spreading, coming nearer; it drowned out the more ordinary noise of the city. The hum of engines and ventilators and voices, the distant sirens and the jets high overhead, the rainfall tapping of a million hard-soled shoes on concrete, the rumble of subways and all the buzzing and hissing and whining of the city, all were lost in the wordless bellow of the happy crowd.

Megan turned and called to the others, "It's a parade!" She had to shout to be heard over the noise.

"And they've got a police lineup," Jack announced at the top of his lungs, "so we can't get across the street to the restaurant until it's passed!"

"Why is there a parade today?" Tom asked, puzzled. "It's not a holiday."

"Perhaps it's a local festival? Something the city sponsors?" Claude suggested.

"Or a march of some kind," Megan said. "A demonstration or a protest, maybe. I haven't marched like that in twenty years."

"I can't see anything," Amy said worriedly, "and I *love* parades!"

Claude turned to look at her, then looked at the crowd, judging them.

"Oh, here," Megan said to Amy, "Jack will let you in front— won't you, Jack?"

"What?" Jack said, turning. "I was trying to see if I could spot any banners."

"I said you'd let Amy in front," Megan told him.

Jack glanced sourly at Megan, then at Amy, and then turned back to the street. "Sure," he said.

Uncertainly, Amy slipped from the door, between Tom and Claude, and ducked under first Megan's arm, and then Jack's.

The cheering was almost upon them; Amy turned and looked, and the parade was only a block away.

The vanguard was a line of mounted police, half a dozen men on horseback strung across the street. Behind them marched a row of young women in a uniform Amy didn't recognize—not quite a cheerleader costume, but something similar, with short, tight black skirts, white blouses, blue vests with badges she couldn't read pinned to them. There were twenty or thirty of them, carrying a white banner with blue and gold writing on it, but as the women strutted their knees struck the cloth from behind, sending it bouncing and rippling and making it impossible to read.

That struck Amy as very odd; hadn't anyone told them to hold the banner up a little higher? She almost called out herself, but lost her nerve.

Behind the women the parade seemed to be just a big crowd of ordinary people.

"That's this damn city for you," Jack snarled in her ear. "It's always some damn thing making life difficult, keeping people from getting on with their lives. I mean, who needs a goddamn parade?"

"Oh, Jack," Amy said reproachfully, "I *love* parades!"

"Well, this doesn't look like much of one," Megan said from her spot just behind Jack. "No music that I can hear, no one carrying signs. I wonder what it's about?"

"Oh, who cares?" Amy said. "Let's just enjoy it! Nobody will mind if we're a little late getting back from lunch."

"They probably won't even know," Megan said, "because probably everyone else is out here somewhere watching, too."

"*I* care," Jack said, "but I don't see there's a blasted thing I can do about it."

Tom was beside Megan now, looking over Jack's other shoulder as the horsemen passed. "What kind of a parade is it?" he asked.

"I don't know," Megan replied.

"It's a *long* one, that's what kind it is," Jack added a moment later, as the banner-bearing women marched on past the corner. "Look!"

He pointed uptown, at a blue-mirrored skyscraper a good twenty blocks away; Tom stared.

Then he saw what Jack meant; the reflective sides of the building acted as a mirror, and while it mostly reflected the blue sky and the surrounding towers, the angled portion at the nearest corner gave them a view of the street below it.

The parade was still passing, twenty blocks uptown.

Tom turned to face the street again.

The marchers were ordinary citizens, in ordinary clothes—business suits, blue jeans, summer dresses. Mixed in were a relative handful of people, both men and women, in glittering costumes of red sequins, with red-sequined top hats on their heads or held aloft, whirling through the crowd.

"Join us!" these red-garbed dancers called. "Everybody join in!"

The throng on the sidewalks cheered, and some of them spilled off into the street, past the white-painted police sawhorses, joining the parade.

Amy glanced up at Jack's face, which was set in a frown.

Tom stared, open-mouthed, over Jack's right shoulder; Megan leaned lazily on his left.

Claude remained pressed against the granite, uninvolved and quietly waiting.

Still frowning, Jack looked at the blue glass skyscraper again, then back at the jammed street, and then at the buildings up the block on the far side—particularly the one with the red-and-gold sign announcing PIERRE'S.

"Listen," he said, "this damn parade's going to take forever to get past—see, they aren't even up to Sixtieth Street yet, I can't even see the end. How about if we just cross now, through the parade? Join in, march for a block or two until we can work our way across, and then come back uptown on the other side? I want my lunch."

Megan considered, then nodded. "Good idea," she said.

"Maybe we can make it three or four blocks?" Amy suggested wistfully.

Tom studied the crowd. "It might take that far," he said. "The street's packed pretty tight, but they're moving along at a fast walk all the same."

"Hey, Claude!" Megan called, "join us! We're going to cut across!"

Reluctantly, Claude left his place by the wall and stepped up close behind Tom.

"We don't want to get separated," Jack cautioned, "so stay close here."

He eyed the marchers—thousands of them, grinning and smiling as they walked past, all the endless hordes of them, the glittering red figures in their midst still calling, "Join us!"

Fools, Jack thought, wasting their time—*everybody's* time—like that.

"All right," he said, pushing Amy forward, "now!"

Amy stumbled, and a man in a dark gray overcoat caught her before she could fall.

"Hey, little lady," he said, "watch your step! And step along, join the parade!"

Amy smiled up at him, found her footing, and joined the march.

Jack was close behind her. "Come on," he said, "Come on."

Megan was there, too, making a place for herself in the crowd, pushing aside elbows as she pressed forward.

Behind them Tom was swept up in the march.

And finally, reluctantly, Claude allowed himself to be sucked into the crowd, pressed in among the cheering throngs.

It seemed to Amy that she had scarcely taken a step, and she was a block from the office already, passing a second cross street. She felt as light and airy as a milkweed blossom, and almost danced along amid the marchers.

"I *love* parades," she said, to no one in particular.

One of the men in red sequins smiled at her and tipped his hat. "Glad to hear it, miss," he said.

The others around her smiled as well—a man in a tweed jacket, a woman in evening dress and pearls, a teenaged girl in jeans and a "Just Say No" T-shirt.

Amy looked for Jack and Tom and Megan, and realized she'd somehow become separated from them in the crowd, in what was surely just a few seconds. For a moment she worried, her mouth turned down, her forehead creased.

Then she shrugged. It didn't matter. She could find them later. And she wanted to enjoy the parade.

For a moment, then, she glimpsed Megan, off to her left; she waved and called, "Megan! Megan! Go on without me! I don't want any lunch; I'm going to march in the parade. I'll meet you back at the office later!"

Megan smiled, waved, and nodded.

Just like Amy, she thought, silly little Amy who would never get anywhere because she never worried about tomorrow, never planned ahead, got hung up on every little detail. Let the poor child enjoy her parade.

She turned her own attention to working her way methodically through the crowd, but despite her efforts she found herself carried at least three steps downtown for every step she moved toward the far sidewalk.

She looked around for Jack, trying to spot his familiar frown in the forest of smiling faces. She wanted to ask his help in bulling through the moving mass of people, but she couldn't spot him.

Probably already across, she thought with a mix of admiration and resentment. Jack was someone who knew how to get what he wanted.

It was a shame he never knew how to enjoy it once he had

it, and that he sometimes chose the wrong things to want. Like that Sheila from Accounting—why had he wanted *her?* Or any of the others he'd gone after over the years?

And why didn't he want *her,* Megan Fausel?

And, she asked herself, where was he, anyway?

In point of fact, at that moment Jack wasn't sure himself just where he was.

He prided himself on knowing his way around, and certainly he ought to know every block on the very avenue he worked on, but he had stumbled somewhere, and been swept along with the crowd, and now the buildings on either side looked unfamiliar. He couldn't see Pierre's; the Warner tower ought to be right *there,* but there was another building in the way, one he didn't know. Had the parade gone around a corner without his even noticing it?

He cursed under his breath and began shoving his way through the moving crowd.

"Hey, there," called one of the men in red, "What's your hurry? Come on along, Jack! Join the fun!"

Jack turned and almost snarled. He hated it when people called strangers "Jack" that way—the fool had no way of knowing it was the right name. The man in red was just using it as a generic form of address, and Jack *hated* that.

He pushed toward the sidewalk.

"Not that way," the man in red called, shoving his top hat tightly onto his head and somehow moving easily through the crowd toward Jack.

That was all he needed, some idiot in spangles telling him what to do. He looked around, and saw two other parade marshals, or whatever they were, watching.

He was outnumbered, just himself against the three of them, it seemed.

Where were Tom and Claude? They weren't much, but they might do to back him up against these clowns.

Where had they got to?

As it happened, Claude hadn't gotten to much of anywhere;

from the moment he stepped off the curb he had been swept along, carried downtown by the crowd, unable to make his way across or to resist the steady march without an undignified struggle.

He didn't struggle; he just let the crowd carry him. Sooner or later he'd find a way across.

It was always easiest to go along with the crowd, and Claude always had—though usually not quite so literally. He'd never been one to make waves. If he just did what he was told, things would eventually work out, he was sure. They always had.

So he marched downtown only a yard or so from the sidewalk he'd started from, his feet moving not because he wanted to march, but simply to keep from falling.

Tom had done better, had gotten out into the thick of it, out toward the middle of the street, where he looked about in wonder.

There were people everywhere; when he looked down he could barely see the asphalt for all the marching feet. To his right strode a plump Hispanic woman in a halter top and Bermuda shorts; to his left was an old man with a cane, stepping briskly along, stick swinging but somehow not hitting anyone. A boy in a sailor suit was ahead of him, perhaps ten years old, and Tom marveled at that: he hadn't thought boys that age still wore sailor suits.

One of the women in red sequins was nearby, and Tom called to her, "What's the parade for? What's the occasion?"

"Join in!" she called. "March with us!"

That was hardly an answer; Tom pushed his way toward her as they both marched, but somehow she seemed to effortlessly move farther away, so that he drew no closer.

"Hey!" he called after her, "what's the occasion?"

She was facing away, toward the sidewalk. She called, "Join the parade!"

Tom shrugged, and looked around again.

Now his neighbors were a black man in a trench coat, a

shirtless kid with a bright blue mohawk and black leather pants, and an Asian girl, perhaps eight years old, in a nightgown, clutching a teddy bear.

What was she doing out here in her pajamas, Tom wondered. He leaned over to ask, but bumped against someone's elbow, and by the time he had straightened that out the girl was gone, lost in the surrounding mob.

He turned to the kid with the mohawk.

"Hey," he asked, "d'you know what this parade's all about?"

The kid turned and gave him a glassy stare—Tom could see that the youth's pupils were hugely dilated, his eyes black and bottomless.

"No, man," he said. "Do you?"

"No," Tom replied. "I just got caught up in it by accident."

"Me, too, man," the kid said, nodding. His blue hair waved gently with the motion. "I figured I'd just walk a couple of blocks." He smiled, showing yellowing teeth.

Tom smiled back. "Thanks," he said. He looked around.

Men in suits, women in dresses, a tall blond man in a leather skullcap, a woman in a velvet hood, three boys in street-gang colors over there, and half a dozen of the figures in red sequins, and beyond them all the sidewalks lined with watching crowds, behind them the blank, eyeless facades of the buildings, concrete and glass and brick, and inside the buildings more people, and beyond them more streets, more buildings, more people.

The weight of the city and all its complexity seemed to be pushing at him suddenly, and he shook his head, almost stumbled.

When he had recovered he looked about.

To the left, that was the sidewalk he wanted to reach. Just get to the sidewalk, turn in behind the watchers and make his way back uptown to Pierre's, eat lunch while the rest of the parade goes by, and then back to the office and away from this teeming mass of humanity, back where he could pretend that he was more than just one of the millions of faceless human ants that made up the city.

All he had to do was reach the left-hand sidewalk. He could find out later what the parade was for; it would be in the papers, surely, or on the evening news.

Where had the others gone, anyway? Were they already at Pierre's, waiting for him?

He began to push his way to the side.

"No need to shove!" called a woman in red sequins. "No need for that!"

He looked up, startled, to find her no more than ten feet away.

"Hey," he called, "I wanted to ask, what's the occasion for the parade?"

She smiled at him, showing brilliant white teeth. "What do you think?" she said.

Then she slipped away through the crowd before he could reply.

What did he think? He had no idea!

He didn't *want* to think about it. All he wanted to do was get over to that sidewalk.

Where was Jack, anyway? If they'd told *him* not to shove, they might have had a riot on their hands.

"Not that way," the man in red told Jack.

"You can't tell me where to go," Jack said. "You can't tell me what to do!" He shoved aside a girl in a yellow party dress and made his way one step further toward the sidewalk, even as the crowd pulled him three steps downtown.

Then the man in red was right there in front of him, pushing him back toward the center of the street.

"This way, friend, this way," the parade marshal, or whatever the man was, told him cheerfully.

"You can't push me around!" Jack shouted. "What right have you got to treat me like that? Let me through!" He lowered his head and tried to force his way past the marshal, between the red-sequined frock coat and a man in a stained white apron.

The marshal blocked him and pushed him back.

"Hey," Jack shouted, "hey, you can't do that! You can't walk all over me! I have rights!"

The marshal shoved him again, harder, and he staggered back.

Another marcher, a woman in a black-lace slip, pushed him while he was off-balance, and he stumbled, and another, a man in a gray suit, shoved him, and then there was an opening behind him and he fell.

His head hit the asphalt hard, and the pain fountained up from the back of his skull, and his neck seemed to vibrate with the impact, but before he could think about that the first foot hit his belly and knocked the wind out of him.

He gasped for breath, and a boot came down on his throat and closed his windpipe, leaving him airless and drowning for an endless handful of seconds.

Then the boot had moved on, but a woman's spike heel was digging into his thigh, and a dirty sneaker pressed his shoulder down against the pavement. He waved his hands, struggling to find a grip somewhere; a woolen skirt slid through his fingers as a heavy black Oxford rammed down on his arm, slamming his elbow into the pavement and sending shooting pain out in all directions.

He had his breath back for an instant and wanted to yell, but a shoe caught him in the mouth, and another in the groin, and the weight of a fat man hit his foot and twisted it so that he thought his ankle would break.

And then he lost track of the individual blows, as the pain spread everywhere and the feet struck him everywhere and the parade marched on, oblivious, marched on across him, trampling him.

The last sound he heard, over the cheering of the crowds on the sidewalks, was a high-pitched giggle, as sunlight glittered on red sequins above him.

Amy giggled.

"I do love parades," she told the man beside her, as the two of them watched a juggler ahead. The performer was having a hard time of it in the tightly packed throng, but he was gamely continuing, tossing his glittering gold balls up in intricate patterns, catching each as it came down and tossing it back up—most of the time. He missed fairly often, because of the crowd, and when he did, someone else would catch the ball and throw it back to him.

Sometimes he caught it, sometimes he didn't; if he didn't, someone else would, and they'd try again.

The man at Amy's side smiled.

She smiled back, then stumbled over something, and he caught her before she could fall.

"Thank you," she said.

"You folks okay?" asked a voice nearby; Amy turned and found herself face to face with the white-painted face of a clown in full regalia.

"Just fine, thanks," she answered, grinning.

"Better watch where you step; we've a good long ways to go yet before this parade's over."

"Oh, do we?" Amy asked. "Oh, good! I love a parade. I always want them to last forever."

The clown nodded. "Me, too," he said.

"Yes," Amy said, "It's always such a letdown when you get to the end and have nothing to show for it but sore feet."

"I know what you mean," the clown agreed, "but maybe this time it'll be different."

"Oh, that's silly," Amy said. "How could it be different?"

"Well, look around you," he replied.

She looked.

The crowd seemed to have thinned somewhat. The juggler ahead was tossing handkerchiefs now; a man on stilts, dressed as Uncle Sam, was striding along nearby. Someone was passing out cotton candy, though Amy couldn't see where it had come from.

"It's like a circus," she said.

"Not the parade," the clown said, "I mean the city."

Amy looked up, puzzled, at gleaming white spires, like fairy castles, that had replaced the brick and concrete to either side.

"Oh," she said, not questioning. "Oh!"

"Oh!" said Megan, as she stumbled over something. "Damn it!" She glanced down, not to see what she had tripped on, but to make sure her shoes still had their heels. They seemed intact.

She looked up at the buildings nearby.

"Where the hell are we, anyway?" she asked nobody in particular. "Is this Thirty-fifth Street? I don't see any signs."

No one answered.

She looked about.

The man to her right wore a greasy T-shirt and a black denim vest; she wanted nothing to do with him. On the left, though, was a tall, thin man with a graying mustache, clad in an impeccable blue suit.

"Excuse me," she said, tugging at his sleeve, "but where are we? I don't think I know this part of the city."

She had meant that to be a lie, but looking up again she realized it wasn't. The buildings and streets were unfamiliar.

The man in the blue suit brushed her hand away, then looked her over appraisingly—it struck her as an unusually impolite look for a man of his obvious breeding.

"Ah, my dear," he said, taking up the hand he had just knocked away, "what were you saying?"

"Do you know where we are?" she asked. "I seem to have lost my bearings."

He didn't so much as glance away from her face. "No, I'm afraid not," he said.

"Do you know the parade route?" she asked, "I mean, where we'll come out?"

"Oh, I think it's headed straight downtown," he said, with a smile.

"Thank you," she said, smiling back. She started to withdraw her hand.

He didn't let it go.

"Do you have your ticket?" he asked.

She blinked at him, startled, then snatched her hand away. "What ticket?" she asked.

He frowned at her. "Should have known," he said to himself, as if he had forgotten she was listening. "Well, it should be quite a show."

"What should be?" she snapped. "What's that supposed to mean?"

"Oh, nothing," he said. "Nothing at all."

Claude could see nothing at all that he recognized. The buildings to either side were strange—not just unfamiliar, but unnatural, alien. As the parade swept him downtown they seemed to merge, from separate buildings with their own personalities into a single unbroken facade of concrete and stone, one with few windows, and those small and high and oddly placed.

He could see no doors.

And the sidewalks had narrowed, almost vanished. There were no watching crowds anymore; the parade surged up over the curbs and filled the street from side to side, an unbroken mass of humanity, himself trapped in its midst. It was as if the entire population of the city was crowded onto this single thoroughfare.

The air had grown thick and polluted, though the day had been sunny and the air clear when he left the office. It seemed as though the strange buildings were somehow holding in this foul atmosphere.

He didn't understand how this place could be here, how he could be in it. The parade had made no turns, and yet this was definitely not the familiar avenue; he knew he had never seen anyplace like this in the city, ever before, and he had driven all through downtown. He had driven, safe in his car, past the streetwalkers and the old men clutching bottles and the young men with their little plastic packets and vials, very pleased that he was better than they; yet he had never seen anyplace like this, anything like these blank gray walls.

He had driven through rain-slick, gleaming black nights when the streetlights shone from the wet pavement and the police cruisers sprayed red and blue light across the asphalt, watching it all from securely behind the tinted glass of his windshield, and he had seen buildings of concrete and stone and brick and wood, buildings that were rubble and charred timbers, buildings that were steel frame and unadorned, and he had never seen anything like these featureless barriers to either side.

The people around him had somehow changed, as well—they were gaunt and hollow-eyed, staring straight ahead. No one was cheering anymore; all he heard was the shuffling march of thousands of feet. He could see none of the red-dressed marshals; everyone around him, men and women both, wore suits of gray and brown and black, drab and hostile.

Something was clearly very wrong here, something was happening that he didn't understand. He realized he should have followed the others, fought his way across the street instead of allowing himself to be propelled along.

It was too late now, though; there was no longer any sidewalk on either side. Near panic, he watched helplessly as the crowd trudged onward, carrying him with it.

At least, he thought, we'll come to an ending somewhere. This weird parade can't go on forever; they'll have to disperse eventually, and I'll be free, I can find my way out and go back.

He looked ahead, and realized that the street was, indeed, coming to an end. It turned into a ramp, leading upward into a miasmic haze of pollution; the marchers were continuing on up the ramp.

He looked up, rising up on his toes to see over the heads of those in front of him, trying to make out what stood at the top of the ramp.

At first he saw nothing but blank grayness.

Then he saw the ovens.

And the marchers marching on, carrying him with them.

He began screaming, but it made no difference, no difference at all.

Megan had been trying in vain to reach the sidewalks, had tried shouting and pushing, but it made no difference at all; she was still in the same spot in the crowd she had been in for blocks, being carried helplessly forward. And now, ahead, she saw that the parade was reaching its end, marching into a gigantic stadium.

She didn't remember any such stadium being downtown.

"What is this place?" she asked.

"The Arena, of course," the mustached man replied.

"It is?" She tried to remember whether she had ever heard of a city arena, and thought she had; wasn't that where the hockey team played?

"Certainly," the mustached man told her. "Can't you tell?"

"No," Megan replied, defensively, "I've never been here before. I'm not a hockey fan."

"Oh, it's not hockey they play here," he said. "What ever gave you that idea?"

She shrugged. "What is it, then?"

He made no reply, but smiled and looked away.

They were under the arches of the stadium, amid a maze of concrete pillars and chain-link fence, and although the crowd seemed to be thinning, Megan had been swept through one gate and was approaching another before she was able to stop her forward motion. "Tickets!" a uniformed man was calling. "Tickets!"

The mustached man had pulled a blue pasteboard from his breast pocket; the greasy fellow dug one out of his jeans. The ticket taker waved them through.

Megan looked for some way out, but could find none, and then she was at the gate, people behind her forcing her forward.

"Ticket, lady?"

"I'm sorry," she said, "I don't have one. I must be here by mistake. Could you direct me to the exit?"

"No ticket?" The man looked her over critically. He was young and blond and trying unsuccessfully to grow a beard. "That way," he said, pointing off to the left. "You go down that way and through the red steel door. Any problem, ask the guard."

"Thank you." Megan turned left.

The crowd was suddenly all behind her, she was in the clear, and she found herself in a narrow, shadowy passageway between two tall fences—both of them, she noticed, topped with coils of barbed wire.

She walked on, nervous—this place made her nervous, being alone made her nervous, and she still didn't understand how she had come here. She could hear the crowd roaring in the distance, like a heavy freight passing just out of sight.

She glanced back, thinking she might go back and ask the ticket taker to repeat his directions, but she could no longer see him; she must have been walking longer than she realized.

Then she saw the red steel door ahead, illuminated by the glow of a sign, the uniformed guard a dark shadow to one side. She tugged her jacket straight, brushed back her hair, and strode forward.

Tom strode forward. If he couldn't get out of the parade to the side, and if the mob behind him wouldn't let him stop, then he would fight his way up to the front, up to those cheerleaders or whatever they were, and the mounted policemen, and he would get out that way.

No one tried to stop or slow him, and he pushed easily through the mass of cheering, marching people.

There were certainly a lot of them, and so varied—it was as if all the world had come out to march.

There was a woman in a black string bikini; he paused for a second to stare. And there was a man wearing nothing at all, he realized, a great fat man with short black hair—hadn't anyone else noticed? Tom wondered if the man would be arrested.

It wasn't any of his business, of course, and he pushed onward, past a boy in a loincloth and a girl in a purple down-filled parka, a young woman in full harlequinade, an old man in blackface, a mime in whiteface.

The clown smiled at Amy. "We're almost there," he said.

She smiled back at him. "And my feet don't hurt at all," she said. She danced a little pirouette to demonstrate. Her fellow marchers applauded, and somewhere overhead a bird whistled appreciatively.

Amy curtsied in response, then looked up.

They were at the end of the street, where the gleaming pavement ran up to broad marble steps, and at the top of the steps glittered immense crystal gates. Faintly, Amy could hear people singing somewhere.

The gates were closed; the marchers were lined up along either side of the steps, waiting.

Amy stopped. "What's everyone waiting for?" she asked, worried.

"For you," the clown told her.

"Me?" Amy shrank back. "But who am *I?*"

"Well," the clown asked, grinning, "who *are* you?"

The guard smiled at Megan. "Name, please?" he asked.

"No, I just want to get out," she said. "I'm here by mistake."

"I need your name, please," he said.

She frowned, and then decided it didn't matter. "Megan Fausel," she told him.

He glanced at a clipboard on the wall behind him, and nodded.

"Go right out, Ms. Fausel," he said, rolling back the heavy steel door.

"Thank you," Megan answered, stepping through.

It was dark on the other side, not just dim as the passageway had been, but utterly black; that wasn't right. She knew it couldn't be night yet, and besides, the city was never dark, not really.

She was still in the stadium somewhere. She blinked, trying to adjust her eyes, and then light sprang up, blinding her anew. She shielded her face with one arm.

Dimly, through the glare, she could make out the interior of the arena. All around her were tiers of seats, all of them filled, men and women and children, and they were all staring down into the arena, staring at *her,* and she was caught in the spotlight, on the sand floor of the arena.

"There's been a mistake," she said, turning.

The red steel door was closed. She pushed at it, but it didn't move.

The crowd laughed, an immense, overwhelming sound, and she realized they were all laughing at *her.*

She pounded on the door, and her banging was lost in the redoubled laughter of the audience.

She turned, trying to gather her dignity, trying to keep from crying in embarrassment, and marched over to the stands, to find herself at the foot of a sheer concrete wall some nine feet tall.

The spotlight followed her, and the crowd quieted, watching her intently.

She put her hand on the rough concrete and began following the wall.

There had to be an opening, a way out, somewhere.

The crowd seemed to be hushed in anticipation of something, and Megan wondered uncomfortably what it could be. She stumbled along the wall, and found nothing but solid, bare concrete—no doors, no steps, no way up into the stands, no way out.

When she had gone halfway around a circle, she found a door, at last—a black steel door hung from a rail, much like the red one she had entered by.

The crowd was utterly still.

Megan hesitated. She tugged at the door.

It moved slightly, but she released it again, didn't push it open.

Something was wrong here, she knew from the crowd's silence. She put her ear to the black door and listened.

Something growled, a deep, inhuman growl, close behind the door. A terrifying, powerful growl—a *hungry* growl.

Megan shivered at the sound.

The crowd laughed. She looked up at them.

"Open it!" someone called, and amid renewed laughter part of the crowd began to chant.

"Open it!"

"Open it!"

"Open it!"

"Oh, God," Megan said. She sank to her knees on the sand.

"This can't be happening," she said. "This can't be happening to me. I'm just an ordinary person, I never did anything terrible; why am I here?"

No one answered; the chanting died away, and the laughing, and an uneasy, anticipatory silence fell.

A nervous giggle sounded somewhere high above.

And then a rumble sounded, close at hand.

The black door was opening.

"I'm just Amy Drinkwater," Amy told the clown, and the singing grew louder, rising in a triumphant chorus.

"Tell *them,*" the clown said, gesturing toward the gates.

Amy turned. "I'm Amy Drinkwater," she said.

The gates trembled. She glanced back, and the clown nodded encouragement.

"I'm Amy Drinkwater!" she called, and the crystal gates swung open before her, the chorus of song welled up on all sides, sweeping her up the steps into paradise.

Tom swept forward through the crowd, past men in armor and bearded dwarves, past naked women and writhing dancers, and still he could not see the front of the parade.

He could no longer see the sides, either. The avenue had widened, the buildings drawing farther back, until now all he could see, from horizon to horizon, was the marching, dancing throng. The city's buildings were gone; only the street and the people remained, marching on to an unknown destination.

Tom struggled on, trying to find his way out, away from the sweating, singing crowd.

It was several days before he began to wonder why he wasn't tired, and weeks before he began to worry.

THE LOOKING GLASS HAND

MELISSA MIA HALL

"In the mid seventies my mother worked for United Way in downtown Fort Worth," says Melissa Mia Hall. "Their offices were above a bus station. Sometimes I had to take her to work or pick her up. One afternoon I arrived a little early and had to wait in my car. It was a hot day; I had on cut-offs and a halter top. The windows were down on my '66 Chevy and a businessman in an expensive car drove up. He got out, leered at me, and began making offers. I told him to leave me alone. He kept leering and being generally obscene. I was terrified, rolled up the windows and locked the doors. Luckily, he got the message and left. I was barely nineteen, and the sordid experience of being propositioned provided a jolt I won't soon forget. Consequently, my halter top was soon resigned to a drawer and I'm still hypersensitive to men who look at my breasts instead of my face."

Hall, who is in her early thirties, ("a.k.a. thirty-something"), was born and grew up in Texas. She's been a bookseller, a fashion copywriter, a free-lance photojournalist, and a teacher. Most recently, she has published short stories in A Whisper of Blood, Skin of the Soul, Razored Saddles, and Post Mortem.

Mom hasn't come home and Dad never did. I can handle it. I'm good at that kind of stuff. Ricky and Milly are minding pretty well so far. I can make them real scared if they don't mind. Real scared. I say, "No TV after nine o'clock," and Ricky, he screams some, but I hit him good on the head and he cuts it out after a while. He just likes to see how far he can push me. I just push back. I let him eat all the peanut butter he wants in the morning when he's been good. Milly isn't as easy to deal with as Ricky. I can just stare at Ricky mean-like and he starts to tune up. Milly's more—weird. I think she knows something's wrong, even though she's just a baby. We been in this place since winter. It's not a bad complex. I smile at the manager every time I go down to get the mail. Our rent's only a week past due. I broke open Mom's safety box. There's enough for maybe half a payment. That'll stall her.

I need someone to call. I wish Nanny wasn't dead. Nanny would know what to do.

I can't let Ricky eat all of that peanut butter. Not even when he's been excellent. Got to make it last. Milly's crying again. I wish she'd shut up.

"What's the matter with you?" She's wet her pants. "You little brat—how many times are you gonna do this? You're too big to be wetting your pants. I oughta spank you—" My hand tingles. I really want to spank her; I do. I want to spank her till her little pink butt bleeds; but I won't. Mom says I'm a good boy. I am, but it sucks. It really sucks.

Summer's almost over. I don't want to go back to school. I don't want to go back to anything. It's so dumbass.

"Kiss my ass; kiss my ass; kiss my ass . . ." Ricky's given himself a moronic haircut. He's greased himself some spikes with Mom's Vaseline and put some of her red lipstick on his eyebrows. Retarded punk.

"Get me a washrag, you little pervert."

He blows me a kiss and does some kind of war dance. "Say please."

"Please, you little fart."

Ricky's grin slides off and he stops dancing.

Milly stops crying and stares at me. "What're you looking at?" I shake her, then feel like a shithead. "Sorry, kiddo."

The washrag suddenly appears at my elbow. Ricky gives me a silly grin. I pull off Milly's panties and wipe her off. "No more pee, Milly, no more pee on panties, got it?"

"No more pee. No more pee," Milly repeats. "No more. Pee pee gone gone."

"She can't pee again, not ever? How come, man, that's brutal, bru-tal. I can pee anytime I want to—in the toilet bowl—in the toilet bowl." Ricky wiggles his scarlet eyebrows and takes the washrag back carefully, holding it out from his body. "Stinky—stin-key."

"Get me another pair of panties."

"You get 'em."

"Do it or die," I tell him and he disappears. Milly waits patiently. "Listen. You can pee—on the pot, now—just not on your panties. Okay?"

Ricky rematerializes holding out some faded Snoopy panties. I help the kid put them on and then I don't know what to do next. I want to wash my hands. I would like to drink a beer. But there's only half a six-pack left and I need to keep them for a special occasion. The air conditioner's not working right. It's too hot.

"I wanna go outside and play." One eyebrow has been smeared. Ricky scratches his ruined hair.

"I don't care what you do—just be back when you get hungry and don't get into any bad crap, okay?"

"Okay, dude. Can I have a peanut butter sandwich to take with me—please? Can I have a Coke?"

"No Coke, no sandwich."

"Please—"

"I said, no."

"Well, kiss my ass; kiss my stinking ass—"

"Can it Ricky or I'll beat the shit out of you—do you hear me?"

"Shut up, Barbie—you look just like a Barbie without any tits."

I slap him across the face and he sticks out his tongue.

Damn him for bringing up Barbie. I glance at Milly and yep, she's tuning up.

"Bobbie—Bobbie—I want Bobbie."

Ricky killed Barbie yesterday—while Milly watched. Zip—right out the window into the Dumpster. Excellent aim, totally perfecto mundo. And I figured Milly never played with it—she always sleeps with Cooterbear. I guess I figured wrong.

"I want Bobbie!"

"Sorry, Charlie," Ricky says. I grab his arm and twist it. He goes pale. "Lemme go!"

"You little bastard."

"Lemme go; I'm sorry, okay—I'm sorry. I'll go get it. Okay? Okay?"

I twist his arm tighter, till it really hurts. Milly goes quiet. She runs out of the room. And I let go. Ricky runs, too, faster than a speeding bullet. I head for the living room, neutral territory. Ricky's gone and left the front door open. I slam it shut. Milly's come back, sucking her thumb and dragging Cooterbear.

Tomorrow is my birthday. I will be twelve years old. I wish it was thirteen. Then I'd be somebody. Teenagers can *do* things. Teenagers are old. But old enough to be young enough. Young enough to know something. Do the right thing. Nanny said a boy with my IQ will always do the right thing. But I don't think that's true.

Sort of.

I kick the damn door a couple of times, just to watch Milly jump.

"Listen, I'll be in the bathroom for a little while. You stay right there, okay, Milly?"

"Okay." She nods like a little robot. O-kay.

I go to the bathroom and drop my jeans. I look down at my penis. I wish it would grow. Maybe if it would grow bigger, I would be bigger. All I can do now is to be big pretend-like. It's not good enough.

I wish I would die.

* * *

Mom's address book has very few numbers in it that haven't been crossed out. We are always starting new somewhere and cutting old ties. Cutting old ties. I cut Daddy's ties, all three of them, when I was Ricky's age. So I didn't yell at Ricky when he cut his hair. No point. It felt good cutting Daddy's ties. Like I was cutting him up, cutting him into long, stringy pieces. I don't remember his face anymore and I sure as hell don't know where he is.

"I am not beholden to nobody," Mother has said over and over. Me neither, but I need to talk to someone about Mom not coming home this time. She's done this before, but never for this long. Most of her boyfriends don't like kids hanging around when they screw. So she takes off sometimes. Everyone's entitled to a little R and R, as she has told me time and time again. That's cool—I can handle it.

I go check on the kid. She has peed on the carpet like a dog. But her panties are off and wadded carefully into a corner of the sofa.

"No pee on panties." Milly shakes her curly head. I'm so mad I could kill her.

"Mil-ly—damn you—why, why can't you go to the fucking bathroom?"

She shakes her head. "Bubba in bathroom pee pee."

You spank dogs with a newspaper. Maybe I should do that. Stick her nose in it. I'm so tired. That bitch should be home. That bitch doesn't give a Goddamn shit about us.

"I am free—I am free and that's the only reality." Mom's favorite words. She said, "Nobody can ever tie me down anymore. I do what I want to do, when I want to do it." So she had Milly. Her daddy is not the same daddy as mine and Rick's. I could call him if I knew his name but I don't know it. He lives right here in this city maybe and I could call him if I knew his name but I don't know it. Mom said he was Somebody Important. He gave her a gold bracelet. Course she took it with her. Too bad. I could've hocked it.

Let the damn pee stink the house up. I'm not cleaning up pee anymore. I'm sick of it.

"Poo poo——"

"Not on the floor!" I get the kid and haul her into the bathroom. I sling her on the pot.

"Rob-in, where's Momma?"

Robin. She said my name right. Usually she just says Bobbin or Bobby. "That's right. Rob-in——that's my girl!" She's got the *R* down perfect. She smiles like sunshine. She's so cute sometimes.

"Robin, Robin, Robin," she chatters over and over. Her poo poo begins to stink up the bathroom.

"Hurry up."

She doesn't ask about Momma again. I wipe her and flush the commode.

Jake Harris told Mom that Robin was a girl's name. So for a while my name turned into Rob, and at school, it's still my main name, but every time I walk into this place, I become Robin again, even if it's a dweebish, feeble sort of a name. I've always been Robin inside because I want to be. I like birds, always have, even if, say, I'm shooting them with Darrell Blake's air rifle. I don't like killing them, so I don't usually do that. I like watching them fly. I like the way they head on out, not caring. I love the little ones that tackle a big wind like it's nothing, the bluejays that dive-bomb cats and the little ones that fight crows. Another neat thing about my name is this and it's a really a bad-ass idea: I'm Robin——robbin', like, I'm *robbing* you. It's not that I want to be known as a thief, but I like the twist on the word. I'm Robbin'. So, many times I've slipped money out of Mom's purse when she's drunk or stoned and out of that place in the drawer with her diaphragm and she never even realized it. I'm robbin' you blind, I'd think——and now, look at me fly. No one will ever catch me. No one, not ever. I'm going to be smart at life, at doing stuff. I'll always escape because I'm a thievin' bird. I got my hands in the cookie jar and I got my hands wherever it is they don't belong. I got the money. I got the smarts. I can handle anything.

I fly in my dreams a lot.

You can watch TV anytime and see how people get away with murder. And stealing and hurting people. Doing things. I don't do drugs. I just say no. Unlike Darrell and other kids I know. Like Sandra, she's so hot and spreads her legs in a flash if you'll just give her something so she can get something to make her high—high in the sky and flying, as she puts it. I can relate to that—but screwing her, I haven't done that yet. It makes me sweat too much. I can't stand for my hands to sweat. You can't touch a girl if your hands are all wet. I can't, anyway. Not yet.

Jake wasn't such a bad guy. He never slapped us around and he took all of us to the movies a couple of times.

This latest dude is a prize asshole. Just look at this picture of him in his neat haircut and his fancy-pants suit. "He's established, honey, real on target, you know?" Mom told me. "He'll do anything for me. This is my ticket out, Robin. This time everything's going to be great," she said. And she got in his car and they drove off. She took one suitcase, a carry-on bag. I don't even know who he is. Not even where he worked. She just took off. But I've got this picture of him. I could give it to the FBI. They ought to be able to find them.

"Cookie!" It's brat baby. "Cookie—I wanna cookie—" the little beggar's pulling on my shirt.

"Tell Rick."

"Ricky gone."

I fold the picture in half and stick it in my pocket. "Still?"

Night's falling. I'm hungry. We'll have scrambled eggs and toast and the last of the Velveeta cheese. We'll have a feast. But we'll wait till Ricky comes back. I'll get her one of the last vanilla wafers. They're sort of stale, but Milly won't mind, as long as it's sweet. She sucks on those cookies like they're pacifiers.

She wants to play with me. I rub her curls. She sucks the cookie. "Go watch TV," I tell her and I plop on the sofa. Wards-of-the-state-to-be? Not if I can help it. I'm worried about that dweebil weevil Ricko. He should've been home hours ago. I can't remember where he went. I got mad or something. Rick went out to play; that's all. God, I'm sweating but it's actually cooled off some. I shouldn't be sweating. He'll be back. I know he'll be back.

It's time for a beer. I need it. I'm just hyper. I need to chill out, kick back and get reasonable. Mom will be back, too. She will come back. I know she loves us. We're her kids. She carried us in her body; you don't forget something like that. It's heavy shit, carrying babies around inside your body. I'm glad I can't do it. Maybe we were just too heavy. Maybe each time one of us got out she got weaker. Maybe she just got sick of looking at us. Big fucking deal. Bitch. Well, maybe we're sick of her. Yeah.

The front door bangs open. It's the little pervert, Ricky. "It's about time, you moron. Time to eat—what the . . . ?"

Ricky's standing here with a dumb, shit-eating grin on his face, reeking of garbage and looking like the *Night of the Living Dead*. Holy-moly—holding that dumb Barbie doll. "I got it, Milly; I got your doll!"

Milly turns from the flickering TV screen, her big blue eyes like stars. Her mouth rolls into an O.

Rick runs over to her and throws the doll in her lap and dares me to make fun.

I will not cry. "Go get washed up while I fix dinner."

"Peanut butter?" he asks.

"And eggs and cheese—whatever you want, okay?"

"Okay."

*   *   *

Barbie and Cooterbear sit at the table with us. Both of them are wearing ketchup. Milly's been sharing her food with them. They've eaten more than she has. All she wants is cookies and milk. I've begun stealing stuff at the grocery store, gas station and convenience store nearby. I've done it very carefully. Just little things. I'm Robin, after all. I only steal what Milly has to have or Rick. Milk, cookies, peanut butter. I bought the eggs. I am making some money. I baby-sit Tina Green's little girl, Tiffany. It helps. I have her tomorrow, in fact. Tina asked me yesterday how my mom is doing. I told her she has a new man. "All right, good for her—get down on the town. I bet she's having fun. Is he cute?" I told her he was and she sighed. "I got to get me a new man." Tina's husband died in a car wreck. Every time I think about that, I get scared and think about Nanny. Nanny died that way too, and ever since she died life has simply gone from bad to worse, no getting around it. Nanny watched out for us. Nanny took care of us. She could cook, too, and she could laugh with you, instead of *at* you. She didn't beat us and she paid attention and she wasn't mad all the time.

He's licking his plate. "Stop that, Ricky."

He ignores me.

"I said, stop acting like a pig."

"Kiss my ass; kiss my ass—"

"Keep that up and I will." That threat shocks him. He wipes his mouth on the ragged blue dish towel he always keeps close by when we eat and considers the prospect of my lips on his behind. It does not present a pretty picture.

"Well, yuck, yucko—don't you dare."

"Then remember you've got some manners somewhere in that feeb' brain of yours."

"You kiss my ass and I'll kill you, you queer piss-booger."

"Stop talking like a lowlife."

"I'm serious, bubba booger." Rick has a strange look on his face.

"Calm down—you're the idiot who keeps singing 'kiss my ass' till I want to puke."

Ricky won't look at me. He's rubbing his face with the towel again. His eyebrows are back to their natural color and the Vaseline he used to make his hair spikes stick was washed out when he took a quick shower. Now his hair hangs down in strings and damp curls. He looks so little sitting across the table from me and real scared. "I don't mean it, man."

"So don't say it. Guess we ought to start watching our language. School's fixin' to start, you know. Guess we ought to do something about that hair, too. I don't think you should go there looking like that. You look—"

"I like the way I look." He's kicking the table with his worn high-tops.

"Well, just a little, I'll cut it just a little, okay? You wouldn't want Mom to come home and find you looking like a space alien."

"I want to be a space alien."

"You can't always get what you want." Momma loved that old Stones song. She used to quote from it at least once a week.

Ricky's not listening. He's staring at Milly in her high chair who's fallen fast asleep. I go get her. Rick wipes her face with his trusty towel and we take her to Mom's bed. That's where we all sleep at night. Together. I like to pretend it's our nest out in a forest where the trees are higher than the sky and the stars shine through the branches with a white fire. It's peaceful there, quiet and safe. Ricky climbs into bed with Milly. He curls around her, yawning. He drops off to sleep like it's nothing. For me, it takes hours. I turn off the light and shut the door. I'm glad they are safe tonight. I'm glad we're still together. I shut off the lights in every room, except one in the living room. I have to watch the news. Mom always watched the news every night. "You have to stay informed," she always used to say. "There's no excuse for ignorance."

She wasn't a bad person. She had a college degree. She just

didn't know how to make money and she didn't like us. We weren't good enough. Maybe she wants to come back and he won't let her. She was always stupid about guys. Maybe he killed her. Yeah, that's it. She wouldn't just leave us.

It was neat, Ricky finding that dumb doll in the Dumpster and bringing it back to Milly. He's not such a bad kid.

"Here's Tiffany's bankie and here's her cereal and bananas—and some chocolate chip cookies for all you guys. And if you have any problems, just call me and here's the number and my extension. You're such a good boy, Rob, to do this for me. I'll pay you Friday. I don't know what I'm going to do when you go back to school next week."

It's on the tip of my tongue to tell her that I'm not going to, but I don't.

"Where's Candy? Did she get a new job? What's that new boyfriend do? What's his name? She's so secretive about men. Why? Does she think I'd try to muscle in?"

I shrug my shoulders. She's suspicious. As if I don't have enough problems. They'll probably cut off the telephone next week.

Tiffany tries to pull on her mother's fake-leather miniskirt. "Don't honey, you'll snag my hose. Go on and play with Milly." She glances at her watch and frowns. "Gotta run, but you holler if she's any trouble. And tell Candy to call me as soon as she gets back. I need to talk to her." The door clicks as it shuts. I stare at the kids. My body is like, numb-like. Cold. But I'm sweating. Tiffany grins at me. Already, she's a flirt.

"I'm not gonna get married, ever."

"What?" I try to focus on her twirling form. She suddenly plops at my feet with a "ta-da" and a flurry of handclaps. "Nope, not ever."

"Aw, sure you'll get married. You'll marry me, maybe?" I tease her. Pretty baby. I want to pick her up and smell her sweet hair. Her momma uses a shampoo that smells like

Christmas morning. I try to grab her but she wiggles out of my grasp and stands before me, hands on her little hips, her lower lip stuck out and serious. Like a teacher, for Christ's sake. "I'll never get married 'cause I don't wanna get pregnant."

"Why? Don't you want to have a baby someday?"

"No, 'cause the baby'd kick my stomach out." She loses interest in me and goes over to Milly.

Rick comes out of the bedroom, still sleepy. He heads for the kitchen for some milk and then comes to me. He hands me the scissors. "Just do it—fast." I sit him down in a chair and go to work on his hair, very carefully. The scissors are sharp. His neck is so thin I could cut it in two and probably do him a favor. But I don't.

I'm not going to get married, either. Then I remember the time I saw Sandra at Darrell's apartment. In the bathroom. But I don't want to think about that. It's too much trouble and makes me sad.

Nanny was nice. I wish I could talk to her. She liked Grandpa. I don't remember him. She never said anything bad about him. It must've been a good marriage. They never got a divorce. He just died.

"Ya'll be good. I'm going to the bedroom for a nap. Ricky, keep an eye out."

"I wanna go outside and play."

"No, stay here."

"What are you going to do?"

"Think."

"Can I help?"

"No. I told you what to do. Watch the kids for a few minutes. That's all." Ricky shoots me the finger as I go back to mother's bedroom. I have to be alone. I shut the door. I sit on the edge of the bed and look at the looking glass hand on the dresser. Nanny's looking glass hand that holds mom's rings and some cheap gold-tone necklaces. Nanny said whenever she wanted to know what the future held—and that wasn't very often—she'd look into the palm of that glass hand and she would find an answer. She told me that it was only something she would do if life had gotten so out of hand that she felt desperate and truly frightened and God had quit answering her prayers—or maybe, God's voice had gotten so faint that she could no longer hear it. I never believed Nanny. Nanny liked to tell stories. It is just a hand made out of white glass. It's not a magic mirror. I never saw Mom look into the palm; she didn't believe Nanny, either.

I go to the dresser and pick up the hand. A necklace swings. There's a ring with a fake ruby. I take it. I know who would like this. Sandra. I'll give it to Sandra.

"I'll be back later, kids. Be good."

"Where you going?" Rick tries to make me stop. He runs in front of me and holds out his arms. I push him out of the way.

"I'll be back."

The kid's frantic, still trying to block me. "Don't go—don't go, Robin; I promise to be good! Don't go Robin—"

"I'm just going to see Sandra," I whisper, sliding away from his grabby little hands.

"Oh," he says and I am out of there. Free.

Sandra answers the doorbell in a pink T-shirt that barely covers her rear. She has dark circles under her eyes and her dyed-blond hair is dirty. She stinks of cigarettes, B.O. and cheap cologne. "Yeah?"

"Hi."

"Hi, yourself. Come on in, Robby."

"You by yourself?" I don't want to be too eager. "Today is my birthday," I announce brightly, hating myself for being so obvious.

"Well, happy birthday, cutie. Thirteen big ones?"

"Yes," I lie, and we go sit on her bed.

"You're getting on up there, Robby. In a couple of years you'll catch up to me." She sits back against a stack of pillows. "Oops—no, I guess you'll never catch up to me. I'll always be older, right?" She giggles.

"Your dad's already gone to work?" I ask, though it's ridiculous. If I thought her father'd be here, I never would have come.

"Yeah." Her vague green eyes stare at the ceiling. She points at the faint spots on the ceiling. "Those are pretend stars—the constellations—I pasted them up there last year. At night you can see them, like real stars. Isn't that neat?"

"Sure is." I scoot closer to her. "I brought you a surprise."

She looks at me hopefully. I hand her the ring. She's surprised. "Take it," I tell her. She puts it on the first finger of her right hand.

"Wow, Robby boy, what's this for? Are we going steady now?" She's making fun of me.

"Sandra?" I can't say it. She's not wearing a bra. Her soft tits are pushing against the thin T-shirt. I blush. She ought to wear a bra.

She sighs. "I know, it's your birthday." She has bad breath. But she kisses me and it's not so bad. I'm so scared I'm trembling. And then, I'm not so scared and I'm just sweating a little bit. I almost tell her about mother. I'm singing inside "Happy Birthday, to me" I think her legs are gonna open to me and even though she smells, it will be okay. But then she just laughs and gets up and nothing has happened. I am still me. She says, "Wanna Diet Coke?"

The policemen are in the apartment when I get back, grilling Ricko. The little pervert panicked when I didn't come back for two hours. He had to call Tina and blab out every damn thing. Everything. And now what are we going to do? We lose everything, every damn thing. He didn't know. He's just a kid, an idiot kid. My brother, and he keeps hanging on me and crying like a tiddysuck. More than Milly. Milly just hugs Cooterbear and watches. They keep asking questions I can't answer. Why don't they just leave us alone?

And Tina, wonderful nosy Tina, here she is holding Tiffany and giving me such go-to-hell looks like I'm a monster or something. Like I'm responsible, like I'm Candy Bernice Brown. I tell them, "I don't know where she is and I don't care where she is. It's not my problem, okay?" After all, I'm a good boy and I can handle it.

But they're going to make us leave. Protective custody? Foster homes? "You've done it this time, you little bastard," I kick Ricky away from me and then feel like the ultimate shithead. I tell him, "Sorry, Ricky, I'm sorry." There's a policewoman who keeps saying, "We want to help you. Let us help you . . ." I don't trust her. I cannot trust anyone. Not ever.

So we've got to pack a bag and leave.

"We'll try to find her," they say. "Everything's going to be just fine."

Tina tries to kiss me before she leaves. I guess some of her anger must've been zapped by Rick's bawling. Her lips brush my forehead like dry leaves. God, how I hate her. She holds Tiffany to her breast like she's a diamond.

"I'll help you pack," the policewoman named Joyce says.

"I can do that—let me do that." If she'd just give me some space.

Joyce looks at her partner. They agree on some silent question.

I go to Mom's bedroom to get the suitcase she left, the big one. I begin to stuff it. Ricky follows me and Milly follows him. She puts her Barbie in under Rick's blue dish towel.

"We're going on a vacation," I tell them. Joyce comes in, checking on us like we're a bunch of morons. She doesn't trust me. We're even.

"Come here, sweetheart." She scoops Milly up into her arms and leaves the room.

"Will they find Momma?" Rick asks.

"I don't know."

"Are we going to jail?" Rick's trying not to cry. His drying tears have made white streaks down his round cheeks. Man I love that jerkoid squirrel butt. I ruffle the top of his pitiful hair.

"Nope."

"If you go to jail, I'll go to jail. I don't mind."

I keep packing our junk, can't look at him or I'll cry and I refuse to be an idiot crybaby fruitcake.

"Are you mad?"

"No."

"O-kay." Ricky jumps on the bed and looks down at me. He slowly begins to jump up and down on the bed. The suitcase bounces. "Stop it, Ricky." I catch the crooked smile on his face. It snaps in two as he falls.

"She's not coming back, is she, Robin?"

I've got everything packed. Except the hand. I've got to take the hand with us. It's a family heirloom. Nanny. I loved Nanny. She was a big woman, tall, with a round stomach and flabby upper arms. I used to make them wiggle and she would laugh. She would laugh hard. She said, "One time, when I was pregnant with your momma, I was having some problems. I looked into the hand and saw everything would work out— that my baby would live." "What did you see?" I asked her. "I saw your mother, pretty as you please, all grown, looking back out at me. I knew, even though the doctors said I couldn't carry to term, that my baby would live." I could tell Nanny believed what she'd told me.

"But how does it work?" I asked her, time and time again. "How do you make the hand work?" "Well," she said, "you have to believe the question as much as you do the answer."

Go figure. I don't know what she meant. But right now, I've got to try. My mouth waters. The looking glass hand sits there on the dresser just waiting for me to ask the question. I want the truth.

I go to the dresser and my hand closes around the glass wrist. I hold it level with my eyes. I look into the glass palm. I see just a faint reflection of my stupid face. My hand shakes and the jewelry left entwined around its fingers shivers lightly. I must concentrate upon my question. One old wedding band falls off and Ricky scrambles to pick it up. Good riddance to bad rubbish. I hate my mother. I hate my father. I hate every person on the planet Earth. Tell me; tell me the future. I want to know now! My eyes are bulging out of their sockets.

I'm looking down hard into the palm of the hand and it rolls into a fist.

I know what I see.

Nothing.

It was just a story Nanny made up. She was always making things up, trying to make it all better and it never was. Christ, she believed in luck. She threw salt across her shoulder and said, "Get behind me, Satan." It was stupid. I don't believe in anything.

"Robin, we're about to leave," that policewoman hollers from the living room.

"Where we goin'?" Rick says, as if I could tell him.

My fingers encircle the glass wrist. "You go on in there—"

Rick tugs bravely at the heavy suitcase and pulls it off the bed. It lands on the floor in a soft thump. He'd already closed it shut. No room for the glass hand. He drags it across the floor. "You coming, right-o?" His eyes are black marbles, round, frightened. "Please come, Robin, okay?"

He knows. Somehow, the little jerk knows. I get my backpack from underneath the bed and finish stuffing it with what I'll need. The cheap jewelry and the hand might bring something and the camera I stole out of the backseat of a car day before yesterday. That might bring some bucks.

"How long this vacation gonna be?"

I won't look at him. "Close the door."

Rick shuts it with his body.

"What's going on in there?" Joyce, the policewoman says. She does all the talking. I wonder what her partner's doing? Going through the kitchen? You can't tell me that they don't do that. I holler that I'm getting a poster off the door and she says I can't bring it with me, so hurry up. She says, "We can't wait all day—" and I know she doesn't give a shit, that this is probably the last call of the day.

"Listen," I tell Rick, "you've gotta go with Milly and take

care of her. You can handle it. And I'm going to go find Momma and that fucking bastard she's with." I wad the last T-shirt, my jacket and Mom's address book into the pack. I'm sweating bullets.

"I wanna go with you." I'm headed out the window. If I do it right I won't break nothing. It's a ways down, but hey, I'm cool, I can jump. Yeah, right. I'm certifiable if I think I'm some kind of hot-ass stuntman. Look at that. "You can't," I tell him, easing down the ledge. I'm afraid he's going to cry. He can't cry. "Only tiddy babies cry, Ricky. You're a tough guy, like me."

His round eyes and round cheeks redden. He's trying not to cry, honest to God. From the parking lot some hypnotic rap tells me to hurry up, my man and I gotta go. I've really gotta go now. I can do it now. Be strong.

"You want to help me?" I whisper.

"Yeah!" Ricky says, nodding. His wet eyes sparkle. He's falling for it.

"Okay, stud, listen: I gotta get out of here without them stopping me. I gotta go find your mom and then we'll come back for you. I promise. It's our secret, okay?

"Right now I want you to go back in there and throw the biggest shit-kicking, wall-eyed fit you can throw—I mean, act like a pure-d madman so I can get away. Okay?"

I'm sliding all the rest of the way, a dangling man. The sun's a UFO. I look back at the Rick-man through sweat. "Bye, Space Alien."

"Bye, Robin." He waves a little hand and I'm gone. I'm flying. I hear the screams and ugliest cuss words Ricky knows. The policewoman's madder than hell. The last I hear of Rick is a radical musical version of "Kiss My Ass" and a thin whistling cry from Milly, "Robbie . . ."

I land on the ground, and roll into a wilting bush. A few scratches, but I'm okay, nothing's broken. I hit the pavement, and run across the parking lot. Lots of cracks. No one ever bothers to fix them. There'll always be another earthquake.

The cracks just get wider. I keep looking over my shoulder, thinking they're coming. They're going to try and stop me. I get past the complex. I weave in between broken-down cars and the ones that still work, just barely. I slip into the shadow of a Dumpster and catch my breath. I've got to hurry. I run a long time. Then I realize no one has come after me. No sirens. No voices. Nothing.

I'm free as a bird. No one's gonna put me in a cage, not no way, not no how. Besides, they'll be better off without me. That's what Mom, the bitch queen slut, thought. Why are adults such liars?

I'm an adult now. I lied to Rick.

I keep looking over my shoulder.

Then it dawns on me—they're not ever going to come after me. They're probably relieved. One less mouth to feed.

Vacation in hell and there ain't no Holiday Inn.

I come to the highway. It's a big one with lots of lanes. Express yourself. Oh damn, it's busy. I make a mad dash across to the median. I flatten myself against the divider. Nanny told me she heard on the TV that one time a man who'd been hit by a car drug himself here, all bleeding and hurt, and he just sat here for days before anyone would stop to help him. He was in a coma and they all thought he was just drunk or doped up.

I could die here, too.

It's getting late. Rush-hour traffic. Rush *hours*. Someday cars will run on air, a teacher of mine said. He said he saw it in a movie, so it must be so.

Maybe I'm in a movie.

I forgot to bring food.

I'm a sorry A-double ass.

I think they just drove past in the squad car. I think it was them, really. They were laughing and Milly waved bye-bye.

That Joyce woman knew all along I was running away. She gave me all the time in the world to make my getaway. She didn't want to be bothered with another brat. One less mess of red tape, one less kid to deal with. Yeah, I think I remember the policeman saying to his partner, "Jesus H. Christ, not another one," and then she said, "Three."

I rummage through my pack, hoping for a Snickers all soft and mushy.

A car stops.

It's a rich man in one of those big fat-cat Mercedes. He looks like a commercial for American Express. His Rolex (hey, I seen 'em) catches the rays of the setting sun. My ticket out of here.

"Get in, kid," he says through clenched teeth.

I get in. He smells like a forest but his eyes are blue ice. He steps on the gas. We fly forward, fast, into traffic, like man, he knows where we're going.

"Are you hungry?" he says.

"I'm always hungry," I say as his right hand encircles my wrist.

MAKE A WISH UPON THE MOON

CHARLES L. GRANT

"My wife and I were mugged in New York City several years ago,"
Charles L. Grant tells us. "In Times Square, in fact. Some kids tried to
grab my wallet and my wife's necklace. Kat grabbed her necklace back;
I pushed the kids away. Afterward, when we told our New York friends
about it, they weren't surprised about the mugging—but they were
shocked that we actually fought back. Conditioning, I guess."

Grant, the former president of The Horror Writers of America, has won
many awards for his short stories, novels, and anthology editing.
Stunts, his long novel exploring random violence, appeared in 1990.
He lives, with his wife, the writer Kathryn Ptacek, in New Jersey, where
he collects bad movies on laser disc.

He danced, you know. Every night, in the street. We'd sit
here on the stoop and watch him. Every night that summer.
We used to think he was just one of the crazies, or drunk, or
something, you know what I mean? Like, what kind of guy
would do that, out in the middle of the street like that?

I wish I'd known.

Of course, it was different around here then. That empty lot down there on the corner, it used to be a luncheonette, with some guy who taught piano in a studio upstairs. Drove us nuts, trying to eat burgers and listen to scales at the same time. When the building burned down, some kind of stupid-ass riot over one thing or another, they never replaced it. Kids play there now, in the rubble. With the rats. And the druggies. Not even the folks who don't have anyplace to bed down will live there.

And over there, just up from the fire hydrant, in number 48, look real hard you can still see a little of the pink paint Maria Latines used to mark her door. She couldn't see all that well, and all the brownstones look alike, so she painted it one morning so she could spot it without her glasses, since they were broken most of the time.

The summer he came to dance, in fact.

The summer she left.

I said her name was Maria, right?

Yeah.

Maria.

And all the windows were intact, too. Now, they look like teeth sometimes, y'know? When the light catches the broken glass just right, it looks like some old woman sitting there, waiting for something to eat. Some meat. One of us. Broken glass everywhere. But not then. Then, you look down this side of the street, down the other, there wasn't even a piece of cardboard or newspaper taped over a busted pane. Nobody would let it happen. A kid threw a ball or a rock or something through a window, it was replaced before nightfall.

Always.

Not that the city wasn't falling apart even then. Drunks came from the bars, pissed on the cars, went back to Mars or wherever the hell they came from; Hector Pollman, down there in number 109, he went to jail for killing his wife with a frying pan and a butcher knife, hanged himself in his cell before Christmas; in this building right here, in the apartment right above mine, there was Regina Imatto, prettiest and dumbest hooker you'd ever want to meet. She got beat up twice a week and three times on Sunday, it seemed, and never even considered finding a new line of work.

"No taxes, Barry," she'd tell me, sitting right here on the stoop, right where you're sitting now, as a matter of fact. "No taxes, it's worth a bruise now and then." She'd smile and squeeze my hand, point to sky and kiss my cheek. "Relax, okay? Relax, take it easy, make a wish on the moon and make us rich, okay?" Then she'd laugh and go inside.

She's gone, too.

Damn.

I had dreams once, you know, some of them because of that dancing idiot. I dreamed, just like in the movies, that I'd show her the error of her ways and marry her and we'd move out of this hell and into another state where you can see green and blue and birds and . . .

Where the moon still shines.

Don't laugh.

Look up.

You see any stars?

No, because of all the damn lights and the damn pollution and the damn city doesn't care because it only wants its people to look straight ahead, look down, into the gutter.

But back then, back that summer, you could always see the moon.

You can't see it now.

Look all night, you'll never see it, not once.

No, it's not because of the height of the buildings or the season or the beer or anything like that. It's not an illusion.

Logan Street just doesn't have it anymore.

See, the night he came down the sidewalk the first time, we were all out here on our steps. Radios and stereos going in some of the apartments. Fights coming from others. Sirens and horns out there in the city. And we were watching some kids cheat like hell in some kind of crazy baseball game. I think they were making the rules up as they went along. Shouting, laughing, cursing, laughing again. Cars were at the curb. Old Lady Kettle was in her window—that one, right across from us on the first floor—leaning on her arms and these huge old breasts like flattened pillows, wearing the same print dress she wore to her old man's funeral I don't know how many years ago. Mrs. Schoolcraft was in the window right above her, talking all the time, yelling at the kids. She was a widow, too, married sixty years, I think, and all she had left was the street. Everybody was out that night, and Regina was coming up the other way, just swinging her hips, swinging her purse, laughing at something and calling out to the other guys on the other stoops. No one in the neighborhood messed with her, see. She was family. A little on the black sheep side, but she was family. Maria was crossing over to come see me. She liked me. About my age then, pretty as a Latin dancer, you know?—slim, dark, with eyes that could tear your heart out when she was mad, and could tear your heart when she cried. I could hardly talk to her, though. Something about her, she made my tongue stupid, you know what I mean? A hundred times I wanted to ask her out, and a hundred times I asked her instead about her job, about the weather, crap like that. So she was heading my way, and Alberto the hot dog man, he had set up his cart up the street a little, in front of 55. Teenagers all around him, making fun of his eyepatch, he'd painted a dragon on it when he was drunk on New Year's Eve. He didn't care. He slopped on the sauerkraut and mustard and laughed back as he took their money.

Normal night.

Hot as hell.

The kind of night that even when you were sitting, like you and me, just shooting the shit, you'd work up a sweat.

And the moon.

You know, people say the soul of a neighborhood, it's in the people who live there. Like Maria and Mrs. Kettle, what was left of Hector Pollman's family, Alberto, people like that.

They're wrong.

It's the moon.

You look up at it when things are great, and you think that even you can go there someday and bring a piece of it back for your buddies, for your lover; you look up at it when things are rotten, and it's like it's telling you, Don't sweat it, man, I'm here, you can talk to me. Make a wish.

It's not crazy, not really.

Think about it.

Think about the street that night.

Can you see it?

Can you hear it?

Can you smell the heat and the oil and the sweat and the bodies?

I was wearing a T-shirt and soccer shorts, deck shoes and no socks. Max Rineberg was with me. He lived in the basement apartment. Down there in the well at the bottom of the steps, see? Where all that garbage is now. That was his place, where the barred windows are.

Anyway, we were talking about getting out. That's all we ever talked about, I guess. What else you going to do when you live in a place like this on a night like that? Somebody had knifed a six-year-old kid in the subway, a bunch of church people went nuts up on the North Side and ransacked some stores, two guys jumped from a window in some downtown hotel, the Mob bumped off a couple of federal informants down by the river . . . all in one day.

Summertime as usual.

"Look, Tremain, it's just not the same anymore," he said. He was a little guy with lots of frizzy hair on his face, practically none on his head. Like Regina, he was about my age, only his voice kind of belonged to a little kid. He hated that. He was always trying to make it sound deeper, only sometimes he forgot. "I've been talking with this guy in Los Angeles, he might have a job for me."

I didn't believe it.

He was always talking to some "guy" somewhere who always "might" have a job for him.

That was his dream.

"You going to take it?"

"In a second, Tremain, in a second." He also never called me by my first name. He never called anybody by their first name, except the ladies.

Regina came up the steps then, giggling to herself, short hair like fire stuck to her head because she'd been sweating so much. We didn't ask where she'd been. She stopped at the door and said, "Who the hell is that, Barry?"

I looked where she was pointing.

It was him.

He had a wool Navajo vest on but no shirt, jeans that looked like they would fall off in a strong wind and tied around his waist with a thick piece of rope, and sandals without socks. There was no telling how old he was, he had that kind of face, and he had more hair than I'd ever seen on one man in my life. Not really long, but thick and puffed and flowing, like a kind of mane.

The kids hanging around Alberto's hot dog cart whistled at him, but he didn't pay them any attention. He just stepped into the street, right into the middle of the baseball game, and started dancing.

I swear to God, he started dancing.

Stood right there at the manhole cover and started waltzing around it in these tiny little circles. Nice and slow. Humming to himself. Kept his hands in his pockets the whole time. Nice and slow. Humming.

It didn't take long before Gary Pollman, he must have been about twelve, went up to him and told him to move, he was blocking the game.

The man kept dancing.

Waltzing.

Humming.

Looking at the ground, looking up at the sky.

Now, you gotta understand that Gary, at twelve, had decided he was the man of the house after his old man died and he had moved in with his aunt and grandmother. Old before his time. And the bossiest little kid in the state, I swear to god. He also carried—if you know what I mean. So Max figured two minutes tops before the kid pulls out a blade and threatens the guy with a free blood tattoo.

Gary didn't.

Oddly enough, he backed off after some more yelling, some real imaginative cursing, and talked the rest of the gang into moving the game down the block a little.

"Damn," Regina said, shaking her head. "Weird."

Max snorted.

I didn't think anything of it. Weird, on *this* block, was a way of life sometimes.

So the three of us—Regina, she came back to sit beside me—we watched the dancing fool to see how long it would be before he got tired and moved on.

Three hours.

Just after midnight.

No break, no drink, looking up at the sky and down at the ground.

Three hours, and he walked away.

Just like that.

"Man," said Max, "I wish I had some of what he's on."

"Pig," Regina said flatly and went inside, brushing her hand over my shoulder. No invitation. She liked me; she didn't like Max, he was always trying to grab her.

Most of the stoops were empty by then, the game long over, Mrs. Kettle and Mrs. Schoolcraft back in their dens. That's when I realized that Maria had never made it across the street. I looked up at her window, but the light was out, and it kind of bothered me because maybe, I thought, she didn't want to be around Regina. Guilt by association, something like that. Or maybe she thought I liked Regina better than her.

Damn.

Some days you just can't do anything right, even when you don't do a damn thing.

The next day it was even hotter.

The subway broke down under the river at four o'clock, a bunch of people got sent to the hospital.

Some guy on the news tried to fry an egg on the marble steps in front of Town Hall and almost did it.

A fire broke out in a restaurant over in Little Warsaw, nine people died and a dozen firemen were overcome by the heat.

Then the sun went down.

And Jesus . . . lord, Gary Pollman was killed.

He was running parked cars. You know how it's done, right?—starting at the end of the block, hopping onto the first hood or trunk and then running over the roof, jump to the next car, see how far he can get before he either slips and falls, the cops come, or somebody stops him.

Somebody stopped him.

Nobody saw who did it, everybody heard the shot.

One minute he's standing on a roof, laughing his fool head off, the next minute somebody put a hole in his head.

Cops all over the place, his grandmother and aunt screaming and tearing at their hair, ambulances, spinning lights, people pouring out of their apartments like they were ants that had had hot water dumped into their hill. The police talked to everybody, even me and I had just come home from a movie—I don't know what it was, but the air-conditioning was great.

Anyway, the next thing you know, the street is empty. All the windows open, shapes and shadows moving in the rooms.

And he comes back.

Dancing around the manhole cover.

Mrs. Kettle screams at him, Doesn't he know a kid's been murdered, ain't he got any respect for the dead? But the guy just keeps on waltzing, hands in his pockets. Looking up at the sky. Looking down at the ground.

I don't know when he left. Max wasn't around, there was nobody to talk to, so I went inside and tried to get some sleep.

It didn't work very well.

I had dreams about winter, about the moon, about Maria, about Regina, about losing my job.

When I woke up, I felt like I was dead. But at least it was cooler, a lot cooler, and I guess it wasn't until two or three days later, not too long after poor Gary was buried, that the damn heat came back. Like it was never gone, y'know? Like all those days like spring never existed.

The heat came back.

Mrs. Schoolcraft died of a heart attack.

The heat came back.

The dancing man never left.

I was down there on the sidewalk, right by the black iron railing that kept people from falling into the well where Max's apartment was. I was waiting for him, we were going over to Murphy's, a bar we know, and I was getting pretty damn impatient. He wouldn't answer the phone after we'd made the date, wouldn't come to his door, and I was about ready to go by myself.

I heard a cry.

Not a scream, but a small cry, like a hurt animal.

I looked around and saw the waltzing fool, and saw Regina right beside him. One palm was against her cheek, her eyes were wide like he'd just told her all her family had been murdered, and she looked right at me, and didn't see me.

Son of a bitch, I thought, and ran over, but she was already walking back toward our building. Quick. Heels cracking on the soft blacktop. I glared at the guy, but he ignored me.

Looking up.

When I jumped the curb and took hold of her arm, she pulled away with another cry.

"Hey," I said. "Hey, kiddo, it's me."

She turned around. There were tears in her eyes. They wouldn't fall, but they were there.

When she tried a smile, I wished she hadn't. It made it look like she'd just taken the most god-awful medicine in the world.

"What'd he say to you?" I asked angrily, pointing back at the fool. "He try to hustle you? What'd he say?"

"Nothing." She shook her head. "Nothing, Barry."

She looked up quickly, looked back at me and, before I could stop her, leaned into me and kissed my cheek. "Goodbye," she whispered. "I think I might love you."

I was so stunned I just stood there, while Mrs. Kettle, who'd traded her print dress for a black one in honor of Mrs. School-craft's funeral that morning, laughed and announced the scene to the neighborhood. I told her to shut the hell up and ran after Regina, but she was already on her way up the steps.

"Hey!"

She opened the door.

"Hey, damnit!"

She looked over her shoulder, looked away, and went inside. The door closed, and for some reason I couldn't go after her. It was too final. Even now I can't tell you why I knew that; I just did. So I hustled back to the fool in the street and grabbed his elbow, stopped him from dancing, and only barely stopped myself from screaming in his face.

"What did you say to her?" I demanded, my voice so low it sounded hoarse. "What the *hell* did you say to her?"

Not old. Not young. I couldn't tell even from that close the color of his eyes.

But he made me feel cold.

I wasn't scared, not exactly, and he didn't look like some creature or monster or vampire or anything.

But he made me feel cold on the hottest night of the year.

"What?" I said.

"You know," he answered.

And once again I just stood there like a jerk while he walked away, up the street, and I didn't move until he'd disappeared around the corner. Then I ran to Max's, leaned over the railing, and screamed at him to get the hell out here, now, before I kicked his damn door to pieces.

I could hear Mrs. Kettle laughing.

I could hear the bells on Alberto's hot dog cart.

I yelled again, and he came out, buttoning some truly awful Hawaiian shirt and grinning like a jerk.

"You rang?"

"I'm thirsty!"

He saw the mood right away and tripped coming up the steps. I know it was supposed to make me laugh; it didn't. I just stormed off to the bar, him nearly running to keep up, and it wasn't until I'd downed a couple three beers that I told him what happened.

He had no answer, and I hated him for it. He was supposed to know everything. He was always there for me, Max was. When my folks died, he was there; when I lost that stock market job and had to lug crates in a warehouse, he was there; when I got my new job—trainee in an ad firm downtown— he kept me at it, telling me about my bank account, telling me not to sweat the snide bastards in the suits, pretty soon I'd own the place and fire their tight asses.

I believed him.

I always believed him, and thanked him just about every night, though never to his face.

So we're there in the bar, and I guess I got drunk.

I think Max helped me home and poured me into bed.

I know that the next afternoon after I got home, when I went up to Regina's, she had already left. The building manager was there—a piece of work I wouldn't wish on my worst enemy—and he told me she'd moved out that morning, right after dawn. He was ticked because she woke him up to give back the key and demand a check for her security deposit. And no, he didn't know where she was going, good riddance, he didn't need nutso people like that messing up his life.

That night, while the waltzing man was in the street, I asked the moon what the hell was going on.

I didn't get an answer.

And it went on like that for over a week.

A fire. A robbery next door that ended up in a killing. Stolen cars. A kid crushed under a van, the guy who was driving it nearly beaten to death by a mob.

The dancing man.

Maria and I finally went out a couple of times. Just to the movies. No holding hands or anything, but it was okay. It was, in fact, about the only okay thing going on that year. Then, one night, we were on the steps with Max, me in the middle, and we're watching the waltzing fool.

It was quiet.

The city all around us, and all we could hear was the guy humming, his feet scraping on the street. Looking up. Looking down.

"His wife left him," Maria finally decided. She had leaned her forearm on my leg, her hand draped over my knee. I don't know if she knew it, but it was driving me up the wall. "That's why he's that way."

"Bullshit," Max said. "He's just nuts."

"Have you ever talked to him?"

"Are you kidding?" Max laughed, pulled at his beard. "I bet he doesn't even speak English, for god's sake."

Quiet.

"It's very sad," she whispered.

I was going to make a joke then, but I looked over and saw her face, and damn if she didn't look like Regina the night she left.

It scared me.

I put my arm around her shoulders.

She didn't move.

Max, however, winked at me and excused himself loudly, telling the whole block he had to use the john. He belched, scratched himself, and started down to the sidewalk.

The dancing man looked up.

Max paused, glanced over his shoulder, winked at me again, and walked into the street.

"Hey," I called. I didn't want him to do it.

But Max didn't pay any attention. He was shorter than the guy and had to look up, but his back was to us so we couldn't see his expression. I did see the dancing man's right arm move, like he was taking his hand from his pocket. Max looked down. The man's arm moved again. Max took one stumbling step back, took another, took another, until his heel caught the curb. He nearly fell as he turned, walked quickly to his steps and started down without looking up at us.

"So, Max," I said, "what'd he say?"

He didn't answer.

The next sound I heard was his door slamming open, slamming shut.

I shrugged—"He's a little nuts himself"—and that's when I saw that the moon was gone.

No big deal. Not then. It was late, the moon sets, what the hell. So I gave Maria a quick kiss, and she kissed me back, and the next thing I knew we were in my bed and I was in heaven and I didn't even dream about Regina that night.

She loved me; she said so; I said it back and felt like crying.

Next night we camped on the steps and made all kinds of plans for getting out, buying a little house, finding new jobs or maybe just commuting, giggling and laughing like happy drunks and Mrs. Kettle across the street yelling out the news. I didn't care. I kissed Maria so hard and so long, Mrs. Kettle shut up.

Then I said, "Maria, I'm going to get you the moon for a diamond ring." Stupid, right? What the hell, I was in love.

Except that she said, "That's sweet, Barry, but there is no moon tonight."

The dancing man came, but this time, while he danced, he kept looking at us.

"Of course there's a moon. It's too early for it to—"

It wasn't there.

The man danced.

Looked down.

Looked at us.

I grabbed her hand and nearly pulled her down the steps. "C'mon. It's just low, that's all."

"Barry!"

But she was smiling, and we hurried to the end of the block and turned the corner, walked one block north and I pointed up. "See? There it is, big as ever."

She nodded. "So why can't we see it from our place?"

I nearly laughed aloud. *Our place.* Jesus, thank you!

We kept on walking, looking in store windows, grinning at kids out too late, acting like damn idiots until we reached Margal Street. It was empty. Hell, it was deserted, and looked like someone had dropped a bomb in the middle of it.

"Barry?"

She was looking at the sky.

I looked.

The moon was gone.

"Weird."

"Spooky."

It was back when we walked another block.

I frowned, checked the city, decided we were nuts but pulled her along anyway until we found another place where nobody lived, where the buildings were black with dead fire or crumbling or gone.

No moon.

"Take me home," she said. I could feel her shivering as she hugged my arm. "Please, Barry? Take me home?"

We went home. We didn't make love, but we slept together and that was fine with me. Everything was fine.

Until the next day, when I went down to Max's place to tell him the good news—hell, I wanted him to be my best man—

and found him in the bathroom. In the tub. Dark water. White face. Beard matted with blood.

I went a little crazy, I think, after that. And then I went into like a zombie state or something. I did everything I had to, from bringing in the cops to calling Max's father to calming Maria down to signing all the forms to talking to a funeral guy; I did it all without thinking. One foot in front of the other. One word after another. Not thinking, not crying, not angry, not anything. I moved and I talked, and when the dancing man came that night, I decided to kill him, because everything had been fine until he came along. Somewhere deep in that state I was in, I had been thinking without realizing it. You probably figured it out a long time ago, but hell, I was in love, I was home, there was a nut in the street, just another nut, who the hell knew, you know what I mean?

Maria had gone back to her place.

The street was empty when he finally arrived.

I waited for him by the manhole cover.

He didn't dance that night. He stood in front of me, hands in his pockets, and waited for me to scream at him.

I didn't.

I couldn't.

I looked up and there was no moon; I looked down and saw something softly glowing in each of his pockets.

He nodded. Once. Very slowly.

"I don't believe it," I said, feeling angry now.

"I showed your friend." His voice was winter. Not snowmen and sleighs; a vast field of white where nothing grew but the wind. Don't think desolation, though. Think rage, cold rage. "I'll show you too, if you ask me again."

I looked around, but there was nothing to see. All the streetlights were out, the windows dark, and I could hear, I could actually hear, the rust growing and spreading on the cars at the curb. I knew then that this is what he told Regina, showed Max, showed all the rest without actually speaking—

the neighborhood was dying, and if you don't leave, you're going to die with it.

I didn't believe it.

"Why?" I asked, angrier, sadder.

He looked at me then, really looked, and I saw a smile there, and a tear, before he turned and walked away.

I followed. "Hey, damnit, what the hell's going on?"

He walked on.

I looked back, nearly stopped, because Maria had come back to the stoop, her suitcase at her feet. I gestured to her— *stay where you are, I'll be right back*—but she only shook her head.

The dancing man moved on.

I took a step back toward Maria, back toward the fool, and in that single, damning hesitation she picked up the suitcase and climbed down the steps.

And walked away in the other direction.

"Maria!"

Not even an echo.

So I chased after the man instead, catching up with him just as he reached the intersection, grabbing his elbow and nearly yanking him off his feet.

"Tell me," I demanded, nearly snarling at him, ready to strangle him.

"You know," was all he answered, and walked across the avenue.

Several cars blared their horns at him, a bus shrieked, a van swerved, and when the traffic cleared, he was gone.

Just . . . gone.

All the moons from all the neighborhoods with him in his pocket.

You can't do this! I screamed after him, not making a sound; *you can't, this is my home, bring it back, for Christ's sake; for Christ's sake, bring it back!*

Then I did go crazy, I really did.

I sprinted down the street, ignoring the heat, kicking trash cans, kicking cars, chasing after Maria until I realized she was gone, so I ran back the other way, kicking trash cans, kicking cars. I ran until I fell flat on my face in the middle of the block. I wasn't worried about anybody running over me. Cars didn't come into Logan Street anymore. And I didn't care about Mrs. Kettle or Alberto or anyone else seeing me, because sometime between the time I had chased after the fool and had chased after Maria, they had already left.

You know, he had said.

Twice he had said, *You know.*

The neighborhood had no soul, and those who loved it either died or ran away.

Except me.

You're right; I didn't run.

I was too angry; I was too scared.

And he was right, too—I knew just what to do.

So now I've told you once.

If I tell you again . . .

Oh don't worry, I won't show you my hands, you can just come with me for a while, keep me company, while I go over to Maple Street. Common name, right? Nice people there.

They have a moon.

I'm going to waltz it down and bring it back.

And if it doesn't fit, goddamnit, I'll find another one. The city's filled with them, you know. Bright streets, lively streets, and lots of nice people who don't know they're dying. A lot of nice people who don't know how mad I am.

Find a place to sit down, and watch me dance, hands in my pockets, looking up, looking down.

You can even try to warn them, but I know just what they'll say:

Don't sweat it, man, don't sweat it, he's just another crazy, we get them all the time. Sit and watch a while, have a beer, have a smoke.

And if you think you feel lucky, make a wish upon the moon.

ASH

JOHN SHIRLEY

"One day I realized I was, in part, responsible for all the suffering, neglect, hunger, abuse and misery of the city," John Shirley says, "and that realization was real, genuine horror." He adds: "You're own similar realization is forthcoming."

Shirley, thirty-seven, lives in San Francisco, where, among other things, he is currently the leader of the rock band The Panther Moderns. Much of his short fiction was collected in Heatseeker, *and his novels include* Dracula in Love, Cellars, In Darkness Waiting, *and the new Ziesing publication,* Wetbones.

A police car pulled up to the entrance of the Casa Valencia. The door to the apartment building, on the edge of San Francisco's Mission district, was almost camouflaged by the businesses around it, wedged between the stand-out orange and blue colors of the Any Kind Check Cashing Center and the San Salvador restaurant. Ash made a note on his pad, and sipped his cappuccino as a bus hulked around the corner, blocking his view through the window of the espresso shop. The cops had shown up a good thirteen minutes after he'd called in the anonymous tip on a robbery at the Casa Valencia. Which worked out good. But when it was time to pop the armored car at the Check Cashing Center next door, they might show up more briskly. Especially if a cashier hit a silent alarm.

The bus pulled away. Only a few cars passed, impatiently clogging the corner of 16th and Valencia, then dispersing; pedestrians, with clothes flapping, hurried along in tight groups, as if they were being tumbled by the moist February wind. Blown instead by eagerness to get off the streets before this twilight became dark.

Just around the corner from the first car, double-parking with its lights flashing, the second police car arrived. By now, though, the bruise-eyed hotel manager from New Delhi or Calcutta or wherever was telling the first cop that *he* hadn't called anyone; it was a false alarm, probably called in by some junkie he'd evicted, just to harass him. The cop nodded in watery sympathy. The second cop called through the window of his SFPD cruiser. Then they both split, off to Dunkin' Donuts. Ash relaxed, checking his watch. Any minute now the armored car would be showing up for the evening money drop-off. There was a run of check cashing after five o'clock.

Ash sipped the dregs of his cappuccino. He thought about the .45 in the shoebox under his bed. He needed target practice. On the slim chance he had to use the gun. The thought made his heart thud, his mouth go dry, his groin tighten. He wasn't sure if the reaction was fear or anticipation.

This, now, this was being alive. Planning a robbery, executing a robbery. Pushing back at the world. Making a dent in it, this time. For thirty-nine years his responses to the world's bullying and indifference had been measured and careful and more or less passive. He'd played the game, pretending that he didn't know the dealer was stacking the cards. He'd worked faithfully, first for Grenoble Insurance, then for Serenity Insurance, a total of seventeen years. And it had made no difference at all. When the recession came, Ash's middle-management job was jettisoned like so much trash.

It shouldn't have surprised him. First at Grenoble, then at Serenity, Ash had watched helplessly as policyholders had been summarily cut off by the insurance companies at the time of their greatest need. Every year, thousands of people with cancer, with AIDS, with accident paraplegia, cut off from the benefits they'd spent years paying for; shoved through the numerous loopholes that insurance industry lobbyists worked into the laws. That should have told him: if they'd do it to some ten-year-old kid with leukemia—and, God, they did it every day—they'd do it to Ash. Come the recession, bang, Ash was out on his ear with the minimum in retirement benefits.

And the minimum wasn't enough.

Fumbling through the "casing process," Ash made a few more perfunctory notes as he waited for the armored car. His hobbyhorse reading was books about crime and the books had told him that professional criminals cased the place by taking copious notes about the surroundings. Next to Any Kind Check Cashing was Lee Zong, Hairstyling for Men and Women. Next to that, Starshine Video, owned by a Pakistani. On the Valencia side was the Casa Valencia entrance—the hotel rooms were layered above the Salvadoran restaurant, a dry cleaners, a leftist bookstore. Across the street, opposite the espresso place, was Casa Lucas Productos, a Hispanic super-market, selling fruit and cactus pears and red bananas and plantains and beans by the fifty-pound bag. It was a hardy leftover from the days when this was an entirely Hispanic neighborhood. Now it was as much Korean and Arab and Hindu.

Two doors down from the check-cashing scam, in front of a liquor store, a black guy in a dirty, hooded sweatshirt stationed himself in front of passing pedestrians, blocking them like a linebacker to make it harder to avoid his outstretched hand.

That could be me, soon, Ash thought. I'm doing the right thing. One good hit to pay for a business franchise of some kind, something that'd do well in a recession. Maybe a movie theater. People needed to escape. Or maybe his own check-cashing business—with better security.

Ash glanced to the left, down the street, toward the entrance to the BART station: San Francisco's subway, this entrance only one short block from the check-cashing center. At five-eighteen, give or take a minute, a north-bound subway would hit the platform, pause for a moment, then zip off down the tunnel. Ash would be on it, with the money; escaping more efficiently than he could ever hope to, driving a car in city traffic. And more anonymously.

The only problem would be getting to the subway station handily. He was five-six, and pudgy, his legs a bit short, his wind even shorter. He was going to have to sprint that block and hope no one played hero. If he knew San Francisco, though, no one would.

He looked back at the check-cashing center just in time to see the Armored Transport of California truck pull up. He checked his watch: as with last week, just about five-twelve. There was a picture insignia of a knight's helmet on the side of the truck. The rest of the truck painted half black and half white, which was supposed to suggest police colors, scare thieves. Ash wouldn't be intimidated by a paint job.

He'd heard that on Monday afternoons they brought about fifteen grand into that check-cashing center. Enough for a downpayment on a franchise, somewhere, once he'd laundered the money in Reno.

Now, he watched as the old, white-haired black guard, in his black and white uniform, wheezed out the back of the armored car, carrying the canvas sacks of cash. Not looking to the right or left, no one covering him. His gun strapped into its holster.

The old nitwit was as ridiculously overconfident as he was overweight, Ash thought. He'd never had any trouble. First time for everything, Uncle Remus.

Ash watched intently as the guard waddled into the check-cashing center. He checked his watch, timing him, though he wasn't sure why he should, since he was planning to rob him on the way in, not on the way out. But he had the impression from the books you were supposed to time everything. The reasons would come clear later.

A bony, stooped Chicano street eccentric—aging, toothless, with a squiggle of black mustache and sloppily dyed black hair—paraded up the sidewalk to stand directly in front of Ash's window. Crazy old fruit, Ash thought. A familiar figure on the street here. He was wearing a Santa Claus hat tricked out with junk jewelry, a tattered gold lamé jacket, thick mascara and eyeliner, and a rose erupting a penis crudely painted on his weathered cheek. The inevitable trash-brimmed shopping bag in one hand, in the other a cane made into a mystical staff of office with the gold-painted plastic roses duct-taped to the top end.

As usual the crazy old fuck was babbling free-form imprecations, his spittle making whiteheads on the window glass. "Damnfuckya!" came muffled through the glass. "Damnfuckya for ya abandoned city, ya abandoned city and now their gods are taking away, taking like a bend-over boy yes, damnfuckya! Yoruba Orisha! The Orisha, *cabrón!* Holy shit on a wheel! *Hijo de puta!* Ya doot, ya pay, they watch, they pray, they take like a bend-over boy ya! El-Elegba Ishu at your crossroads shithead *pendejo!* LSD not the godblood now praise the days! Damnfuckya be sorry! Orisha them Yoruba *cabrones!"*

Yoruba Orisha. Sounded familiar.

"Godfuckya Orisha sniff 'round, *vamanos! Chinga tu madre!"*

Maybe the old fruit was a Santeria loony. Santeria was the Hispanic equivalent of Yoruba, and now he was foaming at the mouth about the growth in Yoruba's power. Or maybe he'd done too much acid in the sixties.

The Lebanese guys who ran the espresso place, trying to fake it as a chic croissant espresso parlor, went out onto the sidewalk to chase the old shrieker away. But Ash was through here, anyway. It was time to go to the indoor range, to practice with the gun.

* * *

On the BART train over to the East Bay, on his way to the target range, Ash let his mind wander, and his eyes followed his mind. They wandered foggily over the otherwise empty interior of the humming, shivering train car, till they focused on a page of a morning paper someone had left on a plastic seat. It was a back-section page of the *Examiner,* and it was the word *Yoruba* in a headline that focused his eyes. Lurching with the motion of the train, Ash crossed the aisle and sat down next to the paper, read the article without picking it up.

Yoruba, it said, was the growing religion of inner city blacks—an amalgam of African and Western mysticism. Ancestor worship with African roots. Supposed to be millions of urban blacks into it now. Orisha the name of the spirits. Ishu El-Elegba was some god or other.

So the Chicano street freak had been squeaking about Yoruba because it was getting stronger. His latest attack of paranoia. Next week he'd be warning people about some plot by the Vatican.

Ash shrugged, and the train pulled into his station.

Ash had only fired the automatic once before—and before that hadn't fired a gun since his boyhood, when he'd gone hunting with his father. He'd never hit anything, in those days. He wasn't sure he could hit anything now.

But he'd been researching gun handling. So after an hour or so—his hand beginning to ache with the recoil of the gun, his head aching from the grip of the ear protectors—he found he could fire a reasonably tight pattern into the black, man-shaped paper target at the end of the gallery. It was a thrill being here, really. The other men along the firing gallery so hawk-eyed and serious as they loaded and fired intently at their targets. The ventilators sucking up the gunsmoke. The flash of the muzzles.

He pressed the button that ran his paper target back to him on the wire that stretched the length of the range, excitement mounting as he saw he'd clustered three of the five shots into the middle two circles.

It wasn't Wild Bill Hickok, but it was good enough. It would stop a man, surely, wouldn't it, if he laid a pattern like that into his chest?

But would it be necessary? It shouldn't be. He didn't want to have to shoot the old waddler. They wouldn't look for him so hard, after the robbery, if he didn't use the gun. Chances were, he wouldn't have to shoot. The old guard would be terrified, paralyzed. Putty. Still . . .

He smiled as with the tips of his fingers he traced the fresh bullet holes in the target.

Ash was glad the week was over; relieved the waiting was nearly done. He'd begun to have second thoughts. The attrition on his nerves had been almost unbearable.

But now it was Monday again. Seven minutes after five. He sat in the espresso shop, sipping, achingly and sensuously aware of the weight of the pistol in the pocket of his trench-coat.

The street crazy with the gold roses on his cane was stumping along a little ways up, across the street, as if coming to meet Ash. And then the armored car pulled around the corner.

Legs rubbery, Ash made himself get up. He picked up the empty, frameless backpack, carried it in his left hand. Went out the door, into the bash of cold wind. The traffic light was with him. He took that as a sign, and crossed with growing alacrity, one hand closing around the grip of the gun in his coat pocket. The ski mask was folded up onto his forehead like a watch cap. As he reached the corner where the fat black security guard was just getting out of the back of the armored car, he pulled the ski mask down over his face. And he jerked the gun out.

"Give me the bag or you're dead right *now!*" Ash barked, just as he'd rehearsed it, leveling the gun at the old man's unmissable belly.

For a split second, as the old man hesitated, Ash's eyes focused on something anomalous in the guard's uniform; an African charm dangling down the front of his shirt, where a tie should be. A spirit-mask face that seemed to grimace at Ash. Then the rasping plop of the bag dropping to the sidewalk snagged his attention away, and Ash waved the gun, yelling, "Back away and drop your gun! Take it out with thumb and forefinger only!" All according to rehearsal.

The gun clanked on the sidewalk. The old man backed stumblingly away. Ash scooped up the bag, shoved it into the backpack. *Take the old guy's gun too.* But people were yelling, across the street, for someone to call the cops, and he just wanted *away.* He sprinted into the street, into a tunnel of panic, hearing shouts and car horns blaring at him, the squeal of tires, but never looking around. His eyes fixed on the downhill block that was his path to the BART station.

Somehow he was across the street without being run over, was five paces past the wooden, poster-swathed newspaper kiosk on the opposite corner, when the Chicano street crazy with the gold roses on his cane popped into his path from a doorway, shrieking, the whites showing all the way around his eyes, foam spiraling from his mouth, his whole body pirouetting, spinning like a cop car's red light. Ash bellowed something at him and waved the gun, but momentum carried him directly into the crazy fuck and they went down, one skidding atop the other, the stinking, clownishly made-up face howling two inches from his, the loon's cocked knee knocking the wind out of Ash.

He forced himself to take air and rolled aside, wrenched free, gun in one hand and backpack in the other, his heart screaming in time with the throb of approaching sirens. People yelling around him. He got to his feet, the effort making him feel like Atlas lifting the world. Then he heard a deep,

black voice. "Drop 'em both or down you go motherfucker!"
And, wheezing, the fat old black guard was there, gun re-
trieved and shining in his hand, breath steaming from his
nostrils, dripping sweat, eyes wild. The crazy was up, then,
flailing indiscriminately, this time in the fat guard's face. The
old guy's gun once more went spinning away from him.

Now's your chance, Ash. Go.

But his shaking hands had leveled his own gun.

Thinking: The guy's going to pick up his piece and shoot
me in the back unless I gun him down.

No he won't, he won't chance hitting passersby, just run—

But the crazy threw himself aside and the black guard was
a clearcut target and something in Ash erupted out through his
hands. The gun banged four times and the old man went
down. Screams in the background. The black guard clutching
his torn-up belly. One hand went to the carved African grimace hanging around his neck. His lips moved.

Ash ran. He ran into another tunnel of perception; and
down the hill.

Ash was on the BART platform, and the train was pulling in.
He didn't remember coming here. Where was the gun? Where
was the money? The mask? Why was his mouth full of paper?

He took stock. The gun was back in his coat pocket, like a
scorpion retreated into its hole. His ski mask was where it was
supposed to be, too, with the canvas bag in the backpack.
There was no paper in his mouth. It just felt that way, it was
so dry.

The train pulled in and, for a moment, it seemed to Ash that
it was *feeding* on the people in the platform. Trains and buses
all over the city pulling up, feeding, moving on, stopping to
feed again . . .

Strange thought. Just get on the train. He had maybe one
minute before the city police would coordinate with the BART

police and they'd all come clattering down here looking to shoot him.

He stepped onto the train just as the doors closed.

It took an unusually long time to get to the next station. That was his imagination; the adrenaline affecting him, he supposed. He didn't look at anyone else on the train. No one looked at him. They were all damned quiet.

He got off at the next stop. That was his plan—get out before the transit cops staked out the station. But he half expected them to be there when he got out of the train.

He felt a weight spiral away from him: no cops on the platform, or at the top of the escalator.

Next thing, go to ground and *stay*. They'd expect him to go much farther, maybe the airport.

God it was dark out. The night had come so quickly, in just the few minutes he'd spent on the train. Well, it came fast in the winter.

He didn't recognize the neighborhood. Maybe he was around Hunter's Point somewhere. It looked mostly black and Hispanic here. He'd be conspicuous. No matter, he was committed.

You killed a man.

Don't think about it now. Think about shelter.

He moved off down the street, scanning the signs for a cheap hotel. Had to get off the streets fast. With luck, no one would get around to telling the cops he'd ducked into the Mission Street BART station. Street people at 16th and Mission didn't confide in the cops.

It was all open-air discount stores and flyblown bar-b-cue stands and bars. The corners were clumped up, as they always were, with corner drinkers and loafers and hustlers and people on errands stopped to trade gossip with their cousins. Black guys and Hispanic guys, turning to look at Ash as he

passed, never pausing in their murmur. All wearing dark
glasses; it must be some kind of fad in this neighborhood to
wear shades at night. It didn't make much sense. The blacks
and Hispanics stood about in mixed groups, which was kind
of strange. They communicated at times, especially in the drug
trade, but they were usually more segregated. The streetlights
seemed a cat-eye yellow here, but somehow gave out no
illumination—everything above the street level was pitch
black. Below it was dim and increasingly misty. A leprous mist
that smudged the neon of the bars, the adult bookstores, the
beer signs in the liquor stores. He stared at a beer sign as he
passed. "Drink the Piss of Hope," it said. He must have read
that wrong. But farther down he read it again in another
window: "Piss of Hope: The Beer That Sweetly Lies."

Piss of Hope?

Another sign advertised Heartblood Wine Cooler. *Heartblood,* now. It was so easy to get out of touch with things.
But . . .

There was something wrong with the sunglasses people
were wearing. Looking close at a black guy and a Hispanic
guy standing together, he saw that their glasses weren't sunglasses, exactly. They were the miniatures of house windows,
thickly painted over. Dull gray paint, dull red paint.

Stress. It's stress, and the weird light here and what you've
been through.

He could feel them watching him. All of them. He passed a
group of children playing a game. The children had no eyes;
they had plucked them, were casting the eyes, tumbling them
along the sidewalk like jacks—

You're really freaked out, Ash thought. It's the shooting. It's
natural. It'll pass.

The cars in the street were lit from underneath, with oily
yellow light. There were no headlights. Their windows were
painted out. (That is *not* a pickup truck filled with dirty,
stark-naked children vomiting blood.) The crowds to either
side of the sidewalk thickened. It was like a parade day; like

people waiting for a procession. (The old wino sleeping in the doorway is not made out of dog shit.) In the window of a bar, he saw a hissing, flickering neon sign shaped like a face. A grimacing face of lurid strokes of neon, amalgamated from goat and hyena and man, a mask he'd seen before. He felt the sign's impossible warmth as he pushed through the muttering crowds.

The place smelled like rotten meat and sour beer. Now and then, on the walls above the shop doors, rusty public address speakers, between bursts of static and feedback, gave out filtered announcements that seemed threaded together into one long harangue as he proceeded from block to block.

"Today we have large pieces available . . . the fever calls from below to offer new bargains, discount prices . . . prices slashed . . . slashed . . . We're slashing . . . prices are . . . from below, we offer . . ."

A police car careened by. Ash froze till he saw it was apparently driving at random, weaving drunkenly through the street and then plowing into the crowd on the opposite side of the street, sending bodies flying. No one on Ash's side of the street more than glanced over with their painted-out eyes. The cop car only stopped crushing pedestrians when it plowed into a telephone pole and its front windows shattered, revealing cracked mannequins inside twitching and sparking.

Shooting the old guard has fucked up your head, Ash thought. Just stare at the street, look down, look away, Ash.

He pushed on. A hotel a hotel a hotel. Go in somewhere, ask, get directions, get away from this street. (That is not a whore straddling a smashed man, squatting over the broken bone-end of a man's arm to fuck it in the back of that van.) Go into this bar advertising *Lifeblood Beer* and *Finehurt Vodka*. (Christ, where did they get these brands? He'd never . . .)

Inside the bar. It was a smoky room; the smoke smelled like burnt meat and tasted of iron filings on his tongue. One of those sports bars, photos on the walls of football players smashing open the other players' helmets with sledgehammers; on the TV screen at the end of the bar a blurry hockey game. (The hockey players are *not* beating a naked woman bloody with their sticks, blood spattering their inhuman masks, no they're not.) Men and women of all colors at the bar were dead things (no they're not, it's just . . .), and they were smoking something, not drinking. They had crack pipes in their hands and they were using tiny ornate silver spoons to scoop something from the furred buckets on the bar to put in their pipes and burn; when they inhaled, their emaciated faces puffed out: aged, sunken, wrinkled, blue-veined, disease-pocked faces that filled out, briefly healed, became healthy for a few moments, wrinkles blurring away with each hit, eyes clearing, hair darkening as each man and woman applied lighter to the pipe and sucked gray smoke. (Don't look under the bar.) Then the smokers instantly atrophied again, becoming dead, or near-dead, mummies who smoked pipes, shriveled—until the next hit. The bartender was a black man with gold teeth and white-painted eyelids, wearing a sort of gold and black gown. He stood polishing a whimpering skull behind the bar, and said, "Brotherman you looking for de hotel, it's on de corner, de Crossroads Hotel—You take a hit too? One money, give me one money and I give you de fine—"

"No, no thanks," Ash said, with rubbery lips.

His eyes adjusting so he could see under the bar, in front of the stools—there were people under the bar locked into metal braces, writhing in restraints: their heads were clamped up through holes in the bars and the furry buckets in front of each smoker were the tops of their heads, the crowns of their skulls cut away, brains exposed, gray and pink; the clamped heads were facing the bartender who fed them something that wriggled, from time to time. The smokers used their petite, glimmering spoons to scoop bits of quivering brain tissue from the living skulls and dollop the gelatinous stuff into the bowls of their pipes—*basing the brains* of the women and men clamped under the bars, taking a hit and filling out with strength and health for a moment. Was the man under the bar a copy of the one smoking him? Ash ran before he knew for sure.

Just get to the hotel and it'll pass, it'll pass.

Out the door and past the shops, a butcher's (those are not skinned children hanging on the hooks) and over the sidewalk which he saw now was imprinted with fossils, fossils of faces that looked like people pushing their faces against glass till they pressed out of shape and distorted like putty; impressions in concrete of crushed faces underfoot. The PA speakers rattling, echoing.

"*. . . prices slashed and bent over sawhorses, every price and every avenue, discounts and bargains, latest in designer footwear . . .*"

Past a doorway of a boarding house—was this the place? But the door bulged outward, wood going to rubber, then the lock buckling and the door flying open to erupt people, vomiting them onto the sidewalk in a Keystone Kops heap, but moving only as their limbs flopped with inertia: they were dead, their eyes stamped with hunger and madness, each one clutching a shopping bag of trash, one of them the Chicano street crazy who'd tried to warn him: gold roses clamped in his teeth, dead now; some of them crushed into shopping carts; two of them, yes, all curled up and crushed, trash compacted, into a shopping cart so their flesh was burst out through the metal gaps. Flies that spoke with the voices of radio DJs cycled over them, yammering in little buzzing parodic voices: "This is Wild Bob at KMEL and hey did we tell ya about our super countdown contest, we're buzzing with it, buzzzzzzing wizzzz-zzzz—"

A bus at the corner. Maybe get in it and ride the hell out of the neighborhood. But the bus's sides were striated like a centipede and when it stopped at the bus stop its doorway was wet, it fed on the willing people waiting at the bus stop, and from its underside crushed and sticky-ochre bodies were expelled to spatter the street.

"*. . . one money sale, the window smoke waits. One money*

and inside an hour we'll find the paste that lives and chews,
prices slashed, three money and we'll throw in a——"

He paused on the corner. There: the Crossroads Hotel. A
piss-in-the-sink hotel, the sort filled with junkies and pen-
sioned winos. Crammed in between other buildings like the
Casa Valencia had been. He was afraid to go in.

Across the street: whores, with crotch-high skirts and bulging, wattled cleavages and missing limbs that waved to him
with the squeezed out, curly ends of the stumps.(It's not true
that they have no feet, that their ankles are melded into the
sidewalk.)

"One money will buy you two women whose tongues can
reach deeply into a garbage disposal, we also have, for two
money——"

The whores beckoned; the crowd thickened. He went into
the hotel.

A steep, narrow climb up groaning stairs to the half door
where the manager waited. The hotel manager was a Hindu,
and behind him were three small children with their faces
covered in black cloth (the children do not have three disfigured arms apiece), gabbling in Hindustani. The Hindu manager smiling broadly. Gold teeth. Identical face to the
bartender but long straight hair, Hindu accent as he said:
"Hello hello, you want a room, we have one vacancy, I am
sorry we have no linen now, no, there are no visitors unless
you pay five money extra, no visitors, no——"

"I understand, I don't care about that stuff," Ash babbled.
Still carrying the backpack, he noted, taking stock of himself
again. *You're okay. Hallucinating but okay. Just get into the*
room and work out the stress, maybe send for a bottle.

Then he passed over all the money in his wallet and signed
a paper whose print ran like ink in rainwater, and the manager
led him down the hall to the room. No number on the door.
Something crudely pen-knifed into the old wooden door-
panel: a face like an African mask, hyena and goat and man.
But momentum carried him into the room—the manager

didn't even use a key, just opened it—and closed the door behind him. Ash turned and saw that it was a bare room with a single bed and a window and a dangling naked bulb and a sink in one corner, no bathroom. Smelling of urine and mold. The light was on.

There were six people in the room.

"Shit!" Ash turned to the door, wondering where his panic had been till now. "Hey!" He opened the door and the manager came back to it, grinning at him in the hallway. "Hey there's already people in here—"

"Yes hello yes they live with you, you know, they are the wife and daughter and grandchildren of the man you killed you know—"

"What?"

"The man you killed, you know, yes—"

"What?"

"Yes they are in you now at the crossroads and here are more, oh yes—" He gestured, happy as a church usher at a revival, ushering in seven more people, who crowded past Ash to throng the room, shifting aimlessly from foot to foot, gaping sightlessly, *whining* to themselves, bumping into one another at random. Blocking Ash, without seeming to try, every time he made for the door. Pushing him gently but relentlessly back toward the window.

The manager was no longer speaking in English, nor was he speaking Hindi; his face was no longer a man's, but something resembling that of a hyena and a goat and a man, and he was speaking in an African tongue—Yoruba?—with a sound that was as strange to Ash as the cry of an animal on the veldt, but he knew, anyway, with a kind of *a priori* knowledge, what the man was saying. Saying . . .

That these people were those disenfranchised by the old man's death: the old armored-car guard's death meant that his wife will not be able to provide the money to help her son-in-law start that business and he goes instead into crime and then to life in prison, and his children, fatherless, slide into drugs, and lose their hope and then their lives and as a direct result they beat and abuse their own children and those children have children which *they* beat and abuse (because they themselves were beaten and abused) and they all grow up into psychopaths and aimless, sleepwalking automatons. . . . Who shoved, now, into this room, made it more and more crushingly crowded, murmuring and whining as they elbowed Ash back to the window. There were thirty in the little room, and then forty, and then forty-five and fifty, the crowd humid with body heat and sullen and dully urgent as it crowded Ash against the windowframe. He looked over his shoulder, peered through the window glass. Maybe there was escape, out there.

But outside the window it was a straight drop four floors to a trash heap. It was an air shaft, an enclosed space between buildings to provide air and light for the hotel windows. Air shafts filled up with trash, in places like this; bottles and paper sacks and wrappers and wet boxes and shapeless sneakers and bent syringes and mold-carpeted garbage and brittle condoms and crimped cans. The trash was thicker, deeper, than in any airshaft he'd ever seen. It was a cauldron of trash, subtly seething, moving in places, wet sections of cardboard shifting, cans scuttling; bottles rattling and strips of tar paper humping up, worming; the wet, stinking motley of the air shaft weaving itself into a glutinous tapestry.

No, he couldn't go out there. But there was no space to breathe now, inside, and no way to the door; they were piling in still, all the victims of his shooting. The ones killed or maimed by the ones abandoned by the ones lost by the one he had killed. How many people now in this room made for one, people crawling atop people, piling up so that the light was in danger of being crushed out against the ceiling?

One killing can't lead to so much misery, he thought.

Oh but the gunshot's echoes go on and on, the happy, mocking Ishu said. *On and on, white devil cocksucker man.*

What is this place? Ash asked, in his head. Is it Hell?

Oh no, this is the city. Just the city. Where you have always lived. Now you can see it, merely, white demon cocksucker man. Now stay here with us, with your new family, where he called you with his dying breath . . .

Ash couldn't bear it. The claustrophobia was of infinite weight. He turned again to the window, and looked once more into the air shaft; the trash decomposing and almost cubistically recomposed into a great garbage disposal churn, that chewed and digested itself and everything that fell into it.

The press of people pushed him against the window so that the glass creaked.

And then thirty more, from generations hence, came through the door, and pushed their way in. The window glass protested. The newcomers pushed, vaguely and sullenly, toward the window. The glass cracked—and shrieked once.

Only the glass shrieked. Ash, though, was silent, as he was heaved through the shattering glass and out the window, down into the air shaft, and into the innermost reality of the city.

CITY HUNGER

CHET WILLIAMSON

Chet Williamson explains the roots of this story this way: "It was born from the seeds of an idea I had when I was in New York City one time—how easy it would be to kill someone you don't know, and just walk away. My own Imp of the Perverse is thankfully not strong enough to persuade me to such an action, but I still wanted to take a closer look at the rage that is always simmering just beneath the surface of the city."

Williamson and all his imps (as well as his wife of twenty years and their son) live in Pennsylvania. Currently the vice-president of The Horror Writers of America, he has had work nominated for the World Fantasy Award, the Bram Stoker Award, and the Edgar. His novels include Reign, Dreamthorp, Ash Wednesday, *and* McKain's Dilemma.

It would be easy to kill in this city, he thought as he walked up Fourth Avenue, past the blacks and Chicanos who lined the streets, some talking roughly, others shuck-'n'-jiving, pushing each other in friendly tussles that he knew could explode into something very unfriendly in a matter of seconds. The whores, pimps, three-card-monte dealers eyed him as he walked past. He tried to look mean, but not so mean that anyone would feel threatened by him, feel called upon to defend their street.

Smiling or not, everyone on Fourth Avenue between 41st and 93rd looked mean, even the elderly Jewish couple who, out of some unknown necessity, were forced to walk past and between the loiterers, glancing from side to side with angry, defiant eyes, the old man with his hands shoved in his pockets against his worn wallet, the old woman clutching her husband's arm and her tired purse with equal, white-knuckled force.

He passed them and walked more quickly, the promised haven of his hotel a few blocks further on. Ninety-fourth Street was less densely populated, and he almost relaxed before the siren blared, its shrieking tearing into him like a woman's scream. Another one, he thought. Another crime, maybe another death. Jesus, what was happening here where violence lay just behind everyone's eyes? The city hadn't been like this when he was a kid, had it?

He looked at the trash in the street, at the weathered store-fronts gated and shut like victims' mouths in the late Sunday afternoon gloom, and thought of a song lyric from the sixties, something about asking a city what it had been doing that had made such a ruin out of it. And it *was* a ruin, he thought. It looked bad, smelled bad, even *tasted* bad, and he licked the inside of his mouth, trying to banish the flavor of charred metal.

The hotel gave him scant relief. The clerk was rude, he had to pay in advance, and the bellman was perfunctory and received his overtip with a less-than-gracious mumble of thanks. Everybody was a monster.

Everybody.

And again he thought, it would be easy to kill in this city.

The thought occurred to him again as he walked alone up City Park Boulevard that evening. He had friends on West 119th just off the park, whom he visited whenever he was in town, and he had always felt somehow safe walking on this street. But he could never, he told himself, sit on those benches under the trees after night came, the way the old men sat on them every few blocks or so. It would be so easy for someone to kill them. There one sat, eyes closed in some cheap-wine dream.

He glanced around. There was no one else on the street in front or behind him, only an occasional car at this time of night. If there were any watchers in the buildings across the street, they would have to be on the first two floors, as the thick trees hid the higher floors from view.

So easy, he thought, to kill the old man. Anyone walking by could do it. One quick thrust with a knife, and into the night. Just another random act of violence in the beautiful city.

He smiled grimly and walked on. But the thought walked with him, creeping into his mind until, when he turned the corner at 119th, he was convinced that he could do it and get away with it quite easily. At that same moment, two young black men stepped out of a doorway in front of him. One had a knife, the other a small but deadly-looking pistol.

"Let's have it," the knife said.

He stood there, blinking at them.

"Come on, fucker," the gun sneered. "Wallet."

When the truth of the situation came upon him, his hand darted to his hip pocket. "Hold it!" the young man with the knife barked. "Slow."

He realized his mistake and took the wallet out very slowly.

"On the ground."

For an instant he thought they meant him, that he was to lie on the ground to be shot the way it had happened to that reporter years before in Central America. He opened his mouth to beg, to plead for his life, but only a dry clicking came out.

"The wallet, asshole."

The lump in his throat melted, and he set the wallet on the ground.

"Now walk. The way you came from. And don't look back."

He did as they ordered, turning the corner and walking again down City Park Boulevard. The old man was still on the bench.

Two blocks away he stopped at a phone booth under a street light and called his friends, who told him to take a cab the short distance to their place. They'd meet him at the door and pay the driver.

He explained the situation to the cabbie who picked him up. Instead of showing concern, or even interest, the driver shrugged, said, "Long as I get paid," and did not speak again.

You bastard, he thought, burrowing into the cab's backseat. *You sonuvabitch! I've been robbed, threatened, violated!* And at that moment it was not the robbery that bothered him nearly as much as the driver's uncaring response to his plight.

He leaned forward. "They had a gun," he said through the hole in the plastic shield. When the driver didn't respond, he repeated, "A gun. And a knife."

The driver sighed. "You was lucky you was just robbed. Last week a guy and his wife got killed right around the corner I picked you up."

He didn't answer the driver, but sat back again, laughing silently in the darkness. *Killed. That's what I should've done—gotten killed. But would anyone have paid attention even then?*

In less than a minute they pulled up in front of the building his friends lived in. They met him as he got out of the cab, and paid the driver for him. Their response surprised him. They seemed concerned that the mugging had happened on their street, but did not find it remarkable that it had happened at all.

"There's no escaping it, I'm afraid," said one over drinks in the apartment.

"No use even reporting it, really. How much did you have?" asked the other.

"Around fifty in cash, two hundred in traveler's checks."

"Traveler's checks, that's good."

"But my credit cards," he said, "driver's license, social security, owner's cards . . ."

"Kiss them good-bye," his friend said, "unless you want to go through every garbage can between here and 160th."

When he looked at his friends, they seemed like strangers, sitting there smiling smugly. It was as if they were *glad,* not that it had happened to him, but glad that it had not happened to them. He still felt angry, and was starting to feel uncomfortably disoriented as well.

"You just take this so casually," he said, an edge to his voice. "You're used to this?"

The one shrugged. "It happens. You live with it. What can you do?"

"Did it ever happen to you?" he asked.

"Yes," the other friend said, the smug smile gone. "A few years ago."

"And what did you do?"

"I thanked God I walked away alive."

There was silence for a moment. Then his friend asked him, "Well, where shall we eat?"

He shook his head. "I've lost my appetite," he said, and stood up. "And I'm tired. I'm going back to the hotel."

They tried to talk him out of it, but he refused. They did, however, walk him to the corner of City Park Boulevard and waited with him until he hailed a cab. He noticed on the park side around 115th Street the old man, still dozing, unharmed on his bench.

I'd like to kill him.

The thought came as a surprise to him, and the strength of it was enough to make him gasp.

It would be easy to kill him.

He remembered that he had had that thought earlier, walking past the man what had seemed like years before. But then it had been black fancy, nothing more, a morbid fantasy he'd concocted to shore up his feelings of inadequacy in the face of the brutal metropolis that surrounded him.

It was different now.

He *wanted* to kill the man, to walk up and shoot or stab or strangle or beat him, and let all that venom the city had poured into him rush right back out again. He was in a jungle, and animals kill in a jungle, so why should he be any different?

If *he'd* had a gun, then it might have been different. He could have *shot* those two bastards, killed them both and walked away and never heard a thing, just *shot* them in their mother-fucking *heads,* that would've been good, so good, to see their black faces explode into bits, and the looks on those faces as the bullets flew, well, that would've been goddamned *good.*

But he hadn't had a gun. A gun or a knife or any goddamned thing to defend himself with. But *now* he could. So easy here, it's just so easy.

"Forget what I told you," he said to the driver. "Take me to Liberty Square instead."

It was bright as day when he got out of the cab. He paid the cabbie from the fifty dollars his friends had loaned him, and started looking in novelty stores. The third one he entered had knives.

He chose a folding one with a pearlescent handle and a six-inch blade that widened to an inch thickness at its base. It was twenty dollars.

He felt quite confident as he left the store. The shopkeeper hadn't looked at him at all, hadn't glanced at his face once during the whole transaction. A good sign. He started walking uptown, the knife handle cool against his thigh through the thin material of his pocket. At 107th Street he took out the knife and opened it, his fingers wrapped in a handkerchief so no prints would be on the blade. Then he wrapped the handle in the white cloth, and, clutching it, slipped the blade carefully into his pocket.

When he reached the park, he walked casually up City Park Boulevard on the park side. A few people passed him, but no one looked at him. He had a bad moment when a whipcordthin young black, hands jammed into denim pockets, passed him so closely that their shoulders brushed, making him draw the knife halfway from his pocket. But the young man kept moving without looking back or saying a word, so he slid the knife back, and walked on.

The old man was still there on the bench, his eyes closed, chest rising and falling heavily. The sidewalk was otherwise empty, only an occasional passing bus or cab marring the silence.

He tightened his grip on the knife and looked at the man. Jesus, but he was ugly. The man wore no hat, and in the dim light that filtered through the leaves of the overhanging trees, he could make out a scabrous network of flaking scalp and thick, blue veins that gleamed dully. The nose was battered and bulbous, a drinker's nose, and the half-opened mouth was pitted with holes where teeth had once been.

Here was the city, he thought, with all its decay and wretchedness and horror, a rotting corpse that doesn't know when to lie down and be dead. A gutless, heartless monster that can turn even a civilized, sensitive man into . . .

The thought ended as his knife sliced across the old man's neck.

At first he didn't realize he had actually done it. It was the bubbling that gave him that awareness. The old man made no outcry, for he had nothing left to cry with. The eyes opened for only an instant before they began to glaze over, and the whole body went from sleep to vibrant life to sleep again.

He looked down at the red knife in his hand as if it belonged to someone else. He had *intended* to do what he had done, but he had never actually believed that he *would* do it. And then he looked about in panic for the one who *really* had slashed the man's throat, while he had been standing there, only thinking about doing it.

He was alone.

And it had not worked.

The anger, the frustration, the overwhelming fear—they

were all still there. There had been no catharsis, none of the purging relief he had hoped for, none of the triumph he had thought he would feel. Instead, a new terror had joined the others—the terror of self-betrayal.

He looked up and down the street. There were no pedestrians, and the cars passed too fast for anyone to notice him. He dropped the knife, free of prints, behind the bench as he had planned a long, long time ago, and crossed the street, quickly walking west on 115th for three blocks, where he turned and walked downtown on Sixth. At 97th he turned right, and in another few blocks was at his hotel.

The night clerk didn't notice him as he came in, and he met no one on the elevator. As he approached his room, he heard voices inside, and had the impossible thought that the police were already there, waiting for him. But then he remembered that he had left on the television as a ploy to scare off burglars, and opened his door.

The curtains were drawn, and he closed, locked, and chain-locked the door. Then he turned off the television, and slowly took off his clothes, examining each garment for the slightest trace of blood. There was none, not even on the handkerchief with which he'd held the knife.

He sat naked on the bed, the clothes in a pile at his feet, and after a while the lights began to hurt his eyes. He turned them off, pulled back the curtains, and opened the window. Then he stared into the pale gray city night, and thought about why he had slain the old man.

And as he gazed out over the dusty, cyclopean blocks that made up the city, honeycombed with windows and doors that led only into one another, he knew. The city had made him do it, had forced him to betray himself.

Even now it seemed alive, stretching down far away to where yellow lights gleamed dully on the river, dirty rooftops flexing like terrible muscles layered with tar paper. The city undulated beneath his window, billions of tons of sentient steel and concrete and glass, a gigantic phantasmal maw that would suck out the evil in man like a whale sucks plankton from the sea.

And then something else moved, deep in the valley of shadow between two dark hulks, something wet and slick and viscous, something that crept up the walls of the buildings, giving them a sleek, shiny look like buildings a quarter of their age, making them glow hot crimson in the harsh light caught by the mist and the dust that lay over the city.

He could see it climbing up all the buildings now, covering the streets like a red tide, slipping over roof edges, glazing windows with a ruby film, coating the city with blood. He stood shivering, unable to look away as the gleaming surface began to slide up the sides of his hotel, pulsating with fierce joy, and, he fancied, expectancy.

When it touched his fingers on the windowsill, he screamed at the heat of it, pulled his hand away, and threw down the sash. In a few seconds it had covered the window, and through the red pane the red city faded into blackness. He stumbled blindly into the bathroom, and brought out towels and washcloths, stuffing them along the edge of the windows in the fear that there might be a gap somewhere in the thin metal. He remembered the lights then, and turned them on.

When he saw what lay pressed against the glass, he closed the curtains, sobbing all the while, and ran to the door, jamming his clothes into the quarter-inch space where it refused to meet the floor.

Then he waited, naked and trembling, until morning, like some morsel of food caught between a behemoth's teeth. After a time, he slept, huddled on the floor midway between window and door, and awoke chilled. From the light bending around the edges of the curtains, he knew it was morning.

He pulled the curtains aside just enough to see the glass of the window. It was clear and uncovered, and through it he could see that the day was already bright and sunny, the sky blue and cloudless. He opened the curtains all the way, and looked down and out across the city to the river.

The scene was gray and dirty, but oddly unmenacing, with no trace of the wetness that had redly stained it the night before. Even so, he had to escape, to run from this metropolis that seemed to feed on rage and hate, turning them into murderous energies. He had to flee before—

And he laughed weakly as the cliché came to mind—*Before I kill again. Stop me before I kill again.*

He turned on the television while he dressed. The picture was unwatchable, but he could hear the morning news. There was no mention of a murdered wino on City Park Boulevard. When he called the number of the businessman with whom he had an appointment later that morning, he was answered by a machine that requested him to leave a message, and he explained that an emergency forced him to return to his home office, but that he would be in touch soon.

When he finished packing, he opened the door to the hall hesitantly, but the hall was empty, except for maids' carts and the remnants of a few room-service breakfasts. It was after he'd checked out and stepped into the street that the terror hit, cramping his gut with a spasm of pain that staggered him. Passing faces turned his way, but looked aside quickly. No one stopped. Finally the bell captain came from inside the lobby.

"You okay, sir?"

He nodded, afraid to look into the man's face.

"You sure? You need a doctor?"

"No," he grunted. "Cab. Could you get me a cab?"

Once inside the Checker, with his legs stretched out and his eyes closed, the pain left him, like a fist unclenching after hours of steady gripping, and he was able to analyze his feelings. A combination of things, he thought. Nerves above all, especially after walking outside, on the same sidewalks and streets which last night he'd seen—not imagined, but *seen*—engulfed in blood. And where last night he'd killed.

He had not come to terms with it, not totally accepted it. He would have to, though, have to accept it and rationalize it.

He'd known, even last night, that it hadn't been *him* really, but something else with him, beside him, something born of the city that hungered for what he had done, that had made him kill as a butcher makes a steak out of a steer. It had fed on him.

Suddenly he wondered if they'd even found the old man, and the vision crossed his mind of hundreds of people walking by the bench while the old man sat there, dead and stiff. He told the driver to turn around and go up City Park Boulevard.

The bench was empty, and people walked by it as if it were just another bench. No police photographers were taking pictures, no detectives were measuring and peering, no bystanders gawked at dark stains. It was, he thought as the metallic taste seeped into his mouth, as if it had never happened at all.

A block later he croaked, "City Station," in a dry, raspy voice. While the cab was stopped at a light at 78th Street, he became aware that someone was watching him through the window. It was a short, fat Hispanic in his fifties, who had stopped as he was about to cross the street, and was gazing at him with intense fascination. He shrank down into the seat as the light changed, leaving the staring man behind. He didn't look out of the window after that.

They hit the traffic jam at 54th, and were locked in like tar. All around them horns blared and drivers swore, while the garment workers stolidly wheeled their racks among them like cowbirds frisking amidst angry bulls.

He glanced at his watch. Ten minutes until the train left. If he missed it he would have to spend at least another three hours in the city. Making his decision, he pressed a ten into the driver's hand, climbed out without waiting for change, and started to walk the four blocks to the station.

It was a mistake. The Hispanic had been only the first.

Other eyes now looked into his. Two white men who argued on a corner stopped as he approached them, and turned their pockmarked faces toward his. He scurried past, only to be confronted by a trio of black youths who looked at him in the same way, breaking their formation to let him pass. Then a swarthy man cleaning his nails with a long pocketknife scrutinized him. So it went for four long blocks.

To enter the train station, he had to walk out upon a balcony that overlooked the concourse. From there, steps descended to left and right. Pausing for a moment to catch his breath, he leaned on the balcony rail and looked down.

Faces below looked back at him, dark flowers turning toward a black sun.

The violent, the derelict, the ones who wore the strange hunger around them like a cloak, all gazed up, and each ravenous mouth smiled at him, and each pair of aching eyes hailed him, calling him *comrade, friend, brother.*

He closed his eyes and turned away. When he opened them again, he was looking at the stone floor, at cigarette butts, gobbets of spit, ghosts of evaporated puddles of urine, deckle-edged.

Turning to the right, he stumbled down the steps, looking over the railing just once, seeing the faces looking up at him. He made his way to a bench and sat down, but felt the comradely stares on the back of his neck like a hot boil near to bursting, turned in spite of himself, looked, saw what he knew he would.

With a sob he rose, grasped his bag, and ran to the men's room. The door was open, and he dashed in, yearning for the splash of cool water on his hot face.

There were three of them bent over a fourth. They turned like wolves, but their challenging glowers softened immediately to grins of shared secrets, and one of them gestured to the unmoving body on the floor, an unmistakable offer to share the feast.

Bile lurched into his throat. He swallowed it down, and backed away until he felt a smooth, yielding panel against his spine. It was the door of a booth, and he pushed it open with his back, still watching the feeding wolves. He kept moving in until the back of his legs bumped the knees of the man sitting on the toilet.

Startled, he turned around, and saw the scabrous head, the ruined face of the wino whose throat he had cut the night before.

The shock that seared him dwarfed his previous fears. He could not breathe, and for a few seconds he felt as though his heart had discontinued its rhythm. But then he dragged in a harsh and ragged breath, and saw that the old man did not move, that he still wore the deep, red, fatal smile below his chin. Best of all, the eyes were closed. They did not stare into his with fellowship and unwanted compassion. There was peace here, and acceptance. A peace he had declared.

He moved all the way into the booth, pushed the door closed, and shot the bolt. It had taken him only moments to decide that the dead man's company was to be preferred to that of the living.

Soon, with no faces to call him brother, he was breathing normally again, and he waited by the dead man's side until, through the open door of the men's room, he heard his train and its track announced. Then he unbolted the door and walked out of the room, now empty of the living, and hurried, eyes on the floor, to the stairway that led down to his train.

It was there at the platform. He boarded, and went all the way to the last seat in the last car, where he pressed his steaming face against the coolness of the window and breathed deeply. The vapor distorted his reflection against the black glass so that his image seemed to be smiling at him. But he was unable to tell whether the smile was one of relief or of recognition.

Then he knew that wherever he would go, the city would be home from now on. And a new and greater fear grew within him, for he was afraid no longer for himself, but rather for those people he loved, the people who would look at him with their own unbearable gazes of love and brotherhood in the place he used to call home, the place toward which he was traveling with a red, aching, unquenchable thirst, unappeasable hunger.

THE WHITE MAN

THOMAS F. MONTELEONE

Thomas F. Monteleone tells us about "the night a guy with a knife rousted me in a New York subway. Without even thinking, I turned on him and cranked up my best Norman Bates stare and a leering Tim Curry-as-Pennywise grin. I started chanting some nonsense syllables and the mugger became absolutely freaked. Sensing he'd tapped into a psycho's private world, he ran into the next car. I kept babbling from relief and nervous humor. It was a weird scene."

Monteleone, forty-four, has been a full-time writer since 1978. A former vice-president of The Horror Writers of America, he has published eighteen novels, two collections of short fiction, and has edited four anthologies, among them the recent Borderlands *and* Borderlands II. *He lives in Baltimore, where he plays racquetball and spends a lot of time fooling with computers.*

The city as Beast.

A hackneyed image if there ever was one; but oh, so appropriate, don't you think? Dark, lumbering, labyrinthine, voracious, Gothic, insensate, dangerous. The word's so apt, so utterly fitting, thought Sammy Deller. He was driving his modest vehicle uptown on Utica, intending to leave town for a few days, as he considered his turf in such a cerebral fashion. Yeah, it's a fucking beast all right, and we all ride along in its belly. But one of these days, the bastard was going to take a serious, big-time dumpola, and we were all going in the shitter.

Sammy smiled at his attempts to wax metaphorical. He was no dummy. Everybody'd always told him that. The business about images and metaphors had hung with him from his earliest days at the City Community College, with his freshman English professor. Dr. Tessier told Sammy he had the brains to make it, to be smart, to be whatever he wanted to be. But that was back when he was still thinking about things like skills and dreams, and a grown-up-peoples' job.

A-mind's-a-terrible-thing-to-waste.

What a bunch of sucker bullshit that was. Yeah, sure, he was going to take a gig breaking his chops and sucking up to his boss's rump, for what? A monthly salary that wasn't enough to make him get out of bed? And that don't even talk about the bleeding you get from the IRS. Well not me, thought Sammy. No freaking way, man.

Indeed, Sammy listened to a different beat—the pulsing rhythms of the city. From the funk of its tin-speakered jamboxes across the river, to the deep, muffled murmurs of its Porsches and Mercedes. From the syncopated racket of its west-side factories to the blood-pumping backbeat of its Platinum Row clubs. Yeah, the city was alive, all right, and it was certainly a Beast. Always hungry, always moving, always ready to eat your ass up.

Sammy Deller understood the city's biorhythms, its biochemistry, and he would always survive there. But he would do it *his* way—only his way. He might be a very Heavy Number on the crack market, but nobody would ever figure him for it. No, man. Sammy was way too hip, way too sly, to be like his colleagues. His car was an Accura Legend, his clothes off the racks at Macy's, and his house a modest brownstone on the edge of the Hungarian neighborhoods. Instead of gold chains, he invested in Krugerrand certificates; he took a course in commercial real estate development and he was, with the help of a couple slick Jew lawyers, buying up little pieces of the Beast.

Because Sammy knew there was a shitstorm coming. Not when, or maybe exactly how, but he knew it was surely on its way. The drugs of choice in the city were quicklime to the soul, dissolving everybody from the Canal Street junkie to the Worthington House CEO. Eating them up, down to their narrow-ass bones.

Oh yeah.

There were some nights when Sammy would be sitting on the deck off his third-floor bedroom, maybe a little Wynton Marsalis on the CD player, maybe even some Taj Mahal if he was feeling his roots; but whatever it was, it would be turned down low enough to not disturb his urbanely gentrified neighbors, and he would be thinking about what was *really* going on down deep, down at the shadowed core of the Beast.

You didn't need to be a brain surgeon to feel the churning and the burning, way down in the dark, soft parts. The crack and the heroin and all the other junk was tearing the guts right out of the city and it just wasn't going to just hang out and let it happen. There was something brewing in the back alleys where the only gods or demons you'd ever find are going to be the ones that have already gone crazy. Something slipping up from the sewer grates like greasy smoke, like a poisonous vapor. Sammy would listen to a full-octave run on the scales on Marsalis's golden trumpet and he would just nod his head. It was one of the great paradoxes of the city that such order and beauty could, like, coexist with the dark dreams of the Beast.

Because Sammy knew what the drugs really were: the toxic waste of lost dreams, of shattered souls, and of broken hearts; the hard shell-casings of spent ambitions, of crushed-out hopes; the empty husks of things now dead, juiceless and gone, just gone forever like the fractured stones of ancient places like Troy and Ur. And when you got right down to it, that kind of stuff was infinitely more radical, more heavy than all the muggers and the factory pollutants and exhaust fumes and liquor-store killings and race gangs the city could ever bring into being.

Because those things were *parts* of the Beast, and it could always survive the demands of its own nature. Sammy was worried about other things.

He pulled up to a light and watched the people flow past his hood. He'd reached the outpost borders of two different neighborhoods, and he always found it interesting to see how sections of the city—the "good" ones and the "bad" ones— lacked any visible lines of demarcation, and yet there were borders just the same. Whether he was walking or driving, he would try to spot the exact place along a block or at a particular intersection where you could say, Yeah, *here* it is—this side's cool, this side's fucked.

But he never could. As much as he knew about the city, as comfortable as he was within its depths, even Sammy Deller couldn't nail down the exact places on the map where the Beast changed aspects. He was moving again, and suddenly the sidewalks didn't seem as trashy and the shops' wares didn't seem so tacky, and the people didn't seem so sweaty, maybe not so dirty under their collars and cuffs and dreams. He drove on, heading west until he reached the block where his house hugged the borders of the city's Hungarian stronghold.

There was a wire out on the street that one of the narcotics dicks had a burr up his ass, and was looking to haul Sammy in for some "routine questioning." Right. That's why he was calling it a day real early. Time to catch a train upstate for a few days till the detective found another supplier to roust. Just pull up, throw a few things in a Gucci bag and get outta Dodge. He could buy whatever else he needed when he got off the train.

But as he found a space along the curb, Sammy saw the kid sitting on his front steps—like he was waiting for him.

*   *   *

Sunlight from the late summer afternoon almost forced its way into the shadows of Kovacs's shop. Dust motes drifted lazily through the warm beams and fell across the pawned pieces of a thousand lives. Battered guitars leaned against porcelain mantel clocks, while a shelf of cameras stared its multifaceted eyes at a flock of taxidermied birds. Hunting rifles and power tools stood guard over smudged-glass cases of pocket knives and watches. Beyond the chockablock interior lurked a deeper set of shadows wherein a caged old man sat counting out the hours of his life.

Zoltan Kovacs fumbled a pack of Chesterfields from his shirt pocket. The arthritis in his ropy-veined, liver-spotted hands would sometimes turn his fingers into hard, bent talons that were almost useless and sung with a cold and special pain. He shook a nonfiltered cigarette from the pack and awkwardly thumbed his Zippo lighter into flame. He hated the cigarettes, but he hated trying to give them up even more. But what he hated most of all was the whole business of growing old.

Seventy-two years. A long time; and then again, not a very long time at all.

Zoltan inhaled, letting the smoke rake his throat with its hot tines. Sometimes he could almost feel the cancerous oat cells mutating and growing in the soft tissue of his esophagus, his alveolar sacs, and he often wondered why the disease had yet to claim him.

Seventy-two years. He sat in the shadows remembering how one night, when he was forty-five years old, he sat up in bed, fully awake from a stone-dead sleep. He'd been suddenly struck with the realization that in twenty-five years he would be *seventy*. He would be an *old* man. He could remember that night, that moment of total dread, as if it happened only hours ago. He had looked down at his Magda sleeping beside him, outlined by gauzy moonlight, when she still had a firmness in her flesh, a glow of sex and health. He'd fought with himself as to what to do—he wanted to nudge her awake, to sink into her embrace like a scared little boy in the dark; but he also wanted to shield her from the terror he was feeling, the stark fear of dissolution called old age.

The twenty-five years had fled from him like a guilty thief. So quickly, so goddamned quickly. His grandchild was the only part of his life that offered even the illusion of hope.

Zoltan exhaled, watched the smoke plume up into the dusty air. The front doorbell jingled and he peered through the steel mesh the salesman had said would catch a .38-caliber slug like Yogi Berra gloving a fastball behind the plate. Looking up he saw the thin black man jitter into the shop carrying an expensive camera in both hands. He was basketball-player tall, but lacked the musculature. Cheeks sunken, his shiny blue-black face was all angles, like that of a Nigerian tribesman.

"Hey man!" he yelled through the mesh in a voice mixed with equal parts of panic and desperation. "How much can I get for this thing?"

"I'll need to get a look at it," said Zoltan. He spun a Plexiglas drum until its air-lock-like opening faced the customer. "Put it in the drum."

"Hey, look, it's worth plenty, all right? It's a Hassle-Bomb."

"Hassel*blad,*" said Zoltan as the junkie put the camera on the dolly. It spun slowly into the pawnbroker's crimeproof cocoon and he picked it up. Model 2000-FCM. Expensive. Professional.

"So whaddya think, man? It's worth somethin', ain't it?" The junkie shifted from foot to foot, clenched and unclenched his fists. Sweat beaded on his eggplant-smooth flesh.

"I'm going to need your warranty card and a matching serial number," Zoltan said softly.

"Say *what?*" The junkie's eyes flicked in their sockets, everywhere but straight ahead, as though he continually sought an escape route.

"This is a very expensive piece of equipment—only used by professional photographers. I'm going to need proof of ownership before we can do business."

The black man's lips twisted into a snarl. "What you sayin', Jack? You sayin' I ain't no photographer!"

Zoltan grinned wryly. "Well, let's just say I'm not going to mistake you for Ansel Adams."

The man became more jittery, confusion capered across his face. "Anvil *who?*"

"Sir, I'm going to need proof of purchase and ownership," said Zoltan as he placed the camera on the dolly, spun it back to the junkie. "Or we have no business to conduct."

The man reached angrily for the camera. "Man, what-the-fuck, man? I need some money! Now, Jack!"

"I'm sorry. I can't help you." Zoltan puffed on his Chesterfield, blew out a thin stream through the mesh.

The man simmered and shook like a pressure cooker. "I oughta just shoot your sorry ass."

Zoltan sighed, performed a dramatic shrug. "Maybe you should. And do us both a favor."

"Whatchoo talkin', man?"

"You wouldn't understand, sir. Why don't you come back if you can find the paperwork I need?"

The junkie backed up, his gaze sizing up the protective cage. Apparently convinced he could mount no assault against it, he sneered at the pawnbroker, gave him the finger, and half-jogged from the shop. Zoltan grimaced, shook his head slowly to himself. The drugs. They were turning people into mindless ciphers. He wondered if it was part of a vast plan, some huge conspiracy to keep the masses occupied and fixated, out of the way. Or was it something far more maleficent, more darkly elegant? The junkies worshiped at the altars of self-loathing and ultimate darkness.

Stubbing out his cigarette, he coughed up thick phlegm. In Eastern Europe, his profession was an honorable one, but here, he was considered as low as his customers. He shrugged again. No matter. It had been enough of a business to support Magda and his family well enough in a city that could be as unkind as it could be bountiful. His life had not been grim or unpleasant. He could not complain too much.

The phone rang him out of his thoughts.

"Kovacs's . . . Hello?"

"Zoltan!"

Magda's voice pierced him with its urgency and his heart immediately revved.

"What? What is it? You are all right?"

His wife struggled to keep the control in her voice. Her words fell out in clipped fragments. "It's Michael! Our Mishka! He is gone! Oh my God! I cannot believe this! Oh Zoltan!"

"Magda, Magda . . . you must tell me! Exactly what happened. What do you mean—'gone'?"

His wife drew a steadying breath, exhaled slowly. "He was playing in the backyard. Like he always does. His sandbox. I was out with him, taking in the wash. I went in with a basket. When I came back, the gate was broken down and he was *gone!* Our little Mishka! Oh Zoltan, my stomach—I am sick!"

"Just now this happened?"

"Yes."

"The gate was latched? Locked?"

"I think so. I . . . I had not checked it. But they broke it in!"

Zoltan stood up, pushed a button that electronically locked the shop's front door. "Stay calm, Magda. I am coming home. You called our Elainna?"

"I called her work-office. They said she was away from her desk . . . !"

"His father, then?"

"Zoltan, I—"

In a totally uncharacteristic display of hardness, Magda had not spoken to Kevin since he'd left Elainna and the boy. Divorce was such an impossible concept to Zoltan's wife that she could never forgive Kevin for doing such a thing to her daughter.

"All right . . ." He sighed. "Then I will do it."

"Yes."

"You will call the police. Now. Yes?"

"Yes! Yes! Please, please hurry."

Hanging up the receiver, he threaded his way through the narrow passage defined by overcrowded shelves of musty boxes and long-abandoned curiosities. He walked to the back door, keyed the alarm system, and exited to lock the door. He did this automatically, thinking of nothing but the image of his grandson, a four-year-old boy with blond hair and dark eyes. Eyes that looked at the world with the wonder and joy of discovering something new about it each day, each hour. The boy was his hope, had become his *meaning* for living. To think of him somewhere in the depths of the city, alone and terrified, made Zoltan feel profoundly lightheaded, as if he were delirious.

My little Mishka . . . if anything happens to you, I will die myself.

He began walking up the service alley towards the noise of the street at its entrance. He found himself generating great tides of anger towards his Magda, already making her responsible for the boy's death—if it came to that. He hated himself for even thinking like that.

Little white boy. Blond hair and the bluest eyes Sammy'd seen this side of an Alaskan husky. Bright, hard, almost frosted blue. Wearing a bright-red jacket. As Sammy approached his house, the kid was looking at him like he knew him, like he was expecting him.

"Say, June-bug!" he said with a smile. "What you doin' on my front steps, huh?"

"Why'd you call me that?"

'June-bug? It just means you're a junior—you know, a kid."

The boy thought about this, nodded as though accepting it as even marginally sensible. "Oh, okay." He said nothing more but continued to stare at Sammy Deller. It was the kind of stare that could start to unnerve you if you let it.

"So," said Sammy as he stood there, feeling a little foolish. "I said what you doin' at my place?"

"Oh . . . I'm kinda lost."

"Lost? Well, where do you live?"

"We live in . . . Milford," he said as though unsure.

" 'Milford'? Where the hell's that?" Sammy tried to figure out what the kid was talking about. "You mean Milford Heights? 'The Heights'—is that what you mean?"

"Yes. That's it."

Sammy grinned. Yeah, the Heights wasn't city turf, but Sammy knew all about it. Big-time white professional suburb north of the city. When cocaine had still been fashionable, he'd shipped a lot of snow up north, up to a lotta lawyers' and accountants' and doctors' cribs. Nowadays, that crowd was gravitating back to the chemical hallucinogens and nonaddictive designer drugs. "Leave the white stuff to the niggers," is how one corporate attorney had phrased it when he thought Sammy hadn't been listening.

Sammy shook his head. Sad, but true. His brothers hadn't been able to shake the crack jones even a little bit, and they remained the backbone of his business. He returned his attention to the little white boy.

"So look, kid, do you know the name of the street you live on?"

"It's a long word. I have trouble remembering it."

"Great. What about your phone number? You know what it is?"

"No . . ."

Anybody else would call the police at this point, but cops were the last people he wanted to talk to—now or any other time. So what the fuck was he gonna do? Dump the kid with one of the neighbors. Yeah, let them deal with it.

"But I'm staying over—at Pop-Pop's. For a whole week," said the kid.

"What's that—you mean your gran-daddy? Where's he?"

"Down here. Somewhere near here."

Sammy brightened. "You mean the city? Downtown? Here?"

"Yes."

"Well, where do they live, junior? I'll just take you there."

The boy shrugged, pointed in a vague easterly direction. "I'm not sure, mister. Up that way, I think. I'm supposed to find a police-man. They always help you if you're lost. But I never found one."

Sammy smiled in spite of the growing sense of agitation building in him. He didn't want to be pullin' no jive with this kid when he should be in the dining car on the Northern Line. Kids acted like wiseguys even when they were this little, even when they didn't know shit.

"C'mon," said Sammy, walking up to his neighbors' front door, a kinda bohemian couple who always let you know they were *artists*. They were always home, let *them* deal with the kid . . .

Only today they *weren't* home.

Probably out buying some art supplies, he thought as he directed the kid down the block. He knocked on enough doors to soon realize he was S.O.L. Nobody home and the kid was starting to feel like a lead weight around Sammy's neck.

"Is it okay?" asked the boy.

Sammy looked down at him and got captured by that frosted blue gaze. "Yeah, it's cool. Let's go find your gran-daddy's place."

The boy nodded and reached up to take his hand. Sammy felt uncomfortable, but he let the little pale hand slip into his, marveling at the softness of the kid's skin—the kind women'd kill for.

"So what's your name, junior?" he said as they began walking back up the block.

"Mikey. But Pop-Pop and Mom-Mom call me 'Mishka.' "

Sammy grinned. "Okay, Mikey. So what was you doin' out in the streets? How'd you get so up and lost in the first place?"

The boy stopped and looked up at him. "I was trying to get away from the white man."

Sammy started to laugh. "Yeah! You and me both! All my life, kid . . ."

But there was something about the way Mikey said *the white man*—putting a slight emphasis on "man"—that told Sammy the kid was talking about no *ofay* dude, no paleface. He looked at him and could see the boy was clearly disturbed just to be remembering something.

"Whatchoo talkin' about—'the white *man*'?"

"He tried to get me. I seen 'im before, other times."

"Where? For what?"

"Behind Pop-Pop's. In the alley. But this time I saw him come. From nowhere."

"Mikey, what's this shi—, this stuff you talkin'?"

"That's why he tried to get me. 'Cause I saw him come."

Sammy had been leaning over, talking to the boy, and he felt a sudden wave of dizziness, a sense of total *unease,* of dread, sweat through him. He stood up and waited for the moment and the sensation to pass. It didn't, traveling instead down to his gut. What the fuck was this? There was something about the way the kid was talking. That matter-of-fact way they all had when they talked about monsters, which told you, Well, sure, you *know* there's really monsters out there, don't you?

"You see what I mean?" said Mikey.

"Yeah, sure," said Sammy. "Now, c'mon, let's see if we can find your gran-daddy."

Sammy took his hand and guided the boy along the sidewalk to the corner. The sun was slipping away as the day started to slip into the grays of twilight, and here he was getting what his North Carolina grandmother used to call the jimjams.

He wasn't sure he could get the kid home before it got too dark, but he was sure as shit of one thing—he didn't want no part of whatever it was Mikey'd seen in that alley.

Zoltan hung up the telephone and turned to regard the anxious face of his wife. "Kevin had to leave for the courtroom," he said.

"Hah! He does not even care that his son is gone!"

"Magda, enough. We both agree that Kevin is probably a bad husband, but I do not believe he is a bad father."

"Hah! His own son!"

"He will be here as soon as he can." Zoltan turned up his jacket collar, headed for the back door, then looked back at his wife. "Keep trying to reach Elainna. I will look around the neighborhood. *Some*one must have seen him."

"He was wearing his little red jacket!" she called after him.

Nodding, he stepped out into the darkening afternoon, and regarded the gate and fence which enclosed the backyard. Magda had been unclear—the gate had not been broken down; it had been *obliterated*. A truck careening down the alley could not have destroyed it more completely. Thinking of the boy exposed to that kind of terrible force made him lurch forward as he forced bile back down his throat. He straightened, stepped over the splintered debris and entered the alley, heading for the street. Dusk would soon be welling up from the shadows to hostage the streets for another night. City, night. The two words clung to each other like animals locked in a death grip. Together they conjured up all the foulness and disease which defined the city after sundown. For there were surely strange things in the black avenues of the city, things brought to hideous life through our devout acts of loathing. A desperate creature gnawing on its own parts to survive, feeding the disease, mutating into something ever darker.

To imagine Mishka wandering through such a gauntlet

dropped the bottom out of his stomach. Why hadn't he listened to Elainna? She'd pleaded with him: sell the big brownstone to one of the yuppie homesteaders who were swarming into the old neighborhoods like soldier ants. With such obscene profits, he could have had his house in the country, the farm of his distant European childhood come round again, and he wouldn't ever be dancing on the wall of total panic if his grandson had wandered beyond the back dooryard.

He would do it, he told himself as he turned the corner and paused on the sidewalk on Grand Avenue, wondering in which direction to begin. He would do it, he repeated to himself as he took steps which would take him west and beyond the invisible barriers of the neighborhood. He would sell and get out. Just give me back my Mishka! If the boy had wandered down the Hungarian streets, someone would have surely seen him, recognized him. Everyone knew Zoltan Kovacs's grandson. The thought made him smile bittersweetly. Yes, at least he'd tried to make certain of that.

He did not want to think some bastard had actually *taken* the boy, that anyone could have *done* something to him. No. He was just lost, that's all. Little boys are curious. They are explorers, and he was out testing the boundaries of his world. We all did it sooner or later, and Mishka had decided it was now his turn, his birthright.

Zoltan tried to hold that thought, to believe in its essential, comforting truth as he walked along, searching the eyes and faces of those he passed, wanting to grab each one of them, and shake them and ask screaming if they'd seen his only grandson. But with each passing step, each moment closer to the darkness, the shards of broken hope fell away from him.

Either it was growing suddenly cooler or his arthritis had decided to cripple him once and for all. His hands and feet had become almost instantly cold and brittle, sending icicles of pain up his arms and legs. No, please, he thought angrily to the pain gods, not now! Just . . . not *now*.

He reached the corner and the wind sluicing up the cross

street slapped his face sharply. The ache from the cold marrow of his bones wanted to bring him down like a felled cow at slaughter, and he wanted to cry out against the pain, absurdly wishing Magda might hold him up as he walked along. Turning into the wind, he winced against its ear-burning whine. A wind so harsh he almost did not hear his name being called.

Well, not actually his *name* . . .

"Pop-Pop! Pop-Pop!"

The small voice cut through the keen of the wind, damped down the pain circuits with its special magic. Zoltan jerked his head in every direction. The boy!

"Pop-Pop!" Closer this time.

And there! Far down the intersecting street, he saw a tatter of familiar red. As he moved closer, he watched it resolve into the red jacket—the absolutely *beautiful* red jacket. Blond hair. Blue eyes. A little boy breaking free of a black man's grasp and running forward. A *black* man! The image blurred wetly, and Zoltan wiped the tears from his eyes. Dropping down to a baseball catcher's crouch, he received the impact of his Mishka. The hinted scent of Johnson's Baby Shampoo still clung to the boy's hair, and Zoltan knew forevermore he would smell nothing sweeter.

"Pop-Pop, you don't have to cry."

"Mishka, Mishka! Are you all right? Where did you go? Who is this man?"

"I had to get away from the white man, and—"

"But he is black . . . ?"

"Not *him,* Pop-Pop! He helped me find you."

Zoltan looked up to regard the lanky black man who'd been walking with Mishka. He was wearing a conservative charcoal suit, a fashionable but not gaudy tie. He looked like a stockbroker or perhaps an FBI man.

"Found him on my steps," said the black man with a self-conscious grin. "You must be Granddad."

"Yes, that's right. Thank you! Thank you!"

"Hey, it wasn't nothin' . . . but you better teach that boy your address—he couldn't remember where your crib is."

Zoltan was nodding automatically as he stood up, holding his grandson in his arms, kissing him repeatedly. He was only half-listening as released tension flowed blessedly out of him.

"Well, I better be goin'," said the black man.

"I never got your name," said Zoltan. "To thank you more properly, I should know your name, sir."

"Well we don't hafta worry about that," said the man. "I got a train to catch, you know?"

He turned to leave when Zoltan blurted out a question which held him fast: "What is this 'white *man*' business?"

"Hey, I don't know—you gotta ask Mikey here 'bout that." The man in the charcoal suit looked anxiously at the boy.

"Who is this man who bothered you? This 'white man'?"

The boy's eyes narrowed for an instant. "I don't know . . ."

Zoltan could see instantly the boy didn't want to talk about it, but that only hardened Zoltan's resolve to get to the truth of it. Some creep who scared children needed to be caught, punished.

"Was he wearing something white?" asked Zoltan. "A uniform? Like the ice-cream man? The guy who drives the street cleaner?"

Mishka shook his head, looked at the black man as if to say, *Tell him I don't want to talk about this.* Zoltan ignored this gesture and pressed onward. Mishka tried to ignore him, to change the subject, to misdirect things by whining and complaining, but Zoltan held fast. Finally, he started talking and what he described did not make sense, and yet Zoltan felt immediately chilled. No, that was not the right word—the word was *scared.*

The black man had remained to hear the whole story, as if he were transfixed by Mishka's words, as if he too suspected he was listening to more than a small boy's fanciful imagination.

It was the simple, matter-of-fact manner in which Mishka finally let go of his tale that made Zoltan consider its grimly real possibilities. The White Man was not really a *man,* the boy explained, but he could think of no other way to describe the thing which took form from the steam vent in the alley behind Pop-Pop's house. Like fog or the steam, he said, but he knew it was neither, because it had taken a *shape* and moved off down the alley. Mishka claimed to have seen it many times, but upon each reemergence, the white thing was bigger, more solid.

"How long have you been seeing the White Man?" asked Zoltan.

"Long time. Since I've been coming to your house. But this time it tried to get me. I ran when it broke through the gate."

"We should call the police," said Zoltan.

"Yeah, right, they gonna believe a story about a monster busting into your backyard," said the black man.

"We don't have to explain it like that," said Zoltan.

"Then why bother?"

Zoltan nodded. His companion was correct. Better to take the boy home, then think about what next to do.

Night had claimed them and Sammy was still hanging out with the old man. The train to catch and the detective who wanted to question him seemed like distant memories. Why the fuck was he hanging around? Simple: he couldn't walk away from the kid's story because there was a small part of him, but a very *real* part, that *knew* that kid wasn't throwing no regular kid-bullshit.

Mikey'd seen *something* bust down that gate, and Sammy's subconscious had a good idea what it might be, but so far it wasn't telling. No problem on that score—Sammy wasn't sure he wanted to know anyway. Part of him wanted to just pull a quick fade and be gone. He'd done his Boy Scout gig for the day, and it was playtime now. Better to forget it all. Catch a serious buzz and forget it.

But he couldn't.

The White Man.

Only it wasn't no *man,* was it, Big Sammy? The image of some shambling, amorphous, white thing persisted in his mind. The notion ragged him like an angry dog on his pants leg; it clawed at the trapdoor to his everyday thoughts.

And that's why he stood in the alley behind Kovacs's house in the middle of Hunkie Town. Now he was waiting—waiting for the old man to come down the back of the rear steps, out the walk, past the debris of rear gate. Time continued to grind past him, but he remained held to what had become an unspoken mission. The neighborhood seemed almost too quiet. There was no wind and he could hear his own breathing as though his lungs were some great laboring piece of machinery.

A slamming of the back door and footsteps on the walk. A dark shape appeared in the alley wearing a golfer's cap and carrying a small crowbar. "So, you have waited for me," said Kovacs.

"You didn't think I would?" Sammy tried to smile, did a bad job of it.

The old man shrugged. "I honestly didn't know. And I am sorry for the delay—my wife was very excited to see the boy safe. And she . . . she was a little more than curious that I was planning to walk around the neighborhood with—I must be frank—a black man."

Sammy laughed. "Yeah, I hear you, Kovac! Well, I don't usually spend my bowling night with fat old white dudes . . . know what I'm sayin'?"

The old man grinned, nodded. "Let's go."

"What's the crowbar for?"

"We will need it to get where we are going."

"Where we goin'?" Sammy asked, already knowing the non-specific answer.

"To look for Mishka's boogeyman."

"This is nuts, you know."

Kovacs shrugged. "My friend, you speak as if *all* of life is *not,* as you say, 'nuts.' "

Sammy said nothing as he followed the old guy down the alley. It had grown dark and cool. Autumn weather teetered on the cusp of winter. They walked to the intersection of the alley and the street. Kovacs kneeled down to insert the tip of the crowbar into a square grate which had been blended into the old cobblestone and asphalt so cleanly that it was almost invisible.

"What's that?"

"Gets you to the steam tunnels," said Kovacs matter-of-factly. He lugged the grate to the side, pulled out a flashlight and shone it down into absolute darkness. "Ready?"

"Man, I ain't exactly dressed for this sorta shit."

Kovacs chuckled. "It is a not a sewer, Mr. Sammy. It is surprisingly clean."

Before Sammy could reply, Kovacs was halfway down into the hole. He followed the old guy down a metal-rung ladder and slid the grate back into place. It clanged shut over his head with a finality Sammy didn't like even a little bit. When he reached bottom, he followed the panning track of Kovacs's light. They were standing in a fairly wide corridor lined with large pipes and ductwork running laterally into infinite darkness in both directions. The temperature was at least twenty degrees warmer than that on the street. Overhead, utility lamps in mesh casings glowed a dull red, but so dimly to be almost useless.

"Okay," said Sammy. "So what's with this place?"

"Steam tunnels, I told you already."

"Never knew this kinda thing was down here. Steam for what?"

"In the old days . . ." said Kovacs as he began walking along, slowly, checking the ways and the shadowed areas beneath and between the pipes, ". . . in the old days, all the skyscrapers were heated with steam. It was also piped around the city to run emergency electric turbines for places like hospitals. The big buildings still use it. These tunnels go *everywhere* under the city."

"Yeah? So how'd you know about 'em?"

"My wife Magda's brother—my brother-in-law—he worked for the City Steam Company for thirty years. Retired, and dropped dead six months later."

Yeah, right, thought Sammy. Nothing to add to that one, pal. They walked in silence for several minutes. The utter sameness of the tunnels with their thick pipes running like packs of rubber-banded asparagus. Then Kovacs spoke:

"You believe the boy, don't you? That's why you're here."

"Yeah, I guess I do."

Kovacs drew in a breath to speak, paused, as he allowed the beam of light to linger on a vertical standpipe. "What is this?"

"Huh?" Sammy drew closer to the old man, looked to what had been pinned under the light. As he bent low he could see what looked like frost clinging to the pipes like niter on cavern walls. No, not frost, but actually some kind of powdery deposit. He touched it and it flaked away in hard crusty pieces. Fragments clung to his fingers. Was he contaminating himself by touching this weird shit?

"Look," said Kovacs, washing the light ahead of them. "More!"

Turning, Sammy actually gasped as he saw the powdery stuff covering everything—walls, pipes, valves, support stanchions. Like snow drifted the morning after a storm. There was something unsettling about the image; it stung the edges of Sammy's thoughts, but he couldn't capture it. Despite the warm, humid atmosphere, a chill rippled his flesh.

Jimjams, Granny. Damn straight.

Kovacs strode forward into the midst of the white stuff, and as Sammy followed, he detected a familiar scent. On the street they called it *bonita,* but he had no idea what its chemical name and makeup might be. A tangy, bittersweet taste, it had always smelled kinda like rotten citrus fruit.

"Bonita," he said softly as he tested the powder on his tongue.

"What are you saying?" asked Kovacs.

"They use this shit to cut heroin," said Sammy.

" 'Cut' it?"

"Straight horse'll O.D. your ass big time." Sammy explained the process of thinning out heroin dosages.

"All right," said the old guy. "So why do we find it down here?"

"Hey . . . beats me."

"And how come, Mr. Sammy, you know so much about the drugs?"

"It's a street thing," said Sammy. "My people grow up knowin' about the street, man."

Kovacs grunted and then moved forward down the tunnel. He didn't have to say a word; he didn't believe that load of crap nohow.

They pressed onward and the darkness seemed to become heavier, thicker. Just more of the jimjams, Sammy knew, but he couldn't shake the feeling they were getting into some seriously deep shit.

"Wait," said Kovacs. "Something up here. Look."

Sammy was almost afraid to see what the old man was talking about. He stepped up beside him, followed the track of the flashlight.

Something half-buried in the drifting powder, leaning against the wall. He didn't have to look twice to know it was what was left of a human body. Kovacs leaned closer, playing the light over its knobby skull like a jeweler getting ready to examine a rare gem. There were pieces of flesh and stretches of tendons still attached here and there, but the bones had a brown, mottled look. No telling how long they'd been sprawled in the tunnel.

"Bums," said Kovacs. "My brother-in-law was always finding them and kicking them out."

"Huh?"

"They like to come down here to sleep in the winter. Warm. Only sometimes, they pick the wrong tunnel and the pipes get too hot. But they're asleep or passed out on cheap wine. By morning the steam heat almost cooked the skin right off them." Kovacs shook his head. "I never thought I'd see it for myself."

Sammy nodded and tried to swallow. He wanted to back away from the body, but he hesitated, instead forcing himself to touch the left radius and ulnar bones of the corpse. Lifting the spindly forearm from the bank of white powder, he revealed the still-gleaming gold band of a Rolex Oyster. Instantly he let go of the arm as if it had grown suddenly hot.

"Ain't no bum wears a watch like this." Sammy's nostrils were twitching like he was allergic to something. But he knew it was a more deeply rooted somatic response, and he knew the white powder which drifted over the corpse like a baby blanket was no longer bonita but the purest cocaine he'd ever seen. It appeared to be growing out of the walls like quartz, crystallized and crusted over. The air crackled with the promise of electric highs. It was like all you needed was to be *near* this shit to get off.

Something very weird here. Too weird.

The old man edged forward, played light about the drifted snow. "Mother of God," he whispered.

Looking ahead, Sammy could see the suggestion of other remains in the vast drifts ahead of them. A half round of skull, an empty socket, a pointing finger of bone—punctuating the purity of the whiteness.

Kovacs grunted. "Maybe we should call the police."

"Hey man, *you* call 'em if you want," said Sammy. "When

we get out of here, I'm pullin' a quick fade and I'm gonna
forget about this place. I've had enough."

Kovacs chuckled darkly. "What is the matter, Mr. Sammy?"

"We're messin' with stuff that's outta our league. It's just
time to call a cab, man. Quit it—before it quits us."

Kovacs looked at him in the dim light, said nothing.

Sammy turned to head back. The old man didn't budge.

"Look, you think you got it all figured out, but you *don't*,
man!"

"What do you mean, Mr. Sammy?"

"Listen, this ain't no big-time drug operation down here.
You've been watchin' too many TV shows! Look at this,
Kovac—ain't nobody dumb enough to leave their shipments
just layin' out like this! You don't know what you're lookin' at
here—this is fuckin' *billions*, man! The whole setup is *wrong*,
Kovac. I'm tellin' you—this is somethin' else."

"And what might that be?" Kovacs's voice had lost some of
its smugness. There might even be a trace of fear somewhere
in there.

"I don't know. 'Cept I know it's some bad shit—you can
go to sleep on *that* one. I say we get the fuck outta here now."

Kovacs appeared to be weighing his words, assaying the
truth of it all. "I believe you," he said. "You are a very scared
man."

"I'm also outta here. You with me?"

He turned and started heading back into the almost total
darkness of the tunnel. The light from the overhead bulbs gave
off a red glow so dim it was almost silly. With each step, the
darkness seemed to tighten increasingly down on him like a
fist. The perspective and geometry of the corridor had
changed, looking totally *wrong*.

"Kovac . . . what's goin' on here?"

The old man eased up behind him, played the light around.
It was obvious this was not the same way they'd come in, but
that was not possible. They'd taken no turns, and yet they

found themselves staring at what appeared to be the entrance to a maze.

"I . . . I don't understand." The old man's voice was crumbling around the edges.

"Man I *told* you!" Sammy half-screamed, knowing he was near panic himself.

"Shut up! Get a hold on things. This way." Kovacs started forward, blindly pushing the flashlight ahead like a weapon you don't really believe will help.

"This way my ass, man! We can't—"

Sammy cut off his own words as he heard the sound.

At first like cellophane crackling, so distant, so soft you'd think it'd be impossible to hear it. Then a rougher, stronger sound. A *ker-rrrunching* sound, like something being compacted, or maybe separating from itself, breaking free. Syncopated, like footsteps or machinery laboring toward a rhythm.

Sammy chuckled softly. It was a pathetic, totally unfunny sound, fraught with the coldest, most dick-shriveling, bowel-loosening fear he'd ever known.

"What *is* that?" whispered Kovacs, moving close to Sammy. It was an atavistic, huddle-close-to-you-in-the-cave response.

"You don't really want to find out, do you?"

Kovacs hunched himself deeper into his heavy coat and surged forward into the maze. The corridor, while not encased in flaking white crust, half-glowed with nitrous deposits as if the white stuff were growing like fungi.

The sounds of relentless, inexorable pursuit covered their retreat into the greater darkness ahead. Something was coming for them, and Sammy knew what it was.

Mikey's White *Man*.

But that wasn't really accurate, was it? It might be white, but it sure-the-fuck wasn't no man.

As they pushed against each other, skittering forward like blind rats, Sammy's mind's eye—that movie theater in the center of your skull where the projector was always running whether you wanted to watch the show or not—was putting it all together: *a stirring in the drifted snow as the first movements define itself as not life, but surely something undead; a shape rising up from the powdery shroud, given soul-animus by the sick sad death-energy of the city itself; born in the belly of the beast and nurtured by the sewer-dark torment and dirty-rain despair of the city's self-made zombies; gathering itself like the baddest storm there ever was, using the bones of its nearest oblation to give it a human-mocking form, it broke free of the deadly permafrost; moving forward with the heavy, unyielding momentum of something once began that would never end, it was the* Zeitgeist, *the driven-mad, burn-out engine of spiritual entropy, the animated dread which waits for all of us—from the first child-nights under sweaty blankets to the last cold breath in a sterilized nursing home—only this time it's the monster spawned from our own self-loathing, a monster from the inside that can never die . . .*

And it was coming for them, no-fucking-doubt.

"I can hear it!" said Kovacs as he waved the light down an endless corridor.

"Ain't no way out," said Sammy, as he collapsed against the wall. His suit had soaked through with the rancid-butter stink of his fear, his chest felt like somebody was sitting on it, and he tried not to think about the gold wristwatch—the wristwatch on that bony arm that had his engraved monogram on the back. A part of him knew the game was up and had grown suddenly weary, suddenly without fight. "Can't get away from it."

And then Kovacs was on him like a bear in a cave, the old man's barrel-chest forcing him up like a giant fist, his garlicky breath fogging his senses. "You *know* something!" Kovacs yelled as he braced him up. "Something you are not telling me!"

He heard it again. A crunching sound. It seemed so much

louder now, echoing and reverberating, baffled and folded over and amplified by the close quarters of the tunnel. The thing would be on them in another instant.

"Relax, old man," he said with an effort to be calm. "It don't want you."

"What are you talking about?" Kovacs's death grip on his shoulders dropped off a notch and the old man's eyes desperately searched for answers in Sammy's own.

There was no time left. How could he explain? How could he lay out the complex geometry of the city's lost souls when there was so little time? Quick: to win, just fill in the entry blank and tell us in fifty words or less *why the city's had enough, and why it's gonna give us back all the terror and the hate we've poured down its craw like steaming raw sewage.* And mail it in with two boxtops from your favorite controlled substance . . .

Yeah, just mail it in.

That's what he could do with his chances of getting out of this one. He looked at the old man, and started talking, babbling really, letting the images and the mixed metaphors fall all over the place, and as he talked, the old man started to put a few of the pieces together and he backed away like he'd just discovered he'd been doing hand-to-hand with a serious big-time your-nose-is-gonna-fall-off leper.

The White Man-that-wasn't-a-man *crunched* onward, so close now he could pick their pockets. Sammy spun away from Kovacs's grip and went reeling, staggering, almost waltzing into its long pale arms.

Zoltan's first reaction was to grab for the crazy black man, but he was too slippery, too quick for that. Sammy dissolved into a darkness which was banished by the white heat of an explosion. A nova filled the corridor with phosphorescent light, the stench of burning flesh, and a scream cut off like the skip of a phonograph needle. In the wake of the stroboscopic blast of light and heat, Zoltan's silhouette was burned upon the wall in negative-relief.

Staggering backward, blinded, he fell against the bulkhead of steam pipes. The aura of their humidity clung to him and he welcomed it like a lover. Slowly his sight crawled back to him and he saw what he knew he would: the vacant expanse of the steam tunnel, devoid of menace or the presence of the black man.

Zoltan drew and exhaled several long breaths, then found his way back to the access ladder. How long since he'd climbed down into this soulless place? As he grabbed the first rung in the dying light of his lamp, he thought of the last moments of Sammy Deller, and Zoltan wondered if the newly crowned gods of the city would be sated for very long on such offerings.

If not, they were all in for a long, cold, and very white winter.

CHANGING NEIGHBORHOOD

LOIS TILTON

"I go into the city only reluctantly," Lois Tilton says. "Nothing whatsoever has ever happened to me there, but it's alien territory; I'm convinced I'll get lost or take the wrong exit on the expressway or not be able to find a parking space. I know better than to think the city is a benign place. The radio tells me every day it's not. I live in the suburbs, but very much look forward to moving to the country. I'm not afraid of the city, but I know it's a place I don't belong."

"Fortyish" Tilton is a lifelong Midwesterner who has sold short stories to a widely varied selection of magazines (among them Weird Tales *and* Fantasy and Science Fiction) *and to anthologies such as* Borderlands II *and* Women of Darkness II. *Her first novel,* Vampire Winter, *was published in 1990. She lives in Glen Ellyn, Illinois, is married, and has two children.*

They were all together in the Maleks' living room when Jon Bronkowski announced they were putting their house up for sale. "Richard and his wife have a new house out in Maple Terrace, and there's a senior citizen's complex almost in the same neighborhood," he apologized. "We'll have our own apartment and we can visit the grandchildren every weekend. This place . . ."

His voice trailed off and he stared down at his shoes. But

Anton Malek didn't have to be told what was wrong with this place, this neighborhood where they'd all lived for over thirty years. He remembered it had been sixteen years ago when they'd all been here in this same room and he had opened up a bottle of Cold Duck to celebrate paying off the mortgage. How he'd lit a match to the papers in the ashtray, and how everyone had cheered when he raised the toast, "Free and clear!"

All their lives they'd worked and saved to make that dream a reality. But now the real-estate agents had told him the house was worth less than twenty thousand, if they could sell it at all. The words they used: "Changing neighborhood. Depreciating property values. Tight mortgage money." But what they meant was, the Maleks just couldn't afford to move out of the neighborhood, didn't have enough money to get away. Property values fell, but taxes kept going up, and so did utilities—water and electricity and gas. You work and save, Anton thought, just the way you're supposed to—and now what? He was gray-haired now, but his heavy frame still recalled a laborer's muscles, rock-hard so many years ago. A lifetime of work.

He forced a grin onto his face and shook Jon Bronkowski's hand in hollow congratulations, but not blaming him. Who wouldn't escape if they could?

"It'll be all right." said Anton to his wife, trying to comfort her when they were finally alone. "Another family will move in and it'll be just fine." But Helen just got up and started taking the coffee cups and untouched cake plates into the kitchen.

He followed, standing over her at the sink. Her head had never reached higher than his shoulder. The noise from the alley was louder here in the back of the house, so loud it was almost impossible to hear each other without shouting. It had been that way ever since the gang started to move into the neighborhood—cars racing up and down the alley all hours of the night, stereos cranked up, blasting out that loud Latin music. They called themselves the Grandios, teenage punks swaggering in tight jeans and open shirts, with a Spanish lilt to their foul language. "At least they're Catholics, aren't they?" Helen had asked once, hopefully.

Anton shook his head, remembering. When the spray-painted symbols first appeared in the alley, he'd gone down to St. Rita's to see the priest there, Father Carrizales. It had been their neighborhood church, where Helen and Anton had been married, but for the last ten years or so they'd been going to St. Stanislaus downtown, where they still said the old Latin Mass. Now, when he walked in the door, Anton could hardly believe how much the place had changed. But then, every-thing in the Church was changing these days, the nuns all wearing street clothes, what nuns you saw anymore, the new Mass—even after all these years Anton still couldn't think of it as the Mass. Now they were closing down the old parishes and schools. It ought to be, he thought, that the Church would be the one thing you could always count on, but it just wasn't true anymore. The priest—at least he looked like a priest, wearing the collar—had made it clear he had other priorities than the punks urinating on the Maleks' garage, throwing beer and wine bottles into their yard.

Anton had protested, "But Father, they use drugs, they have . . . women back there, prostitutes—right in their cars! This is a decent neighborhood, there shouldn't be that kind of thing going on!"

"Well, then, it's a matter for the police, isn't it?"

But Anton had already tried the police, the first time he'd found the paint sprayed on his garage. In the end, he'd put up a fence, though it took most of their savings—over two thou-sand dollars! Still, it made them feel safer, having something between the house and the alley. They thought of getting a dog, but Helen couldn't stand the idea of dog mess in the garden, stepping in it, having to scoop it up. For the most part, though, they simply learned to endure the situation.

But Anton did have a gun, a rifle, properly registered, upstairs in the bedroom closet. Loaded, too. He'd been a rifle-man, back when he was in the army, during the war. Chased the Nazis out of Africa, out of Italy, and now held hostage by a bunch of punks in his own backyard. This was what the country'd come to these days. But at least, he kept telling himself, he could still protect his wife and his home.

In fact, the gang didn't have much of an interest in molest-ing the old people in the neighborhood. They had their own affairs to concern them, their business in the alley that didn't start up before one or two in the afternoon, and so the Maleks could go out into their backyard in the mornings to gather up the bottles and the other, more disgusting objects tossed over the fence during the night. Anton could still work in the gar-den.

But after the Bronkowskis left there were new worries. The house was for rent now, but suppose no one moved in? Every-one knew what happened when the gangs took over a vacant house in a neighborhood. So a week or so later, when a moving van pulled up next door, Anton felt a wave of relief. He put down his hedge clippers and went inside to tell Helen, but she was already watching from the front window. "Who do you think they'll be?" she asked nervously.

People were getting out of a car in front. "So *many?*" Helen exclaimed. "What kind of people are they?"

"Chinese?" Anton speculated. One very old couple, the woman was bent over and tiny, then two middle-aged men, some women, younger men. And the kids—so many kids running up to the house that Anton couldn't quite count them all—at least eight. All living together?

The two houses had originally been identical models—kitchen, living room, dining room downstairs, two bedrooms up. The Bronkowskis, with two boys and a girl, had added a third bedroom about twenty years ago. For so many people? But maybe the Chinese were different, Anton thought. Chi-nese, Korean, or Vietnamese—who could tell? These were probably what they called boat people, he supposed. Hard to

imagine the kind of conditions they were used to. The idea
made him uneasy. This had been a decent neighborhood,
once. Hard-working families, mostly German, Polish, Bohemian. Now what was it coming to? He put his arm around
Helen. He could feel how tense she was, her body stiff and
trembling.

"What's the matter?" he asked, alarmed.

"I don't like it. I don't like it." She had her rosary in her
hands, running the beads through her fingers.

"Why? What's wrong with them?" he insisted, ignoring his
own doubts. But she just shook her head, and she refused to
go out with him to introduce herself. Anton couldn't figure it
out. She hadn't ever acted like this before.

The family next door was named Dinh. Anton could never
get their first names straightened out, and there were too
many to tell apart, anyway. So he simply called the old man
Mr. Dinh. Mr. Dinh's English was slow and stiff, but compre-
hensible. Mrs. Dinh, from the distance of the porch, bowed at
the waist but came no closer, and Anton felt embarrassed that
Helen wouldn't come out to meet her. Oriental women were
shy around strange men, he'd heard.

"I don't understand you!" he said sharply when he came
back into the house. "They seem like perfectly decent people.
Why can't you just come outside and say hello?"

"I don't know!" She bit her lip and clutched her rosary
beads. Her voice was shrill. "There's just something—I don't
know! I just can't, that's all!"

Anton stared at her, shocked. What was it? What was
wrong?

Dinh let himself hope that this time, maybe, it would be all
right. The house had three bedrooms, a large kitchen, and
there was room for a garden out in the back. In all the screaming confusion of moving in—unpacking, settling where everyone was going to sleep—he still found time to glance out

into the yard and think of the plants he could put in yet this spring, squash, sweet potatoes, beans. The sight of all the trash out in the back, near the alley, made him unhappy. There seemed to be some young men hanging out back there. It must be where the noise from the radio was coming from. Someone had knocked over the garbage can. Maybe tomorrow he could start cleaning up.

But he was grateful now to his cousin for finding them this place, this new neighborhood. He liked the big trees out in front of the house. If only they could leave all the trouble behind them, start over again.

His grandchildren were out at daybreak the next day, running through the yard. "Tell them to keep out of the streets," he advised his sons and their wives. "We don't know what kind of neighborhood this is yet. There was noise out in the alley last night. We don't want any more trouble." He glanced anxiously out the window, thinking of the garden he would plant. The kids would help him, weeding, watering. It would keep them busy, under his eye.

But everyone was quickly finishing breakfast, leaving their bowls on the kitchen counter. The restaurant opened at six-thirty, and this neighborhood wasn't so close as the old one. Soon there was no one left but Dinh and his wife, who watched the little ones while the rest were at work.

He sighed. No one listened to him anymore. His own sons. It was this country, things were too strange here. At least it had been an easy night, except for the noise from out back. No bad dreams. Maybe they'd escaped that trouble, the shadow that had haunted them ever since they had come to this country, this city, this place where they didn't belong.

It was as if they were cursed. Escaping the soldiers, the deadly borders, the camps, the ocean full of pirates—only to find the shadow of death waiting here for them, stealing his sons, one by one. They weren't meant to live in this place, this hard, mean city, he knew that now, but it was too late. They could never go back again, and there was nowhere else, nowhere else to go.

The trouble started early in the afternoon, when the cars showed up in the alley, racing up and down, tires screaming, radios blasting. Dinh felt a knot of apprehension rise in his throat. It was a gang out there, he realized now. Yesterday he had been too busy to notice the symbols scrawled in spray paint on the garage. Nervously, he called the kids in from the alley, tried to get them to stay near the house. It was hard, with the older boys especially. In the other neighborhood, they'd always been getting into fights, coming home bloody. Back in the village, when his own sons were children, they had run free in the fields, in the trees, from morning to night. And later, in the camps. But this place was different. Oh, if only Van were still alive—his youngest, his favorite. If only the shadow hadn't reached out for him in the night.

He waited with mounting anxiety until evening, when some of the others would be coming home from the restaurant. "They've been back there almost all day," he told his sons. "I think they're selling drugs."

"I couldn't sleep last night, it was so loud," his oldest daughter-in-law added, the brash one who was always nagging his son to save up for a house of their own.

"I'll take care of it," declared the grandson who insisted on the American name of Dave. He opened the screen door and stepped out into the yard, yelling in English, "Hey, you! Quiet down out there!"

Instantly a dozen punks swarmed into the yard, jeering and laughing. Dinh couldn't make out most of the things they were saying, since it was all half-Spanish, but he recognized the tone. His grandson was shouting back at them, and the rest of the Dinh men started out the door, knowing it was going to be trouble. Dinh's wife wailed as she saw one of the gang pull out a knife, the quick bright flash of the blade.

* * *

"Oh, dear!" Helen cried from the Malek kitchen, clutching at Anton. "I knew it! I just knew it! Someone's going to get killed!"

Anton doubted it would do any good, but he reached for the phone anyway. As he punched 911 he could see that the gang had their victim surrounded, shoving him from one to the other of them, cursing and taunting him. And he was sure he had seen a knife.

"Damn," he cursed tightly, willing the operator to answer. The Grandios had guns—he'd heard shots sometimes at night in the alley. Finally, the operator answered.

Emergency hotline.

"I want to report a gang assault at 25541 West Casimir Street."

I'm sorry, can you hold?

"No, I can't hold! They've got knives and guns out there! Someone's likely to get killed."

All right, sir. Can you give me that address once more? And I'll need your name and phone number.

Next door, women's voices were shrieking in some language he didn't recognize. He wondered if he ought to take his rifle and go out there, but he was afraid, and the self-knowledge shamed him.

Then, miraculously, came the sound of a siren, and the gang dispersed. One punk came running past his back porch and around the side of his house. But at least the police had come. For once. Anton told Helen to stay in the house, then went outside. "I live next door," he told one of the two cops. "I called 911."

"Oh, yeah? You the one said there were guns involved?"

Anton didn't like being treated as if *he* were the criminal, but he knew better than to antagonize the police. Sometimes they didn't care who they shoved up against the side of their squad cars. "They do have guns. I've heard them shooting in the alley."

"Yeah, but you did actually see anybody fire a shot? Just now?"

"Well, no . . . "

The cop shrugged and started to turn away. "One of them did have a knife!" Anton insisted. "I saw him cut . . ." He turned around to try to identify the man he had seen bleeding. There were five or six Asian faces, all indistinguishable, most of them bloody. One younger man was on the ground, protesting that he didn't need an ambulance. "I saw him cut that man!" Anton declared firmly. "I can give you a description." Sure he could: young, black hair, Latin looks. It would fit any one of the punks out there. Oh, what was the use?

The cop looked bored and exasperated. "Maybe later," he said, and walked away.

Anton's shoulders slumped. He'd tried. He'd offered, for a second anyway, to get involved. He was just walking away when old Mr. Dinh came up and took hold of his sleeve. "I hear," he said in awkward English. "You call police. I thank you, helping us."

"Just what any neighbor would do," Anton explained, feeling embarrassed. He hadn't done anything, not really, not like he knew he should have. "Was anyone badly hurt?" he asked awkwardly.

"Not so bad. My grandson's arm . . . but not so bad. Police come."

Anton felt he ought to warn him. "The police . . . don't usually come when there's this kind of trouble. I mean, I wouldn't count on them. The next time."

"Yes," said Dinh, "we know. My cousin . . . he find us this house, rent we can afford . . . he say it safe here. Where we live before, the black people, they call us bad names, beat us up. My son—my third son—die in that place."

"You mean they killed him?" Anton asked, knowing what it meant to lose a son.

Dinh lowered his eyes to the ground, shook his head. "No. He . . . the shadow take him."

Anton was puzzled, but Dinh went on. "My cousin, he tell us, this a better place. No gangs here."

"Well, they don't really give us too much trouble. We just try to stay away from them," Anton said apologetically. "I'm sorry, I don't know what else to tell you. This used to be a good neighborhood, good people." He glanced back at his own house. "I'm sorry, I have to go now. My wife, she gets nervous with this kind of thing going on."

"Yes. My wife, too." Dinh's back bent forward in a hint of a bow. "You go. I thank you."

Summer came abruptly, the long days of heat and scorching dry weather. Anton would go out in the relative cool of the mornings to work in the garden and watch his lawn go brown—impossible to water it with the restrictions. Old Mr. Dinh would be out there with him, trying to grow vegetables in a sunny patch alongside the fence. It was all right in the mornings, just the old people at home, and the Dinh grand-children who were too young to work at the cousin's restaurant.

But in the afternoon the noise started up in the alley, the music, the heated, driving rhythms pounding constantly. With the windows closed to keep out the sounds, the Maleks had to switch on the air conditioner. When the light bill came it was a shock—over a hundred dollars just for June, with the worst of the summer still to come.

Anton thought for a while of getting a job, maybe part time. His city pension wasn't nearly as much as Social Security, but at least they wouldn't cut back on his benefits if he started to bring in a paycheck. But Helen cried and said she couldn't stand it if he left her alone all day.

More and more, he was worried about Helen. Ever since the Dinhs had moved in, something was wrong. At night he would lie in bed, feeling the seismic pulse of sound coming out of the alley, making the whole house vibrate to its rhythm. Even over the drone of the air conditioner he could still hear the tires squealing as the cars raced up and down the streets, and more and more frequently the sound of gunshots. Helen lay next to him, rigidly awake, breathing in whispered prayers. She flinched if he reached out to her. He hadn't been able to touch her in bed for weeks.

The doctor gave her a prescription to help her sleep, but Anton could tell she was lying awake most of the night. It would be simple to blame everything on the gang, the constant noise, but he knew that wasn't all of it. No, it had something to do with the Dinhs. He couldn't understand it, her reaction to them. "I don't know," she said, twisting the chain of her rosary, "it's just something . . . maybe all those kids running around. No, I just don't know what it is. Something wrong, that's all. I can feel it."

He remembered, she'd been like this once before, when their son was killed, insisting she could hear him calling her. And then there'd been that woman who said she could contact Ron's spirit "on the other side." It had been a mess for a while. Anton didn't want to have to go through something like that again.

"Is it Alzheimer's?" he'd asked the doctor. Except that Helen wasn't forgetting things or anything like that. She was just nervous all the time, and couldn't sleep. "Depression, maybe," the doctor had suggested, and prescribed more pills.

But she was getting worse. She kept the house all sealed up now, windows locked and the curtains drawn. She wouldn't even come out onto the porch anymore. It was starting to get on Anton's nerves now. He found himself spending more and more time outside, whenever the weather allowed it.

"My wife," he explained to Dinh as they faced each other

from across the privet hedge, clippers in hand. "She doesn't come out much. All this noise makes her nervous."

Dinh nodded. "My wife, too. She speak not much English. This place . . . she want to go home, but . . ." He sighed. "My village. There, we know everyone, they know us. The land was good, rich. Our house . . . gone now, all gone. Soldiers come, we run away. Now, here, not so good. The kids . . . all the time they watch TV, don't listen to elders. My sons have no more respect. My grandsons . . . I say, stay inside, stay away from gangs." He looked over his shoulder at the alley, and Anton's eyes followed. "They don't obey."

"It's like that everywhere, these days," Anton agreed. He could remember when Ron had been twelve: the boy couldn't so much as sneak a cigarette in the alley without the neighbors calling up on the phone.

"I think sometime, this place don't want us here," Dinh said nervously. "Since we come here. The shadow . . ."

"This shadow, it's not another gang?"

Dinh shook his head. "Last year my cousin bring us here, to this city. He has new restaurant, jobs for us all."

"He was your sponsor, then?"

"Yes, sponsor. He find us house, give us work. I think, maybe bad times are over now. Then my third son, he die. Doctor say, no reason. But the young men here, they die, in night. First, two sons of my cousin. So he bring us here. Van, he was good son. Go to school. College. He do well, good grades. To be . . . electronic engin-eer. We proud. Then, one night . . ."

"I'm sorry," said Anton.

"All young men. All the same, in the night, they die. People say, the shadow take them. This not our place, this country, this city. In my village, even in camps, young men don't die in sleep. Only when we come here." Dinh's shoulders twitched, and he looked nervously around for an instant, as if there might be something behind him, following him.

"We lost our son, too," Anton confessed suddenly. "Eighteen years ago in a highway accident." Their daughter-in-law had remarried, and he and Helen hadn't seen the grandchildren in . . . they must be grown up by now, maybe with kids of their own. He had thought he'd gotten over the pain years ago.

"Only one son?" Anton could see pity in Dinh's face, for a man who would have no descendents to honor his grave.

Anton wished he could tell Dinh how it had been in the old days here in the neighborhood when he and Helen and Ron had lived here together, before the gangs and the spray paint and the drugs and the darkness that seemed to reach out of the alleys to smash every hope and make them live constantly in fear.

But just then he glimpsed a movement of the curtain drawn across the front window of his house. "Excuse me," he said apologetically, "I think my wife . . ."

It was dark in the house, and stuffy, reminding him of an old-fashioned funeral home. Anton felt a brief, angry impulse to rip the curtains away, let in the light.

"You were talking to *them* again."

"Mr. Dinh is our neighbor. I like him."

"There's something . . . something wrong over there. I don't know, I can feel it."

Yes, getting worse. He was going to have to take her back to the doctor. "Never mind. Did you want me for something?"

"We're out of bread. And cooking oil."

"All right, make a list and I'll go to the store."

But as he stepped down from the porch with the list in his pocket, she called out to him, "Wait!"

"What's the matter? Did you forget something?"

"No, I . . ." She was twisting her rosary again. "I don't want you to leave me here alone."

"All right. I'll wait while you go get your purse. You can come with me."

"No! No, I can't go out there. I can't go past that house." Her hands went up to cover her face, and she shook with the force of her sobs. "I can't! I just *can't!*"

Anton finally got her to lie down on the couch and take a couple of her pills. When she got quieter he managed to leave the house long enough to arrange for one of the Dinh grandchildren to make the trip to the store for the bread.

"I'm sorry," she kept saying when he came back, "I'm so sorry. I just can't help it, I'm so afraid."

"I thought your pills were helping you."

"They are, they do. It's just . . . I never feel safe anymore. There's something . . . out there. Those people . . ."

"Helen, the Dinhs are hardworking people, they're Catholics, just like we are. I don't know why you have this . . . attitude about them. They have problems of their own, you know. All the trouble they had coming to this country. And even here they've lost relatives, one of their own children. It just makes it worse to dwell on things, imagine things!"

"I know. I'm sorry but I just can't help it! Sometimes I think, if I could just see it, face it, everything would be better. But I can't. And it's worse, lately. It is. I'm not imagining it. Oh, I know you must think I'm crazy, but I just can't help it!"

Anton was in despair. He sometimes almost wished it *were* Alzheimer's, something he could understand. Then Helen took a breath. "I'd like to go see Father Kaczmerek, talk to him about all this. Maybe the Church can help."

Anton frowned dubiously. No matter how Helen still believed, the Church hadn't been much help lately. And Father Kaczmerek at St. Stan's was an old-school Jesuit with cold logic in his veins, not likely to be too sympathetic to Helen's unnameable fears. But Anton couldn't think of anything better to try, unless he took her back to the doctor again, and that hadn't worked.

"All right," he said finally.

But Father Kaczmerek, as he'd feared, frowned when he

explained his concerns about Helen. "You've considered moving, I suppose."

Anton nodded, feeling shame. "All we have is my City pension. With what's been happening in the neighborhood, the house isn't worth very much."

"Well, the city does have subsidized housing for seniors, you know."

"Yes, Father, I know. We've been on the list for eight months now. But . . ." His hands moved helplessly in his lap.

"Yes, I understand," said Father Kaczmerek. "I'm sorry, I wish I could help you. But you have to realize, the Church's resources are strained. We have to consider the homeless, who are even worse off than you are. At least you have a roof over your heads, your own home."

"Of course, Father. I do understand. That isn't exactly why we've come to you. It's something else, really. Helen . . ." He turned to glance at his wife, who was twisting her rosary. "She has these . . . fears. She's been to the doctor, she has her pills, but she still seems to feel there's something, I don't know how to describe it, really . . ."

"It's something dark," Helen broke in, her voice quite steady. "I can feel it there, by that house. Ever since those people moved in. It's an evil thing, Father. I pray . . . I pray, and maybe that's kept it away so far, but I can still feel it there, waiting."

"The people next door are a refugee family, Father," Anton explained. "The Dinhs. They're Catholics, but I think they go to their own church."

"Well," said the priest after a moment, "it sounds to me, Helen, that what you're suffering from are anxiety or panic attacks. Maybe you should go back to your doctor, see if you should have your medication adjusted." He stood up, bringing the interview to an abrupt close. "I'll pray for you, of course. These are difficult times. We should all pray for strength."

* * *

"My grandson," Dinh said. "My oldest grandson. At night, he have bad dreams. We take him to doctor, give him pills." It was the shadow, Dinh knew it was. The darkness that had followed them since they came to this place, hating them, knowing they didn't belong. It had come last night again. His grandson had felt its smothering presence in his dreams.

"My wife takes pills," Anton said glumly. "They don't work very well, either. She thinks it's something else. She's always been sensitive about some kinds of things. When our son died, she knew. It wasn't until four in the morning that they notified us, but she knew, right the minute it happened. She sat up all night, waiting for the phone to ring. Now—well, we saw the priest, but he just said to take her back to the doctor."

Dinh shook his head in sympathy. He had encountered the American priests. It was almost as if they didn't believe. Back in his village there would have been alternatives, the Buddhist temple or the shaman. People who understood the spirit world, who knew how to deal with such things. But this spirit was not part of the world he understood, and here in this place there was only the doctor, who openly admitted there was nothing he could do.

Dinh walked slowly away to shut off his hose, and Anton missed the cooling backspray. He wiped the sweat from his forehead and sighed. It was the end of July, almost too hot to be outside unless you were in the shade. There was dust and grit all over everything, and the cicadas were filling the air with their high-pitched skirling, almost drowning out the noise from the alley.

It was a relief to get back inside the house with the air conditioner running, though he dreaded the arrival of the bill at the end of the month. It wasn't fair—as soon as summer came, they raised the rates. Nobody ever seemed to care how people living on a pension were supposed to survive.

He looked for Helen, found her in the darkened kitchen making a salad for dinner, slicing up hard-boiled eggs and cheese. No heating up the house cooking a hot meal, not in this weather. The heat ruined his appetite, anyway.

"Almost ready," she told him. "Do you want to pour some lemonade?"

She seemed fine now, after a nap, though last night had been one of her worst. He thought her new pills must be working, finally. Here inside the house, with the curtains shut and the blinds pulled down, she could pretend she was safe from whatever it was outside. Until nighttime, at least.

They watched TV until the late show was over. Helen refused to go to bed alone, and Anton was reluctant to try to sleep in the heat, even with the fan in the bedroom. He glanced at the thermostat on the way back from the bathroom—it was eighty-two degrees upstairs, and that was with the air-conditioning on.

They kept a light on in the hall these days. Helen was afraid to sleep in the dark. Anton lay on his back in the bottom half of his pajamas, eyes open, staring at the ceiling, Helen next to him in her short cotton nightgown. He knew the shape of her without having to look, knew how it would feel if he reached over and ran a hand up to her breast, the sweat-stickiness of her skin under the nightgown. Her breathing was audible; she wasn't asleep. If he moved, he was sure she would flinch away. It was hard, he thought, living this way. Was it simply getting old? Was it the changes in the neighborhood? Or something else?

He rolled to his side, facing the other wall. The beat of the music in the alley pulsed through him, hot music, throbbing like sex. He tossed restlessly on the damp, clinging sheets.

The darkness grew heavy. It spread itself over his face, a smothering weight compressing his chest. So heavy. Hard to breathe—no, someone was screaming!

He woke, gulping air like a drowning man breaching the surface of the water. His heart was racing in terror. *Heart attack,* he thought in a panic, almost reaching for the bedside phone. Then he saw Helen. She was sitting straight up in bed, her breath coming in short, high-pitched cries. Her eyes were huge, black circles in white, staring into nothingness. Anton grabbed her shoulders, shook her once, hard. "Helen! Wake up! It's just a dream!"

Her eyelids fluttered. She blinked, seemed to see him finally. Then she gasped again, this time like a sob. "The dark thing! Like a shadow. Oh, it's there, getting closer . . ."

Anton shuddered, still feeling the suffocating weight of his nightmare. *The dark thing, the shadow. It comes in the night. The young men, they all die.*

She was staring now, eyes still wide with terror, at the window facing the Dinhs' house. Clutching her rosary. Afraid of the shadow. Not a dream. No, it had never been a dream, had it? Suddenly Anton jumped out of bed, pulled back the curtains, pushed up the creaking window sash. The warm damp breath of the night was on his face, and the sound of the music from the alley intensified. The distant street light threw shadows onto the house next door, and just for an instant he thought he could see a deep pool of darkness crawling.

The grandson, he thought. The grandson who had bad dreams. Anton swallowed hard. The shadow. Whatever it was, it was real, it was there, seeking out the boy's life. And Helen had known all this time, had felt it somehow, haunting the Dinhs, shadowing them, waiting for night to take the young men in their sleep.

"It's over there, isn't it? It's over there right now."

Helen said nothing, but he knew he had to do something, wake them before it was too late. Only, what? Call them on the phone? He didn't know their number, didn't even know for sure they had a phone.

Anton flung open his closet door. There was the rifle, already loaded. He pulled it out, ran to the window, looking across the yard to the house next door. He hesitated, cold sense trying to intervene. What was he going to do, shoot at a phantom? A shadow? Shadow of what?

He started to turn away, but out of the corner of his eye he caught a glimpse of something—a splotch against a window of the house, a shifting shape, blacker than night. His hands were sweating, clutching the stock of his gun. It was *there.* For an instant he felt himself smothering under the darkness, heartbeat racing to the breaking point, and desperately he thrust the gun barrel out the window and fired blindly into the night. There was the sound of glass shattering, and then lights turning on inside the Dinhs' house. From the alley came abrupt and sudden silence.

His hands started to shake, and he almost dropped the gun. *Oh God what have I done?* There were people out there, inside the house. He might have hit somebody, killed somebody!

"I've got to go, I've got to tell them—there might be somebody hurt." Not even stopping for his robe, Anton ran out the front door, across the yard, past the shattered window. He pounded on the Dinhs' door.

In a few moments the porch light came on, making him blink, and then it opened and a face was looking out at him—one of the sons or grandsons, he never had figured out which was which. "I'm Anton Malek, I live next door," he started to explain, stumbling over the words, "I'm sorry, I didn't mean to disturb you this late at night, I hope I didn't do any damage—" Trying to articulate what had happened, his voice failed him. The vision from the window now seemed distant and unreal, the insane product of a nightmare. Oh, what had he *done?*

Then Dinh replaced his son in the doorway. For a moment he blinked, recognizing Anton Malek, the terrified pallor on the man's face, as if Malek had come face-to-face with a ghost. He was stammering, "Mr. Dinh, I saw . . . something, through my window . . . I shot at it . . ."

"You? Malek? You shoot the gun?"

"I'm sorry, I don't know what came over me—I thought I saw . . . it was something dark . . ."

Dinh's eyes widened in sudden comprehension. The dream had come tonight in all its oppressiveness, the presence of the shadow reaching out from the streets of the hard, unmerciful city, this alien place, rejecting their presence. He was struggling with it, being dragged down into the dark, when suddenly out of the night came the sound of a shot, breaking glass. He woke, knowing the shadow had fled. And his grandson, stumbling out of the room where he slept, pale and shaking in terror, but alive—alive! Spared, at least for this night.

Now Dinh reached out for Malek's wrist, held it in both hands. The American was standing there in the doorway, in a state of shock. "The shadow," Dinh whispered, not wanting to say the word out loud. "The gun. The shadow . . . gone now."

Anton shook his head in confusion. Gone? He still couldn't make himself believe it had been real, that moment in his bedroom window, seeing what he had seen.

From the alley, the driving beat from the radios started to pick up again, as if nothing had ever happened. "I . . ." he started to say, but then he noticed that Dinh was looking past him in surprise, and he turned around to see Helen standing behind him on the walk, wearing her robe.

"Is it gone?" she was asking, looking from him to Mr. Dinh. "I felt . . . something out here, but then no more. Do you think it's gone now?"

"For tonight," said Dinh, when Anton said nothing, standing numb in his bare feet on the porch. "Maybe not . . . tomorrow."

"I see," said Helen, nodding. She was pulling her robe closer around her, shivering despite the night's heat.

Slowly, Anton reached out his hand for hers, held it closely, pressing the rosary beads into her palm. To Dinh he said, "My wife. My wife, Helen. This is our neighbor, Mr. Dinh."

"I'm pleased to meet you. It's too bad about all this trouble, but I hope you and Mrs. Dinh can come over soon for a cup of coffee and some cake," she said, while they all stood there together under the porch light, a small, isolated island in the surrounding night.

OPEN HEARTS

STEPHEN GRESHAM

"I was in a bookstore once, just browsing," Stephen Gresham says, "when suddenly a young man in a black cape entered the store and announced that he was going to kill everyone there (probably ten, maybe fifteen of us). I was scared to the bone—it was a neon jangle, an intense kind of fear I had never experienced. He appeared to have some type of weapon under his cape, but the clerk (either a very brave or an immensely stupid fellow) calmly talked our executioner out of his plan."

Gresham, age forty-three, has had eleven novels and more than twenty short stories published, most recently Blood Wings *and* The Living Dark. *He lives in Auburn, Alabama, with his wife and sixteen-year-old son.*

The Bleeder called around noon that day.

The usual interrupted transmission. It came through on Tarko's line, and I'll never forget his face, how pasty white it got, how a nervous tic developed at the corner of his mouth as he turned to me, trying to jump-start his speech. His black eyes had frozen. I remember he pointed down at his phone like a big rat was cornered in it.

"Tark?" I said. "Trouble with a customer?"

He shook his head, and I could see sweat beading on his

upper lip. Thankfully, none of the others noticed how freaked he was, they being too busy with their own calls.

"You got a dead line?" I followed. "Some crackle?"

I was eyeball-deep in the bookkeeping. An end-of-the-month Friday. That meant payroll. Checks to write. A mountain of paperwork required by this goddamn city.

"The Bleeder," he said, and his voice somehow sounded as white as his face, if you can imagine that.

Shit, I thought. Hard enough living and working in this foul, filthy, repulsive city without some kook adding to the general scheme of pollution, corruption, crime, unemployment, an out-of-control drug problem, and the worst fucking weather on the planet.

Well, I thought, we've heard from the Bleeder before. He's gotten his jollies scaring the piss outta Tarko—so now he'll leave us alone for a few days.

"Says he's coming," Tarko sputtered. "Says he's going to pay us a visit. At five o'clock."

Tarko had been staring at me right up to those final words, at which point he glanced over my shoulder at the clock on the wall above my desk. And he shuddered.

And I felt tiny, ice-cold, skittery tracks race down my back. It was a day destined to change all of us. Especially me.

I leaned conspiratorially close to Tarko's face; he had brushy bristles of hair in his nostrils and those nostrils were flared.

"Be cool," I believe I whispered. "Don't say *anything* to anyone else. This has to be between you and me, okay? You and me."

He seemed to relax a notch.

The rest of the day passed like a surrealistic dream culminating in a nightmare, and yet I can recall some details with crystal clarity. I think you're gonna want to hear this story about the day the Bleeder visited us.

But bear with me.

It's a hard story to tell.

* * *

The name of our piss-ant little company is Open Hearts Industries, Incorporated, a telemarketing group founded by my brother, Will. We hawk Heartglow health foods: vitamins, diet wafers, iron pills, protein boosters, super energy candy bars (one plain chocolate, the other chocolate with almonds) and even a soda cracker that (I kid you not) is supposed to help your lungs breathe the unbreathable air in this cesspool of a city. Our logo is a big red heart with an open door in the middle of it and smiling faces looking out—not very imaginative. I swear I had nothing to do with the design.

Open Hearts. Yeah, you've probably gotten a call from us if you live in the metro area. As I said, this is Will's baby. Or was. His idea, though he had to fight the city commission to get this operation set up, was to provide jobs for the handicapped, but he wanted the concept of handicapped to be given a lot of latitude, so as it stands, "handicapped" includes obvious physical handicaps—such as blindness or crippled or missing limbs—as well as mental handicaps, individuals with prison records, and another class of people the city labels "the terminally unemployable." Sounds like a disease, doesn't it?

To begin with, I thought of my job as manager of the Open Hearts as temporary. Hey, now I'm not so sure. You see, I was an ad man on Platinum Row, downtown. High profile all the way. Jesus, I had a cushy job, sixty grand a year as a mock-up specialist for Henderson, Quayle & Harmon Associates. Things were seashells and balloons until a few months ago when the company was bought—one of those hostile take-overs you read about. Sure, it was a corrupt, dirty deal—dirty as a rat's ass. But you have to expect that on Platinum Row. It's a mean place. What place in this city isn't? People were let go from the agency. Within weeks yours truly had to dump his glitzy apartment in the Bancroft Towers and sell his Porsche and say bye-bye to all the high-class chicks he'd met. They can smell it when you're no longer rolling in dough.

Times were bleak. Then they got bleaker. A month after the Row stabbed me in the back, my older brother, Will, committed suicide. Word on the street is that he was seduced by corruption—this city, in other words, destroyed another decent soul. One night the blackness beyond darkness called to him and he shot himself up with enough digoxin to kill an elephant. But before he shuffled off this mortal coil, he wrote out this letter requesting that I agree to become manager of Open Hearts until a replacement could be found. I've always been a sucker when it comes to Will.

Yeah, I gotta believe this city killed him.

Or maybe the Bleeder had something to do with it?

We're in the Bush Building, third floor of this three-story scab of a building about eight blocks from downtown. No central heating or air-conditioning. Most of the other offices are empty, gathering dust and harboring the world's largest cockroaches. One office houses the headquarters of a mayoral candidate, another is a front for the local mafia, and one is the center for lesbian rights—the latter has been firebombed a time or two.

Our office space is a rectangular room twelve feet by thirty feet with a wall of dirty, disgustingly smeared windows looking out onto the street and a burned-out building across the way that used to be a warehouse of some sort. It's major-league depressing, and the day the Bleeder came was even more depressing than usual, what with a gray sky that resembled old, dead or diseased skin. A cold, cold wind. We have a space heater, but you'd better stay within five feet of it or you'll freeze your ass off. I have a small desk facing away from the windows. Behind me are three long tables, five chairs and a bank of five phones. Oh, and I keep a gun in my desk: cute little Rossi .38. In this city you need one.

I'll give you a quick sketch of my employees—the "Hearts" as I call them—because there's no story without them. Basically good folks, though they've let me know, in subtle and not-so-subtle ways, that I'll never be able to replace Will. Yet they haven't gone on strike or left threatening notes around.

Okay, on the far left is Molly; she's a plump redhead who escaped the ritzy north side and her rich parents—don't ask me why. She drinks large Cokes one right after another and often gets excited on the phone and hyperventilates. She also occasionally hears voices on her line: sometimes God, sometimes Jesus. Next to her is Tarko from the west side. I believe he's Hungarian or Bulgarian or some "arian"; he's been arrested a few times for shoplifting. He's very thin and has a pathetic beard, and at his feet he keeps a small duffle bag, but it's empty as far as I know. Then there's Dexter, a heavyset black fella, partially blind with very bad knees and a soft, effeminate voice. He's our best hawker because he can plant tears in his delivery whenever he needs to—God, you oughta hear him. Next to him is Trampita. Like Dexter, she's from across the river. She's Hispanic, pretty, small and thin, and has a withered left arm (has to cradle the phone under her chin). She sees things when she hasn't taken her medication regularly or gets too stressed. And finally there's Shondra, a street-smart black who used to be a prostitute. She has a spectacular body; she brings her one-year-old daughter to work with her. The daughter is all messed up because Shondra was on cocaine during the pregnancy; the kid has no name: "Why waste a perfectly good name when she'll never live long enough to turn a trick?"—is Shondra's explanation for that.

All the Hearts are around twenty-one; Shondra's probably a few years older. But (except for Shondra) they work well. We put up some good numbers every month, no thanks to the city, which hassles us at every move. In fact, the Hearts seem to have a curious synergy about them. What I mean is, a bond, a chemistry. For example, last week Trampita's mother got real sick, and so one day when I came to work, four of them— Shondra doesn't go in for this kind of thing—were standing, holding hands in a circle, not exactly praying, just sending out good vibes I suppose. Yeah, you guessed it: Trampita's mother got better. Call it coincidence.

One more thing about the Hearts: each is scared of the Bleeder; Shondra would never admit that she is, but, trust me, she is. But now back to that fateful day. The Hearts had brown-bagged their lunches—chips, sandwiches, et cetera. Like I said, I was doing paperwork. Over my shoulder I heard Dexter's soft, effeminate, non-ghetto-inflected voice delivering our basic sales spiel.

"Mrs. Radinsky, this is Dexter Hollarann of Open Hearts. How are you today, ma'am? . . . Good, good. Mrs. Radinsky, we're not a charity, but our company gives the handicapped a chance to earn money and gain self-esteem by selling Heartglow health products, and each of our callers receives a small commission for each sale. Would you be interested, Mrs. Radinsky, in helping our worthwhile cause? We offer an array of health products that . . ."

I can repeat it in my sleep. Sometimes do. The elderly are our best customers. Especially the well-heeled north-side folks. Well, as I recall, Dexter made a sale. A pretty good one. I called the customer back as usual to recheck the order. Business began to click. Several more sales. A spitting of snow outside, but no one except me really noticed. To tell you the truth, I had almost forgotten about the Bleeder. Just some basically innocuous weirdo—no slasher or subway maniac, I figured.

The Hearts were on fire. Molly was hyperventilating; Tarko was nervously picking up a sale or two, and Trampita wasn't in tears (she cries when she gets rejected on three calls in a row). On the other hand, Shondra was complaining because she had the *F*s and *G*s that day, so she was reading the morning *Pantagraph*, the city edition, and I said,

"Shondra, would you please make some calls, or am I going to have to kick your pretty ass?"

She flipped me the bird.

"Listen to this, creephearts," she said. "Front page has a poll on personal safety in this city over the past five years. Forty-four percent say where they shop or dine is less safe now.

Forty-one percent think walking in their neighborhood at night is less safe, and fifty percent say the likelihood of crime where they work has increased. Guys and gals, we're living in a fucking jungle."

"Make some calls, Shondra," I snarled.

And Dexter added, "I think you're developing an attitude problem, Shondra."

That rattled her cage.

She did a slinky walk over to him and announced loudly enough for everyone to hear over their sales spiels,

"Only reason Dexter's so chirpy today is 'cause Molly agreed to fuck him. Ain't that right, Big D? Gonna shove the meat to her tonight?"

Work came to a halt. Mid-spiel, Molly sorta swooned and crashed her nose into a large Coke. Trampita hung up on someone and started to cry. Tarko's mouth formed a series of tiny O's as, apparently, he tried to imagine the act of sex between Molly and Dexter.

So I said,

"Shondra, was that really necessary? Get back to work."

Dexter himself, flustered and angry and momentarily speechless, finally blurted, "You are trash. Pure trash. I do not think unclean thoughts about anyone."

His bad eye was clouding.

What does Shondra do? She unbuttons about three buttons of her silky, magenta-colored blouse and thrusts a lacy black bra and two ample breasts in his face and laughs like a mad woman.

As you might guess, sales fell off dramatically for the next half an hour. That's when Tarko stood up and said, "It's one o'clock."

Shondra, who was in the act of dialing a potential customer, craned her neck around and said,

"What the fuck's that supposed to mean?"

There was general commotion as everyone in his or her own personal way told Shondra to shut up. And that's when her baby started to cry. She went over and picked it up, and even from where I was sitting you could see that it had turned a funny yellow color, sorta like the pages of old magazines. Her kid did that whenever there was unusual tension in the room. And it didn't exactly cry either—it was more like the gurgling sound of water having trouble squeezing through a drainpipe.

Shondra nailed me with a glare.

"Some kinda bad shit happenin' here, Michael? What's Tark know?"

I had to tell her—and the others—but I added, "Listen, folks, he's probably just a harmless loony who's been living in this city too long. I promise you there's nothing to it."

You think they believed me? Yeah, right.

The city had swallowed us.

We were like microbes in the stomach of a beast.

Ever notice the snow that falls in our fair city? It's gray. Like big pieces of ash. Ashes to ashes. Fits, doesn't it?

By two o'clock it was snowing in earnest. Not sleet. Just ugly flakes of snow driven by a north wind. For the better part of an hour the Hearts had watched the clock and the street and the door and made their calls reluctantly. Not one sale during that time. Molly doodled in her phone book and hummed a hymn; Tarko picked at the hairs in his nose; Dexter ate Skittles; and Trampita kept her handkerchief handy. Shondra smoked and traded the *F*s and *G*s to Tarko for the letter *J*, claiming that people named Johnson and Jones had always been her best customers when she was flatbacking.

By two-thirty everyone was busy again; the sound of their spiels was like Muzak. When I wasn't recording a sale and filling in my ledger, I played the radio, hoping to hear a weather report. The snowfall had a nasty, implacable energy to it, but once or twice I heard the wheeze of a bus, so I knew they were still running.

Three o'clock is our break time. We shut down for fifteen minutes; out in the hallway there are soft drink, candy, and cigarette machines and two filthy restrooms. Trampita asked me if I would stand outside the women's restroom while she went in. Afterwards I bought her a Diet Pepsi and said,

"You're having a good day—three sales—not megabuck totals, but not bad."

She smiled. God, she has the most beautiful brown eyes; I could swim in them. Hell, I could snorkle in them. Has a nice little figure, too. At first I thought it was just good, old-fashioned lust, but the longer I'm around her the more I wonder if I'm falling in love with her.

Shondra noticed my obvious interest in Trampita and whispered an appropriately Shondra comment to me: "Think she'll go down for you, Michael?"

No sooner had everyone gotten back to work when Molly squealed and started muttering some kind of incantation at the ceiling. It took some effort, but I managed to coax an explanation out of her.

"It was the Bleeder," she cried, and all the other Hearts except Shondra issued a startled murmur. The atmosphere in the room couldn't have been any freakier if a truckload of cobras had been dropped among us. I did my very best to calm everyone and had won a general victory ten minutes later, but Shondra popped up and said,

"I wonder what the dude looks like? You know—the Bleeder."

That got everyone going again.

Molly: "He looks like Satan. He's possessed by Satan. I could hear it in his voice."

Trampita: "His face is very ugly."

Tarko: "He has a gun, but he is handsome."

Shondra: "No, dudes like this carry blades, not guns—they like to cut, and they've got scars all over their face."

Dexter: "He looks like anybody you'd meet on the street. He must be lonely."

They were like kids around a campfire trying to scare each other. Needless to say, I didn't add any fuel to the fire.

Right at three-thirty it began to snow like a son of a bitch. A gray-white curtain closed in front of the windows. The Hearts stopped talking about the Bleeder and stared at the snow.

And then Dexter's phone rang. Everybody got real quiet. All eyes were on me waiting to see what I would do. Dexter pushed away from it as if it were a bomb. It rang three times. Four. I felt like ants were scurrying through my veins. Suddenly I grabbed the phone.

"Listen, you crazy bastard, leave us alone. Do you hear me?"

It wasn't the Bleeder. It was the delivery service of Papa Joe's Pizza informing us that because of the weather the large "killer mushroom" pizza Dexter had ordered hours ago would not be arriving.

I apologized and everyone started breathing again.

But it was getting dark. I went to the window and watched for a few minutes and didn't see a single bus and only one taxi. So I whistled as loudly as possible to get the attention of each Heart. They put their phones down and I said,

"This weather's looking serious. If anyone wants to go home now they can."

It was 3:45. For a few moments no one spoke. Then Trampita looked up at me with chocolate mousse eyes and said, "But what if the Bleeder follows us home?"

Good question.

My mind was toying with a response just as Shondra began loading up her baby.

"Not gettin' my ass stuck here during a shitstorm—be seein' you around, creephearts."

For once I thought Shondra made pretty good sense.

Without Shondra's constant flurry and babble, the office almost seemed empty. When I glanced around, however, I could see that our space was very much occupied with concerned souls, and in their eyes I could read their thoughts: *Will would have done something.*

I turned away from them. And the snow continued to fall, and the cold, north wind continued to blow.

We called him the Bleeder because he apparently understood phone lines well enough to tap or "bleed" into them from somewhere in the city. The name made him sound more ominous, more threatening—people will do that, you know—find bogeymen in every dark alley.

But why was he calling us? And would he actually come?

I worked a minute or two longer before sneaking a peek at the Hearts: Molly and Dexter and Trampita were holding hands; I could tell that the simple act gave each of them some comfort. Tarko, he was up standing at the window picking at his sparse beard.

And then he said, "He's watching us."

For all I knew Tark could have been right.

"Might as well sit down and make some calls," I said to him, hoping he wouldn't make a further issue of the matter. "Why don't we all just concentrate on our sales?"

So we did.

For about five more minutes.

At which point there was a pounding on our door.

It was 3:55.

"He's early," said Tarko.

Like a damn fool I went to the door without my gun. I started to open it, then said,

"Who's there?"

The screech and string of profanities could have come from only one source: Shondra and offspring exploded through the door, shivering, quaking, a flake or two of snow in the woman's shimmeringly black hair.

"No buses. Not a taxi anywhere. And the fucking snowplows must be on strike. Something else, too, creephearts—there's a stiff on the front steps."

That brought another series of gasps and murmurs, and then I remember Dexter saying something very peculiar. He said, "Maybe Shondra's the Bleeder." Oh, yeah, I know he was just kidding, just trying to get a rise out of her—and he did, plus a few verbal vulgarities that were actually quite creative. But I'll spare you.

A dead body on the front steps.

I had to check. I had reached the first floor when it hit me: damn, I'd forgotten to bring my gun again. Christ. It was frigging cold and the wind was chattering the glass doors, and there I was, weaponless, and the Bleeder possibly hiding around a corner.

Shondra was right about the body. Definitely dead. An old man in a threadbare parka and a gray, felt hat. His face was the clear, whitish color of an ice cube; his nose was pressed against the top step. I couldn't see any blood, but I wasn't about to roll him over or touch him before the authorities got there. I looked around and saw no one: no traffic, no people and the darkness was closing fast—it was like some episode from "The Twilight Zone."

Back in the office I called the cops after advising the Hearts to get back to work. They popped questions at me, but I disregarded them, giving my attention instead to the dispatch operator who accidentally (maybe purposely) cut me off twice. I mentioned the dead man and the Bleeder and requested the aid of the city's finest and was promptly informed that the Bush Building was in the realignment sector which—translated politically—meant that an officer was no longer assigned to that beat. No squad car in the area, and furthermore the highest priority had to be given to . . . and that's when I hung up.

Priority? Let me tell you about priorities in this city: the quarterback on our professional football team makes enough money *per game* to pay the salary of a beginning city policeman for about three months. Don't talk to me about priorities.

It was 4:00.

Maybe it was because the Hearts had seen me trying, I don't know, but strangely enough they got back to work. All except Shondra, of course, who bitched and moaned and betrayed a little of her fear.

I began to think about what staying overnight in the office would mean. We had a couple of blankets in the storeroom. Candy and soft drink machines in the hallway. (Did Shondra have milk for the baby? Did that pathetic creature drink milk?) We could survive. Depending, of course, upon what the Bleeder chose to do.

I sneaked a peek at the clock.

4:05.

No one was hawking.

"Folks," I said, "I realize that I'm asking you to work under adverse conditions, but let's do it as long as the lines are open." And then, maybe because stress was making an omelette out of my brains, I added, "Bums have died on this street before—we've all seen it happen. No big deal. The cops will get around to picking up the body sooner or later."

"Yeah, and they can bag ours while they're at it."

That was Shondra. She had replaced Tarko at the window and was rubbing one hand over her delectable bottom. I'd never seen her so nervous. The others unenthusiastically lined up a number and started dialing, they, too, uneasy about Shondra's more than evident anxiety.

I believe I was punching buttons on the adding machine when Shondra screamed. It sounded like the hissy squeals a city bus makes when the driver slams on the brakes. Only this was louder. Everyone turned to read her face.

My stomach growled.

"I see him," said Shondra, pressing her fingers very softly and tentatively to her lips. "I see the Bleeder."

Naturally we all rushed to the window.

There was somebody down there all right. A man in a dark overcoat and hat. He was standing by the mail drop box, and he might have been waiting for a bus except . . . except he had positioned himself so that the angle of his shoulders was given to our building rather than the street.

Christ, that's him, I thought.

In some ways he looked like a lonely actor on an empty stage—like all the rest of us in this city—but then again he looked like the malicious stranger we all fear in the deepest, darkest cell of our hearts.

Strange thing happened.

He looked up at our window and our collage of faces.

Everybody jumped back. Trampita cried out and buried her head in my shoulder. Molly's breathing sounded like a copying machine on the blink. Shondra plunged her face into her hands. Dexter and Tarko got superquiet.

I had seen the man's eyes.

He looked, well . . . lost.

When I glanced out the window after consoling Trampita, the man was gone. No one had seen which way he went.

From 4:10 to 4:30, we saw and heard or imagined that we saw and heard and even smelled the Bleeder everywhere. Molly and Trampita heard his footfalls in the hallway. Dexter smelled a fetid odor and wondered about its source. Shondra sat and smoked—and once, I believe I saw her shudder.

The tension bordered upon being unbearable.

Tarko was on the phone at 4:35.

I could tell that he was listening very intently.

His eyes took on that dark, frozen look again, and suddenly he slammed the receiver down and yanked the line out of its jack—did the same for each one of the phones. I sorta grabbed him by the shoulders; he spun around and said,

"He's coming."

Seemed like everyone else started jabbering and crying at once.

I told Tarko to sit down, but he wouldn't. Desperate,

scared, I riffled through my desk drawers knowing I wouldn't feel secure until I had the Rossi in my hand.

It wasn't there.

Panic was a pulsing, screaming yellow light behind my eyes. I tore through the drawers, punching doubts, wrestling with the possibility that I had taken it to my sad-faced little apartment. I was sure of nothing.

Except that I was surrounded by some very frightened Hearts.

Dexter was sitting with his arm around Molly; Shondra was pacing with her baby; Tarko was leaning his head against the window. I saw a tear trickle from one eye; and I began to hold Trampita again, her heart beating like a hummingbird's.

At 4:45, Molly said,

"I was wrong. I just imagined it. I didn't hear the Bleeder earlier."

It was a curious admission; I had no idea then what it meant.

Tarko gave out a funny wail, and Shondra's baby launched into its own weird kind of bawling. The place was a zoo, and all the animals were freaking.

At 4:50, the tension halfway broke.

Molly and Dexter, hand in hand, rose. Trampita joined them out in the center of the office; she invited me with those black velvet eyes of hers, and in a lingerie voice she said, "Please."

Man, I was tempted, but I kept my head. Shondra and Tarko didn't join them either.

4:52.

The wind was howling like an ambulance siren.

4:54.

I heard the front door downstairs bang—could have been the wind, of course.

4:56.

Molly, Dexter, and Trampita had their eyes closed. Praying? I wasn't certain.

4:58.

Tarko sat down; his lips moved as if he were talking to himself; Shondra was sobbing. God, that was something new. Her baby was issuing a totally bizarre kind of metallic hum.

And that wind outside wouldn't let up.

I turned to face the door.

Come on you bastard—let's get this over with.

4:59.

In the eye of the storm.

I remember that I wanted to join Molly, Dexter, and Trampita, but some coldly rational mechanism within me wouldn't allow it.

5:00.

Zero hour.

Nothing happened.

At first.

You see, time got fuzzy.

I felt like I was in some nightmarishly surrealistic movie. There was a slice of fear, and then it was blocked out as if nerve endings had been severed.

Here's what I recall:

Tarko reached into his duffle bag and pulled out a gun. My gun.

And I said, "We won't need that. It's five o'clock. The Bleeder didn't show. See?" I pointed at the clock.

And he said, "Yes . . . he did."

Christ Jesus, no.

Tarko looked at me; a wrinkle squirmed on his forehead.

"No one can live in this city," he said, tonelessly. "No one can *live* here."

I said nothing. I did nothing. I wondered why I hadn't foreseen this.

Stepping toward Molly, Dexter, and Trampita, Tarko raised the .38 and fired. A chunk of Dexter's shoulder tore away, showering drops of blood onto the window. There was screaming, and I whispered, "Oh, God." I started to move to Dexter's side where Molly was clutching at him.

"No," Tarko grunted.

Shondra broke free of her stupor and began babbling. She was holding her baby when Tarko grabbed her and jammed the nose of the .38 into her mouth. Her eyes got as big as golf balls and the same color.

They knew he wasn't a killer—Dexter, Molly, and Trampita—they knew. Over my objections, and as blood continued to seep from Dexter's shoulder wound, they kept their hands joined and closed in on Tarko.

"I could blow her brains out," he exclaimed, his dark eyes absorbing glints of light.

The metallic hum of Shondra's baby grew louder. Trampita reached out for my hand. Her lips formed the words, "I love you." Heart-in-my-throat scared, I touched her love, and we circled Tarko. It was amazing.

In a few moments he released Shondra, and she scampered to a corner like a frightened animal. Her baby was quiet. I thought we had won.

But then Tarko put the gun to his head and watched us.

Dexter was having trouble standing, but our circle held firm.

We held. Oh, my God, we held.

And so, eventually, did Tarko.

The Rossi thudded to the floor.

And we closed our circle to embrace him.

Was Tarko really the Bleeder? In a way, of course, yes. That's not what's most important. We'll try to get Tarko some help.

This huge, ugly city didn't bring down the Hearts.

A handful of love beat it.

You see, this city's like a massive rock. Think about it. A rock nourishes little. Time and the elements gradually reduce it to sand. In the meantime, those of us who live here are like lithophytes, those curious plants that grow on rocks.

Am I going back to Platinum Row? No, I don't think so. I've found a place. A redoubt of humanity, meager as it is. Found it the day the Bleeder came to visit.

Now I sit back and listen to the music.

What music? Here, if you like, you might want to listen, too:

"Mrs. Brown, this is Trampita Lopez of Open Hearts. Ma'am, we're not a charity, but . . ."

THE INJURIES THAT THEY THEMSELVES PROCURE MUST BE THEIR SCHOOLMASTERS

WILLIAM RELLING, JR.

"Cities don't really scare me," says William Relling, Jr., in marked contrast to many of this volume's other contributors. "I'm a dazzling urbanite. I could never live anyplace that doesn't have a major league ballpark within easy driving distance. Not that the city can't be frightening. You just have to learn to live with it. I love the smell of concrete and exhaust."

Relling is the author of numerous short stories, many of which are gathered in his collection, The Infinite Man, *and has also published the novels* Brujo, New Moon, *and* Silent Moon. *Thirty-seven years old, he lives with his wife in Los Angeles.*

AUGUST 28

There was a phone call for me this morning from a man who introduced himself as Mr. Brooks, the principal of J. Danforth Quayle Junior High School. I didn't know the school—it's on the west side of the city—so he gave me the address. He said they're looking for an English teacher to handle the ninth grade. He sounded impressed with my transcripts and my student-teaching record. My being fresh out of college didn't seem to bother him—they'd like to fill the position with a first-time teacher, he said. I told him that I hadn't been offered a job anywhere else yet, and we agreed on a time for an interview. Next Tuesday at eleven A.M.

Annie was very excited when I told her about it. I've no reason to be overoptimistic, but somehow I've got a good feeling about this.

SEPTEMBER 1

I dropped Annie off at the doctor's and drove to the school from there. Mr. Brooks's directions were very good, and I had no problem finding it—smack in the middle of one of the west side's shabbier neighborhoods.

It's a depressing-looking place from the outside: low-slung classroom buildings made of cinder block and poured cement; a ten-foot-high Cyclone fence surrounding the entire property; razor wire wrapped around the top of the fence; an armed security guard at the entrance gate. I pulled the Civic to a stop at the gate, and the guard checked my name from a list on a clipboard and waved me through.

Mr. Brooks was waiting for me in his office in the administration building. He's a pleasant-looking man—medium height, fiftyish, balding, smiles easily. Dark circles under his eyes, though. He motioned me to a seat opposite the desk from him. As soon as I'd settled myself, he offered me the job.

"I'll be straight with you, Mr. Ford," he said. "We need somebody A.S.A.P. As a matter of fact, we're a little desperate."

"I hate to think you want me just because you're desperate," I replied.

He shook his head quickly. "No, no. I just want to be frank with you, that's all. There's a shortage of teachers in this city, especially English teachers. And I'll be the first to admit that Quayle's not an easy place to work. It takes a certain . . . personality. It's a good school, but it's got a reputation for being pretty tough. I'm not talking about its academic reputation, either, you understand. Experienced teachers are difficult for us to keep sometimes."

"How come?"

He shrugged. "Different reasons. Some get tired of dealing with junior high school students—not enough intellectual stimulation, I suppose. Some simply desire a change of scenery. Some don't care for the extracurricular duties that come with the job. And I can't deny that some simply burn out."

We talked a few minutes more, then he took me to my classroom in the language arts building. The room's not much: a thirty-foot by twenty-foot cubicle, with bare walls freshly painted a drab beige color, a scarred and battered wooden desk—*my* desk—standing at the front. Thirty-six desks for students—six rows of six desks each. Two low, metal bookshelves. A blackboard that filled the entire wall behind the teacher's desk.

It's not much, but it's mine.

Mr. Brooks gave me a tour of the school grounds, then turned me over to the school's secretary, Mrs. Campos. She handed me a stack of forms—W-4, health insurance, pension fund, life insurance, Person(s) to be Notified in Case of Emergency. While I was filling out the forms, a tall black man walked in. Impeccably dressed, lean and hard-muscled, built like a gymnast, with close-trimmed hair and sharp features. He looked at me as if he were taking my measure, then came over. The corners of his mouth edged up in a narrow smile. He held out a hand. "You're Mr. Ford, right? The new English teacher? I'm Hoyt, the vice-principal."

He had a strong grip. "Nice to meet you," I said.

"Mr. Brooks tells me this is your first teaching job."

"That's right."

"I think you'll like it here at Quayle," he said. "It's a good place to work for somebody who's looking for a challenge."

I nodded. "I understand you're the one to talk to if I have any discipline problems with the students."

It was as if a thundercloud passed over his face. "There aren't any 'discipline problems' here," he said sternly.

It was one o'clock by the time I left. On the way to the doctor's to pick up Annie I bought a bottle of champagne. She was waiting for me, beaming. We had a double celebration. Not only did I get the job, but in seven months, I'm going to be a father.

SEPTEMBER 7

Back late from a Labor Day barbecue at Annie's folks' house. Her mom and dad are excited about the baby, of course, and looking forward to being grandparents. They're considerably less excited about my new job. I told them how good the pay was—the teachers' strike last spring boosted salaries across the board, especially for new teachers—but they're worried about the reputation that schools have on the west side. Bad enough that our apartment is in a part of the city they don't care for. Or that we live in the city at all.

My father-in-law joked, "Aren't they supposed to give you combat pay when you work in that part of town?" I could tell by the look on my mother-in-law's face that she didn't think the joke was very funny.

SEPTEMBER 8

What an exhausting day. We have six class periods at Quayle, with a forty-five-minute break for lunch. Each period is fifty-five minutes long, with a five-minute break between to give you time to get to your next class. All full-time teachers have five classes and one free period every day. I teach five sections of ninth-grade English. Three are ordinary classes, one is an honors class, one a remedial class. A total of one hundred and thirty-three students—ninety-nine regulars, eighteen honors, sixteen remedial.

Most of the kids seem pretty good. A little rambunctious, maybe, but who wasn't at their age? Still, one hundred and thirty-three kids—it's going to make for a lot of "How I Spent My Summer Vacation" compositions to grade.

S E P T E M B E R   1 1

Today was not a good day. It started off badly, what with Annie suffering her first bout of morning sickness, and went downhill from there.

We had a fight over a stupid issue—she'd mixed up an entry in the checkbook, reversed some numbers, caused us to bounce a couple of checks. She wasn't in the mood to be lectured, but I was sort of itching for a fight, having just survived a long, long week at school. I ended up storming out of the house.

By the time I got to school, a headache was pounding above my right eye. And, wouldn't you know, I had to have a confrontation with a kid right off the bat, first period. One of my regulars, a kid named Morrow.

Another simple, stupid issue. I was giving a spelling test, Morrow hadn't brought a pencil with him. I called him on it, reminding him of the rules I'd laid down the very first day of class. "Hey, I'm sorry, I forgot, all right?" he snapped at me. "No big deal. Don't be such a dick about it."

"What did you call me?" I demanded.

Cowed, Morrow looked away. "Nothin'," he grunted.

"I want you to repeat it."

He glared at me. "All I said was 'Don't be such a dick.' "

My head was ready to explode. I was clenching my fists. The rest of the class was silent, watching Morrow and me. Waiting.

I took a deep breath. "I think you'd better apologize. All right?"

He looked at me with disgust. "I think you can go fuck yourself."

I went to my desk, pulled out a punishment slip, filled it out—all without a word. Gave it to Morrow. "Tell Mr. Hoyt I'll be down to see him as soon as class is over."

Morrow looked at the slip. His eyes got large. "You got to be shittin' me . . ."

"Get out," I said. "Now."

The moment stretched for an eternity. Until with a great show of defiance, Morrow gathered up his books and stalked out of the classroom, slamming the door behind him.

By the time I got to Hoyt's office I was in a more forgiving mood. Needless to say, I felt awful when I found out that Hoyt had thrown the book at Morrow: Saturday morning detention for the next four weeks.

Hoyt wouldn't hear my plea for clemency. "Morrow's a hard-ass," he said. "He belongs more at Juvenile Hall than he does here. A real shit-disturber from the word 'go.' I've had him in my office at least once a month for the past two years. Don't feel bad, Ford. If you hadn't busted him, sooner or later somebody else would've."

Small consolation. I'd been "advised" about Morrow by a few of the other teachers—and much of that advice I took with a grain of salt. But until today things had been smooth between us. I'm sorry that it had to happen.

On the way home I bought a dozen roses for Annie. Lucky for me, she was in a forgiving mood herself. And thank God the weekend's here.

As I do every morning when I first get to school, I went into the faculty lounge to get a cup of coffee and check my mail. Several of my colleagues were in the lounge, abuzz over something that had happened during last Saturday's detention. A shouting match between the vice-principal and a student had escalated into a fistfight. I listened with my mouth agape. Even before I pressed them for details, a tight sensation in the pit of my stomach told me which student it was.

It turned out not to have been much of a fight—Hoyt being older, stronger, quicker—a gross mismatch, in more ways than one. Possessing the entire weight of the school's administration, Hoyt suspended Morrow for two weeks, pending an official investigation to determine whether the boy should be expelled outright.

My ears were hot as I stalked out of the lounge, beelining for Hoyt's office. He wasn't there.

It wasn't until lunch that I caught up with him. I'd cooled down a little, but I was still able to make clear how upset I was that such a trivial incident—for which I bore as much responsibility as Morrow—had mushroomed into something so ugly. At least, I *thought* I made it clear.

Hoyt looked at me as if I were the Man from Mars. "I don't understand you, Ford. Didn't I tell you last Friday what a shit-disturber this kid Morrow is? The little bastard took a poke at me, so I decked him. That's all there was to it. Hell, he's lucky I didn't call the cops and have him charged with assault and battery."

He turned and walked away.

My remedial class met immediately after lunch. Morrow's best friend, a boy named Farr, was there. He did nothing but stare at me for the entire period: a cold, sullen look of accusation and hatred. When the dismissal bell rang and the rest of the kids were filing out, I asked him to come up to my desk.

"I'd like you to do me a favor," I said. "I heard about what happened to Morrow on Saturday. If you see him, tell him that I intend to take a big part in this 'investigation' that Mr. Hoyt's got planned. I think what he did was way out of line, and I'm going to do whatever I can to keep Morrow from getting kicked out of school. Since in a way what happened was my fault, I owe him that much."

I may as well have been talking to the wall. "He don't want no help from you, man," the boy grunted. "He don't want nothin' from you at all. We'll take care of it ourselves."

The implied threat in his voice made me bristle. "What's that supposed to mean?"

Farr smiled chillingly. "You'll see."

I spent the rest of the day turning over and over in my mind what he'd said. I wondered whether I should mention to Hoyt the threatening tone in the boy's voice, but I decided that would only make things worse. I don't trust Hoyt at all. Who knows what he might do?

S E P T E M B E R   1 8

Morrow's "inquisition" was today. Present were Mr. Brooks, Mr. Hoyt, Morrow, Morrow's father, and me.

Hoyt railroaded the boy. The way he described what happened last Saturday made Morrow sound like a rabid psychopath. Hoyt also had the boy's school record—a history of misbehavior, I'll admit, but he painted a picture of Morrow as some kind of vicious archcriminal.

I tried my best to defend the boy. I described the circumstances surrounding my giving him the punishment slip, that it was as much my fault as it was his. For God's sake, I implored, he's barely fifteen years old.

It was futile. Mr. Brooks read a letter from the president of the school board enforcing Morrow's expulsion from Quayle. This meeting was merely a formality. They'd made up their minds days ago to kick him out.

I was watching Morrow and his father as they left Mr. Brooks's office. I felt so sorry for the boy—you could tell just by looking at his father what a violent, brutish, Neanderthal the man was. I shuddered to think of what lay in store for Morrow once his father got him home.

After they'd gone, I said grimly to Hoyt, "I hope you're pleased with yourself."

He looked at me with puzzlement. "What do you mean?"

I shook my head sadly. "Nothing."

I was still feeling glum when I came home. Fortunately, Annie had some good news. She'd gone to see her obstetrician that morning. He'd done an ultrasound and taken pictures of the baby. Though he can't be one hundred percent sure, it looks like a girl.

The doctor had Annie put on a stethoscope and listen to the baby's heartbeat. She said it sounded healthy and strong.

SEPTEMBER 20

Annie and I came out of the apartment this morning, on our way to the deli at the end of the block to have breakfast. The Civic was parked at its usual spot in front of our building. Annie was the one to notice how the car's front end was sagging. I was the one who found out that the tires had been slashed.

I had to wait two hours for a tow truck. I spent the greater part of the day at the tire store, sitting in a smoky, grimy waiting room, watching a football game on an ancient black-and-white television. The TV picture had a tendency to roll every few seconds. And I'm *not* a football fan.

While we were having supper tonight, Annie asked me if I thought somebody had cut the Civic's tires on purpose. Up till that moment, the idea hadn't occurred to me. It was just some stupid, thoughtless prank—what else could it have been? When you live in the city, these things happen.

During lunch today I was given a message asking me to come to Mr. Hoyt's office immediately after school. When I got there, Hoyt and another man—a plainclothes juvenile officer named McBain—were waiting for me. That was when I found out that the same thing happened to Hoyt's car over the weekend as happened to mine. It wasn't just a prank after all.

McBain asked if I had any idea who might have done it. I hesitated for a moment before telling them about my "conversation" with Farr a week ago. Hoyt was angry that I hadn't informed him before. He immediately got up to go to Mrs. Campos's office to check the attendance roster. "Don't bother," I said. "Farr wasn't in class today."

Hoyt turned to the police officer. "Well?"

McBain promised to check on both boys and call us if he discovered anything. He and I left Hoyt's office together. He walked me to my car, and along the way I gave him my version of all that had gone on with Hoyt, Morrow, Farr and me, starting with the morning I threw Morrow out of class.

McBain scowled. "You mean all of this is a consequence of some piddling incident where a kid called you a bad name?"

"It appears that way," I said with chagrin.

"Well, it appears to me that your vice-principal may have overreacted a little. Wouldn't you say?"

"I'd say so, yes."

He shook his head, disbelieving. "You teachers give me a pain," he grunted with bitter displeasure. "Why is it you people always blow things so far out of proportion?"

McBain telephoned tonight, after supper. He'd talked to both Morrow and Farr. Neither had confessed, but McBain is convinced they're the ones who slashed my tires and Hoyt's last Saturday night. He asked me if I wanted to press charges.

I told him to forget it. As far as I'm concerned, things have gone far enough. Since my insurance company paid to have the car fixed, I just want to put the whole mess behind me.

"It's up to you, Mr. Ford," said McBain. "I should tell you, both of these boys have been arrested before, and a few of the charges have been serious, though neither one's ever been convicted of anything." He sighed wearily. "I only wish your vice-principal felt the same way you do. It'd make my job a helluva lot easier."

"What are you talking about?"

"He's suspending the Farr boy for truancy. He also wants me to prosecute both of them to 'the fullest extent of the law.' That's a quote." McBain sighed again. "I hope you don't mind my saying this, but your friend Mr. Hoyt is an officious, hard-assed son of a bitch. You're aware of that, aren't you?"

"I'm aware of that, Mr. McBain," I said glumly. "And I assure you he's *not* my friend."

S E P T E M B E R   2 7

I had a horrible nightmare last night. I don't remember what it was about specifically. Only that something awful happened to Annie, something that scared me badly.

I woke up sweating. I reached for her. She was asleep, lying on her back, her breasts rising and falling beneath the sheet in a gentle, steady rhythm. I laid a hand on her stomach, and for a moment I thought I felt the baby kicking.

When I told Annie about it this morning, she gave me a patronizing smile and said it was just my imagination. She assures me we won't start feeling the baby move for a while yet.

Or is it *September 30?* I'm not sure. It's Tuesday night, but it's late, well after midnight. It must be Wednesday, the 30th. Must be.

I didn't want to come home. I wanted to stay at the hospital with Annie. But I'd been there for nearly thirty hours. No sleep. Dead on my feet. The doctor told me to get some rest and come back in the morning. There's nothing I can do for her. Nothing.

Can't sleep, though. Can't close my eyes without seeing the monitors beeping and clicking, the tiny lights blinking off and on and off and on. The tubes feeding her, breathing for her, keeping her alive. I can't sleep.

It started yesterday. Hoyt came to my room between class periods and told me that he'd talked to McBain again. On Saturday the police picked up Morrow and Farr, charged them with willful destruction of private property, booked them, took them to Juvenile Hall. Held them for twelve hours, then released them in the custody of their parents. Hoyt was unhappy, because it looked as if the charges would have to be dropped. No witnesses, no confessions, no proof.

Then he asked me if I'd got any threatening phone calls on Sunday like he did—a disguised voice leaving obscene messages on his answering machine, promising to fix him good. Annie and I don't have an answering machine, and we were at her parents' house all day Sunday. Hoyt was certain the boys were behind it, getting back at him because "we'd" had them arrested. He said he hoped the little bastards wouldn't try and do something else to get even.

Came home from school on Monday afternoon. Found the note from Annie on the kitchen table. She'd gone out to the market to buy something for supper. Said she'd be back by five o'clock.

By six I was starting to worry. At six-thirty, as I was heading out the door to look for her, the phone rang. The police, calling me from the hospital.

The officer at the hospital was a young woman. Hispanic, I think. She told me that Annie had been found in a park playground a few blocks from our apartment. Unconscious, badly beaten, her skull fractured. Beaten and raped, by more than one assailant. She was in a coma. Bleeding internally. The doctors had to force labor. The baby was stillborn, dead in Annie's womb, killed by a blow from one of the attackers. Six and a half months premature. A little girl.

No suspects. No witnesses. No clues.

Nothing. Nothing. Nothing.

O C T O B E R   2

I make the doctors and nurses uncomfortable. They don't want me around. But no one has the nerve to ask me to leave.

I can read on their faces they don't want me there. *Why* they don't want me is because I'm a symbol of something they'd rather not have to deal with.

No change in Annie's condition. No change.

O C T O B E R   3

Mr. Brooks came to the hospital today, looking for me. He asked how Annie was doing. "No change," I told him. "No change."

He said, "I realize I'm running the risk of sounding insensitive, but do you have any idea when you might be coming back to school?"

I stared at him blankly.

"You have to be realistic about this, Ford," he went on. "I understand how you feel about your wife. But you do have other responsibilities. I've done you a courtesy by waiting until today to talk to you about this. No one feels worse about what happened than I do, but you have your own life to get on with. I've managed to get by with substitute teachers for the last four days, but your students need *you*. I'd like to know when you'll be coming back."

I heard a hollow-sounding voice answering him. "Monday," said the voice. "I'll be back Monday." Only later did I realize that the voice was mine.

OCTOBER 5

Everyone was very sympathetic at school today—my colleagues, the kids, everyone. All of them concerned for Annie, and for me.

I went to the hospital immediately after school. Annie's parents were there. The three of us had dinner together. As we ate, I noticed that there was something different about the way they looked at me. Subtle, but there nonetheless. A look of condemnation. They blame me for what happened to their daughter and their grandchild.

They're right.

OCTOBER 7

I have to be very careful how I put this down. There can be no mistake. I must be precise.

I know who hurt Annie. I *know*.

I arrived at school this morning, went directly to the faculty lounge. Miss Kiley, the history teacher, came up to me and said, "Guess who's back in school? Your old friends, Morrow and Farr."

"Morrow and Farr?"

"They've been reinstated. It turns out the president of the school board superseded his authority when he wrote that letter expelling Morrow without bringing the matter before the entire board first. It was a stupid mistake, but he was doing a favor for Hoyt. They're old buddies. Now the president's being censured by the rest of the board because the boys' families are suing the school for harassment. Hoyt's probably going to be fired for his part in it. What do you think of that?"

The bell rang before I could answer, calling us to our first-period classes. As I made my way to my room, I wasn't even thinking about what Miss Kiley had told me. In the past ten days I haven't had a waking moment when Annie wasn't uppermost in my mind. So Morrow and Farr were back in school—I couldn't care less. So Hoyt was going to be fired—he probably should've been fired a long time ago. I wasn't thinking about Hoyt or Morrow or Farr at all. Until I reached the door to my classroom and heard a sneering voice behind me. "So how's your old lady doin', Mr. Ford?"

I turned around. It was Morrow. My eyes locked onto his.

And that's when I knew. That's when I read in his eyes that he'd done it.

It took a moment for him to read my expression, to realize that *I knew.* The blood drained from his face.

Then I heard another voice calling my name. It was Mrs. Campos, the school secretary. "Mr. Ford! Mr. Ford! Please hurry!"

I followed her back to the office. Annie's doctor was on the phone, calling from the hospital. Even before I picked up the receiver I knew what he was going to tell me.

O C T O B E R 1 0

Annie's funeral was this morning.

The cause of her death was a massive subdural hematoma

from the same blow that had fractured her skull. There was nothing anyone could have done to save her. Nothing.

Today was an Indian summer day—warm and clear, the sky so blue it seemed unreal. At the cemetery I couldn't help thinking that the weather was all wrong. For funerals, it should be overcast and cool, raining perhaps. Shouldn't it?

That's what I've been thinking about tonight, since I came home. The weather. That and one other thing.

I keep remembering the expression on Morrow's face, the look in his eyes, when he realized I knew what he'd done. The look. In. His. Eyes.

OCTOBER 11

Mr. Brooks phoned me this afternoon to ask how long a bereavement leave I'd be taking. I told him I was planning on being back at school tomorrow. He seemed surprised.

OCTOBER 17

I only today got back my journal. My mother-in-law went to the apartment to pick it up and bring it out here to me. I had to allow the doctor to read it first, though, before he'd let me have it.

You might think what happened several days ago wouldn't be as fresh in my mind as the events I used to record on the days they happened. Not so, not so. I remember everything, quite clearly.

On Monday I arrived at school on time. I greeted my colleagues in the lounge, most of whom looked at me as if I were a pariah. I graciously accepted everyone's condolences. The bell rang, and I went to class.

Morrow was there, as I knew he'd be. Since his and Farr's

return to school, the two of them have been model students.
No doubt under pressure to behave themselves, so as to help
validate the lawsuits their families have pending. No doubt.

The class was astounded—or should I say shocked—to see
me. Especially Morrow. All of them sat quietly, watching me.

"Today," I said, "we'll be starting a unit on Shakespeare."

Silence.

I passed out the books I'd brought with me. "I know that
when most of you hear the name Shakespeare, you think, 'Oh,
God, that stuff is *so* boring! All those *thees* and *thous* and
wherefores!' One of the first things I'd like to do is dispel the
notion that Shakespeare is dull. That's not the case at all." I
held up a copy of the book. "This play, for example. *King
Lear.*"

I ordered them to move their desks into a circle, leaving a
cleared space in the middle of the room. My stage.

"The story goes like this," I continued as they leafed
through the pages of the book. "Lear was an old man who had
been king for a long time. One day he decided to retire. His
intention was to divide his kingdom among his three daughters, but only after each one told him how much she loved
him. His two oldest daughters, Goneril and Regan, secretly
hated their father, but they lied to him about how deeply and
truly they worshiped him. When Lear's youngest daughter,
whose name was Cordelia, answered honestly that she loved
him only as much as a good daughter should and no more
than that, he became angry. Because Cordelia wouldn't play
up to his ego the way her sisters did, even though she was the
only one who truly loved him. That's what the play is about:
being blind to who's really good and who's really bad."

I moved into the middle of the circle. "Why so many people
have problems with Shakespeare," I told them, "is because
they just try to read the plays, instead of acting them out as
they were meant to be. To give you an example, I want you
to turn to Act Three, Scene Seven."

Such good children to do as they were told.

"Here's what's happening in this scene," I went on. "Lear has run away from Regan in the middle of a storm, having been humiliated by her and her husband, the Duke of Cornwall. Afraid that Lear has gone off to raise an army against them, Regan and the duke order the capture of the Earl of Gloucester, the king's most trusted adviser, in hopes that they can find out from him what Lear is up to. The earl doesn't know that Regan and her husband have been conspiring with Edmund, who is the earl's illegitimate son, to ruin both Lear and the earl."

By then most of them were looking at me with pained expressions. They had no idea what I was talking about. It didn't matter. "Don't worry," I assured them. "Once we start acting out the scene, you'll be able to follow well enough."

I chose my actors: Regan, Goneril, Edmund, Oswald, three servants. I was to play the Duke of Cornwall myself. "Morrow," I said, "you'll be the Earl of Gloucester."

He rose reluctantly to join the rest of us in the middle of the circle. The scene began. I sent Goneril, Edmund and Oswald on their way. I ordered my servants to bind Gloucester and bring him to me. Regan and I argued with Gloucester, threatened him. His servant attacked me. Regan took my sword and stabbed the servant from behind. The servant fell, uttering to Morrow with his dying breath, "I am slain! My lord, you have one eye left to see some mischief on him!"

"Lest it see more, prevent it!" I cried. "Out vile jelly! Where is thy luster now?"

I leaped at Morrow, knocking him to the floor. I squeezed his head between my hands and pressed my thumbs into his eyes. I felt his eyeballs pop, the blood and fluid dribbling down my fingers.

I heard him scream. And scream. And scream.

And then, they brought me here.

The reason why I haven't written in so long is because after the last thing I wrote my journal was taken away from me. It was for my own good—or so I was told. All I would do was read what I'd written, over and over and over. And when I'd come to the part about what I'd done to Morrow I'd laugh and laugh and laugh.

I finally got my journal back today. Along with all of my other "personal effects." I got them back, because I'm going home. Today.

I find that I'm asking myself again and again: *How can this be?* No one is more flabbergasted than I am that they're letting me go. No one. Don't they realize what it is that I've done? I belong here.

The doctor assures me, however, that I've recovered from the breakdown I suffered as a consequence of the grief I was feeling over the death of my wife. The assault charges against me are still pending, but the lawyer whom my father-in-law hired to handle my case insists that my "diminished capacity" at the time of the incident will be an adequate defense. He seems certain that the case will be dismissed.

I suppose there is a sort of justice after all. The law couldn't do anything *for* me, but neither will it be able to do anything *to* me. There really is a certain irony there, don't you think?

I've spent the evening passing out chewing gum to the few trick-or-treaters who've visited me. Six or seven children, no more. Few people go out on Halloween anymore, the way they used to when I was a boy. You never know what you might find buried in the center of a candy bar these days. A razor blade, perhaps. Or worse.

It's the city. The city breeds hatred and fear and paranoia. These are its survival mechanisms. I understand that now.

There are only two things that matter. Survival. And revenge.

I've had other visitors today, one this morning and one later in the afternoon, just before the sun went down. The first was Mr. Brooks. He remarked upon how well I was looking, and how glad he was that I would be coming back to school tomorrow. I told him I was anxious to be back in my classroom. I thanked him for everything he'd done to help get me released from the hospital. It was his testimony to the doctor that ultimately tipped the scales in my favor.

"My motives weren't entirely altruistic," said Brooks. "You know how much trouble I had finding you in the first place. I didn't exactly have many candidates clamoring for your position."

"I had no idea I was so indispensable," I said.

He nodded. "Of course, everyone regrets what happened. Nobody does more than I do."

"Of course."

"But we're all certain nothing like that will ever happen again. Aren't we."

"Of course."

We wished each other a happy Halloween, and he left. I went out for a while. When I returned, I found a note that had been slipped under the front door. The note was from Detective McBain. He'd dropped by and promised to return.

He came back just before nightfall. I showed him into the living room. He sat down on the sofa. "I can only stay for a minute," he said. "I have some information for you that I didn't want to give out over the phone. I wanted to tell you in person."

I waited.

"Last night," he said, "we arrested two adult males who'd raped and bludgeoned a woman in an alley not too far from here. They confessed to several other rapes in the area." He took a deep breath. "Including your wife."

I was watching him carefully.

"Their blood type matches that of the semen samples we took from her," McBain continued. "What's more important, though, is their confession—they got all the details right. We're certain they're the ones who killed your wife. It wasn't the Morrow boy after all."

I said nothing.

After a time he began to shift uncomfortably, then came to his feet. He looked at me pointedly. "I just thought you'd like to know that," he said. "I thought you'd like to know that we caught the ones who did it."

As he was walking toward the door, he paused to look back at me. "You'll probably be called in to give us another statement."

I nodded.

He showed himself out.

That was hours ago. Since then I've had much time to think about several things. What Brooks had told me, and what McBain had told me. I've had time to think about survival. And revenge.

I thought about all that while I was cleaning the broadsword I'd bought at an antique shop, while I was out this afternoon. On the same trip during which I bought the treats for my handful of Halloween visitors.

I understand very well that I have to do this. I can't think of any other reason why the hospital would have let me go. Why would Brooks allow me back in school? *Want* me back.

The city and I are one. Survival and revenge.

McBain is mistaken, of course. The men they've arrested had nothing to do with Annie. But he couldn't know that, because he never saw the look in Morrow's eyes.

I'm not wrong. I know that. It was Morrow. And Farr, whom I have not forgotten. I haven't forgotten him at all.

Tomorrow, after lunch, we shall continue our study of the

works of William Shakespeare. *Macbeth.* Act Five, Scene
Eight. I've been practicing Macduff's lines. "Hail, King, for so
thou art! Behold where stands the usurper's cursed head!"

I'm so looking forward to this. I think the class will enjoy it,
too. And I hope that my friend Farr realizes what an honor it
will be to have had the starring role.

TALLULAH

CHARLES DE LINT

"I remember when I was fifteen," says Charles de Lint. "I was a run-away and living on the streets of Toronto. This was in the summer of peace, love, and flowers—1967—and things weren't quite as weird as they are on the streets these days. Late one night I was walking through a residential area north of Yorkville (Toronto's version of Haight Ashbury, now all trendy boutiques) with a friend, looking for a place to sleep for the night, when we saw a house with a very scruffy lawn. The grass had to be eight, nine inches high. The place had a deserted air about it, so we decided to see if it was empty. When we tried the front door, it was unlocked, and we found the place long-deserted, except that it looked as though whoever had left, had done so in the middle of a meal and just never come back. There was still food on plates on the table, a sink full of dishes. Everything was there: furnishings, drapes, carpets, beds, closets full of clothes, the works. It was all dusty and had an air of musty neglect. Very weird. Still, we stayed there for a few nights. I never did find out what happened to the people living there."

De Lint, a writer, editor, and accomplished musician, has published almost twenty books, not to mention short fiction and reviews of fantasy, science fiction, and horror. He has served on various awards juries and is a frequent guest of honor at conventions. He lives in Ottawa, Ontario, with his wife, MaryAnn Harris, a fellow musician and artist.

Nothing is too wonderful
to be true.
———MICHAEL FARADAY

For the longest time, I thought she was a ghost, but I know
what she is now. She's come to mean everything to me; like
a lifeline, she keeps me connected to reality, to this place and
this time, by her very capriciousness.

I wish I'd never met her.

That's a lie, of course, but it comes easily to the tongue. It's
a way to pretend that the ache she left behind in my heart
doesn't hurt.

She calls herself Tallulah, but I know who she really is. A
name can't begin to encompass the sum of all her parts. But
that's the magic of names, isn't it? That the complex, contra-
dictory individuals we are can be called up complete and
whole in another mind through the simple sorcery of a name.
And connected to the complete person we call up in our mind
with the alchemy of their name comes all the baggage of
memory: times you were together, the music you listened to
this morning or that night, conversation and jokes and private
moments—all the good and bad times you've shared.

Tally's name conjures up more than just that for me. When
the *gris-gris* of the memories that hold her stir in my mind, she
guides me through the city's night like a totem does a shaman
through Dreamtime. Everything familiar is changed; what she
shows me goes under the skin, right to the marrow of the
bone. I see a building and I know not only its shape and form,
but its history. I can hear its breathing. I can almost read its
thoughts.

It's the same for a street or a park, an abandoned car or
some secret garden hidden behind a wall, a late-night cafe or

an empty lot. Each one has its story, its secret history, and Tally taught me how to read each one of them. Where I once guessed at those stories, chasing rumors of them like they were errant fireflies, now I know.

I'm not as good with people. Neither of us are. Tally, at least, has an excuse. But me . . .

I wish I'd never met her.

My brother Geordie is a busker—a street musician. He plays his fiddle on street corners or along the queues in the theater district and makes a kind of magic with his music that words just can't describe. Listening to him play is like stepping into an old Irish or Scottish fairy tale. The slow airs call up haunted moors and lonely coastlines; the jigs and reels wake a fire in the soul that burns with the awesome wonder of bright stars on a cold night, or the familiar warmth of red coals glimmering in a friendly hearth.

The funny thing is, he's one of the most pragmatic people I know. For all the enchantment he can call up out of that old Hungarian fiddle of his, I'm the one with the fey streak in our family.

As far as I'm concerned, the only difference between fact and what most people call fiction is about fifteen pages in the dictionary. I've got such an open mind that Geordie says I've got a hole in it, but I've been that way for as long as I can remember. It's not so much that I'm gullible—though I've been called that and less charitable things in my time; it's more that I'm willing to just suspend my disbelief until whatever I'm considering has been thoroughly debunked to my satisfaction.

I first started collecting oddities and curiosities as I heard about them when I was in my teens, filling page after page of spiral-bound notebooks with little notes and jottings—neat inky scratches on the paper, each entry opening worlds of possibility for me whenever I reread it. I liked things to do with the city the best because that seemed the last place in the world where the delicate wonders that are magic should exist.

Truth to tell, a lot of what showed up in those notebooks leaned towards a darker side of the coin, but even that darkness had a light in it for me because it still stretched the realms of what was into a thousand variable what-might-bes. That was the real magic for me: the possibility that we only have to draw aside a veil to find the world a far more strange and wondrous place than its mundaneness allowed it could be.

It was my girlfriend back then—Katie Deren—who first convinced me to use my notebooks as the basis for stories. Katie was about as odd a bird as I was in those days. We'd sit around with the music of obscure groups like the Incredible String Band or Dr. Strangely Strange playing on the turntable and literally talk away whole nights about anything and everything. She had the strangest way of looking at things; everything had a soul for her, be it the majestic old oak tree that stood in her parents' backyard, or the old black iron kettle that she kept filled with dried weeds on the sill of her bedroom window.

We drifted apart, the way it happens with a lot of relationships at that age, but I kept the gift she'd woken in me: the stories.

I never expected to become a writer, but then I had no real expectations whatsoever as to what I was going to be when I "grew up." Sometimes I think I never did—grow up that is.

But I did get older. And I found I could make a living with my stories. I called them urban legends—independently of Jan Harold Brunvand who also makes a living collecting them. But he approaches them as a folklorist, cataloging and comparing them, while I retell them in stories that I sell to magazines and then recycle into book collections.

I don't feel we're in any kind of competition with each other, but then I feel that way about all writers. There are as many stories to be told as there are people to tell them about; only the mean-spirited would consider there to be a competition at all. And Brunvand does such a wonderful job. The first time I read his *Vanishing Hitchhiker,* I was completely smitten with his work and, like the hundreds of other correspondents Brunvand has, made a point of sending him items I thought he could use for his future books.

But I never wrote to him about Tally.

I do my writing at night—the later the better. I don't work in a study or an office and I don't use a typewriter or computer, at least not for my first drafts. What I like to do is go out into the night and just set up shop wherever it feels right: a park bench, the counter of some all-night diner, the stoop of St. Paul's Cathedral, the doorway of a closed junk shop on Grasso Street.

I still keep notebooks, but they're hardcover ones now. I write my stories in them as well. And though the stories owe their existence to the urban legends that give them their quirky spin, what they're really about is people: what makes them happy or sad. My themes are simple. They're about love and loss, honor and the responsibilities of friendship. And wonder . . . always wonder. As complex as people are individually, their drives are universal.

I've been told—so often I almost believe it myself—that I've got a real understanding of people. However strange the situations my characters find themselves in, the characters themselves seem very real to my readers. That makes me feel good, naturally enough, but I don't understand it because I don't feel that I know people very well at all.

I'm just not good with them.

I think it comes from being that odd bird when I was growing up. I was distanced from the concerns of my peers, I just couldn't get into so many of the things that they felt were important. The fault was partly that of the other kids—if you're different, you're fair game. You know how it can be. There are three kinds of kids: the ones that are the odd birds, the ones that piss on them, and the ones that watch it happen.

It was partly my fault, too, because I ostracized them as much as they did me. I was always out of step; I didn't really care about belonging to this gang or that clique. A few years earlier and I'd have been a beatnik, a few years later, a hippie. I got into drugs before they were cool; found out they were messing up my head and got out of them when everybody else started dropping acid and MDA and who knows what all.

What it boiled down to was that I had a lot of acquaintances, but very few friends. And even with the friends I did have, I always felt one step removed from the relationship, like I was observing what was going on, taking notes, rather than just being there.

That didn't change much when I got older.

How that—let's call it aloofness, for lack of a better word—translated into this so-called gift for characterization in my fiction, I can't tell you. Maybe I put so much into the stories, I had nothing left over for real life. Maybe it's because each one of us, no matter how many or how close our connections to other people, remains, in the end, irrevocably on his or her own solitary islands separated by expanses of the world's sea, and I'm just more aware of it than others. Maybe I'm just missing the necessary circuit in my brain.

Tally changed all of that.

I wouldn't have thought it, the first time I saw her.

There's a section of the Market in Lower Crowsea, where it backs onto the Kickaha River, that's got a kind of Old World magic about it. The roads are too narrow for normal vehicular traffic, so most people go through on bicycles or by foot. The buildings lean close to each other over the cobblestoned streets that twist and wind in a confusion that not even the city's mapmakers have been able to unravel to anyone's satisfaction.

There are old shops back in there and some of them still

have signage in Dutch dating back a hundred years. There are buildings tenanted by generations of the same families, little courtyards, secret gardens, any number of sly-eyed cats, old men playing dominoes and checkers and their gossiping wives, small gales of shrieking children by day, mysterious eddies of silence by night. It's a wonderful place, completely untouched by the yuppie renovation projects that took over the rest of the Market.

Right down by the river there's a public courtyard surrounded on all sides by three-story brick-and-stone town houses with mansard roofs and dormer windows. Late at night, the only man-made sound comes from the odd bit of traffic on McKennit Street Bridge a block or so south, the only light comes from the single streetlamp under which stands a bench made of cast iron and wooden slats. Not a light shines from the windows of the buildings that enclose it. When you sit on that bench, the river murmurs at your back and the streetlamp encloses you in a comforting embrace of warm yellow light.

It's one of my favorite places to write. I'll sit there with my notebook propped up on my lap and scribble away for hours, my only companion, more often than not, a tattered-eared tom sleeping on the bench beside me. I think he lives in one of the houses, though he could be a stray. He's there most times I come—not waiting for me. I'll sit down and start to work and after a half hour or so he'll come sauntering out of the shadows, stopping a half-dozen times to lick this shoulder, that hind leg, before finally settling down beside me like he's been there all night.

He doesn't much care to be patted, but I'm usually too busy to pay that much attention to him anyway. Still, I enjoy his company. I'd miss him if he stopped coming.

I've wondered about his name sometimes. You know that old story where they talk about a cat having three names? There's the one we give them, the one they use among themselves and then the secret one that only they know.

I just call him Ben; I don't know what he calls himself. He could be the King of the Cats, for all I know.

He was sleeping on the bench beside me the night she showed up. He saw her first. Or maybe he heard her.

It was early autumn, a brisk night that followed one of those perfect crisp autumn days—clear skies, the sunshine bright on the turning leaves, a smell in the air of a change coming, the wheel of the seasons turning. I was bundled up in a flannel jacket and wore half-gloves to keep my hands from getting too cold as I wrote.

I looked up when Ben stirred beside me, fur bristling, slit-eyed gaze focused on the narrow mouth of an alleyway that cut like a tunnel through the town houses on the north side of the courtyard. I followed his gaze in time to see her step from the shadows.

She reminded me of Geordie's friend Jilly, the artist. She had the same slender frame and tangled hair, the same pixie face and wardrobe that made her look like she did all her clothes buying at a thrift shop. But she had a harder look than Jilly, a toughness that was reflected in the sharp lines that modified her features and in her gear: battered leather jacket, jeans stuffed into low-heeled black cowboy boots, hands in her pockets, a kind of leather carryall hanging by its strap from her shoulder.

She had a loose, confident gait as she crossed the courtyard, boot heels clicking on the cobblestones. The warm light from the streetlamp softened her features a little.

Beside me, Ben turned around a couple of times, a slow chase of his tail that had no enthusiasm to it, and settled back into sleep. She sat down on the bench, the cat between us, and dropped her carryall at her feet. Then she leaned back against the bench, legs stretched out in front of her, hands back in the pockets of her jeans, head turned to look at me.

"Some night, isn't it?" she said.

I was still trying to figure her out. I couldn't place her age. One moment she looked young enough to be a runaway and

I waited for the inevitable request for spare change or a place to crash, the next she seemed around my age—late twenties, early thirties—and I didn't know what she might want. One thing people didn't do in the city, even in this part of it, was befriend strangers. Not at night. Especially not if you were young and as pretty as she was.

My lack of a response didn't seem to phase her in the least.

"What's your name?" she asked.

"Christy Riddell," I said. I hesitated for a moment, then reconciled myself to a conversation. "What's yours?" I added as I closed my notebook, leaving my pen inside it to keep my place.

"Tallulah."

Just that, the one name. Spoken with the brassy confidence of a Cher or a Madonna.

"You're kidding," I said.

Tallulah sounded like it should belong to a twenties flapper, not some punky street kid.

She gave me a smile that lit up her face, banishing the last trace of the harshness I'd seen in her features as she was walking up to the bench.

"No, really," she said. "But you can call me Tally."

The melody of the ridiculous refrain from that song by— was it Harry Belafonte?—came to mind, something about tallying bananas.

"What're you doing?" she asked.

"Writing."

"I can *see* that. I meant, what kind of writing?"

"I write stories," I told her.

I waited then for the inevitable questions: Have you ever been published? What name do you write under? Where do you get your ideas? Instead she turned away and looked up at the sky.

"I knew a poet once," she said. "He wanted to capture his soul on a piece of paper—really capture it." She looked back at me. "But of course, you can't do that, can you? You can try,

you can bleed honesty into your art until it feels like you've
wrung your soul dry, but in the end, all you've created is a
possible link between minds. An attempt at communication.
If a soul can't be measured, then how can it be captured?"

I revised my opinion of her age. She might look young, but
she spoke with too much experience couched in her words.

"What happened to him?" I found myself asking. "Did he
give up?"

She shrugged. "I don't know. He moved away." Her gaze
left mine and turned skyward once more. "When they move
away, they leave my life, because I can't follow them."

She mesmerized me—right from that first night. I sensed a
portent in her casual appearance into my life, though a portent
of what, I couldn't say.

"Did you ever want to?" I asked her.

"Want to what?"

"Follow them." I remember, even then, how the plurality
bothered me. I was jealous and I didn't even know of what.

She shook her head. "No. All I ever have is what they leave
behind."

Her voice seemed to diminish as she spoke. I wanted to
reach out and touch her shoulder with my hand, to offer what
comfort I could to ease the sudden malaise that appeared to
have gripped her, but her moods, I came to learn, were mercurial. She sat up suddenly and stroked Ben until the motor of
his purring filled the air with its resonance.

"Do you always write in places like this?" she asked.

I nodded. "I like the night; I like the city at night. It doesn't
seem to belong to anyone then. On a good night, it almost
seems as if the stories write themselves. It's almost as though
coming out here plugs me directly into the dark heart of the
city night and all of its secrets come spilling from my pen."

I stopped, suddenly embarrassed by what I'd said. It
seemed too personal a disclosure for such short acquaintance.
But she just gave me a low-watt version of her earlier smile.

"Doesn't that bother you?" she asked.

"Does what bother me?"

"That perhaps what you're putting down on paper doesn't belong to you."

"Does it ever?" I replied. "Isn't the very act of creation made up of setting a piece of yourself free?"

"What happens when there's no more pieces left?"

"That's what makes it special—I don't think you ever run out of the creative spark. Just doing it replenishes the well. The more I work, the more ideas come to me. Whether they come from my subconscious or some outside source isn't really relevant. What is relevant is what I put into it."

"Even when it seems to write itself?"

"Maybe especially so."

I was struck—not then, but later, remembering—by the odd intensity of the conversation. It wasn't a normal dialogue between strangers. We must have talked for three hours, never about ourselves, our histories, our pasts, but rather about what we were now, creating an intimacy that seemed surreal when I thought back on it the next day. Occasionally, there were lulls in the conversation, but they, too, seemed to add to the sense of bonding, like the comfortable silences that are only possible between good friends.

I could've kept right on talking, straight through the night until dawn, but she rose during one of those lulls.

"I have to go," she said, swinging the strap of her carryall onto her shoulder.

I knew a moment's panic. I didn't know her address, nor her phone number. All I had was her first name.

"When can I see you again?" I asked.

"Have you ever been down to those old stone steps under the Kelly Street Bridge?"

I nodded. They dated back from when the river was used to haul goods from upland, down to the lake. The steps under the bridge were all that was left of an old dock that had serviced the Irish-owned inn called The Harp. The dock was long abandoned, but The Harp still stood. It was one of the oldest buildings in the city. Only the solid stone structures of the city's Dutch founding fathers, like the ones that encircled us, were older.

"I'll meet you there tomorrow night," she said. She took a few steps, then paused, adding, "Why don't you bring along one of your books?"

The smile she gave me, before she turned away again, was intoxicating. I watched her walk back across the courtyard, disappearing into the narrow mouth of the alleyway from which she'd first come. Her footsteps lingered on, an echoing *tap-tap* on the cobblestones, but then that too faded.

I think it was at that moment that I decided she was a ghost.

I didn't get much writing done over the next few weeks. She wouldn't—she said she couldn't—see me during the day, but she wouldn't say why. I've got such a head filled with fictions that I honestly thought it was because she was a ghost, or maybe a succubus or a vampire. The sexual attraction was certainly there. If she'd sprouted fangs one night, I'd probably just have bared my neck and let her feed. But she didn't, of course. Given a multiple-choice quiz, in the end I realized the correct answer was none of the above.

I was also sure that she was at least my own age, if not older. She was widely read and, like myself, had eclectic tastes that ranged from genre fiction to the classics. We talked for hours every night, progressed to walking hand in hand through our favorite parts of the benighted city and finally made love one night in a large, cozy sleeping bag in Fitzhenry Park.

She took me there on one of what we called our rambles and didn't say a word, just stripped down in the moonlight and then drew me down into the sweet harbor of her arms. Above us, I heard geese heading south as, later, I drifted into sleep. I remember thinking it was odd to hear them so late at night, but then what wasn't in the hours I spent with Tally?

I woke alone in the morning, the subject of some curiosity

by a couple of old winos who casually watched me get dressed inside the bag as though they saw this kind of thing every morning.

Our times together blur in my mind now. It's hard for me to remember one night from another. But I have little fetish bundles of memory that stay whole and complete in my mind, the *gris-gris* that collected around her name in my mind, like my nervousness that second night under the Kelly Street Bridge, worried that she wouldn't show, and three nights later when, after not saying a word about the book of my stories I'd given her when we parted on the old stone steps under the bridge, she told me how much she'd liked them.

"These are my stories," she said as she handed the book back to me that night.

I'd run into possessive readers before, fans who laid claim to my work as their own private domain, who treated the characters in the stories as real people, or thought that I carried all sorts of hidden and secret knowledge in my head, just because of the magic and mystery that appeared in the tales I told. But I'd never had a reaction like Tally's before.

"They're about me," she said. "They're your stories, I can taste your presence in every word, but each of them's a piece of me, too."

I told her she could keep the book, and the next night, I brought her copies of my other three collections, plus photocopies of the stories that had only appeared in magazines to date. I won't say it's because she liked the stories so much that I came to love her; that would have happened anyway. But her pleasure in them certainly didn't make me think any the less of her.

Another night she took a photograph out of her carryall and showed it to me. It was a picture of her, but she looked different, softer, not so much younger as not so tough. She wore her hair differently and had a flower-print dress on; she was standing in sunlight.

"When . . . when was this taken?" I asked.

"In happier times."

Call me small-minded that my disappointment should show so plain, but it hurt that what were the happiest nights of my life weren't the same for her.

She noticed my reaction—she was always quick with things like that—and laid a warm hand on mine.

"It's not you," she said. "I love our time together. It's the rest of my life that's not so happy."

Then be with me all the time, I wanted to tell her, but I already knew from experience that there was no talking about where she went when she left me, what she did, who she was. I was still thinking of ghosts, you see. I was afraid that some taboo lay upon her telling me, that if she spoke about it, if she told me where she was during the day, the spell would break and her spirit would be banished forever like in some hokey B-movie.

I wanted more than just the nights, I'll admit freely to that, but not enough to risk losing what I had. I was like the wife in *Bluebeard,* except I refused to allow my curiosity to turn the key in the forbidden door. I could have followed her, but I didn't. And not just because I was afraid of her vanishing on me. It was because she trusted me not to.

We made love three times, all told, every time in that old sleeping bag of hers, each time in a different place, each morning I woke alone. I'd bring back her sleeping bag when we met that night and she'd smile to see its bulk rolled under my arm.

The morning after the first time, I realized that I was changing; that she was changing me. It wasn't by anything she said or did, or rather it wasn't that she was making me change, but that our relationship was stealing away that sense of distancing I had carried with me through my life.

And she was changing, too. She still wore her jeans and leather jacket most of the time, but sometimes she appeared wearing a short dress under the jacket, warm leggings, small trim shoes instead of her boots. Her face kept its character, but the tension wasn't so noticeable anymore, the toughness had softened.

I'd been open with her from the very first night, more open than I'd ever been with friends I'd known for years. And that remained. But now it was starting to spill over to my other relationships. I found my brother and my friends were more comfortable with me, and I with them. None of them knew about Tally; so far as they knew I was still prowling the nocturnal streets of the city in search of inspiration. They didn't know that I wasn't writing, though Professor Dapple guessed.

I suppose it was because he always read my manuscripts before I sent them off. We had the same interests in the odd and the curious—it was what had drawn us together long before Jilly became his student, before he retired from the university. Everybody still thought of him as the Professor; it was hard not to.

He was a tiny wizened man with a shock of frizzy white hair and glasses, who delighted in long conversations conducted over tea, or if the hour was appropriate, a good Irish whiskey. At least once every couple of weeks the two of us would sit in his cozy study, he reading one of my stories while I read his latest article before it was sent off to some journal or other. When the third visit went by in which I didn't have a manuscript in hand, he finally broached the subject.

"You seem happy these days, Christy."

"I am."

He'd smiled. "So is it true what they say—an artist must suffer to produce good work?"

I hadn't quite caught on yet to what he was about.

"Neither of us believe that," I said.

"Then you must be in love."

"I . . ."

I didn't know what to say. An awful sinking feeling had

settled in my stomach at his words. Lord knew, he was right, but for some reason, just as I knew I shouldn't follow Tally when she left me after our midnight trysts, I had this superstitious dread that if the world discovered our secret, she would no longer be a part of my life.

"There's nothing wrong with being in love," he said, mistaking my hesitation for embarrassment.

"It's not that," I began, knowing I had nowhere to go except a lie and I couldn't lie to the Professor.

"Never fear," he said. "You're allowed your privacy—and welcome to it, I might add. At my age, any relating of your escapades would simply make me jealous. But I worry about your writing."

"I haven't stopped," I told him. And then I had it. "I've been thinking of writing a novel."

That wasn't a lie. I was always thinking of writing a novel; I just doubted that I ever would. My creative process could easily work within the perimeters of short fiction, even a connected series of stories such as *The Red Crow* had turned out to be, but a novel was too massive an undertaking for me to understand, little say attempt. I had to have the whole of it in my head, and to do so with anything much longer than a short novella was far too daunting a process for me to begin. I had discovered, to my disappointment because I did actually *want* to make the attempt, that the longer a piece of mine was, the less . . . substance it came to have. It was as though the sheer volume of a novel's wordage would somehow dissipate the strengths my work had to date.

My friends who did write novels told me I was just being a chickenshit; but then, they had trouble with short fiction and avoided it like the plague. It was my firm belief that one should stick with what worked, though maybe that was just a way of rationalizing a failure.

"What sort of a novel?" the Professor asked, intrigued, since he knew my feelings on the subject.

I gave what I hoped was a casual shrug.

"That's what I'm still trying to decide," I said, and then turned the conversation to other concerns.

But I was nervous leaving the Professor's house, as though the little I had said was enough to turn the key in the door that led into the hidden room I shouldn't enter. I sensed a weakening of the dam that kept the mystery of our trysts deep and safe. I feared for the floodgate opening and the rush of reality that would tear my ghostly lover away from me.

But as I've already said, she wasn't a ghost. No, something far stranger hid behind her facade of pixie face and tousled hair.

I've wondered before, and still do, how much of what happens to us we bring upon ourselves. Did my odd superstition concerning Tally drive her away, or was she already leaving before I ever said as much as I did to the Professor? Or was it mere coincidence that she said good-bye that same night?

I think of the carryall she'd had on her shoulder the first time we met and have wondered since if she wasn't already on her way then. Perhaps I had only interrupted a journey already begun.

"You know, don't you?" she said when I saw her that night.

Did synchronicity reach so far that we would part that night in that same courtyard by the river where we had first met?

"You know I have to go," she added when I said nothing.

I nodded. I did. What I didn't know was—

"Why?" I asked.

Her features seemed harder again—like they had been that first night. The softness that had grown as our relationship had was more memory than fact, her features seemed to be cut to the bone once more. Only her eyes still held a touch of warmth, as did her smile. A tough veneer masked the rest of her.

"It's because of how the city is used," she said. "It's because of hatred and spite and bigotry; it's because of homelessness and drugs and crime; it's because the green quiet places are so few while the dark terrors multiply; it's because what's old and comfortable and rounded must make way for what's new and sharp and brittle; it's because a mean spirit grips its streets and that meanness cuts inside me like a knife.

"It's changing me, Christy, and I don't want you to see what I will become. You wouldn't recognize me and I wouldn't want you to.

"That's why I have to go."

When she said *go,* I knew she meant she was leaving me, not the city.

"But—"

"You've helped me keep it all at bay, truly you have, but it's not enough. Neither of us have enough strength to hold that mean spirit at bay forever. What we have was stolen from the darkness. But it won't let us steal anymore."

I started to speak, but she just laid her fingers across my lips. I saw that her sleeping bag was stuffed under the bench. She pulled it out and unrolled it on the cobblestones. I thought of the dark windows of the town houses looking into the court-yard. There could be a hundred gazes watching as she gently pulled me down onto the sleeping bag, but I didn't care.

I tried to stay awake. I lay beside her, propped up on an elbow and stroked her shoulder, her hair. I marveled at the softness of her skin, the silkiness of her hair. In repose, the harsh lines were gone from her face again. I wished that there was some way I could just keep all her unhappiness at bay, that I could stay awake and protect her forever, but sleep snuck up on me all the same and took me away.

Just as I went under, I thought I heard her say, "You'll know other lovers."

But not like her. Never like her.

* * *

When I woke the next morning, I was alone on the sleeping bag, except for Ben, who lay purring on the bag where she had lain.

It was early, too early for anyone to be awake in any of the houses, but I wouldn't have cared. I stood naked in the frosty air and slowly got dressed. Ben protested when I shooed him off the sleeping bag and rolled it up.

The walk home, with the sleeping bag rolled up under my arm, was never so long.

No, Tally wasn't a ghost, though she haunts the city's streets at night—just as she haunts my mind.

I know her now. She's like a rosebush grown old, gone wild; untrimmed, neglected for years, the thorns become sharper, more bitter; her foliage spreading, grown out of control, reaching high and wide, while the center chokes and dies. The blossoms that remain are just small now, hidden in the wild growth, memories of what they once were.

I know her now. She's the spirit that connects the notes of a tune—the silences in between the sounds; the resonance that lies under the lines I put down on a page. Not a ghost, but a spirit all the same: the city's heart and soul.

I don't wonder about her origin. I don't wonder whether she was here first, and the city grew around her, or if the city created her. She just is.

Tallulah. Tally. A reckoning of accounts.

I think of the old traveling hawkers who called at private houses in the old days and sold their wares on the tally system—part payment on account, the other part due when they called again. Tallymen.

The payments owed her were long overdue, but we no longer have the necessary coin to settle our accounts with her. So she changes; just as we change. I can remember a time when the city was a safer place, how when I was young, we never locked our doors and we knew every neighbor on our block. Kids growing up today wouldn't even know what I'm talking about; the people my own age have forgotten. The old folks remember, but who listens to them? Most of us wish that they didn't exist; that they'd just take care of themselves so that we can get on with our own lives.

Not all change is for the good.

I still go out on my rambles, most every night. I hope for a secret tryst, but all I do is write stories again. As the new work fills my notebooks, I've come to realize that the characters in my stories were so real because I really did want to get close to people, I really did want to know them. It was just easier to do it on paper, one step removed.

I'm trying to change that now.

I look for her on my rambles. She's all around me, of course, in every brick of every building, in every whisper of wind as it scurries down an empty street. She's a cab's lights at three A.M., a siren near dawn, a shuffling baglady pushing a squeaky grocery cart, a dark-eyed cat sitting on a shadowed stoop.

She's all around me, but I can't find her. I'm sure I'd recognize her—

I don't want you to see what I will become.

—but I can't be sure. The city can be so many things. It's a place where the familiar can become strange with just the blink of an eye. And if I saw her—

You wouldn't recognize me and I wouldn't want you to.

—what would I do? If she could, she'd come to me, but that mean spirit still grips the streets. I see it in people's faces; I feel it in the coldness that's settled in their hearts. I don't think I would recognize her; I don't think I'd want to. I have the *gris-gris* of her memory in my mind; I have an old sleeping bag rolled up in a corner of my hall closet; I'm here if she needs me.

* * *

I have this fantasy that it's still not too late; that we can still drive that mean spirit away and keep it at bay. The city would be a better place to live if we could and I think we owe it to her. I'm doing my part. I write about her—

They're about me. They're your stories, I can taste your presence in every word, but each of them's a piece of me, too.

—about her strange wonder and her magic and all. I write about how she changed me, how she taught me that getting close can hurt, but not getting close is an even lonelier hurt. I don't preach; I just tell the stories.

But I wish the ache would go away. Not the memories, not the *gris-gris* that keeps her real inside me, but the hurt. I could live without that hurt.

Sometimes I wish I'd never met her.

Maybe one day I'll believe that lie, but I hope not.

SPARE CHANGE

DAVID BISCHOFF

"Cities scare the hell out of me," says David Bischoff. "The worst was the night I decided to go to an all-night horror filmathon at a theater on Piccadilly Circus, London. I was twenty years old and didn't expect the gruesome, weird London street people who hung out in the theater, the perverts who put their hands on my knee, the decontaminant the ushers sprayed down the aisles every hour, the splashes of vomit in the men's room, the incredible grimness of it all—all while horror movies flashed on the screen. Unsettling stuff, believe me."

Bischoff, thirty-nine, is the author of over thirty novels and fifty short stories. His most recent books include Abduction: The UFO Conspiracy *and* Deception: The UFO Conspiracy. *He lives in Los Angeles.*

That was the day that he decided that total annihilation of the world by exploding nuclear bananas might not be such a bad thing after all.

"Spare change?" he'd say.

Or: "Got a quarter, bud?"

Perhaps even, "How 'bout a buck for a down-and-out dude in Washington, D.C.?" This, to the yuppies and the lawyers, briefcasing down K Street or three-piece-suiting up Pennsylvania, the world on their strings and a spit shine on their Guccis.

He sure as hell needed some spare change *this* day.

"Dimes nickels quarters harvesting the bacon," he muttered, and the dawn of the world strobed about him with incandescence. Somehow, though, he focused on the quarters. Change change change, the daily urge for change buffeted him as the sensory salad stopped whirling. The word *change* thundered in him as soon as he got up and off his bench in Dupont Circle with a head the size of a watermelon from last night's Boone's Farm Strawberry. Christ, and his bladder was about to blow, too, so he hiked it on down to the Metro Entrance that Never Was over on P Street, by the Peoples Drug Store. Ha ha, and Peter picked a peck of pickles too, huh, Pal? he thought through the wooze as he limped down the stairs into the predawn darkness filling the cement hole.

Suddenly his sense of smell exploded.

The blast of old and new urine and feces slapped him like a foul garbage bag, and even though he knew he was no rose himself, he had to hold his breath. He'd just have let it go on a tree, but the commuters were starting to come out of the live Metro stops, and there'd be cops around any minute, and chances were they'd spent all last night hosing down blood from crack dealers and were in no mood to let a homeless bum winkle on the shrubbery.

Grimy hands tugged a bloated penis past age-grayed underwear, but he let go too soon.

"Shit!" he said as pee poured down his trousers. He managed to arc the flow away, and let it gush into where it was supposed to go. By the time he was finished and had tucked himself back in, he realized his interior was feeling plenty hairy-ragged.

He bent slightly, and as though summoned by some incantation, demon vomit spiked onto the wall. A rat came through his mouth. A tiny leprechaun sailed out in a boat, grinning. Two frogs and a snake. When he was through, his throat felt as though the puke had had barbs in it, but he felt discernably better. He decided to hobble back to his bench and see if there was anything left in the bottle.

This was when he noticed the tentacle twining around his ankle.

It had come up from between the grates cutting off the steps from the deserted and unfinished section of the Dupont Circle Metro stop, a purple-black tendril lined with obscene suckers, like the lips of lipsticked whores.

The thing pulled on his leg, and he had a sudden dark intimation of some bloated eye swimming in the darkness below, above drooling jaws.

But it was weak today, weak and pathetic . . .

"Cut it, asshole. It's me. You wanna see my pass card?"

He brought his free boot down and stomped the thing good on a meaty part of the limb. It spasmed a bit, and the tip uncurled. There was a whimper from below. He kicked it away with contempt. He hawked up a gob of phlegm and spat into the darkness.

When he got back to today's home base, Jacob was sitting on the bench.

"Hi, Ted," said the slender man, neatly dressed in a beige jumpsuit. Jacob adjusted his glasses for no reason, which was one of his tics, and smiled up from his place like he'd just discovered the Secret of Life. "Let's kill somebody today."

"Guava," said Ted. He looked around for his brown bag.

"No, Ted. *Kill.* A woman, maybe. A little girl? Yes, we'll take off her panties and *spank* her to death. If you can get it up for a change, maybe a poke or two. Before, after? Depends on your taste. Me, I go for after . . . but while the body's still warm. Reminds me of my ex-wife."

The bag containing the bottle of wine had rolled off into the grass. Ted bent over, picked it up and pulled it from the sack. About a mouthful left. Enough. He twisted off the top and drained it. The stuff tasted like strawberry vomit, but hey, it was alcohol.

He tucked the empty bottle in his ratty rucksack and he sat down on the park bench, letting the wine wash out some of the badness of the morning.

"Jake, you are *so* full of shit," he mumbled. "You're so full of zorpa. What the hell do you know?"

A shrink at the Thomas Circle shelter told Ted that he was schizophrenic.

Ted was of two minds about this.

On the one hand, he knew that *something* sure as hell was wrong. He had vague memories of a wife and a family some-wheres down South, a roofing business that went under, debts you wouldn't believe and stress in spades, all heaped on top of the voices that talked to him from time to time and just kept on getting louder as he got older and deeper into shit. Things weren't good, and this wasn't the first day that Ted would experience that ardent desire for atomic defoliation of the rotting harvest that was humanity.

On the other hand, sometimes life got so damned interest-ing that he just didn't care. Like now. Like his arguments with this loon here. Complain as he might, he actually enjoyed Jake and his wild suggestions, his off-the-ceiling comments and opinions. It kept his mind off things like hangovers and tenta-cles coiling around his ankle after a pee.

Jake ignored him. "You ain't worth dick, man. What good are you? You might as well do something *worthwhile*. And I can't think of anything better than *killing* someone."

Ted didn't say anything. He was thinking about today's panhandling. He was going to need some more booze, oh, about midafternoon, and if he didn't find any office worker's breakfast remains in trash cans, he'd have to buy some pet food or something, so he'd better start thrusting out the palm at the Metro stop soon. He looked over to ask Jake if he wanted to help out.

But Jake was gone.

For now.

* * *

"Spare change?"

It was late and it was dark, and Ted had pretty much given up on Dupont Circle and was moving up Connecticut towards Adams-Morgan for the upwardly mobile bar crowd. He was actually feeling semi-okay, too. Yolanda's deli had a special on Schaefer quarts of beer, a buck a pop, and he'd had three of them, along with a half a sandwich someone had given him and a quarter pizza he'd found in the trash outside a carry-out. Sounds weren't overloading his head, and people weren't glowing. If he could just jingle-tingle some more with change, he could liquidate himself with more beer and the bugs would stop crawling up his legs.

The guy, a dopey looker in shorts and a tank top, ignored him. City dweller. Worst kind. They wouldn't give you the time of day. Thing about down-and-out panhandling was the eyes. You get ahold of their eyes, you give a quick squeeze of entreaty, a little pupil-flicker of despair and they think, what's a quarter? Years of quarters, though, inured the residents; they didn't even look at you. Some kind of built-in telemetry signaled instant peripheral response—their eyes went dead, turned the other way, focused on the angst-of-the-day.

The thing was—and Ted had long since learned this—that if you looked desiccated enough, if it seemed like you really needed the money, it didn't matter how heartless the dude or dudette was, they had this inner bum-budget. They assuaged some inner guilty-conscience node with a few quarters a week dropped in begging cups. This, plus the freer hands of tourists and suburbanites, was what kept people like Ted in wine and beer and whatever; food could be found in trash cans, soup kitchens and charity wagons. Trouble was, in the last couple years, perfectly healthy young black men discovered that it was a lot easier and a lot more fun to hustle The Man for quarters than to hod the bricks their education allowed in the way of employment. That cut into the quarter market, definitely. Still, as pissed as it made Ted (when he was lucid enough to be angry), he far preferred this to seeing these homeboys dealing crack.

As it happened, though, as old Ted schizoed up past the Royal Palace of nude dancing and angled on up Florida Avenue toward the restaurant land of 18th Street, it was crack that finally convinced him that the human race was worthy of a total nuclear and fruity death.

On up past the Embassy Theatre and 19th Street, Florida gets curiously dark and mangy, no streetlights to speak of, a regular little armpit in the affluent body of the Dupont Circle district area. It is here, in shanty-shacklike row houses without air-conditioning, that the city's slums are foreshadowed. A baby's howl, the sound of gurgling sewage pipes, the scutter of a fat rat amongst garbage: a mere few sensory impressions in a ripe summer stew. Tonight, the infamous Washington humidity was up, like an unwelcome cowl of steam over your face. One of the nice things about mental illness, though, was that you didn't notice stuff like discomfort too much. There were far too many other interesting things to pay attention to, like giant ants invading the White House, and adenoidal voices from Venus describing the mating habits of pygmies.

Just outside Johnson's Pro-Service barber shop stood a clot of young black men, and Ted sensed the tension half a block away. Something bad was going down, no question, and he was thinking about cutting across to the other side as he approached them, when a shot sounded like a muffled elephant's fart.

A moment of total stillness, and then suddenly the homeboys scattered. Two tore past Ted, and he could see the fear in their eyes, but there was something else: a wild excitement, a thrill far deeper and darker than the shadow land where he lived. A single figure of the group remained, and it was slumped on the ground amidst a spreading pool of darkness. Normally, Ted, a survivor, would have cut and shuffled with the rest, but something took him by the scruff of the neck and dragged him over to the fallen man.

"Ted," said the man. "Ted."

The young man lay spread-eagled on the concrete, a blossom of blood on his chest, seeping into the pool. His black eyes were closed, and his black mouth was shut, and he was dead, dead, dead; but somehow, he spoke to Ted.

"Ted. Take my gun. Kill the bastards. Kill the fucking crack bastards. Kill them all."

And Ted listened, because, with a sudden mystical vision, he saw that there was a halo around this fallen man's head, and that, far from being just the average Lamont or Dalroy of drug-soaked streets, he was, in actuality, Jesus Christ Himself.

"Jesus!" said Ted.

"Take the gun, Ted. Take the gun. They're not worth saving, Ted. I renege on the crack dealers. Send them to Hell. Send them to Hell!"

By the man's hand, alongside a cellophane Sandwich Saver bag holding crack rocks, was a Glock 17 pistol. Where Jesus had gotten the gun, Ted didn't know—the D.C. police had recently switched from revolvers to the semiautomatics as a move to counter the incredibly hi-tech weapons like the Intratec TEC-9 favored now amongst drug dealers.

Could Jesus Christ have gone undercover for the D.C. police?

Ted reached down as though powered by Strings From Above. His fingers closed around the handle of the gun and pulled the thing up. It felt unreal, but an instinctual *rightness* coursed up Ted's arm. This was a gift from Heaven. A mighty, swift sword. A surge of anger swept through Ted, and he knelt by the dying Jesus Christ, and he said, "Human beings deserve total nuclear destruction, my Lord. Destroy us all!"

"No," said the black Jesus. "Just D.C. crack dealers, Ted. Just the black-heart crack dealers."

Holding the gun, a flicker of memory shivered through his mind. He'd used one before. Not a Glock. Something else, somewhere else, some other time, when he was a different person. The odor of military rose up from dusty boot camps and the taste of war and sting of the tropics. Just as soon, something clamped down ("No!") and the subdrug nothing-ness of his past returned.

The air filled with rising sirens.

Ted sensed the coming light.

He looked down once more at the dead Jesus, and the neon halo crowning his head arrowed up and struck the Glock in a burst like microcosmic fireworks.

In his head, Ted heard a new voice, and it said, "Kill them, Ted. *Kill them!*"

Ted turned and melted down a side alley, feeling the dark-ness cover him like a damp and electric home.

Crack.

This town used to be a nice place to deteriorate in.

Oh, nothing like the tales Ted heard of Florida and New Orleans, and that fabled down-and-out mecca, Venice Beach of Los Angeles. But in the center of government, a down-and-outer got some attention, some handouts, and getting swept under a rug with spare change in your pocket and Salvation Army soup in your stomach was better than, say, in New York, where the nicest thing that happened to the homeless was maybe they got run over by a subway train.

Crack.

Now, though, there was this *drug.* You smoked it and *wham,* for maybe a few minutes you got bliss like you never thought possible. Only, of course, chances are you get hooked, or even if you don't, you want it again, sure enough.

Crack.

Now tell me (Ted would tell one of the members of his Dupont Circle Sunbathing Club when he wasn't too crazy or too drunk and the demons of his mind were having a coffee break), you got a choice: you can make four ninety-five an hour, max, at a McDonald's, or you can pull down a few thousand a week selling cocaine by-products. The only thing between the two choices were a few morals and some integrity, and there was precious little of *that* in this fucking country today. Plus, drug dealers were heroes in some of the neighborhoods. What you got, buddy, Ted would say, you got a crazy funhouse mirror of fucked-up American society. What you got is black people fucking up their own people with drugs, black people wasting other black people with high-power ballistics, black people selling their souls to the people who made the real money, The Man they so despised.

Now The Man would always be The Man, but there was a point in life, you gotta take a crummy job, or hell, even bum change offa people instead of dumping your little stinky hate-turd in the cesspool that was Black American heritage.

But no, Irv the Peg-Leg would say. Hell, that ain't human *nature,* Teddy.

Maybe, Ted would say. Maybe, then, what humanity needs is an atomic *enema* with a bunch of apricots!

This was a constant thread in Ted's rants, so much so that the bums on Dupont C. would call him Mr. Fruit Nuke sometimes. Now, though, with a Glock in his pocket, a Glock that held seventeen hollow-point 9-millimeter rounds in its magazines, he was ready to visit critical mass upon the dregs of human evil, atom by foul atom.

And Jesus Christ Himself told him to do it.

Thing was, you didn't see too many dealers here in Northwest.

No, he'd have to go to the Northeast, mostly.

First, though, he wanted to make a dry run. Up past Utah, on the wrong side of 16th Street was a place called Meridian Park, only people never called it that, they called it Malcolm X Park or sometimes Needle Park, and if you threw a rock at the right time at night, you'd hit a drug dealer.

Ted figured he'd visit old Malcolm X Park. Just once. To try out his trigger finger. It wasn't all that far away and bums didn't look too out of place up there.

He gave it a day. He waited till after dark, and all day long the gun was heavy in his old coat, like a dead baby in his stomach.

He didn't drink cheap booze. He didn't eat much either, and he was too nervous to panhandle. What he did was to bide his time and talk to the voices bubbling excitedly in his head.

He gave it till past two, when business would be lonely in the park, and then he shambled up 16th, crept into the shadows beneath the south wall, and ascended the stairs.

The dealer was leaning against a lamppost, looking this way and that for potential customers. He was black, but he wasn't dressed particularly fancily. Street dealers were not pimps, and they didn't parade around in glitz, they wore normal clothes, their one tip-off generally the shiny new editions of Air Johnsons or whatever athletic shoe was the jive vogue of the moment. This homeboy, he was no exception. The Etonics were so white they fairly glowed in the dark. He wore a dark jacket, as the dealers generally did to house their wares as well as a firearm, but beneath it was a white see-through nylon tank top for ventilation.

Gripping the Glock beneath his own jacket, Ted walked toward the dealer.

"Yo! Friend!" he called, and the black dude spun on him showing white teeth in a very black face.

"What chu doin' here, bro?" There was a look of recognition in the man's aspect; he'd probably seen Ted around Dupont. "Don't you look for no spare change from me!"

He had to get closer, though. "I . . . I thought you might be able to sell me something," said Ted.

"Nothin' *you* can afford, that's for sure!" The dealer grimaced. *"Woooo!* You wanna get downwind from me? You ass is *ripe!"*

Close enough. Ted pulled the gun from beneath his coat, pushed the muzzle into the dealer's chest and pulled the trigger, once, twice.

Hollow points flatten upon entry into a body, and they tend to lodge. But these were fired at such a close range, they tore straight through the dealer's torso, exiting with a great slap, carrying along chunks of lung and bone and heart with them, splashing the pavement with blood. The dealer had seen what was coming, though; it was in his eyes when they went out: the Glock, his death, the intense disgust and dismay at being taken out by a *bum*. But death was death, and the eyes slapped on that blank hood of nothingness as the body flopped onto the cement, did an obligatory little spasming rap number ("Crack and death, they are my jones," Ted heard the little fading death-voice in his head, "and now I'm trash, so bury my bones!") and then was still.

The pool of blood spread like red piss.

The shots had been muffled by the body, but they were audible. Although the voices were starting to roar again in his head like hornets coming home to their nest, Ted knew that he had to get out of here, get out quick, 'cause in five minutes there'd be cops sniffing around this body like buzzards.

As he left, heading down 15th, hurrying, hurrying, hurrying back to Dupont home base, bumland, Ted felt a slow ecstasy of exhilaration.

He'd done this before, he knew. Somewhere, somehow, and he recalled now steamy jungles and foreign voices and the insanity of gunpowder in the air.

He'd done it before, and liked it then, and he'd done it for his country then, and now he was doing it for Jesus, and it felt good, good, *good*, an orgasm of release and righteousness.

And as he cut down New Hampshire toward the Promised Land, he knew he'd do it again.

* * *

He did.

He took a bus this time. A bus to the Northeast. A late bus it was, and he took out a dealer on 5th Street, a single bullet to the back of the head, close range, brains brains brains. And once more the charge, the release, the hosannas of the cherubim and seraphim amidst the hornetsbuzz voices and the words of Jesus again, "This is my killer of crack monsters, of whom I am well pleased."

The next stop was two nights later, this time in the Southeast, not too far from the Capitol Building. Late again. A hurried approach, a whisper, a shot in the eye. This time, Jesus told Ted to cool it a bit, check out this blasted black body, like specifically the hip pocket. Sure enough, there was a great big wad of twenty-dollar bills, favored dealer currency.

Back in the shadows, Jesus said, "Rest my son. Get some food. Get more ammunition. Wait a few weeks."

And Ted saw the infinite wisdom of these words, for too many similar killings would point attention to him. No, he waited, and sure enough, the three (or four?) he'd done were swallowed up by the welter of murders promising to top five hundred this year alone.

Ted bought two new magazines of ammunition from a shop up Georgia in the Northeast. He bought himself some good wine for a change and shared it with his buddies in the Dupont and they peed with gladness into the dead Metro stop.

Late, late, in the depth of the night, he awoke on his bench and he heard the Call.

The Sacrifice. It was time for the Sacrifice.

Ted was disturbed, for he had just done a sacrifice a few months back, and the Dark God demanded one generally once a year. Fortunately, Ted had a spare bottle of California zinfandel, so he pulled it out of his sack and trudged drunkenly to the dead Metro entrance. The familiar shitpeevomitdeath odor was particularly strong tonight, and Ted could smell the seaweed and dead fish of the Dark God splashed in.

"Here you go, you greedy bastard!" he growled. He hurled the bottle (a good one, a whole one, and it did his alcoholic heart harm to see such delicious stuff go to waste) and watched as it crashed against the rusted bars, splattering into the darkness.

A tinkling, a slinking, a sucking.

And then, suddenly, out of the black slithered the tentacles. Ted hardly saw them coming; they snaked about his legs and his arms, and pulled him down into the deeper filth and smell, down to bang against the grating.

And they were *thicker*, this time.

More powerful.

From the depths, a half-luminous something shimmered, and Ted, in his near-unconscious state, could barely make out the click of octopoid beak, the wink of squamous eye.

"Blood, Ted. I smell blood on you," said the surf-on-rocks voice. "I hunger, Ted. I hunger."

This one was harder.

He had to have more time with this one, so he followed him for a while until the dealer turned into an opportune alley. Desperation spiking a new energy into him, he raced around the other way, and waited at a corner for the man—a boy, actually, looking more like L. L. Cool than Amos 'n' Andy Dopepeddler—to come round. When he did, he took one step then jammed the long knife up under the left of his rib cage deep into his heart.

He'd bought the knife at the army-navy store over in the seedy part of Georgetown by Key Bridge. He'd learned how to use it in the Marines. Ted knew that much now, that he'd been in the Marines, that he'd been to Nam, and he remembered now why he never, ever went down to the Viet Nam Memorial on the Mall. He never went 'cause he was too damned scared he'd find his own name chiseled into the rock.

The guy just kind of sighed as Ted held him steady and felt

the blood stream out of him, heard the gush of shit and piss as the guy's sphincter and bladder relaxed. Ted then gentled him down to the cobbled ground under a staircase and set to work.

The Dark God was hungry for more than wine.

Ted pulled off the dead guy's decorative chains and his expensive silk shirt, and set to work.

Ted had bought the long knife especially for its serrated edge. He used it to cut open the abdomen, and then saw through organs and connecting membranes. He pulled a black Hefty garbage bag from his jacket and heaved the still-warm viscera into it. Then he cut out the heart and what he could of the lungs (which was not much) and added these to the gory collection in the bag.

The next part was trickier. But the Dark God had been specific. Just guts wouldn't do today, oh no. The Dark God wanted much more.

Ted stood up from his bloody work and looked around for what he needed. It took a while, but he knew he'd find it; they were all around Washington. He found it behind a bashed-in fence of a tenement. A cinder block. He took the cinder block over to the dead man and dropped it on his head. The skull cracked. Ted lifted up the block and dropped it again, this time adding a little momentum to its fall with his arms. He'd been afraid that the crack would be too loud on the first throw, so he'd been a little careful. Now, though . . .

He smashed the cinder block down a few more times for good measure—there'd been no specifics about undamaged goods. Then he took his knife, pried upon the cranial bones and dug out as much of the pulpy brainstuff as he could, adding it to the garbage bag like a little more meat to a stew.

He brought his hand away and he realized that there were a few chunks of gray matter still clinging to his hand through a sheen of red. Up against the distant light of a sodium street-lamp, the stuff glistened—and then it commenced to sparkle like organic diamonds. A surge of energy seemed to run up Ted's arm like static electricity, and a vision roared through his head like heroin through an overdoser's ganglia.

Ted saw the past. He saw the present as well, and up ahead—well, there was the future, too. It was an unbroken panorama of disgrace, degradation and squalor, a junkyard of dreams and hopes, a swamp of sin and suffering. Not good, not evil, not anything; the detritus of chaos. The afterbirth of nothingness and pointlessness. Existence was, Ted knew instinctively now, a joke, a state where even nihilism was a romance; a fluke in the wormiest sense. Its denizens mere pieces of shit, warm and stinking for a cosmic breath or two and then sinking back into the universal sludge.

And the gods . . .

"No," said Ted. "*No!*"

Clutching his plastic bag close to him, he stumbled away from his kill.

This time, Jesus had absolutely nothing to say about anything.

Jake said, "You know, this has been fun."

Ted, drunk on Crown Royal cognac, looked up blearily. Sure enough, there he was. Jake. In his jumpsuit. Dupont Circle was swimming blearily all about, dusk and dust. Ted lifted the paper bag and took a sip.

"Yeah. Glad you took my advice. And the crack dealers— you know, that's a good idea too. Does the community some good." Jake tapped the *Post.* "You're gettin some press, too. Did you look?"

Ted bent over and read the headline: " 'CRACK THE RIPPER' SERIES OF DRUG MURDERS STUNS DISTRICT"

Ted didn't read the article. He knew the gist.

"How much ammunition you got left, Ted?" said Jake.

"Magazine and a half."

"Say Ted, you know, dealers are all well and good—but you know, they're pretty small potatoes. Take a look at this other article over here."

Jake turned deeper into the A section. Something about drug distributors and their high-powered lawyers.

"Say, Ted," said Jake, and there was a mischievous glint in his dark eyes, "what do you call a busful of lawyers at the bottom of the Potomac River?"

Distantly, Ted heard the slither of leather slime and gurgle of a Call from the sewers, hissing, "Yes, Ted! Yessssss!"

The building was about as high-rise as Washington, D.C., got. It gleamed in the morning light, steel and glass and money.

Ted walked in. He carried a briefcase in his left hand, leaving his right hand free. Ted had managed to scrub the caked blood from beneath his fingernails in the cheap hotel room he'd rented. He'd also given himself a long hot bath, cut his hair into a semblance of decency, got a good sleep and then slipped into the suit he'd bought with his money from the dealer kills.

The security guard hardly noticed him as he walked to the elevator and took it to the ninth floor, which was totally devoted to the firm of Brandon, Bosworth & Cox.

"EAST COAST DRUG DISTRIBUTION NETWORK TO BE REPRESENTED BY WASHINGTON D.C. LAW FIRM," the *Post* had said.

Ted remembered lawyers. Ted had had a lawyer. Back in his business in the South; yes, Ted remembered him now. A smiling, glad-handing fellow. Expensive, but worth it, his business associates had said. He'll dig you out. He'll keep the creditor dogs at bay. Instead, what he'd done was to suck out what funds Ted had left, and then upped his price along the way. All the while, smiling, smiling, smiling . . .

The number nine hummed to a halt and the doors smoothed open. Ted stepped out toward the receptionist behind the glass doors marked with the firm name. Although he looked presentable enough, he still had a slight shuffle to his gait, which the receptionist picked up on immediately.

"May I help you?"

"I'm here to see a lawyer," he said, and his voice was the final clue. The receptionist, a cool blonde in a bright blue puffy blouse, raised eyebrows behind aqua designer glasses. Her hand reached for the phone to call security if she had to.

"I'm sorry, they are all presently in a morning meeting," she said crisply.

Ted picked up on the tension in her voice. "And where might that be?"

"If you could leave your card or a name and a phone number where you can be contacted . . ."

Ted coughed. "Shit," he said, and he pulled out the Glock. "Where's the fucking meeting, lady!"

She told him, and then he pistol-whipped her unconscious.

Marching down the corridor toward the end of the hall, toward the muffled voices speaking professionally on matters legal and otherwise, Ted felt the righteousness of anarchy course through his sinews like molten lightning. He felt the thunder of justice echoing hollowly in his veins. These people . . . these and their ilk were the corrupt container that allowed the cesspool of chaos. These people, these lawyers . . .

(What do you call a busload of lawyers at the bottom of the Potomac?

A start.)

Grinning, Ted opened the door and started firing.

Ted has his own room now, and he likes it. There are no edges here, nothing sharp or dangerous with which he might hurt himself. They took his Glock away, but secretly this is a relief to him; it reminds him too much of his time with the military.

They have him on medication, and life is a pleasant blur

rather than an unfocused fuzz of detritus and booze. Oh, there were a couple of weeks of unpleasantness, drying out, but past that, these drugs were so much more effective. Lithium, Thorazine, whatever—Ted has heard the pharmaceutical mutterings of the psychiatrists, but he is too unfocused to catch all the names. Drugs, so many, many drugs . . .

St. Elizabeth's. Another name he's heard. That's where he is: St. Elizabeth's. He vaguely remembers that this is where they kept John Hinckley a while after his brave and valiant attempt to liberate the country from Ronald Reagan, and that Ezra Pound, the poet, stayed here for a while. Sometimes he fancies he talks to Pound's ghost, but it is dim, so dim in his mind now, what with the drugs, that neither Jesus nor Jake nor any of his other voices talk much.

Except, of course, for the Dark God. He is there and always will be there.

Now, as Ted sits on the corner of his bed, it is late. Today, he has heard the psychiatrist in charge of his testing, Dr. Benton, talking about a transfer to Clifton T. Perkins Hospital for the Criminally Insane. It looks, says Dr. Benton, like a case of schizophrenia. The man is unfit to stand trial for his crimes.

This is fine, Ted thinks now. He was getting tired of sleeping outside, anyway. Besides, he has done his duty, he has made his contribution to the commonweal.

As Ted the homeless bagperson, anyway.

The hour is well progressed into the stillness and darkness of the evening, and he judges it is time now.

The creature who once had been called Ted stands from the edge of the bed and slowly walks to the seatless commode.

No, he thinks, as slowly the darkness congeals about him and his limbs metamorphose, the Dark God is never gone. He has been here all along, from the very beginning, coaxing, teasing, gaming . . .

And now His work proceeds.

The tentacle that was once an arm wriggles down into the toilet. Down and down and down, through the sewer system it wriggles, through the pipes, through the shit and the cesspool, the bloated tampons and torn condoms. The creature slinks after it, boneless and home again, slithering and shambling through the sewage.

There is work to be done, and an insatiable hunger to feed.

There is darkness and hate and anger to plant and spread.

And one day, perhaps, its mission will be complete, the universe will once again slide back into the metaphorical ooze of peaceful nonexistence.

And life once more will be a dream . . .

This time with meaning.

THE CITY NEVER SLEEPS

GENE O'NEILL

"It struck me as odd," Gene O'Neill says, "when I learned that some of my New York City writer friends found the country disquieting—you know, that feeling that 'something' malevolent was lurking in the darkness on camping trips. I wrote 'The City Never Sleeps' to reflect my own (and what I'm sure must be the more common) feeling: that there is something even more disquieting about the city."

O'Neill, who has been a Marine and has spent time working on seismic crews, has seen better than forty of his short stories in print, and has also won the Jerry Lewis/MDA Writing Award (1981) for nonfiction. His most recent piece of short fiction, "The Beautiful Stranger," appeared in the January 1991 issue of Starshore.

> Day time
> night time
> week in week out
> the city never sleeps
> ——RAP-TRANS GRAFFITO

Knox spots an opening and guns his Comet onto the West-side Freeway behind an old flatbed. Then he begins to relax, loosening his tie and trying to ignore the heat that even at seven A.M. is muggy and oppressive, making his underarms and crotch feel gritty. He cracks the window, hoping for a breath of fresh air, but just as he starts to suck in a deep breath, the derelict ahead belches out a thick cloud of dirty exhaust that drifts back and engulfs the Comet. "Jesus Christ," he swears half-heartedly, cranking the window up. He glares at the back of the truck driver's head, then sighs, and for a moment considers the possibility of riding Rap-Trans rather than fighting this mess every morning and evening. But he knows from graphic examples on the nightly news that wearing a suit on the train is just asking for trouble from one of the gangs that prey on commuters. Besides, all that graffiti and filth is too much to take—one of the stenos in the office told him an incredible story of coming home late at night and finding a used condom on the empty seat next to her. So, Knox shakes his head and resigns himself to driving the old car. After all, it could be worse, he tells himself, thankful that it's only a few miles from their apartment in the Towers on the north side to his office downtown.

Momentarily he glances west of the freeway and frowns at the Wasteland—as the media dubs the projects—the multi-storied gray buildings rising up out of a desert of cement and asphalt, not even a tree adding color to the monotonous landscape; then he quickly shifts his attention to his left, trying to spot the newest sculpture across the northbound lanes. Last Friday the partially completed work appeared to be something really large, maybe a dragon or a dinosaur. Ahead, the freeway splits, the left lanes curving east to cross the river on the Westside Bridge into the downtown area—

The sculptures are gone!

The flat stretch of bank between river and freeway is completely devoid of the folk art constructed from driftwood, tires, plastic bottles and other debris washed up from the waterway bisecting the city; the ingenuity of anonymous artists responsible for the informal project that has eased commuter frustration for decades. But it's all gone, even the old stuff.

He knows there must be some reasonable explanation for the sudden disappearance over the weekend, but he can't think clearly, the disappointment adding to the discomfort of the heat which is continuing to rise. At the tollbooth—the latest dodge by the mayor to add to the machine's insatiable coffers—Knox hands the collector a five and asks, "What happened to the sculptures?"

She hands him back a book of tickets, her long fingernails painted in a Flo-Jo style. "Sculptures?" she asks flatly, as if it's a word she doesn't understand.

"Yeah, the ones over on the curve," he says, with an impatient gesture over his shoulder toward the empty bank.

"Doan 'member no sculptures over there, and I been here since they started up the toll," she says, bending slightly at the knees so she can see his face, the boredom gone from her voice.

Another uniformed woman appears and hands the collector a box of ticket books. "Say, Tina," the collector asks, her tone playful, "y'all ever see any sculptures out there?" She points a red, white, and blue fingernail toward the riverbank. "Man here wants to know."

Tina snaps, "No," looking at Knox suspiciously, her expression saying: *Hey motherfucker, you some kinda nut?*

The collector shrugs at Knox, a smile on her face, as the horns begin honking back in line.

Knox pushes the Comet up the curving arch of the Westside Bridge, searching the news stations on the radio, trying to pick up something about the strange disappearance. Nothing. He hadn't read anything in the newspaper over the weekend, either. It's like they never existed, he thinks.

In the city, in the middle of the financial district, Knox leaves the car in his rented space at the garage. Then, waving absently at the attendant, he hurries around a stalled car in the driveway to the street, narrowly avoiding a collision with a bike.

"Wake up, dude!" the messenger yells over his shoulder, as

he expertly negotiates the channel between parked cars and traffic. He is dressed in a black Jack Daniel's cap, a T-shirt with a photo of the rock group Second Coming, patched jeans, and pink high-topped Converses, his garb not unlike others of his trade, but in sharp contrast to the dark suits crowding Center Street this morning.

Knox tightens his tie despite the heat and follows the flow of suits into his office building. After emerging from the revolving front door into the lobby, he slips to the right to catch his breath.

"Mornin', suh, how y'all?" the old man greets him from the alcove, his broad smile softening the hostile impact of his battered brown face—the flattened nose, the scar tissue over both eyes. It's Frisco Jack.

"I'm fine, Jack," Knox replies. "How's it going?"

"Bidness good," the black man says in a drawl, nodding down at the shoes lined up to be shined. "But always got time fo' y'all." He indicates the empty chair on the one-seat shoeshine stand wedged in the narrow space.

Knox likes to get his shine in the chair, exchanging sport banter with the old boxer, who was never a contender but fought all the best West Coast middleweights in the fifties.

"Maybe I'll have more time tomorrow morning," Knox says, sliding back into the steady stream of suits.

"Yes, suh, I'll be here," Frisco Jack says, grinning a farewell.

The next morning Knox is up at five, planning on going into the office early, but spending a few minutes getting his shoes shined. After all the rabble-rousing on TV by militant black leaders, it's comforting talking to the polite old black man. Frisco Jack is almost a friend . . .

But in the lobby Knox stops suddenly—

The shoeshine stand is gone!

They've replaced it with a Coke machine. There's absolutely no trace of the old man, the floor around the machine glistening the same color as the rest of the lobby. Jesus, Knox thinks, he's been shining shoes in that same spot for over ten years. A few suits pass by, but Knox is too stunned by the disappearance to stop anyone and ask what happened to Frisco Jack.

A short while later, Knox finds himself on the elevator, on his way up to Feldman & Associates, which occupies the top floor of the building, the twelfth. Still dazed, he shuffles past reception, which is unmanned at this hour, down the hall by the steno pool and private offices of the associates, and pauses to look out over the feedlot—fifteen divided cubicles, all exactly alike with desk, phone, and computer terminal, the working places for the lowest members of the company, the assistants. He notices the light on in his neighbor's cubicle and raps on the partition lightly with his pen. "Good morning, Bennett," Knox says with a cheerfulness he doesn't really feel.

Bennett glances up from his work and mumbles, "Morning." He's a large man who looks like he'd be more comfortable someplace other than squeezed into a stall in the feedlot.

Knox lingers in the doorway. "Say, do you know what happened to Frisco Jack?"

Bennett looks up again, an annoyed expression on his face. "Frisco Jack?" he repeats.

"The man who runs the shoeshine stand in the lobby."

"You trying to be funny, Knox?" Bennett says sourly. "There's no shoeshine stand in the lobby."

With a sinking feeling in his stomach, Knox protests weakly, "Yes there is, the one in the alcove by the front door."

Bennett drops his pencil. "That's a Coke machine, man."

Knox raises his hands in a gesture of supplication. "Okay, sorry, I'm going." He slips into his stall.

There are two more stacks of client-transaction folders piled next to the stack he left unfinished yesterday. He groans. Looking over the volume of work makes him forget the old man. He checks his in-basket, hoping to find something from personnel. There's an associate position open in the company's branch out in the country west of the city. For a moment he feels a tweak of paranoia, wondering if his boss forwarded his request to personnel. After all, the man had been weird when he accepted the application: *Knox, don't you know people only come here? No one leaves the city.* The sensation passes as Knox recalls seeing the man initial the request. With an effort of will he sinks down in his chair and reaches for the first folder.

Heather meets Knox inside their apartment door, number 626, with a pitcher of margaritas in one hand and two glasses in the other. She looks serious, wearing her dark blue satin number, her eyes picking up the deep color and sparkling with a hint of inner joy. He knows she's about to burst with a secret.

"Hello, hon," she whispers in his ear, after giving him a quick peck on the cheek.

"Hello," he replies, relishing her fresh, clean smell as she directs him to a spot on the couch.

Heather's expression remains grave, but as she pours him a drink a little dribbles over the edge of the glass, and she bursts into a giggle.

"Hey, babe!" he protests loudly, laughing and licking up the icy froth from his hand. But he cooperates, playing his role and asking, "Okay, Heather, what's going on? What's the occasion? I know it's not our anniversary . . . not my birthday. What's up, babe?"

With a staged look of nonchalance, she says, "Well . . . ," dragging out the suspense as she pours herself a drink. Then she raises her glass in a toast, and says, "To the future poppa!"

"What—?" Knox blurts, choking on his drink, as he struggles to get to his feet. "You went to the clinic today?"

She nods, unable to restrain the smirk of self-satisfaction.

"You're really pregnant this time?"

"That's right, boy," she clowns. "You knocked me up."

"I can't believe it," he says, hugging her tightly. They've been married four years, with nothing but a series of false alarms. Gently, Knox pushes Heather away, examining her carefully for some physical sign in addition to the silly grin. "When?"

"About seven months."

Suddenly he shivers, the air-conditioning sobering his mood. They can't raise a baby here in the Towers . . . or anyplace in the city for that matter. The promotion and move to the branch office is critical now. They would *have* to leave the city . . .

Knox keeps on a happy face during the elegant dinner, not wanting to spoil any part of Heather's celebration. But he can't shake the memory of his supervisor's strange words: *no one leaves the city.* Later, he forgets his concerns during their joyful lovemaking.

Thursday morning on the way to work, Knox rehearses his speech for his appointment with personnel. He'll go over his merits, mention the time he's spent as an assistant with outstanding performance reports, emphasize his desire to work and live in a smaller, less urban place, and then cap it all by mentioning the baby—the company likes family men . . .

After the eleventh floor, Knox is the only one remaining in the elevator, which strikes him as a little strange. But he shrugs, and on the twelfth he stops in the public restroom to check his appearance before heading down to personnel. Then he hurries out of the restroom, but stops short and looks around.

Feldman & Associates is gone!

He wanders around the empty floor in a daze. He should talk to someone, he tells himself . . . but whom? No one is here, not even old Bennett.

Down in the lobby, Knox has a flash of brilliance and stops to check the directory:

Edelman Publications
Fancy Foods, Inc.
Gant, William, D.D.S.

Feldman & Associates is not listed. With another burst of inspiration, he moves to the phone booth and flips through the Yellow Pages. . . . No Feldman & Associates there either. For a moment he considers calling Heather. But what can he tell her? My employer doesn't exist? Jesus. What the fuck is happening? he asks himself, fighting back the mixture of anger and panic. First the sculptures, then Frisco Jack, now the company.

Later, Knox finds himself in the little park around the corner, where he occasionally eats lunch with some of the other assistants. But it's much nicer this time of day without the lunch-hour hustle and bustle. He feels too emotionally drained, too exhausted to even think. Looking around, he finds a nice shady spot on a bench, sits down, unknots his tie, slips off his shoes, and lets out a long sigh. For lunch he buys a hot dog and root beer, neither on Heather's list of approved consumables, but he doesn't even give it a second thought as he wolfs down his food. He tosses the cup and wrapper into the trash and spots someone's discarded newspaper. He proceeds to leisurely read the entire thing.

During the afternoon, Knox is nagged by the sense that he should be doing something, but he remains in the pleasant little park, too comfortable, too detached, idling time away, just watching people coming and going, but not thinking about the disappearances.

Friday morning, Knox gets up early, dresses, acting as if he's going to work. He still hasn't told Heather about not having a job anymore, and he hasn't decided what to do, although it has occurred to him that he might need psychiatric help. He drives downtown.

It's a rare morning, clear and cool, the pollution index low. So Knox decides to go over to the big park. But he doesn't even get out of the car. The thought of all the crap the tourists leave behind at the zoo, museum, and tea gardens is just too depressing.

So he spends the day driving, the traffic surprisingly light. At dinnertime he heads home, knowing he will have to tell Heather everything.

From the freeway the red light atop the Towers flashes like a beacon to Knox. He takes his off ramp then makes a sharp circle back into the building's parking lot.

In the elevator Knox punches the sixth floor and tries to structure what he wants to tell Heather. When the door slides open, he hurries down the corridor to their place, all the apartments exactly alike except for the numbers: 616, 618, 620, 622, 624—He's reached the end of the hall, but there's no 626.

Their apartment has disappeared.

Knox is stunned. After a few moments he glances across the hall at the nearest door on that side: 625. The odd numbers descend back toward the elevator, each one exactly like its neighbor. Jesus.

In the lobby, Knox checks over the occupant register. But he's forgotten the apartment number he's looking for; and as he reads through the listings, he sees no familiar names. In a state of confusion, he shuffles to the pay phone, digging change from his pocket. Then he dials a number and deposits the amount requested by the operator. The phone rings four times before it is finally answered—

"Yes, hello."

Knox sighs with relief after clearing his throat. "Hello," he says, his voice barely more than a whisper.

"Is that you, son?"

He nods, then realizes she can't see him. "Yes, Mom, it's me."

"Well, how are you?" asks his mother, a tentative edge in her voice. "Is everything all right?"

Knox shrugs, knowing everything is not at all right.

"Where are you, son?"

"I'm . . ." Knox looks over the surroundings. "I'm not sure, Mom. But I need someplace to stay—"

"Have you been drinking, again?" she asks in an accusatory manner. "I just wish you'd settle down . . . maybe get married."

The words stab into his chest. He stifles a moan. "Mom," he murmurs defeatedly, "I need someplace to stay tonight."

"Well, no problem, son," she replies soothingly. "You know you're always welcome at home."

He smiles, feeling a glimmer of elation growing. If he can just make it home, he knows everything will be fine. He thanks her and hangs up.

Then he dashes out to his car and drives back to the freeway, heading north to the valley beyond the city.

At the tollbooth to the Northside Bridge, he glances in the mirror, unable to shake the feeling that he's being followed by . . . *what?* He doesn't know. He just feels it, and it dampens his growing elation.

Halfway across the bridge, Knox leaves the city limits, and he sucks in a deep breath. I've made it! he thinks. I'm free.

A half hour later as he enters the valley, he notices something unsettling in the hills—the lights, once infrequent dots, are now almost contiguous clusters. He frowns, and with an effort shrugs off the feeling.

A few minutes later he brakes and pulls into his mother's driveway. Inside, he convinces his mother that he is not drunk; and even though he isn't hungry, he lets her fix him a snack. Later he takes a long shower. Then, at last, he crawls into bed between fresh, crinkly sheets, listening to the old fridge kick on for a few minutes. Then it's quiet, dead silence out here in the country, and Knox drifts off into a deep sleep.

Something is wrong.

Knox pushes himself up on his elbow, looking out into the darkness through the open bedroom window. It's the sounds:

cars and trucks, brakes squealing, horns blaring,
a siren wails like a wounded animal,
people talking, laughing, shouting,
music blasting,
and gunshots.

The city never sleeps.

LOCK HER ROOM

ELIZABETH MASSIE

"My visits to the city are limited by choice," Elizabeth Massie states. *"There I have seen an old man claw my own discarded, rancid sandwich from the trash can I'd just tossed it in, then open it and chew on it as if it were a feast. I've stepped around people on sidewalks; I've seen blood hosed from pavement. I've stood, apprehensive even among friends, while waiting for the subway train. I've read the garbled, violent screams from the graffitied walls of buildings. I've felt the despair and the need and the hate and the hunger. And I've felt the city try to drop its heavy, numbing coat of indifference over me. The masses have their drugs to blind them. The city's own drug is detachment. It wards off the true overpowering horrors which exist in the streets. And so I run home again. I write my angry letters to our leaders and send my donations to charities. And pray for those left behind."*

Massie, a teacher, has published short stories, poems, nonfiction, and wrote a PBS television special which won a 1990 Parents' Choice Award. Her first novel, Sineater, *will be published in England by Pan Books. Married and the mother of two children, she lives in Waynesboro, Virginia.*

Curt and Malcolm had said, "Hang tough, little John. Cool to be cruel. We all done this, it's called solitary. We'll be back." And then they were gone. And of course, Johnny believed them. But that was three days ago.

Johnny Morris wasn't so sure anymore.

Johnny wet his pants for the third time in seventy-two hours. He stood still, let it go, enjoyed the feel of the wet and warm, and then did not give it another thought. What the hell else was he to do, with the hall door boarded up and the bathroom door locked? Johnny's fine motor skills weren't as well developed as many of the other kids in the high school, and so his attempts at picking the bathroom lock had been a waste of time and knuckle skin. Not that he didn't have time— time was the one commodity of which he had an overabundance. A place to take a piss or dump, warm clothes, and food were items that were sadly lacking.

And so, after spending the first several hours of his confinement in the subterranean locker room kneeling on the floor in front of the bathroom key hole, cramming anything small and sharp in and jangling it around, he gave up and peed in the corner by the last row of lockers. The corner became his john. He sat on a bench, sang to himself, masturbated, and slept a little.

Curt and Malcolm didn't show up. It had been more than a day, Johnny knew. He could see the ebb of light outside the tiny, ceiling-high windows, and he had seen the light come back hours later. And so Johnny began picking at the bathroom door keyhole again. Not so much for a cleaner place to relieve himself this time, but because he thought there might be another door in the bathroom, a door leading out to the hall.

If Curt and Malcolm had forgotten he was down there, he would need a way out. True, he would have to face the music, but he'd worry about that when it happened. It wouldn't be the first time he'd had his face kicked in by someone he cared about.

But the lock never gave, and Johnny's obscenities did not bring the door off its hinges. There was no way out of this hole, save for the whims of his friends who had put him there. Johnny paced and cursed, kicking up dust balls and slamming his feet through the piles of mildewy socks and shoes that littered the locker-room floor. A headache came in a bright shot of pain, and then subsided.

After the second day had come and gone, Johnny, in boredom, wet his pants to see what it felt like. Wasn't much to it, but it was something to do.

He found a water pipe running the length of the room, and he worked a crack free. The water spilled out in irregular drops. He drank some and let the rest run to the floor, through a pile of crusted towels, and out the drainholes.

The basement locker room had not been used for students in almost two years. Pollard Street High School no longer offered an official physical education program to its youth. The knifings and the drugs and the bench-top sex had ended dressing out and showers. Now, physical education consisted of letting the students wander about in the fenced, black-topped area outside the cafeteria for twenty minutes a day, girls separated from boys, seniors separated from freshmen. Security guards watched from their corners and from the cafeteria steps, hands ready on hip-carried guns and walkie-talkies. The principal declared that wandering the blacktop fit into the category of physical activity, thus covering school board requirements, and feeling justified, locked the basement gymnasium. Door handles were strung with chains. The boys' and girls' locker rooms were boarded up with assorted nails and planks.

No one was even allowed in to claim their gym suits and jockstraps.

Johnny looked at the newest wet spot on his pants, rapidly growing cool, touched it, then sat again on the bench.

Fucking three days now. Cool to be cruel, no shit. How tough would he have to hang? How tough could he hang with no food? Until his stomach caved in? His head began to ache again.

He wished once more that he had a watch. His friends all had watches, and not cheap little wristband shit. They had gold chain watches, watches that they could swing around and show off with. Watches bought with money they'd gotten in any way they could, from hustling male tricks on the streets to playing carry men for the bigger dealers to rolling the little Jesus-trash students here at school. But Johnny was just a ninth grader, and he was still earning his way. He knew he needed to do what was said without crying, and so far, he had done well. He had helped pick pockets of teachers, had been watchman when ice was passed along in the halls, and, a few days ago, had helped kidnap the little Jesus-trash bitch and stuff her into a locker along with her stupid blue purse to see how long she would live.

That had been a burst of fun. "Lock her in the lock her room!" Carl had crowed. All had chimed in, "Lock her room, lock her room!" Everyone was high and elated after it was done; Malcolm magnanimously gave Johnny two free hits.

Johnny crossed his arms. He thought they were looking thin, although it was hard to tell, as Johnny had never been much on the muscle scale. And now he was enduring what his big buddies Carl and Malcolm said all worthy Pollard Street kids endured. Solitary. Solitary would make him a man. It would make him keen and hungry and ready for the world.

The only thing was, it wasn't exactly solitary.

Johnny scooted his butt around on the bench and looked at the first long row of lockers. Nope, this wasn't a genuine solitary confinement. The little bitch was in locker number 35.

It wasn't such a big deal. She had been in the locker almost a full day longer than Johnny had been in the locker room. She didn't say a word, and she didn't bump around. Even when the boys had snatched her on her way to sixth period on Monday and had dragged her, bumping and flopping down to the basement where they pried the boards from the locker-room door, she didn't say much except, "Why are you doing this?" That was the way the Jesus-trash kids were. It seemed like there were always a few kids in each grade who were quiet and solemn and didn't go with the flow of the vocal and violent majority. Neither Carl nor Malcolm knew if they were religious kids. For all the little they said, they could have been Buddhists or Muslims or Hindus. The boys just called them Jesus trash because it was like they wanted to be crucified. Their silence begged for it. Screw them, they deserved to be victims, Carl had told Johnny. Rid the school of deadwood. Help the city trim its worthless overload.

Johnny looked at locker number 35. The bitch had been in the locker for four days. Maybe she slept all the time. Maybe she had died the first night.

She hadn't been an ugly girl. More like not there. Plain hair and plain eyes and not a bit of the makeup the girls that hung with Carl and Malcolm wore.

Johnny's stomach growled, and for the first time, he realized that going without food was going to hurt bad. He had fasted before, unintentionally, when on a drug weekend. But there were no drugs here. "Man," he said. No food, no drugs. How the hell long would they leave him here? Didn't they even want to come see if the girl was still alive?

He lifted his head and shouted to the ceiling, "Cool to be cruel! Solitary's gonna make me a man."

He licked his lips and looked at the window. It was still light, but he had not kept good track of time, so it could have been breakfast time or suppertime. Why the fuck hadn't he stole himself a watch when he'd had so many chances?

One o'clock, two o'clock, red o'clock, blue o'clock.

Where is thumbkins? Where is thumbkins? Here I am, here I am. How are you this morning, noon, afternoon, evening, who the hell knew? Johnny stood and drove his foot into the base of the nearest locker. It collapsed inward with a groan. Old MacDonald had a clock, with a tick tock here and a tick tock there.

"I'm hungry, you shits! What time is it?"

Johnny listened to his voice thump and die against the far wall of the locker room. Then he looked at locker number 35. He walked down the row and stopped in front of it.

He scratched his eyebrows, and crossed his arms. Then he said, "Hey, bitch."

There was no answer. Johnny bobbed his head and worked his shoulders, as though he were speaking to someone who could see him.

"Bitch, you got a watch in there?"

He pulled his nose and sniffed. He looked over his shoulder and back again. Bitch was dead, no two ways about it. Four days, man. Had to be. He'd have to wait on the boys. Fuck it all. His stomach growled angrily, and there were teeth in the growl. It made him catch his breath. For a moment, he felt dizzy.

Then a voice from inside locker number 35 said, "No."

Johnny flinched. His eyes widened, and a bubble of spit popped out. But then he pulled it together. Can't lose cool, no sir. "No watch?" he said. Goddamn it, she was actually conscious.

"I'm sorry. I never wore a watch. It would have been stolen."

"Shit," said Johnny. "Have any lunch in that purse?"

"No lunch."

"Shit," said Johnny. Then he shifted his weight and looked at his toes. He had opened a conversation with this girl. Was he now supposed to just go on back to sitting on the bench and waiting for his buddies? He wished he'd left it alone. He wondered if she was getting really thin, even more thin than he was.

He strode back to the end of the bench and sat for a while. He played with his dick, he chewed loose skin from beside his fingernails. He stretched out and tried to doze.

After what could have been minutes or hours, he went back to the locker.

"Got any dope?"

There was silence for a moment, and the voice said, "No dope."

"Man, you ain't no fucking good for nothing, are you?" Johnny kicked locker number 35 and it rattled. He'd kicked so hard that his toe hurt, and he took off his shoe to examine the damage. His nail had broken off short, and a little blood was soaking the sock.

"I bet I die of infection," he said to himself, but the voice in the locker answered, "It's not that bad."

Johnny looked up at the vent holes in the locker. He half expected to see little eyes peeking out at him. But the holes were too small and the locker too dark.

"How do you know?"

The voice said, "I know. Just wash it clean. It'll be all right."

"Fuck you," said Johnny. "Why should I do anything you say? We crammed you in a locker to see how long it would take you to die. What do you think of that?"

There was no answer.

Johnny sighed, and looked at his toe. His head began to swim, and he shut his eyes. Colors moved in a slow, nauseating pattern behind his lids. He opened his eyes again. He had a sudden urge to reach out and touch the locker, but he balled his fist instead.

"We gonna die of hunger in here, you know? If the boys don't come let us out."

The voice didn't answer. Johnny spit on his toe and wiped it off. He looked at the window. The light was fading.

"I been in here more than three days," he said to the locker. "They said they'd come back. Said I'd be a man. Fuck their shit-wipin' asses. They lied to me."

The voice said nothing.

"You think they lied?"

The voice said, "I don't know."

"Well, I thought you knew everything, bitch!" Johnny

stormed back to the far end of the benches. He buried his face in his hands and tried to will his headache and stomachache away.

When it was dark, he went back to the locker. There was no way the girl would still be alive. It was stupid trying to talk to her. She was nothing, just a Jesus-trash kid, just somebody he and his friends had put in a locker to die.

But for some reason, he wanted to talk. He had to talk.

"Hey," he said. He stood before the locker, and tipped his face to try and see up the locker vent holes. "Hey, you still there? Ha, ha, that's a joke."

"I'm here."

"We're gonna die. But it don't matter, does it? I mean, just two less people to worry about is all I can say." Johnny held his breath. It was suddenly important that she not agree with him. He'd been in violent fights, and could have died many times. But here death had no glory. Death here, death now, would be the death of a cockroach, stepped on by a careless boot.

The thought chilled him.

"You don't want to die, do you?" said the voice.

Johnny laughed, a coarse, barklike sound. "Sure, bitch. I want to die. What do you think?"

"I think life wants itself."

Johnny sat on the bench in front of the locker. He crossed his arms against his complaining belly. "Don't talk weird. You don't make sense."

"Life insists on living. It's a power. Life wants to hang on, life wants to live."

"Shit," said Johnny. He leaned over, and looked up through the vent holes. There was nothing. "Too many people in the world. Life ain't worth nothing. Blast a cop, blast a dirty old man, blast a mama. Ain't worth nothing."

"Life never lost its value."

"Hey, you know everything, tell me how to get out of here! I'm sick of you, I'm sick of this fucking place."

A panic suddenly dug its claws into Johnny's lungs. Sweat burst out onto his face. He jumped from the bench and picked it up over his head. His muscles screamed. He screamed. He hurled the bench to the wet floor, and the legs splintered into vicious shards. "Sick of this fucking place! I want out! Let me out!" The sound of his own cries horrified him. His heart spun and thundered against his chest. He felt as if he was underwater and could not breathe. "Oh, God, let me out! I don't want to die!" He charged the door and slammed his shoulder into the wood. The door did not give. "Oh God please please let me out!"

No one opened the door. He could not get out. He limped back to the locker, and sat on the floor amid the pieces of the broken bench. He began to cry.

"Please help me. I want to get out."

The voice said nothing.

"I'd help you but I don't know the combination," Johnny said. He shuddered, and he dug his palm into the tears on his cheeks. "I swear to God I don't know it."

Locker number 35 was silent.

"I'll say life is a fucking power if you want me to. It's a power, okay? I feel it, okay? That make you happy? I really feel it, no lie. Now help me, please!"

Then the voice said, "What do you think I can do for you?"

"I don't know. But you's one of those smart kids. I could tell by looking at you. Think of something."

"Cool to be cruel."

"What?"

"Isn't that what you and your friends say?"

"Uh . . ." said Johnny.

" 'Cool to be cruel.' It's this year's school motto. Last year it was 'Get 'em while they're down.' This year it's 'Cool to be cruel.' "

Johnny dragged a set of fingers through his hair. His hands were cold. "Yeah, that's it."

"Cool to be kind, Johnny."

Johnny rubbed his cold hands together and looked up at the locker.

"Life is power, it wants to go on." The voice was gentle and steady. Johnny wished he had a sledgehammer for the combination lock, and that wish stunned him. "But life needs help. Try this instead: 'Cool to be kind.' "

Johnny slowly got up on his knees. This time, he let his hand brush the surface of the locker. It was surprisingly warm. "Cool to be kind," he muttered.

"Do you understand?"

Johnny pressed his hands firmly on the locker. It was warm, and from within, he could smell something sweet, like flowers his mother sometimes brought in from the street vendor. The warmth was beautiful; the scent caressed his heart.

"Johnny?"

God, she knew his name. Johnny put his forehead against the locker.

"Yes," he said.

"Say it, Johnny."

"Cool to be kind."

"Put your mouth to the vent holes."

Johnny raised up. He closed his eyes. He put his mouth to the holes. Something warm and sweet flowed out and onto his tongue. He licked and swallowed. He let more pour into his mouth. The taste was heaven. He knew he would live. A glow swelled in his gut. The glow was life and love and hope. He thought if he could see himself at that moment, he would be sparkling.

And then the liquid stopped. Johnny slowly opened his eyes and pulled back from the locker. Streaks of red zigzagged down the front of the locker door, bright, shining rivers of glistening scarlet. When he wiped his mouth, thick red came away on his fingers.

"Oh, God," he whispered. The glow, the sparkling, squeezed his head like a wonderful tourniquet. He said, "Girl?"

The voice said nothing.

"Hey, girl, you saved me. You really saved me."

There was silence.

In the silence, among the wood shards, Johnny curled up and began to drift into sleep.

But there were more voices, loud, harsh, laughing voices from beyond the locker-room door. Johnny's eyes opened, and he spun up onto his knees. A splinter from the bench drove deep into the flesh of his shin.

There was a sound of hammering and cursing and shouting. The door crashed open. Carl and Malcolm stood grinning with claw hammers and crowbars in hand. Several others crowded in behind them, looking over their shoulders.

"Fuck you, little John! You made it!" said Malcolm. He nudged Carl in the ribs.

"You're one tough-hanging bastard," agreed Carl. All the boys shook their heads as though incredulous.

"See you found water," said Malcolm as he stepped over a water pool on the floor and came to stand beside Johnny. "I told Carl you wasn't no stupid shit, you could find something to keep you wet."

"Even if you had to drink your own pee." Carl giggled. He was on something, and his eyes flashed white. "Drink your own pee, little John?"

"No." Johnny stood up. His arms prickled.

"Fuck it, look!" said one of the boys. "He got blood on his mouth!"

"Bite off your dick, little dick?" said Carl. "He lived to be a man, but bit off his dick to do it!"

"No," said Johnny. Then he said, "You gonna let the girl out?"

Carl looked confused. "What girl?" he said.

Malcolm said, "Oh yeah, we did cram a Jesus-trash kid up in a locker, didn't we? Man, when was that? Last week or last month? I can't even remember which locker it was."

"Number 35," said Johnny. "We put her in four days ago."

"So you want to see if she's still living?" asked Carl. He leaned over to Johnny and coughed in his face. Spit flew. "Think she bit off her dick to stay alive, too?"

"Don't know the combination," said Malcolm.

"You have a crowbar," said Johnny.

"What difference does it make, John?" said Malcolm. "Let's go. School's out. I got stuff to do."

"Number 35. Use the crowbar."

"Fuck it, why not?" said Malcolm. He squinted at the row of lockers until Johnny pointed at the right one. Malcolm raised the bar and gawked at his friends. "Like opening one of them time capsules."

The crowbar arched and fell against the lock. The lock swung crazily. Malcolm aimed and swung again. The lock broke free.

Johnny grabbed the handle. She saved me, he thought. *Life wants itself.* His head and chest still tingled with the power. *Cool to be kind.* He pulled the door open.

Malcolm and Carl fell back, their faces contorting and their eyes rolling. "Shit, oh, man that's gross! Leave her the fuck there and let's go."

Johnny stared into the locker.

The girl was dead.

"Come on, little John!" The boys reached for Johnny's arm, but he shook them off.

The girl's head was tilted down and hung against her chest like an obscene, deflated balloon. Obviously, her neck had been broken when the boys had stuffed her into the locker four days ago. Her eyes were wide and yellowing and sightless. Her face had begun to swell. The lips were cracked and peeling, a ghastly purple color. The ripe stench of decay was heavy. One hand was lifted and stiff, the fingers curled as if in a blessing.

The fingertips were lined up with the locker holes. The ends of the fingers were pulpy and red, as if they had recently bled.

"Take her on a date, why don't you?" shouted Carl as he and Malcolm and the other boys hurried from the locker room. "You's a sick man, little John!"

Johnny caught his chest in his hands. He stared at the girl in the locker.

Life had the power. It wanted to go on. It wanted itself.

"Oh God," said Johnny.

He slowly shut the locker door.

"Cool to be kind," he said. He looked out the open locker-room door to the hallway. The walls of the hall were dark and damp and barren, exactly as they were when he had been put into solitary. He listened, and could hear the thumping and laughing and shouting of Carl and Malcolm as they ascended to the first floor of the school.

Johnny slowly walked to the door. His toe hurt and his hands were cold and his stomach began to growl again. But the tingle remained; the sparkling tickled his brain and sent sparks through every nerve in his body. He had never been so completely afraid, nor so completely sure.

Fear and power took him upstairs to face life.

WELLSPRING

LEE MOLER

Lee Moler says, "Something eerie happens every time I go into the city: I become so small that I'm invisible. You could die leaning against a wall and no one would notice until you fell over, and then it would only be your blue color that caught their attention. It's scary and liberating at once."

Moler, forty, was born in West Virginia and now lives in Bel Air, Maryland, with his wife and two children. A former soldier, disc jockey, janitor, and bureaucrat, he has published short stories in Borderlands, Borderlands II, *and the Horror Writers of America anthology,* Freak Show. *His novel, a thriller entitled* Baltimore Blues, *was released by St. Martin's.*

Roger Rhodes felt a distinctly sexual thrill as he stood in front of the giant window in his office. It was the same thrill of anticipation he used to get when he knew he was going to score with a girl for the first time. Somewhere in the hundreds of scores, that thrill had disappeared, along with most of the other ones. That was the thing most people didn't realize about being wealthy: after a time new thrills get harder to find. Some guys bought sports teams when they reached that stage. Others got into perversion of one form or another. Of course, as far as he was concerned, sports teams were just another perversion; going down to the locker room and slapping a bunch of naked dummies on the ass, letting them pour champagne on your head. Bullshit. Owning sports teams was for guys who got picked last for the team when they were kids, even when they owned the ball. All bullshit. When you got as rich as Rhodes, you had to make your own thrills. You had to have imagination.

He looked out the window and felt the thrill again, a little shock wave running between the center of his chest and his crotch, an involuntary intake of breath as he looked out from the seventy-fifth floor to where the river divided the city into past and present.

The side where Rhodes stood was a slab-glass card game played by gambling addicts coked on money. This was where the deals went down in elevators and up in smoke. Here was where the players gave each other the triple-speed double cross while they ate hundred-dollar lunches and watched the cabs bleat at each other like poor people. Paper property was bought, carved, parceled, shipped, reconstituted and put into play again. Today it was a service economy—a big card game where the deck was reshuffled after every pot. Rhodes knew it would fold when the action moved to another city, but what the hell, he was a player not a civilian. At a party one time an old guy asked him what it was he made and Rhodes told him he made out.

Across the river was the land of the dead. The old factories seeped poisons into the water as they sank slowly into the mud flats. Chemicals rose off the river in a greenish fog which swirled through the rusty air around the tops of the slowly failing smokestacks. The green fog was always there, drifting halfway out into the river before being sucked back by the slow-roiling suction of decay. Sometimes Rhodes would stand at his window and pick out one noxious tendril as it reached directly for him and then withdrew like an alien thing that couldn't stand organic life.

The old section of the city was called Industrial Island, even though it was a peninsula that hooked out into the widest part of the river to form what used to be a harbor. It was connected to the newer business section where Rhodes stood by a tunnel and to the rat warren of old houses behind it by a flaking suspension bridge. It was there that the old factory employees collected their welfare checks and had their cancer funerals.

Rhodes gave a short laugh when he thought of the way those people were always bitching and moaning about their lost jobs and the lack of city services in their neighborhoods. The poor dumb fuckers. They lived next door to a place where the Nazis would have sent the Jews, and they were worried about their jobs. The eight-foot wire fences should have told them something, or the danger signs, or the memories of what they worked on when they had jobs. But they said nothing. Oh there was the usual group of sandal wearers who tried to make trouble, but when they found out the grass roots had died along with the rest of the vegetation on Industrial Island, they'd gone off to get themselves arrested in warmer climates.

"Hell," Rhodes said aloud, "someone should tell the poor dumb bastards, but it won't be me. I'm having too much fun."

The sexual thrill shot through him again and he looked at his watch. Only three more hours until sundown. He went to his desk and opened the bottom drawer, searched through it and then pressed the button on his intercom. "Janice, where are my binoculars?" he said into it.

"You left them out here, Roger," Janice said in her throaty contralto. "You asked me to clean the lenses."

"Well did you?"

"I, uh, I've been pretty busy today. I could do it right now if you like."

"Forget it. Bring them in."

"Really, it would only take me a minute."

"I said forget it." Jesus! He didn't give a damn if they were clean or not. It was just that she'd given him three good blow jobs and he'd decided to let her do something personal so she'd know he liked her.

"Here Roger," she said, leaning over his desk. "I cleaned them on the way in." She straightened up and looked down at him expectantly. Janice was a tall redhead with a tiny waist and twin rockets to go along with her contoured lips, but the thrill was gone. It would be the fourth time and he knew how it would go. She'd expect to get off her knees and onto his couch, and then she'd want to hang around afterward and talk career advancement. The whole thing would turn into a bore. "Thanks, Janice," he said. "That's all for now."

"Really?" she said, surprised.

As she moved toward the door, he noticed her fine pillowy ass, but what the hell? He'd see one just like it tomorrow or the next day. He never quite knew what he'd see on the island. Rhodes walked to the window with the binoculars and stared across the river. Now he could see inside the fog to where it rose out of colored puddles to turn paint into slime and metal to rust.

Shermer Vinyl Products was in the center of the island, two miles east of the old Daw Chemical plant and three miles west of what used to be Arlon Paints. Jesus, talk about the place where the sun never shines. He'd acquired Shermer as part of the Nucron takeover with the intent of dumping it for some quick cash. That was just before some sandal wearers got the ear of a lint-head liberal congressman and the EPA had shut the place down because it was leaking enough dioxin to melt the soles of your shoes. The lint-head was up for reelection, so the EPA investigated Daw and Arlon and found out they were planting a big crop of PCB, DDT, and a string of other letters Rhodes had never even heard of. Hell, it wasn't worth cleaning the place up so, he'd done the same thing as Daw and Arlon, fired all the workers and let the plant sit. The place was impossible to sell, but it showed a hell of a nice loss at tax time. Not that it wasn't a pain in the ass. He had to put up the fences and only ex-cons were willing to work the place as security guards. They stole everything they could just for practice and maced a few people on the subway, but for two dollars over minimum wage they were willing to look the other way when Rhodes went there to play Feudal Prince.

It was a real kick thinking of himself that way, and who deserved it more? He sure looked the part; six-four and a silver-haired fifty-two years old, only five more pounds than his college weight, a face like Charlton Heston without lockjaw. By God he was a prince, and the pencil dicks at EPA had crowned him. They'd made Shermer Vinyl Products into his own game preserve. Oh yes, absolutely: a theme park for adults. Going there was like being a kid and stepping into a tall damp forest where you don't know what might be behind the next tree, the only thing you know is that it's yours and you have the right to kill it.

The first time he'd wondered if he had the nerve to actually go through with it, but that certainty pulled him through, that princely assurance that it was his property and any pests were his rightful quarry. And what a thrill when he found that, not only could he do it, but it also made him feel good. Sometimes he thought maybe it was turning into an addiction. He'd tried to hold it to once a month, then twice. That worked for a while, but now, after four years, he was having trouble staying with once a week. But what the hell, there were always more homeless. No matter how many he killed, there were always more. You'd think Industrial Island was some kind of goddamn health spa, the way they came. They lived in the empty factories and deserted warehouses like rats; no drinkable water, no plumbing, right in the epicenter of Dioxin Lagoon. Hell, the security guards wouldn't even go in there to chase them out. Rhodes would, though; the Prince. He wondered if they knew about him. Maybe they thought he was the Grim Reaper, or God. What the hell, he was doing the miserable wretches a favor.

They didn't know it though. That was the great part. They always tried to get away and he had to hunt them down. Some of them even tried to fight back with rocks or knives, and that worried him, not because he was afraid but because he wasn't. He was too important to get killed by some rummy who got lucky, but without that possibility there would be no kick. And what were the odds? He had the decontamination suit, the night-scoped Weatherby 380, and the same kind of shotgun microphone the networks used to pick up sideline fuckyous at football games. No, it was just dangerous enough to be fun.

Rhodes took one last look through the binoculars, hoping to see one of them. It would be such a special thrill to stand at a great distance and see the one he would kill at close range that night. As always, though, he saw nothing but smokestack shadows making bile-colored crosses on the rusty ground. Only two more hours and their Prince would come.

"He's coming tonight," said Rees. "I can feel him looking at us."

"I know," answered Bell. "I can feel him too, from right up . . . there." Bell's finger pointed out over the water to a sheet-glass mirror of a building that reflected the sun into the eyes of the drivers below. Rees's own eyes hurt as he saw it.

"My eyes hurt," Bell told him, and of course it was true even though Bell was completely blind.

"It's the building," Rees told him. "The sun off the glass is hitting the drivers in the eyes."

Bell gave a short laugh and spit up some blood. "Mirrored buildings," he said. "Just like their limos. This aversion the rich have to being seen. I think it's more a desire not to see the blood, a way to stay focused on the score."

"He wears a silver suit when he comes."

"No mystery about that, is there?" They both laughed.

"He's looking for us, right now," Rees said through the laughter.

"But he can't see us."

"I still don't believe this."

"Believe it kid," said Bell. "It's a gift."

"It's gonna kill me."

"Every gift has a price." Bell laughed again and spat up some more blood. He took a pint of muscatel out of his pocket, poured a big dollop into his mouth, gagged it down, and offered it to Rees.

"Nah," said Rees. "I don't use the cheap stuff. That's not the reason I'm here."

"I forgot," replied Bell. "You're one of the innocent ones."

"Come on."

"I mean it," said Bell. And he did. The booze had put him on his path. He was one of the "unfortunates" they talk about in AA who aren't helped by anything. He'd tried of course, even managed to keep his job as one of the best reporters in the city. But every day he saw the papers closing, the jobs leaving, the survivors murdering each other. The flame that powered the city was being extinguished; the day-night rhythm replaced by the fish-eye fluorescence of an eternal television dawn. He didn't have the face for anchor work or the stomach for sound bites. All he had to offer was a talent for telling the truth, and on television the truth was anything that could be stated in thirty seconds.

He was a man in love with words and he was being forced to watch his lover being slowly strangled by a cancer of "dialogues" inflicted by a virus of bottom-line positions. In his grief, he rediscovered the fact that the alchemy of liquor is to change self-pity into the more socially useful emotion of self-hatred. Self-hatred allowed him to serve as an example, a warning, a raven perched on the shoulder of society. So he crucified himself with bourbon and hung himself on the hill for all to see, but they preferred to look away. And rather than endure their ignorance, he preferred to sail down the river of whiskey and out into the alcohol sea, where waves of vodka washed him into storms of hair tonic and Sterno then onto the shores of a cistern in the factory's basement.

One icy night, when he was too sick to be drunk on the pint of T-bird he'd found in a frozen stiff's pocket, he'd fallen down a flight of metal stairs onto a steel grate where he'd looked down two flights into a nest of rats and steam-pipe insulation to see a mercurial white glow coming from a hole in the floor. It looked like a light of some kind, maybe a bulb that would warm his hands, so he found another flight of stairs and followed them down a rusting wall to where a hole had been broken in the foundation, allowing him to crawl through and nestle with the rats in the insulation. He'd leaned on an elbow and looked over the edge of an old sump pump where the white stuff collected.

It came from everywhere, sweating out of the walls, dripping from broken pipes and bubbling up from the bottom of the hole. There was a nonspecific glow off it like the one on the ground during a full moon in winter. If he turned his head, the stuff seemed to change depth and consistency. He knew it was some kind of leftover toxic waste, but then so was he. The stuff in the hole became hypnotic. It seemed to burn with the same dead blue heat as his heart.

He waited a day after the vodka ran out and then stuck his hand into the cistern. It was cool at first, like a liniment, and after a few seconds he could feel it penetrating the pores of his hand. It didn't burn, though; it just felt like it was filtering through his skin to the bone. He sniffed it, and under the metal chemical smell, he detected a sharp stab like alcohol. He waited another day before he drank some.

The second it hit his stomach he knew it would kill him. The cool liniment feeling spread outward, shriveling his balls into what felt like two raisins on a dead vine. Then he was on his knees, the top of his head being sliced off from the inside, then the air pouring into his head and down through his body, leaving him as rigid and empty as a metal cup.

When he woke up, he was blind. But he could remember his Social Security number and his mother's middle name. And, even though he couldn't see a lick, the shape of the room and the factory grounds seemed to be imprinted on the inside of his eyeballs. Stranger than that was another feeling which came up through the soles of his feet; something he couldn't identify, powerful yet unformed, like somebody just out of earshot was trying to yell to him. The next day he drank some more.

The feeling through his feet was stronger. It wasn't a person who was yelling to him, it was a thing, or things. In the following days and weeks he dosed himself daily and began to realize that the things were the things of the factory. He was starting to feel the place through his feet and ears, sensing the shape of its rivets and girders, the vibrations of the wind through the empty places. The differences between the rustle of paper and the flap of tin became magnified into something as clear as Braille except that it required no learning. It came to him along with a sensitivity to minute changes in heat. Like a snake, he could tell when another creature was nearby by its body heat and how near it was by the amount of that heat. He fed himself by grabbing passing rats with snake-arm strikes and curing them in the stuff from the hole before he ate them.

He knew by the blood he coughed and the petrified feeling his insides were getting that it was killing him, but since he'd been dead to the world for some time, he deemed it a fair trade. The stuff was just making his death official, and in the process was giving him a power he had never had in life. He could see by feel better than he'd ever been able to see with his eyes, without color but with absolute positional precision. He felt that his new death was carrying him close to the sky rather than into the ground. He could remember things; how many people were on the *Titanic,* what the chances were of crashing in an airliner. And there was more. He was now past thinking. He knew things, things like why he was put on earth, why he'd made the choice he had, why at the end of his life it was going to be worth something.

Rees was the reason. He and the new ones like him who weren't on the streets because they'd decided to be but because the people on the other side of the river had decided it for them. They'd worked in the factories and bought their little row houses and sent their kids to their little schools, all the time knowing they were living small but thinking they were doing right. Then, in the space of a few years, their lives had been bought out from under them and trashed by the very poisons they made. Houses unsalable, middle-aged bodies unemployable, birthdays unenjoyable. Those were the new ones; on the streets with their whole families.

So they'd begun showing up at the factory. They knew it was condemned, but what else were they going to do? They were old city to the core and everything about the old city was condemned. They came in from the back where the houses now stood empty but guarded. At first the scum security service tried to run them off, but there was no way all those boys with new shoes and old prison tattoos were coming in where the water glowed. Without encouraging it, Bell had become a kind of advisor to the new ones. He'd lived in the factory longest and was able to tell them about every corner where they might find soft bedding and some warmth. Pretty soon they were staking claim to boiler rooms or offices and fixing them up as best they could with whatever they'd been able to carry on their way out of normal human life. After a time, the place had become like some kind of street-rat condo. Except the new ones didn't consider themselves street rats. They still thought they were people and tried to act like it, going out to look for work and trying not to look too disappointed when they came back.

It was inevitable that Bell would have to decide whether to tell them about the liquid. Rees was one of the first to get there and one of the smartest. A factory maintenance man, he'd lived in the shelters until he got wind that the social workers were planning to take his kids because his old lady was on the sauce. She'd taken to turning tricks and he'd taken off with the kids. It didn't take Rees long to follow Bell to the cistern. Bell warned him, but Rees said it must be the dose that caused the blindness. Bell asked him what about his new old lady whom he'd met while scrounging a junkyard for old car seats. That stopped him for a while, but then the shooter had started coming; not often at first, but then more often. When it got to once a month, Rees had told Bell that he had to have some of the stuff. What were they going to do, call the cops? Even if they believed it, they weren't about to spend any time staking out Industrial Island. Their answer would be to kick everyone the hell out. Rees said they were probably all dying from just being around the stuff, so it was only a question of degree. It was the end of the line but it was home. People were having babies there. Someone had to do something.

So Bell had mixed the stuff down with whiskey and fed it to some rats until they found a mixture that didn't kill them instantly or blind them. And Rees drank it. He kept on drinking it until he started to feel the place the same way Bell could. Like Bell, he knew it was accelerated death, but in the process of dying he became part of his surroundings. He often thought that the stuff was burying him into the ground where it lay before he even died and that was why he could feel everything like it was at the end of his fingers.

He could even feel across the river to where the new city was dying like the old one. They didn't know it yet, over there with their briefcases and suits, but they were dead. They didn't make anything but money. Rees didn't know much about money, but he knew the city and he could feel the emptiness at its center. He could put his hand on the ground at river's edge and feel the paper walls and subcode foundations laid by crews of cokeheads bossed by political nephews. He could feel the new city shake in the wind and know that it was afraid of the dark to come when the suits with the play money went to play somewhere else. He could see the empty offices staring at him, the mouths of the half-full parking lots gaping at him like hungry babies. He could feel the popcorn lightness of the monied but joyless young people who soaked in their flopsweat as they were blown down cracking streets by winds from Japan.

It wasn't imagination. It wasn't wishful thinking. It was sight and feel and smell. Others on the island had begun to drink the stuff and they all confirmed it. They would look at each other and nod when they heard the tunnel under the river groan like a distended gut. It was all dying; killed by people like the shooter.

"He's on his way now," said Bell. "I think he's on his way right now."

"You're right," answered Rees. "I felt the light shift in his office as he left."

"And when it shifted?"

"He gave it that special bounce he gets when he comes here."

"That poor sonofabitch. How dead does your life have to be to get off on something like this?"

"Oh, I don't know," said Rees. "I think I'm going to get off on it a little."

"Proves my point exactly." They both laughed, Bell coughing up more blood than Rees.

Rhodes felt the thrill strongest now, just like when you see a girl naked for the first time and know she's going to be yours in only a minute, or however long you want to stretch it. He looked down the legs of his silver jumpsuit to where his feet squished through some kind of slimy green shit. No telling what it would do to him if he didn't have the suit, but no problem. Some people had the suits, some didn't. That's life.

He'd paid off Zeke at the gate and walked up the old

asphalt road to the big square where the trucks used to back up to the loading docks. He stopped, put the Weatherby to his shoulder, and looked through the sniper scope. It was a moonless night, but he could see the old buildings outlined perfectly in a kind of grainy green. The last time out he'd bagged a woman as she tried to scoot around a corner of the plant manager's office. It had been a hell of a shot, nailed her through the shoulder and had to finish her off with one through the head. The poor bitch was covered with some kind of sores. He'd turned her over with his foot before he finished her and she'd looked up at him like she thought her life was worth something. Jeez, he'd done her a favor. He never left them wounded, no matter where he had to follow them.

Nothing at the manager's office. He scanned left and then right, slowly right toward a holding shed, and then a sliver of light. Yes. One of them heading around the corner. On the dead run he hit the corner of the shed and stopped. Once a wino had clipped him with a rock as he rounded a corner. Rhodes took a step out and pointed the Weatherby . . . no one there, but that flash of light again up ahead on the loading dock, running toward a door. He sighted and fired.

Rees touched the loading dock wall and felt the vibration as the shooter's cheek hit the stock of his rifle. He ducked as the bullet slammed into the wall above his head, then leapt through a glassless window frame. He could feel the footsteps following him, could feel them as though they were walking on the bottoms of his own feet. When he got to the opposite end of the long room, he reached up and put his hand on the broken end of an old water pipe. He could feel microscopic puffs of air hitting his hand at a rapid rate. The shooter was breathing heavily, thirty, thirty-five a minute, not in as good a shape as he ought to be. Maybe never had to work this hard. Or maybe just excited by the chase.

* * *

Christ this was great, a lot like fucking but maybe better, on your own, no one to satisfy but yourself. The guy was leading him a chase. Must be a young one. Good. The young ones were usually too smart to come out at night. He sighted through the scope as the guy went through the door, but it wasn't a good angle. He pulled the rifle down and followed, thankful for the two sessions of squash he'd played that week.

Rees was through the door and heading down a long hall. He ran with his fingertips pressed against the wall, feeling for the vibration of stock against cheek, but it didn't come. The shooter was slow getting into the hall, so Rees waited, a step from the door at the other end. When he saw the silver suit, he stood flat against the door, a perfect target, and as gun came up to cheek he saw the man's heavy breathing pull his right elbow down. The shot would go wide to Rhodes's right. Rees stepped aside and raised a hand to catch a splinter that flew off the doorframe as a bullet slammed into it. Then he stepped through the door onto a metal grate and began clambering down a series of rusting ladders. At the bottom of the second one he stopped to spit out a mouthful of bloody phlegm. He ripped a piece of flaking skin from his palm. The exertion was accelerating the rotting effect of the liquid, but as he placed his raw palm against one of the ladder's rungs he felt rust sift slowly into his blood, too slowly. The shooter had stopped. He was hesitant to come down the ladder. Rees smeared some of the blood from his palm against the ladder and made a wounded sound in his throat.

Never leave them wounded. That was the rule. He'd pulled it to the right in the hallway but the bastard must have been hit by a ricochet. Nothing to do now but go down the ladder.

He sighted through the scope first, looking for a knife, wishing for a pistol. The Weatherby was awkward in tight spaces. Seeing nothing, he fired a shot down the ladder just in case and went down, remembering that it was just dangerous enough to be fun. When he got to the bottom, he pulled out a flashlight and looked around. Blood on the ladder. He had hit the bastard. Only one way he could have gone from here. Nothing to do but go down the next ladder.

When Rees got to the bottom of the third ladder, he turned and ran into a concrete tunnel for twenty yards, turned right into another tunnel and waited. The air was cold. It moved in planes, the molecules in flux like dust motes in light. But there was no light. He was twenty feet underground, under the old mixing vats, in the drain where the toxins were flushed into the river. The shooter would have the scope and a flashlight. But the scope would be dim in the nonlight and he'd have to put down the light to fire his rifle. Rees had the city. He could hear power lines burning with electrons outside in the dirt. He could feel the tunnel sag miles away as cars crossed under the night. He felt the wind blow against the old-town suspension bridge, causing its foundations to pull against the joints of the sewer line. He felt the bridge's solidity forcing the river away toward the glass towers on the other side. The water was eating away at the new shore, but no one over there saw it. Rees placed his tumorous back against the tunnel and felt the city breathe in slow expansion that stressed the concrete like the flexing of a muscled arm. He had the city. He edged down the tunnel to a door and waited.

Jesus, it was so dark that, even through the night scope, all Rhodes could see was a kind of underwater green blur. He took a flashlight out of a pocket on the side of his silver pants and pressed the button. A beam of light cut through the damp air, but the darkness was so absolute that the effect was more like drilling a hole than turning on a light. He could see where he pointed the beam but nothing to either side of it. As a result his eyes tended to follow the play of light rather than what was at its end. He had to force himself to look for his quarry. For a brief instant he considered turning back, but he never left them wounded. That was the rule and somewhere at the bottom of himself he was certain that to duck a self-imposed rule would change him forever. He'd begin to think of himself as ordinary, and in so doing might become ordinary. He was Roger Rhodes. He followed no one's rules but his own, but those he followed to the letter. Hell, what could happen? The sonofabitch was wounded, probably losing blood, it would be nothing but target practice. All he had to do was find him. He played out the beam in a slow circular motion and moved down the tunnel, balancing the rifle's stock in the crook of his left arm, his right hand on the trigger. Jesus it was dark. There! A shadow. Rhodes dropped to his knee and raised the rifle. Sighting through the scope he saw that it was nothing but a right angle where the tunnel turned. He lowered the rifle again and moved toward it, smiling grimly, his breath quickening.

He was coming. Rees saw the tunnel of light reflecting off the adjacent wall in a rhythm he knew the shooter couldn't detect. But Rees could judge the man's step by the swing of the light. He could feel the heightened breathing in the slight spray of light as the beam hit the wall but wouldn't stay focused. He knew by the cone of darkness to the shooter's left that he was carrying the rifle in the crook of that arm; unconsciously sure that he was protected in that direction. Rees edged down the hall to a door at the end. He knocked softly and placed his hand on the knob.

*   *   *

What was that? A bump, three of them, not more than thirty, forty feet around the corner. He had the bastard now. It had been fun, but now the party was almost over. Christ, the fucker was probably passed out from blood loss, probably hit his head on something as he fell, or was trying to find a way out, trying to climb the walls. Why did they always try to get away, like it meant something to spend another day in the shit that was their lives? Instinct, he guessed. They couldn't help it. Rhodes quickened his step, hit the wall with his back as he got to the turn, held the flashlight along the Weatherby's stock, and jumped into the next tunnel, landing in a shooter's crouch.

Rees saw the beam coming, straight ahead, no play, on the tip of the rifle, saw it hit above the top of the door, knew by its momentum it would swing across and come back on him, so he waited. When the light hit him, he looked up for the instant of shock he knew would enter the shooter's brain and then slipped through the door just ahead of the bullet.

Goddamn the guy was quicker than he expected, but it was getting close. Rhodes chambered another round and rushed the door. When he got there, he could tell in a glance it swung inward, so he kicked the rickety bastard open and jumped through the opening . . . and was struck in each eye by a solid bar of light that traveled back through his optic nerve and hit him in the back of the head with a rocket of blindness. The pain would have dropped him to his knees, but something was supporting him under each arm.

As Rees and another man held the 200-watt floodlights an inch from each of the shooter's eyes, four others seized him

under each arm, held him while Rees got the gun, held him
tighter as Rees put the gun to his head and told him not to
struggle.

It was dark again and they had him. With his own gun to
his head they were dragging him across a room. He could feel
his heels scraping cement. They pulled him upright and sat
him in a chair, at least six of them. They stank like the river.
No one had said anything. Maybe they weren't going to kill
him. Maybe they didn't know he was the one who'd been
coming for them. He could tell them he was a cop hired to
look into it, or a private detective, or some kind of security
guard hired by the owner.

"You're the shooter," he heard a parched voice say. "We
want you to see something."

When they turned on the lights, Rhodes almost vomited
into the hood of his decontamination suit. He was looking at
two moving death masks. They were white as the moon, hair
gone, except for errant strands growing wild like stalks in a
burned-out cornfield. Patches of skin were peeling off their
cheeks in translucent sheets, and the faces seemed to leak
blood—small trickles of it were oozing from the corners of
their mouths. Blood was also seeping from the arms of these
people, dripping out like oil through cheesecloth. It soaked
through the garbage surplus they wore and crusted on the
arthritic knobs of their long-nailed hands. He could see it
smeared on the silver sleeves of his suit. But it was the eyes.
Jesus, it was the eyes that made his hair begin to stand.

The eyes were alive, as separately alive as if they'd come
from somewhere out of the sky or ground to hold the ruined
bodies upright with their power. The older man's pair were
completely and inhumanly black—iris, pupil, and what used
to be white, all black. They shone like diamonds recom-
pressed into gem-coal. Moving in their flaking sockets like

snakes, they struck at his face from every angle. The younger man's eyes had reversed. The whites now black, the center now ice white. Rhodes felt like their eyes were turning him inside out. He gagged and felt feverish. It was hot in the room, and not because of his silver suit, because the men at his side were stripping it off him. He could feel the sticky air against his skin.

"I'm not who you want," he said. "The owner heard about the shootings and sent me to look into it. The police wouldn't help so he—"

"You're the shooter," said the older one. "My name's Bell and I know you. I've known you for a long time, but I couldn't do anything about you, 'cause I'm too old."

The old man was blind. That accounted for the distant shine, but the black . . . "I'm not, really—"

"Cut the shit," said the old one. "I know you."

"No! I'm not. How could you? You're blind."

"The heat," he said. "Everybody's got a heat shape. I saw it the first time you were here. I saw it again across the river."

Rhodes jerked backward in the chair. "No, no. That's not possible."

"You ever heard of infrared, you dumb fuck?" asked the younger one with the reverse eyes.

Panicked now, Rhodes looked from one captor to the other. The old one leaned closer. Rhodes retreated as far as the chair would allow. "I can see the fear," the old one said. "You're scared out of your britches right now, and you oughta be. You been comin' out here and killin' us like we were rats. That's what we were to you: rats. But now we gotcha. Don't we?" The old man laughed and coughed. Rhodes retched again as what looked like a blob of bloody lung landed at his feet.

"Makes you sick, huh asshole?" the young one sneered.

"What . . . what are you going to do?" asked Rhodes. "You know if I don't come out, the security men will come looking for me."

"Shit," said the old man. "Those parolees wouldn't come in here even if they *liked* you."

"You're ours," said the young one. "You're completely ours. How does it feel?"

What Rhodes felt was a loosening in his bowels. Oh God. The thought of crapping himself frightened him more than anything that had been said. That couldn't happen. It couldn't. "Go ahead," he said. "Do what you're going to. Let's get it over with."

"Okay," said the young one, and the men at his sides lifted him from the chair and half-dragged him across the room to the edge of what looked like a large sump hole. "Look down," said the voice in his ear, and when he did, what he saw was a narrow well full of a silvery glowing substance with the elusive shimmer of mercury. He thought in a moment of frozen panic that they were going to throw him in the stuff, but then he realized it was too narrow. "Rees is my name," said the young one. "And that stuff's the reason you couldn't hit me with the rifle. It's the reason Bell can see you even though he's blind. And it's the reason we look like we do."

Rhodes tried with some success to keep a tremor out of his voice. "I don't understand."

"We made a trade," said Rees. "Our lives for some dignity. We decided on dead power over live shit. You think we're shit, but we can see, smell, hear, and feel with far more intensity than you can."

"What do you mean?"

"I mean we drink the stuff, you dumb fucker, and it kills us. But while we're alive we're more than we were before, more than men. And just because you like to be around us so much, we're going to make you a member."

Before Rhodes could move or run, four of them had pushed him to the floor and had pinioned him there on his back, arms and legs outstretched, head bucking frantically, the indignity of the position worse than what might happen. But then he realized indignity was nothing compared to what was happening. Two men took his head in their scaly arms and held it while another pinched his nose shut, and then Rees appeared over him, a cup in his hand.

"We drink it," Rees said. "We drink it and get strong as we die. We go down as supermen instead of living garbage, and since you're already such a superman, we thought you'd appreciate this."

Rhodes twisted and fought and gagged and spit, but they only held his nose tighter and came back with more. In the end he was forced to swallow what must have been close to a cup of the silvery liquid. It was a cool fire expanding through his gut, and although he prayed it was his imagination, he thought that, somewhere near his liver, he could feel it begin to kill him.

Then they lifted him to his feet and Rees stood before him, bull's-eye eyes triumphant. "Now you're going to die, Mr. Rhodes," he said. "Just like you always were. Everybody dies. Did you forget that? No matter what score you keep or how far ahead you are, everybody dies. Now you're on the other side."

Rhodes didn't know he was crying until he felt the tears on his cheek. "Good God, you've killed me."

"That's what it feels like on the other side."

"What is it?" Rhodes asked, thinking maybe there was something he could take, something the best doctors anywhere could give him if he could just get to them in time. "What is it?"

"We don't even know," Rees answered. "But it makes you see, so see." He stepped back and raised his arms as though unveiling a statue.

Rhodes looked beyond the arms and saw why the place was so warm. It was a nursery. There were little watercolor pictures of bears and bunnies painted in crayon and stuck to the walls with tape. There were fifty-gallon drums filled with burning wood and vented to the outside with what looked like old car exhausts. There were broken bassinets scrounged from dumps and makeshift cribs made from car seats. As near as he could tell, there were over thirty of them. And now that his initial shock had worn off, he could hear the sound of crying—high-pitched but muffled wails, as though from heads covered by pillows.

"Come on," said Rees. "Look." Rhodes felt himself being shoved forward, toward the rows of bassinets. He didn't want to see anything. He could feel cancer growing inside him. "No more," he pleaded, but they pushed him forward. And what he saw caused him to forget what might now be growing inside him and stand in wonder, mouth open, nakedness forgotten. Before him, in rows, in their thrown-together cribs, attended by their half-dead mothers, were what looked like thirty miniature teenaged children. They were the size of babies, but their faces were old, fully developed, the eyes studying him with knowing maturity. Some of them had facial hair, little mustaches, the beginnings of beards or breasts. And when they cried, the sound seemed to come from far away, as though their vocal cords weren't new but old and worn from use. It was as if some tribe of headshrinkers had cut the heads off young adults and attached them to the bodies of babies, and it was the bodies that seemed to be protesting, forcing somatic distress signals through unwilling throats. Rhodes was unable to speak, unable to believe he wasn't dreaming.

"There's not a one of them over ten months old," said a voice from behind him. "They can spot their mothers at a mile. They can catch a fly out of the air. Some of them can write what they hear before they've learned to talk, and some of them have learned to talk." It was Bell who was speaking, but Rhodes couldn't look away. "By the time they're three they'll be able to see through walls. By the time they're ten they'll look like they're forty. And by the time they're twenty they'll be dead. I know. The stuff's inside me. It makes you know. You know too, don't you?"

Rhodes's knees buckled and they helped him back to the

chair. Bell leaned close, but what did it matter? Rhodes was on the verge of lapsing into a kind of catatonia when the old man slapped him hard across the face, leaving a smear of polluted blood on his cheek. "Listen, goddammit," Bell screamed. "Some of us have put ourselves down here, but others were sent by you and your kind across the river, where it's the future you're supposed to be making. Well right here is your future. Mutant babies who're born with a hate for you in their hearts and a power in their minds that'll bring that hate right into your guts. These people come out of the city, the real city that you thought you put on the shitpile. This is what we're makin' across the river from you fuckers in the suits and razor-blade smiles. This is the city, just as much as your half."

Bell leaned even closer. His breath smelled like formalde-hyde mixed with bleach. His skin smelled like a dead dog's ass. For a second, Rhodes thought the old man was going to kiss him, but instead he whispered, conspiratorially, in a hyp-notic rasp choked with blood, "We've sent out some people to other cities. With the power, and the death. And we'll die, but our babies will breed. We don't know what they'll be like, but their parents have the power, and the ones to follow may not need the liquid. They can track you by heat and find you by night and see you through the shape of the hate you cast through the daylight, and they'll kill you. If you try to wipe out this city, or drive them out of this last home, they'll come for you and kill you, and they'll always be watching, wherever you go, whatever you do. We're the city, whatever you've made of us. You have to live with us. You've cracked the world in two. You can try to put it back together or kill a half of it, but we've got the power of death: we don't care, got no place to go but straight to your heart, no place to run but straight to the grave. See us. Hear us when it's quiet in your office and you think the world's under control. Do something. Make something that feeds the city iron and steel instead of paper and promises. Give us something to think about except killin' you. And you got the chance, 'cause we're human even in our death. We're better than you are or deserve to be. That shit you drank was nothin' but a little Sterno mixed with vodka. A pussy like you will probably get nothing more than a bad hangover and some important memories."

The following morning, Roger Rhodes stood at his seventy-fifth-floor window looking through a pair of binoculars. He was staring down at the sidewalk below, where a bag lady browsed the trash cans. Suddenly he swung the binoculars up and out over the river. The green fog ghosted through the blackened iron as always. Shadow crosses still latticed the ground. Everything was as ever. But they must be there, he thought; there must be some sign, some movement. How could there be such an alien world with no sign, and why did he want to see it anyway? The old man had told him what he'd drunk was fake, so why look? Why the feeling that he had to look? Two sweeps through the fog with the binoculars and then he'd turn away, just two more sweeps and . . . Rhodes stumbled backward; a pain through his eyes like the binoculars contained spikes. "See us," he heard the old man say.

Rhodes walked shakily back to the window and looked down at the street again. The bag lady was still there. As if someone had tapped her on the shoulder, she looked up; and in an instant like the one between the beats of a wing, her eyes met his and the look burned down into his stomach with a familiar cool heat that spread through his body. The old man said what they'd given him was fake, but Rhodes knew. In that moment, from seventy-five floors up, he knew the woman on the street. Maybe the old man lied and he was really dying.

Rhodes dropped the glasses onto the carpet and went to his desk. "Janice," he said weakly into the intercom. "Bring me the files."

"What files, Roger?"

"All of them."

"I, uh, I don't know what you mean."

"I mean I want to see some sort of file on every one of our holdings."

"That will take some time to get together."

"Let's start, then, Janice," Rhodes said softly.

"Any particular areas you want to see first?"

Rhodes stared at the intercom, thinking of iron and steel, and time. "Yeah," he said. "Find a file on a company that makes something that strikes you as beautiful out of steel—beautiful, in any way you define that word. Find me something to make."

"Are you all right, Roger?"

"Just hurry," he said. "Hurry and I'll see."

AT THE END OF THE DAY

STEVE RASNIC TEM

"I honestly love city life," says Steve Rasnic Tem, *"but I think the city has a peculiar sort of dual nature in its encouragement of anonymity. I grew up in a very small Southern town, where everyone knew practically everything about everyone else. When I moved to the city, I became an unknown, an anonymous creature, which I greatly prefer. In anonymity, there is always this sense of opportunity and unlimited freedom—once you become known, then people start defining you, limiting you, and you have to force yourself not to hear those voices. This is the sort of thing I see in city faces. The other side, of course, is that a sense of community becomes tragically fragmented. Architects and planners try to create this community by building monuments, great stadiums, and auditoriums, which the populace is to be proud of, to take mutual pleasure in. But that's a rather pathetic substitute for community. After years of living in the city, I still can't get used to the fact that when there's an accident, or a crime, everyone doesn't just naturally leap in to help. And then there are street people—we had them in the small town where I grew up, but we knew them by name, we talked to them, fed and sheltered them. I can't remember ever pretending not to see one. That would seem to be a property of 'city eyes.' "*

Tem, forty, was born in Virginia and currently lives in Denver, with his wife, the writer Melanie Tem, and their four children. He's published many, many short stories, as well as the 1987 novel, Excavations. *In 1991 an English publisher will bring out a chapbook of five original*

Tem ghost stories, Absences: Charlie Goode's Ghosts, *and his first collection of short fiction will be published in France.*

At the end of the day Sam has one final package to deliver, a perfect cube a foot on a side wrapped so tightly in its heavy brown paper that not even a stray microbe could get in, and thinking this increases his sense of urgency more even than the bright red envelope marked URGENT affixed to the top of this package and containing the day's final, imperative and unequivocal message.

For hours Sam has searched his maps of the metropolitan area—maps so complete, complex, and expensive they remain unavailable to the average commuter—but he is still unable to find the address. Earlier calls to the dispatcher have confirmed that the address is a true address although the dispatcher herself—a voice soft, yet utterly convincing—cannot help him with its exact location. A thorough perusal of the twelve volumes of executed and planned revisions to the city's constantly changing street nomenclature and arrangement—stacked in order within his delivery van's oversized glove compartment—provides no significant clues, although there are sixteen similarly named streets, avenues, drives, places, courts, ways, and circles. Despite its apparent futility he has hunted down each one in the seemingly unlikely event that a mistake in address has been made.

By the end of the day all urgent packages and messages within the city limits (including extended suburbs) must be delivered. At the end of the day who can know what disaster might follow if such a delivery has failed to go through?

At the end of the day Sam wonders if there will ever be a time when his job ends at the end of the day. At the end of the day Sam is still driving his van up and down the same streets, endlessly circling the same routes where every day he delivers packages wrapped in plain brown paper to people who are rarely at home to accept them. Sam wonders, briefly, if any of these absent recipients might imagine that magic played a part in these timely, mysterious deliveries, but he admits to some difficulty crediting the average person with such imagination.

At the end of the day Sam tries to remember if his job has ever been any different than it was today. He began the job when he was eighteen, right out of high school, intent on earning a few dollars while he decided what his heart's work might be. Delivering the packages had been a game, and an opportunity to learn the routes which might some day lead into his future. His father had once told him that sometimes what you like to do has little relation to what you can get paid to do. Sam discovered times had changed—now it had almost no relation.

At the end of the day Sam dreams about an early-morning ambition he once had to be a poet. Now the dispatcher's soft but unerring patter is the poetry that fills him like alcohol: "Four thirty-two, four thirty-two, Park Avenue, Trader Bill's, four forty-four, Wilmott Square, three-two, three-two." But the dispatcher's voice faded out hours ago, and he is lost with his delivery, packing his lost message through the late after-noon, the message itself no doubt a longed-for poem, and his quest fit subject matter for poetry.

At the end of the day fatigue is a shadow-self just beginning to separate from his skin, adhering stubbornly to his body, waiting for the dying sun to change its color. Sam wonders what a sun the blue-gray color of death would do to the shape and texture of the human shadow. He suspects that it would do nothing, for the combination of polluted air and skyscrap-ers filtering the sun has already resulted in many blue-gray sunny days. And he has simply become used to these shadows whose tone and color remind him of the face of his grand-mother a few hours after her death.

Those shadows with legs stagger out of alleyways as if intent on stealing his package and plagiarizing his message, but he is highly skilled at the wheel, sailing around them so closely they spin so quickly that blood flies from their mouths like song.

At the end of the day shadows form with little resemblance to the objects casting them. Behind a street sign looms a giant, upraised fist. Bus benches front a broad torso broken in half. Corner streetlights hang below huge, shadowed eye sockets. The spaces between tall buildings are filled with gray, unfocused limbs attempting to crawl their way back into the roar of evening traffic. Now and then Sam vaguely recognizes a profile or a stance. Over the years he has known some of the men and women who built, formed, and poured these inhuman monuments. But as the pace of the day wears to its end, his sense of recognition fades, the transition into night making him an alien plying his vessel through the narrow lanes of fragmented landscape.

Out on the main streets there are few pedestrians, for this is rush hour and most have retreated to their cars for the long, anxious ride home. But he knows that there are those who cannot afford cars, who take to the sidewalks and the buses. There are those who cannot afford homes, who cannot afford even a shadow, and who look exactly the way their missing shadows would look. Gray and smudged as if they had struggled against erasure. These people live in the alleys and doorways and under the bridges, where countless shadows collect. There they blend together and blend with the night. Sometimes streetlights send them running, but few of the streetlights work downtown. The city does not pay its bills.

Someone else is unable to return home at the end of the day, he knows, someone trapped in an office positioned awkwardly between dead streetlights, anxiously awaiting the arrival of the urgent package Sam has been ferrying through every section of the city. His client is late. Sam is even later. But far later still, he suspects, is the city itself, changing its names and hiding from its tired messengers.

At the end of the day he thinks about his children, and how they must anticipate his arrival. How the three of them will line up at the base of the stairs as he enters the front door, each with a question, a request, or the gift of today's story. It is the stories he likes best, and he will devote the most time to these, the daily retellings of how the world is both the same and constantly changing, perspectives he misses on his repetitive routes delivering messages and packages across the city. The questions are sometimes almost as interesting, inquiries as to the nature of life, the world, and the end of the day. He seldom has answers—his life as deliveryman having limited his insights—but the questions make all of them think, and it is his children thinking that he prizes above all else. The requests are seldom true requests but merely excuses for talking; having been filled by the endless chatter of hot exhaust expanding and contracting metal all day, he is more than happy to listen to his children's aimless talk.

Awaiting a change of light he stares down at the package also waiting, resting solidly across his right front seat. At the end of the day he again wonders why he never looks inside the packages he delivers, why he never reads the messages. There is always ample time for such surreptitious activity. With the current volume of traffic no one really expects him to deliver either packages or messages on time. And yet so many are marked URGENT. So many, he is told, must be delivered by the end of the day.

In fact, he has long suspected that the messages he delivers are never very urgent, for if they were his clients would use the telephone or the fax machine. He has wondered if, rather, what he delivers are scattered moments of contact, simple statements of existence from random citizens to other random citizens, with the unpredictability of his delivery times an essential part of the message. During holiday seasons there are always many more such messages to deliver. He sometimes considers inserting his own messages into his deliveries for random distribution, but thus far has not had the courage.

But at the end of the day the particular package in question seems much more than this. At the end of the day his final message seems an essential delivery. At the end of the day it seems the job he took on after high school has all come down to this. He can feel his van deteriorating, bolts and washers and scattered bits of metal dropping off from the stress of his final delivery.

At the end of end of at the end of the rat a tat tat tat . . .

At the end of the day he wonders what his wife is cooking for dinner. The traditional role she has taken in their lives has always made him feel guilty, but although he has attempted to convince her many times to continue her career, she has adamantly declined, preferring the company of their children with their endless supplies of questions, requests, and stories. In recent years his attempts to get her out of the house have been rare. At the end of the day he envies her place in their home.

He suspects his wife could have done his job better. He suspects his wife would have delivered this package by the end of the day. She has always been far more controlled than he, far more organized.

He maneuvers his van through city divisions which seem to vary greatly in climate. The poorer sections of the urban sprawl always seem colder. At times he switches on his heater. After a few blocks a quick change to the air conditioner engenders a whine of stress in the engine compartment behind the thin metal wall in front of his knees.

At the end of the day various city walls are coming down, some at the express instructions of the city fathers, instructions he himself had delivered on earlier days when he managed to get all messages and packages out before the end of the day. But there are always those which crumble unexpectedly, leaving piles of rubble with which his van must dance.

At the end of the day the various models of automobile seem to regress, as if the day's passage has taken years off the streetscape. The foreign cars are the first to disappear. Ancient Fords and Studebakers fill the poorly paved roads. The bordering buildings warp their architectures in the twilight, as if shifting in earthquake trauma or melting beneath the last rays of a thermonuclear sun. A rain of darkness pours down across his windows. A layer of memory disappears each time the blades wipe across the windshield. Half-forgotten faces fold and gather in the gutter line. The streets along the edge of darkness become a litany of all that has been lost and that he is likely to lose.

At the end of the day the pavement begins releasing its heat and the air loses its color a small portion at a time. Darkness fills all empty spaces and someone remembers to turn the stars on. He sometimes wonders if that someone can go home now, his or her job completed. For himself, he still has this one more delivery, one more package and message he cannot make himself forget, perched patiently on the front seat of his van.

In the darkness, familiar directions become untrustworthy dreams. New street signs appear, providing a fresh supply of obstacles. Shadows spread and ignore their loyalties. He sticks his head out the driver's-side window and attempts to find his way by smell. In the past he has been good at smelling despair and hunger and the locations of those waiting long hours to receive a delivery.

When the light dims at the end of the day it always seems a sudden event, even though the sun may have been sinking or the clouds rolling in for hours. But beyond his consideration the day is suddenly gray or amber, depending upon the time of the year, and he feels a strain in his eyes as they attempt to see all the details they are used to seeing. He feels dangerous driving a vehicle at such times, and is surprised at the end of the day to find that he has failed to run over any of the shadows.

The deepening night is like black snowfall, a mass of dark flakes carved from the giant ball waiting at the end of the day, the flakes gathering first in the corners and hiding places of the world, finally filling up the very air he breathes. Every morning he has breathed it out again, but a sooty residue of the previous night always remains inside him, in his heart and blood, in his thoughts and the words he uses.

He does not believe anyone would mind his peeking inside the package. He cannot believe anyone would deny him his right to know the final message. But he must hurry, he thinks, and decide what he must do, for the address scrawled on the bright red envelope might suddenly appear at any time.

But at the end of the day time passes slowly. Each block is longer and the intervals between lights stretch out lazily. He remembers all the dead ones, the ones who were former lovers, family members, even the dead strangers named by the newspapers. He can almost see them fleeing the headlights. At the end of the day he speculates about what their lives have become. At the end of the day he can feel the shadow of their fatigue in his hands clutching the steering wheel.

At the end of the day the lines of the streets disappear and he follows the final sparks of head- and tail-lights into the night. Static fills all positions on his radio. He drives through a landscape of black birds, thousands of birds gathered under his wheels, no light to reflect their colors or everyday shapes, wings overlapping until they are one solid, mobile mass rocking his van with their movements. He drives through a landscape of broken trees, their ragged ends scratching at the night. He drives through a landscape of window frames and door frames, their buildings transparent and filled with black.

At the end of the day he imagines that somewhere else, beyond the limited vision his windshield provides, events of terrible beauty are taking place. Faces are melting and hair is burning. Somewhere beyond his vision his children's lives are turning to smoke. In his undelivered package he believes there must be revelations about the causes of such events. In his unopened message there may be instructions concerning what to do at the end of the day. At the end of the day he will have no one to tell him stories, no one to make requests, no one to speak the orders.

Sam opens a window to feel the dark air, and his fingers come away raw and blistered at the end of the day so that he can barely grasp the steering wheel.

And yet there is still this one more delivery to make, one more service to perform. As his route stretches out into darkness the lights in the houses dim to amber, then fade to black. Body heat escapes through open windows and chimneys, causing the neon signs to burn noticeably brighter. At the end of the day the city burns its citizens for the fuel that keeps the buildings tall, the concrete rigid, that prevents the asphalt from melting into a viscous sea. Sometimes there are power failures. Sometimes the tires on his van adhere to the road, making this final delivery more difficult at the end of the day.

At the end of the day all the customers have forgotten their orders. At the end of the day there is no one left to receive his package. His message is written in a forgotten language. There are no more tongues wrapped around difficult communications. In the empty streets there are no more tongues. The windows of the stores are grimed. Abandoned cars join together into metallic reefs to block his passage. At the end of the day all the vessels lie empty. At the end of the day torn scraps of paper, discarded messages, litter the plazas and lawns. At the end of the day everything sleeps. There is nothing else to do at the end of the day.

In the dark faraway he hears his wife and children calling him. His shift should be over by now, they tell him. He should be coming home. But at the end of the day there are very few roads fit for travel. At the end of the day he has lost his name. At the end of the day he cannot find his way home.

But at least he knows he still has his unopened package. At least at the end of the day he can imagine its contents. He can recite the poetry of its unopened message. Because it is urgent. Because it is essential. And because it is all that he has.

THE ASH OF MEMORY, THE DUST OF DESIRE

POPPY Z. BRITE

Poppy Z. Brite's tale: "When I was very young, in New Orleans, my family used to take me to the French Quarter on weekends. My father was interested in magic, and we would go into all the voodoo shops. In one shop—a particularly little, dark one back at the end of a winding French-quarter alley—there was a skeleton in a glass case. The skeleton frightened and fascinated me. I remember having dreams in which it would sit up from its case, smiling like a dear friend. This memory made such an impression on me that I wrote a story about it. But after that, I asked both my parents about the place. They both remembered the shop perfectly, but said there had been no skeleton in a glass case. Did I make up that detail? Or (improbable) was I the only one who noticed it?"

Brite, who was born in 1967 and spent her early years in New Orleans, now lives in Athens, Georgia, with her cats. Her short stories have appeared in The Horror Show, Borderlands, *and* Women of Darkness II. *She has been nominated for a Bram Stoker Award.*

Once, I thought I knew something about love.

Once, I could stand on the roof of the tallest skyscraper in the city and look out across the shimmering candyscape of

nighttime lights without thinking of what went on down in
the black canyons between the buildings: the grand melo-
dramatic murders, the willful and deliberate hurt, the com-
monplace pettiness. To live is to betray. But why do some
have to do it with such pleasure?

Once, I could look in the mirror and see the skin of my
throat not withered, the hollows of bone not gone blue and
bruised around my eyes.

Once, I could part a woman's legs and kiss the juncture like
I was drinking from the mouth of a river, without seeing the
skin of the inner thighs gone veined and livid, without smelling the salt scent and the blood mingled like copper and
seawater.

Once, I thought I knew something about love.

Once, I thought I wanted to.

Leah met me in the bar at the Blue Shell. It was six o'clock,
just before dinnertime, and my clothes were still streaked with
the dill-cream soup and Dijon dressing we had served at
lunch. The fresh dill for the soup had come on a truck that
morning, in a crate, packed secure between baby carrots and
dewy lettuces. I wondered how many highways it had to
travel between here and its birthplace, how many miles of
open sky before the delivery man lugged it up to the twenty-
first floor of the posh hotel. "The Blue Shell on Twenty-one"
read the embossed silver matchbooks the busboys placed on
every table, referring not to avenue number but to floors
above street level. Way up here they kept it air-conditioned,
carefully chilled . . . except in the heart of the kitchen, where
no amount of circulated air could compete with the radiant
heat of a Turbo Ten-Loaf bread oven. In addition to the residue of lunch, I felt sheathed in a layer of dry sweat like a dirty
undershirt gone wash-gray with age.

The bar on ground floor was as cool as the rest of the hotel,
though, and Leah was cool too. As cool as the coffee cream

when I took it out of the refrigerator first thing every morning. For her appointment today she had dressed carefully, in the style affected by all the fashionable girls this year. Leah was one of the few who could get away with it: her calves were tight and slender enough for the clunky shoes and the gaudy, patterned hose, her figure spare enough for the sheath-snug, aggressively colored (or, for a very special occasion, jet black) dresses, the planes of her face sufficiently delicate to sport the modified beehive hairdo, swept up severely in front, but with a few long strands spiraling carefully down the back. "There was a long waiting line," she told me, toying with the laces of her shoestring bodice. I imagined her sitting in one of the anonymous chairs at the clinic, hugging herself the way she did when she was defensive or less than comfortable—an unconscious gesture, I was sure. My cool Leah would never have chosen to do something that so exquisitely exposed her own vulnerability.

I was supposed to feel guilty. I was supposed to feel neglectful because I hadn't been able to get anyone to work lunch for me; thus I had sent fragile Leah into a dangerous situation unprotected, into a situation of possible pain without the male stability she craved. Something in me cringed at the accusation, as if on cue. Until now I had only sipped at the boilermaker I'd ordered; now I drank deeply, and was vaguely surprised to see it come away from my lips half-drained. The taste was good, though, the sour tangy beer washing down and the sweet mash of the whiskey lingering. Bushmills. The kitchen staff drank free after getting off a shift, and the bar brands were damn tasty.

"They hurt me," she said next. "I don't see why I had to have a pelvic. Jilly didn't have to have a pelvic when she went to her private doctor. They just tested her pee, and when they called her on the phone later, the nurse already had an appointment set up for her."

"Jilly's boyfriend designs software," I told her. "Jilly can afford to see a private doctor."

"Yes, but listen." She spoke excitedly, mouthing her words around the various straws and skewers they'd put in her drink. She drank fruity, frothy stuff, drinks you couldn't taste the alcohol in, drinks that more properly belonged on a dessert plate with a garnish of whipped cream. A dark red maraschino cherry bobbed against her lips. "Cleve went with me today. He says he's got some money saved up from his last gallery show. If you help too, I'll have enough. I can have the operation at a private doctor's office—the clinic's going to call and make me an appointment." Her hand set her drink down on the bar, found mine, tightened over it.

I noticed the way she said *operation* before I thought of anything else. Casual, with no more pain in the twist of her mouth than if she were saying *new dress* or *boyfriend* or *fuck*. Like something she was used to having, that she couldn't get used to the idea of not having whenever she wanted it. It wasn't until my next swallow of whiskey that I registered the name she'd spoken.

"Cleve went with you?"

Again the casual twist of the lips, not quite a smile. "Yes, Cleve went. You couldn't get off work. I didn't feel like doing it alone."

I remembered standing in the kitchen two days ago, slicing a carrot into rounds and then chopping the rounds into quarters. I kept my eyes fixed on the big wooden cutting block, on the knife slicing through the crisp orange meat of the carrot, but in the corner of my vision I could see Cleve twisting his battered old hat in his hands. Between his long fingers, the hat was like an odd scrap of felt. Cleve's hands were large enough to fit easily around my throat; Cleve stood a head and a half taller than me, and his arms might have been strong enough to throw me half the length of the kitchen. But I knew he would let me kick his ass if I wanted to. If I was hurting so bad that I wanted to pound his head against the floor or punch him in the face until his blood ran, then he was prepared to let me. That was how deep his guilt went. And that was how bad he still wanted Leah.

"I can't work for you Wednesday," he'd told me. "Any other day I'd do it, you know that. I've got to see this gallery owner, it's been set up for weeks."

He wouldn't meet my eyes. I thought he was just upset at the idea of me having to run the kitchen alone, having to make the thousand little decisions that go with the lunch rush while all the time I worried about Leah . . . imagining her getting off the bus at the last stop before the clinic, having to walk through blocks of the old industrial district. Other parts of the city were more dangerous, but to me the old factories and mills were the most frightening places. The places where abandoned machinery sat silent and brooding, and twenty-foot swaths of cobweb hung from the disused cogs and levers like dusty gray curtains. The places that everyone mostly stayed away from, mostly left alone with the superstitious reverence given all graveyards. But once in a while something would be found in the basement of a factory or tucked into the back room of a warehouse. A head, once, so badly decomposed that no one could ever put a face to it. The gnawed bones and dried tendons and other unpalatable parts of a wino, jealously guarded by a pack of feral dogs. This was where the free clinic was; this was where certain doctors set up their offices, and where desperate girls visited them.

And while Leah was making her way through this blasted landscape, while I was slicing goat cheese for the salads or making a delicate lemon sauce to go over the fresh fish of the day, Cleve would be ensconced in some art gallery far uptown. I pictured it like the interior of a temple: lavish brocade and beaded curtains, burning sachets of sandalwood and frankincense, carpet lush and rich enough to silence even the tread of Cleve's steel-toed cowboy boots. There Cleve would be, kicking back in some cool dim vast room, trying to say the right things about the colorful paintings that came from some secret place in his brain, about the sculptures he shaped into

being with the latent grace of his big hands. I liked the idea
of Cleve bullshitting some spotless hipper-than-thou gallery
owner, someone who attended the right parties to see and be
seen, someone who had never been to the old industrial district or any of the rough parts of town except for a quick
slummy thrill, someone who never got mustard all over his
shirt or scalded his hands in hot dishwater.

But Cleve hadn't been bullshitting anyone except me.

Leah extricated her hand from mine and adjusted the hem
of her skirt over her knee. Her fingernails were painted the
cool blue of a blemishless autumn sky; her movements were
guarded and deliberate. I caught the glimmer of her frosted
eyelids, but in the semidarkness of the bar I could not see her
eyes.

I took a long drink of my boilermaker. Warm rancid beer;
the flat taste of whiskey settling spiderlike over my tongue.

One of Cleve's passions was his collection of jazz and blues
records, most of them the original pressings. No digital
techno-juju or perfect plastic sound, just the old cardboard
sleeves whose liner notes told the stories of entire lives. Just
the battered vinyl wheels that could turn back time and rekin-
dle desire, just the dark sorghum voices. Billie and Miles, Duke
and Bird . . . and more obscure ones. "Titanic" Phil Alvin, Peg
Leg Howell. I had given him a bunch of them, and he knew
I loved them too. One night he willed them to me over a case
of Dixie beer. (Cleve had made a special trip to New Orleans
when the Dixie brewery finally closed, and there were still a
few cases stashed in his studio closet; I had helped him drink
another five or six.) "Jonny, if I got jumped by a goddamn kid
gang on my way home—" he paused to light a Chesterfield
"—or if I walked in front of a bus or something, you'd have
to take 'em, man." He gestured around the room at a series of
little jewel-box watercolors he was doing at the time. "My
paintings could go their own way—shit, they can take care of
themselves. But you have to take the records. You're the only
one who loves 'em enough."

The records were Cleve's sole big indulgence. The rest of his extra money went to buy paints and canvas and an occasional luxury like groceries. He never collected them out of any kind of anal retentiveness, any desire to possess and catalog. It was just the feel of good heavy vinyl in the hands, the fragrant dust that sifted from the corners of the dog-eared cardboard, the music that spun you back to some grand hotel ballroom where you danced beneath a crystal chandelier . . . or some smoky little dive renting space in the basement of a whorehouse. The records were magic rabbit holes that led to the past, to a place where there was still room for romance. And I loved them as much as Cleve did.

And right then, in that moment at the bar as Leah withdrew her hand from mine, I could have taken a hammer and smashed the records all to bits.

We walked the four blocks from the hotel to the train tunnel half-staggering, almost drunk off our one drink apiece. Leah had not eaten because of her appointment; I, after wracking my brain to concoct delicious menus day after day, could hardly eat at all. Forsaking a free dinner at the Blue Shell meant we would go to bed hungry. Our refrigerator at home was empty of all but the last parings of our life together: an old rind of cheese on the shelf, a vegetable or two that neither of us would ever cook withering in the drawer, a flask of vodka I had stashed in the freezer.

As we left the hotel behind, the street grew shabbier. The buildings along here were old row houses of brick and wood, once fashionable, now unrenovated and nearly worthless. Children and teenagers sat on some of the stoops, hardness aging their faces, their grim eyes urging us past. Most unnerving were the houses that stood vacant: I could not imagine what face would look out from the dirty darkness behind the windows. Leah pulled my arm around her. I felt her skin and muscles moving under the thin dress. I thought of that strength moving with me, around me, like snakes wrapped in cool velvet. We had not had sex in three weeks, had not made love in so much longer than that. Whenever I was not with either Cleve or Leah, I imagined them together, drowning in ecstasy, dying their little deaths into each other.

Cleve had told me first, as soon as he realized that Leah didn't intend to. Away from the kitchen, away from work, in a neutral bar with a fresh beer in front of me, he confessed in a hesitant voice, telling me what a dumbfuck he was and how anyway there was only *lust* between them, no love, not seeing how that would hurt the worst. He bought me another beer before I finished my first one. Maybe he just wanted to know where both of my hands were.

Leah was in bed but not asleep when I went home. She'd heard me coming up the stairs and fumbling with my key, and rolled over when I came in. Some nights she slept naked; tonight she was wearing something as sheer and weightless as ectoplasm. I saw the line of her shoulder silhouetted in filmy silver-white, somehow more erotic than the curve of her hip or breast. I sat on the edge of the bed.

"I waited up for my story," she said. It was our custom for me to tell her a tale before we fell asleep at night: sometimes just a shred of hotel gossip or a memory from childhood, sometimes a dream, one of the plans I only told her and Cleve, one of my schemes to get away from the kitchen and into a grander, larger, more leisurely world. These were made of the finest ego-spun gossamer and collapsed in the telling; nonetheless it was pleasurable to tell her, like placing a drop of my heartblood on her lips.

"I'm not telling you a story tonight," I said. "Tonight it's your turn."

She didn't move then, only looked up at me with her eyes dark in the darkness of the room: she knew I knew. And four weeks later she finally came up with a story to tell me in return for all the ones I'd given her. She was carrying a living, breathing, bloodsucking piece of meat inside her, and it might be Cleve's meat, and it might be mine.

* * *

Leah always liked to feel passive when she had sex. No, it wasn't just that she *liked* to: she *needed* to feel passive, needed to feel she was being acted upon. I could kiss her anywhere, manipulate her knees and elbows and the strong curve of her back, pretend she was a department-store mannequin I was posing for some pornographic window display. She would press her face into a pillow and whimper, enjoying the power of pretended helplessness. I could dine on her tangy juices all night if I wished, I could stay inside her as long as I pleased, come when I wanted to. Only when I asked her what *she* wanted would Leah get angry. She had to be the little girl; she had to have someone take control.

Not on the morning of her operation. I woke in the still, stuffy light of predawn, unsure what had caused me to surface. I thought I had heard a distant sound, something separate from the intermittent cacophony of voices and sirens that punctuated the night. A train whistle miles away, or a telephone ringing in a far-off room.

Then, before I even knew Leah was awake, she sat up and in one liquid movement was straddling me. I had not felt her body close to mine in so long that it startled me into immobility. Even when I pressed up against the urgent sharpness of her nipples, up into the syrupy heat of her crotch, I wasn't ready.

She tensed above me. In the waxing light I saw surprise on her face, and faint annoyance. She began to grind against me. In the unfamiliar position I could not think how to respond. Leah hardly ever got on top—maybe five or six times in the three years we had been together. It didn't fit her penchant for being acted upon, and it played up the fact that she was almost as tall as me. She had told me that one of the things she liked best about Cleve was his bigness. His hands could enfold hers as if her hands were baby birds. Her bones felt more delicate when she pressed them against the solid bulk of him.

My overactive imagination served me up plenty of Leah-and-Cleve snapshots, plenty of inevitable intimate moments, generous helpings of feverish speculation. I was helpless to push these out of my mind once they held sway, but that was not the worst thing about them.

The worst thing about them was that occasionally—usually when I was feeling low and tired and ugly—these thoughts would give me a moment of masochistic excitement.

I thought of Leah's flower-stem spine pressed flush against Cleve. I thought of him kneeling above her, his back covering hers, his big hands cupping the tender weight of her breasts. I knew Cleve preferred to fuck doggy-style. He was a confirmed butt man, loved to ride between those sweet snowy globes. I thought of him just barely entering her, the petals of her opening for him, slicking him with her juice. Cleve had a thick penis, heavily veined and solid-looking; he told me the only time a girl had blatantly propositioned him was once when he had been modeling for an art class.

Imagining it going into Leah, searching out the fruit of her heaven, I began to get hard too.

She grabbed me and then suddenly I was deep inside her. One thrust upward and I felt I was pushing at the heart of her womb. She came the way women do when they only need one good deep touch: quick and hard, with an animal groan instead of the little feathery noises she often made. I thought of the lump of meat that grew inside her, thought of bathing it with my sperm, melting away its rudimentary flesh, melting away the past few months and their caustic veneer of pain. Then I did come. The sperm didn't reach far enough: it pulsed out in long, aching spasms that flowed back down over us, into the sticky space between our thighs. The months of pain did not melt away. The lump of meat remained—it would have to be scraped away, not drowned in the seed of sorrow.

As she was pulling away from me, the telephone did ring. The noise jarred something in me, a faint, grating edge of déjà vu: I wondered again what had woken me. Leah hunched

over the receiver. "Yes," she said. "Wait—let me get something—" She grabbed a pen from the bedside table, a glossy
magazine from the clutter on the floor. Her breasts hung ripe
as fruit when she leaned over. She scratched something on the
cover of the magazine. I rolled my head sideways on the
pillow and looked. *217 Payne Street,* she had written—the
doctor's address, which the clinic wouldn't divulge until the
morning of the abortion. An address in the disused industrial
district of the city.

"Thank you," said Leah, "yes . . . thank you." Gently she
placed the receiver back in its cradle. The weak light was
growing brighter behind the dirty curtains. Leah got out of bed
and hurried to the bathroom. I was still lying there when she
came out thirty minutes later. She did not look at me. She
pulled fishnet stockings the color of smoke up over her long
smooth thighs, fastened a wisp of a garter belt around her
waist, zipped up a sleeveless, black-lace shift. Then she sat on
the edge of the bed and cried.

I held her hand and touched her face with all the tenderness
I could summon. Her mascara did not run—some new water-
proof kind, I supposed. Her lipstick was perfect. I tried to
comfort her, and all I could see in my mind was Leah lying
back on a stainless steel operating table, some black-rubber
vacuum-tube apparatus snaking up into her. Her labia were
stretched wide as a screaming mouth and she was wearing
nothing but the lacy garter belt and the fishnet stockings.

It was an image Cleve would have appreciated.

"Yes, Jonny, I know you try to be sweet to me. You're a
saint, Jonny. But you know what you have? Only that damned
little-boy sweetness. You can't take care of me. You could
cook me a million gourmet dinners and when I finished them
I'd still be lonely. Cleve has a special kind of sweetness—"

"I know, I know. Cleve's sweet the way a dumb dog is

sweet. You like 'em big and stupid, right?" When I was with Cleve I could not hate him. Only my arguments with Leah could convince me that Cleve had ever meant me any harm, and only then could I say cruel things about him. We had started arguing on the way to the doctor's office. Walking through the abandoned factory district made me tense—the landscape was falling to waste, long stretches of broken glass gleaming dully here and there like quicksilver sketched onto a monochromatic gray photograph. The silence in the empty, shabby streets seemed deafening. Leah mistook my own silence for indifference: I wasn't listening to her gloomy prattle, wasn't even thinking of the ordeal about to happen to her.

The buildings here loomed low and oppressive, blotting out the sun. Years ago this place had been a toxic hell of factories and mills. We passed smokestacks blackened halfway down their towering stalks with soot and char. We passed burned-out lots that made me think of cremation grounds. The smell of death was here too—the odor of burning crude oil is somehow as humanly filthy as the odor of corrupted flesh. These places had been abandoned over the past twenty or thirty years, as the heart of the city's industry gradually moved north to the silicon suburbs. Out there you could live your whole life shuttling between a superhighway, an exit sign, a gleaming building made of immaculate silver glass, a house and a yard and a wide-screen TV and the superhighway again.

More frightening to me than the empty lots, more oppressive than the huge corrugated-steel Dumpsters that overflowed with thirty years' forgotten trash, were the dead husks of the buildings. Some of them went on for blocks and blocks, and I could not help but imagine what it would be like to walk through them—endless mazes of broken glass and spiderweb and soft sifting ash, with the corners laved in shadow, with the pipes and beams zigzagging crazily overhead. I thought of a poem I had written once for some long-ago college class, in some idealistic day when the city was far away and I only

cooked the food I wanted to eat. A few lines came back to me:
*When the emptiness in you grows too large/ You fill its vaulted
chamber with the ash of memory/ With the dust of desire.*

"I don't want to fight," Leah said suddenly. "There's not
enough time, it's too soon. Hold me, Jonny. Help me——" She
pressed me back against a wall and covered my mouth with
hers. Her lips were lush, her tongue was moist and searching,
and again I was reminded of loving her. Not the sterile and
functional fuck this morning, but the real love we had once
shared: the soft friction of skin, the good long thrusts, the
liquid sounds of pleasure. But these memories were receding
rapidly. Soon they would be just a point of brightness on a
dark horizon, and I knew now that they could never return. As
I kissed Leah I became conscious of the rough bricks at my
back, of the vast empty space behind me. I grasped her shoulders and gently pushed her away. "Come on," I said. "You
can't be late. What are we looking for——Payne Street?"

She nodded, didn't speak. We kept walking. In all the
blocks since we'd gotten off the train, we had only seen two
or three other people: sad silent cases who walked with their
heads down, who looked like they might vanish from existence as soon as they turned the corner. Now it seemed we
were alone. The streets grew ever shabbier and emptier; a few
of them had signs whose letters were half-obliterated, spelling
out cryptic messages, pointing to nowhere. None of them
looked like they might have ever said Payne Street. At one
corner, a long spray of dirt lay across the sidewalk. Leah could
not quite step all the way over it, and when we were past I
saw a dark crumb stuck to the heel of her shoe. The delicate
tired lines around her mouth and eyes seemed etched in dust.
I began to feel that the landscape was encroaching upon her;
she would leave here forever marked.

If it could erase the mark of Cleve from her, or rather the
mark of her love for Cleve, then I would bless this blasted
landscape. Maybe then I could love her again.

I thought I wanted to.

Soon it was obvious that we were getting to the fringes of the industrial section. The buildings here were more cramped and ramshackle. If anything walked here, it would be the wraith of a drudge worked to death in the sweatshops, dead of blood poisoning from a needle run through her finger. Or perhaps a tattered ghost, a hungry soul mangled by machinery from a time that knew no safety regulations. The sidewalk was fissured with deep cracks and broken into shards, as if someone had gone at it with a sledgehammer. I saw weeds sprouting at the edges of the vacant lots, leaves barely tinged with green, as furtive and sunless as mushrooms.

"You think the doctor's office burned down?" I said.

The look from beneath Leah's eyelashes was pure sparkling hate. Leah disliked getting around the city, and when she had to find a place by herself, she got panicky and sometimes mean. "He said we should come out of the tunnel and turn left. It was supposed to be three blocks down past the cotton factory."

"They had cotton *mills,* Leah, not factories, and any one of those buildings we passed could have been the one you want. By the time we walk all the way back there, we'll be a half hour late." A little flame of rage snapped in my chest. If she didn't have her directions straight, and if we arrived too late, we could miss the appointment. Appointments with a private doctor who would perform this particular operation were difficult to get, so difficult that if Leah missed this chance, she might be too far along by the time she could get another.

Without a word, she wheeled and started walking back the way we had come. I had to hurry to keep up with her; despite my anger, there was still the old reflexive fear that she might twist her ankle in one of the cracks or break into a run and escape from me or fall into a giant hole that would open like a mouth in the ground beneath her feet. You hold onto what you have; you do not give it up easily, even when you know it is poisoning you.

We walked quickly for a long time. Leah was sure we had

turned at a certain corner; I didn't remember, and we argued over that. Somehow she managed to bring Cleve's name into it. "If you were with *Cleve,*" I said furiously, "you wouldn't be bitching at him. You'd be all contrite and saying how stupid you were to get lost. You'd whine until you tricked him into taking care of you."

Leah spun on her heel. "Well, Cleve *isn't* here, is he? He had to hang his stupid gallery show today—he couldn't come! I'm stuck with you!"

"He was never going to go. He said you and I should go alone—said maybe that would help you decide. Make you quit stringing me along, I guess he meant."

"Yes, that was what he said he told you. But Jonny, I was going to meet him this morning. I was going to tell you I wanted to go by myself, that I'd decided I had to do it alone. Then I was going to meet Cleve at the train station. But when I called him this morning, the bastard backed out. He decided to spend the day playing with his damned pictures."

Only the fact that I was still somehow pitifully, stupidly in love with Leah allowed me to do what I did then. I turned and ran from her. If I had stayed I could not have kept my fingers from around her throat; in my head I would have been choking her and Cleve at once. Never mind the total illogic of it; never mind that both Leah and Cleve knew I would never have let her go off alone; never mind that I did not really believe Cleve would betray me so completely, not even for Leah, not even though I knew he was pitifully in love with her too. Something had woken me up this morning at the first pale light of dawn; it could have been a cry down in the street, or a jet plane arrowing through the smog far overhead. Or it could have been Leah murmuring into the phone, cursing her conspirator in a whisper when she realized he wasn't coming. Then replacing the receiver ever so gently—wanting to slam it down—and flowing over on top of me. Making love to me to spite Cleve, even if only in her head.

I had the spreading cancer of jealousy in me; it had been

eating away inside me for a long time. Now at last I thought I was in its death throes, suffering its final agony. And, like any dying man, I tried to run from it.

We had already lost the way we had come by. Now I ran deeper into the maze of streets, not looking or caring which way I went. For a few moments I sprinted, desperate to get away, wanting nothing but to run and run. Then the sound of Leah's heels ticking frantically behind me began to slow me down, began to pull me back to here and now and what I thought I wanted. I walked fast, jogging when she got too close, not letting her catch up with me but not completely losing her. I was afraid I might never find her again; I was afraid of having nothing to crawl back to.

Then I turned a corner and didn't look over my shoulder soon enough. When I did glance back, Leah was gone.

I froze. How could I have lost her, not meaning to? I waited a few seconds to see if she might follow. If I ran back around the corner and she was still coming, my game would be up—it would be as good as admitting that I hadn't wanted to run away at all. But if she'd gotten disgusted and started back to the train station, I had to catch her. I had to get her to that appointment if I still could. If she needed dragging there, I would drag her.

I came around the corner and the sidewalk was empty. For a moment I vacillated between anger and the stark terror of abandonment. But farther up the street, at the mouth of a narrow alleyway, I saw a smudge on the sidewalk—darker than the drifting ash, and shiny. I walked back to it. The smudge on the sidewalk was blood, twin patches of it ground into the cement. A few feet away, half-hidden beneath a blackened flake of newspaper, lay a tube of scarlet lipstick.

Leah had tripped over her heels, fallen, spilled her purse, skinned her knees brutally on the broken sidewalk. But where had she gone after that?

I looked down the alleyway. No one there. Nothing—
—except a sign.

I hadn't seen it at first. No one walking quickly past would have noticed it; it had been placed only three or four feet up the wall, at waist level instead of eye level. And it was so faded, the edges of the letters seeming to blend into the dusty brick, that it could hardly be read. But I imagined Leah sitting up after her fall, her smoky fishnets torn and the raw ganglia of her kneecaps screaming, her eyes filling with tears. She would have sat there for a moment, dazed, not quite able to get up. And the sign might have caught her eye.

Pain Street, it said.

The alleyway led between two empty factory buildings.

Suddenly the sky seemed too wide and bright and heavy, the silence too big. A fragment of sidewalk shifted under my foot. I saw little drifts of refuse piled against either wall of the alley—soot and ash, more bits of charred paper, the razor confetti of broken glass. I did not know if I could set foot in the alley; I did know, however, that I could not go home alone.

One wall was blank and featureless all the way to the back of the alley, where more trash was heaped. At my approach, a bottle rolled lazily down but did not shatter. I thought I had walked into a cul-de-sac until I came to the end of the alley. There, set back in an alcove of crumbling mortar, was a heavy steel door wedged open with half a brick.

Someone had taken a nail or a shard of glass and scratched the number 217 on the door.

The door made a gritty ratcheting noise as I pulled it open, but there was no trash in front of it, and the hinges swung easily. Someone had opened it before me. I paused for a moment, drinking in what little dirty sunlight managed to filter into the alley. Then I stepped inside. It was easy. Leah always led me to the places I feared most, and I always followed.

The air inside the building was as cool and dim and stagnant as the air in a sarcophagus. In the dark rafters and pipes of the ceiling it hung like a cloud of bats waiting to fly, rustling their parchment wings, exuding their arid spice smell. *The ash of memory,* I thought dreamily, *the dust of desire.* Walking in this air was like moving through a syrup of fermented ages; the silence in here could wrap you up like cloth and preserve you for a thousand years. As my eyes adjusted to the light, shapes began to resolve themselves around me: a huge mesh of Gigeresque machinery, cogs hanging in the air like dull toothy moons, rubber belts and hoses gone brittle with dust, steel spires soaring up to the apex of the great vaulted chamber. And a row of hooks as long as my leg, sharp metal hooks that looked oddly organic, as if they should be attached to the wrist-stump of some enormous amputee.

I walked a few steps into the chamber, and my foot punched through something dry and papery. A giant vegetable bulb, I thought, like an onion or a shallot kept too long in a root cellar, rotten and desiccated from the inside. Not until I pulled my foot back did the fragile rib cage crumble, collapsing the swollen shell of the belly and exposing the scrimshaw beadwork of the spine.

A younger woman than Leah, almost a child, half-buried and half-dissolved into the grime and ash of the factory floor. Most of the face was gone. I saw scattered teeth gleaming in the dust like fragments of ivory. But the curve of the cheekbone—the tiny hand—surely she could not yet have been sixteen. And I wondered why she had come at all, with the once-ripe swell of her belly; she had been too far along in her pregnancy to have hoped to live through an abortion.

I could go no further. I could not walk that gauntlet of machinery, not even to find Leah. I could not turn my back on it either. I stood over the husk of the young girl, and the machinery stretched out mutely as far as I could see, and time hung motionless inside the old factory, not disturbed by me or Leah or anything in the city. It seemed impossible that just a few miles away the trains were still running, the drugs were still changing hands, the endless frantic party went on as if time could not be stopped.

Very nearby, magnified by furtive echoes, I heard the click of a high heel.

"Leah," I called, not knowing if I hoped to save her or if I wanted her to save me. "Leeeeah . . . " When she walked into the far end of the chamber, I could no longer be ashamed of the pleading note in my voice. Her face was smeared with tears and makeup. The blood from her scraped knees had begun to cake, gluing her torn stockings to her legs. Her face twisted with relief and she started toward me, her arms out as if in supplication. In that moment Cleve might never have touched her, never have tasted her. We might have gone home together, might have slept in each other's arms again. I might have rested my cheek on the burgeoning mound of her belly, and found peace.

Then the machinery kicked on.

It had not been used in a long time, long enough to let the young girl fall away nearly to bare bones, and it filled the air with dust as thick as whipped cream. Only dimly did I see the first hook lifting Leah up and away from me, as if she had raised her arms and flown. I stood there dumbly for several minutes, unable to grasp what had happened even as her blood fell upon my face and my outstretched hands. A high-heeled shoe dropped to the floor in front of me, missing my head by an inch. I did not move. I stared up, up at the swirling clouds of dust, up at the figure that hung suspended like an angel in black lace. When the dust cleared Leah was slumped over limp, her head hanging upside down, her hair like a bright banner in the dusk of the room. The hook had punched into her back and out through the soft flesh of her abdomen, but her face was perfectly calm. I was calm, too, an absolute calm like the equilibrium of particles in a solution. Should I have been frightened? Perhaps. But somehow I knew that even if I walked up to one of the machines and touched it, I would not be hurt. They did not want me.

The metal of the hook was beaded with bright blood. On its sharp tip was a thick gobbet, darker than the rest and more solid-looking. It looked like nothing but a piece of meat—meat that had ceased to live or breathe or suck.

I no longer thought I knew something about love.

Now I *knew* what love was all about.

I have described the scene to Cleve as well as I could, and asked him to paint it for me. When he has captured it as closely as possible in the jeweled watercolor tones that he loves—the soft gray dust, the banner of her hair, the red so clear and vital it hurts the eye to see it—he will mat and frame it and we will hang it on the wall.

Cleve's work has become somewhat fashionable among the gallery crowd, and he has begun getting shows uptown, where the art patrons don't think they've gotten their money's worth unless they pay upwards of five hundred for a piece. We have both cut back to half time at the Blue Shell. Whenever we have a night off, we try to work our way through the last of the Dixie beer, and we listen to Sarah Vaughan or Mingus or Robert Johnson, and when the music ends we sit and stare at each other, and a thousand secrets pass between our eyes.

I hate to look in the mirror. I hate to see the beginnings of an old man's face. I hate the loose skin of my throat and the hollows around my eyes. But I know what Leah's eyes must look like by now.

Sometimes we talk about magic.

In a city of millions, an ancient city overcrowded and mean enough, a kind of magic could evolve.

Ancient by American standards isn't very old. Two or three hundred years at most . . . and the abandoned mills and factories are no more than sixty years old. But I think of New Orleans, that city mired in time, where a whole religion evolved in less than two hundred years—a slapdash recipe concocted of one part Haitian graveyard dust, one part juju from the African bush, a jigger of holy Communion wine, and a dash of swamp miasma. Magic happens when and where it wants to.

In a great, cruel, teeming city, one could create one's own magic . . . intentionally or otherwise. Magic to fulfill desires that should remain buried in the deepest pit of the soul, or just to get through the desperate hustle of staying alive from day to day. And out of the desperation, out of the hunger for bread or love, out of the secret hard bright joy at the madness of it all—out of these things something else could be born. Something made of bad dreams and lost love, something that would use as its agent the abandoned, the forgotten, the all-but-useless.

The obsolete engines, the rusted cogs . . . and the steel hooks that stay honed sharp and shiny. The machinery of a forsaken time.

The love that no one wanted anymore.

I go up to the roof of Cleve's building and I look out over the city, and I think about all the power waiting to emerge from its black womb, and I wonder who else will tap into this homegrown magic, and I howl into the wind and rejoice at the emptiness within me.

And nowhere else on the horizon have I ever seen so many billions of lights . . . or so many patches of darkness.

HELL TRAIN

GARY L. RAISOR

*Gary L. Raisor has this story to tell: "Many years ago I worked the night
shift near skid row. I was coming back from lunch and it had been
raining heavily, making it difficult to see. Passing near a row of run-
down bars, I came upon a parked ambulance with its lights flashing.
At first I didn't see whom they had come to pick up, but then I saw the
old man lying in the street. He was dead, a victim of a hit and run, and
I can still see his hand sticking out from beneath the sheet they used to
cover him, as though beseeching someone to help him. Many yards
down the street was a pair of shoes that belonged to the dead man. He
had been knocked out of them. That was difficult to see, but the thing
that really stuck with me were the onlookers at the scene. There was
absolutely no trace of compassion or pity on their faces. An old man
had died on that rainy street, alone, and nobody gave a shit. I often
wonder how he came to such a fate."*

*Raisor, who "grew up in a town so small that both 'City Limits' were on
the same street," has published short stories in* Night Cry, The Horror
Show, Cemetery Dance *and numerous anthologies. Recently, he sold
his first novel, and is also the editor of the well-received anthology,*
Obsessions, *which appeared in early 1991. He lives in Kentucky.*

With thanks to Joe Lansdale, Alan Rodgers,
Al Sarrantonio, and Dave Silva
for all their help along the way.

It was cold. Quiet.

And lonely.

The loneliness made a man hear things that weren't there.

Stan Macklin, track inspector, stared into the distance and wondered if his ears were playing tricks on him. Someone was moving around in the darkness up ahead, just far enough from the light so he couldn't make out who it was.

But that was impossible. This stretch of track was supposed to be closed down for the next four hours. His fingers danced a nervous two-step on the handle of the handcar that had brought him here, as he tried to decide what to do. His fingers stopped and he listened. The footstep didn't sound right. This was crazy—they didn't sound quite . . . human.

Despite the cold, a trickle of sweat wormed down his face, causing him to pull out a handkerchief and start mopping. His job was inspecting track and, damn it, that's what he was going to do. He'd been doing it for damn near forty years now and he took the job seriously. A lot of people's lives depended on him.

Stan swung down and reached across the handcar to drag out his toolbox. Even though the dented blue metal container weighed close to sixty pounds, he handled the weight easily. A large man, he had been stooped and worn some by the years, but like the tenements of the city he called home, he expected to be around a while longer.

The years hadn't taken much of his strength. His mind might be another story.

The last several nights had been filled with dreams. He ground his teeth at the lie: They weren't dreams, they were nightmares. There was no other word for them. Scattered debris popped up from the depths of his mind and floated past, leaving gooseflesh in its wake.

Nightmares.

Caught between waking and sleeping.

Nightmares—

—*of standing in a vast subway tunnel that seemed to stretch out forever into the distance. Beneath his feet, the earth was damp and the odor of ancient rot filled his nostrils, as though the ground here was untouched by even the memory of sunlight. Overhead the light was a sullen yellow, dim, casting the tunnel into permanent twilight.*

When Stan stared down the track, he saw a distant, shadowy dot that was no larger than the head of a pin moving toward him. It appeared to be moving slowly, and yet it was somehow closing the distance between them with incredible speed. Bearing down on him. Somewhere, farther back, the sound of screeching metal reached his ears, and Stan thought he could make out clouds of spark-filled smoke billowing up behind.

Something was out there and it was coming toward him with unnatural speed—

—and Stan had sat up in his sweat-soaked bed before whatever was coming down the track had gotten any closer.

He was relieved, because there was something unnatural about the whole damned thing. Sleep had been impossible for the past three nights.

Maybe he was going fucking nuts, but he still had a job to do. With an eye honed by forty years of experience, he looked at the rails and began tightening a bolt that had worked loose. The wrench slipped and the skin on his knuckles that Dr. Antonelli had so intricately stitched hit the rail and popped open. Blood spurted. He winced and dropped the wrench. Harsh echoes faded down the tunnel.

For a moment he thought he heard movement again, but when he shone his flashlight into the murkiness, he saw nothing.

"Too many years alone down here," he said under his breath, "can make you hear things." He gave the rail a kick as he picked up his toolbox and dropped it back on the handcar. "Make you talk to yourself, too."

Yanking out his last good handkerchief, he wrapped his injured hand. A frown settled on his face. Dr. Antonelli sure had a strange way of stitching up a man's hand.

A dry rustling sound came, died. Stan crouched down and put his ear to the rail.

There was only silence.

Something on the wall caught his eye and anger welled up, pushing everything else aside. "Goddamn graffitti artists," he said as he stared at the swirls of color that disfigured the concrete. "Always messing up everything. Sons of bitches oughta have a spray can jammed up their asses and lit." He grinned. "Now there's an art exhibit I'd pay good money to see."

The neon paint was shaped into words, but they were like no words Stan had ever seen before. They looked foreign, like something on the menu over at Chen's. There was a painting, too, really sick shit, dismembered people being served to featureless monsters who stood back in the shadows and looked out with yellow eyes that glowed.

Whoever had done this was good because the paintings looked almost . ... *real.* Silently he mouthed the words on the wall. Stopped. They made him uneasy.

An itchy sensation swept over him, the kind of feeling that meant someone was watching. Turning, he sent the light from his flashlight probing into the dark crevices overhead. Two red eyes looked back without fear.

A scuttling noise followed.

Something ran across a beam in the ceiling, causing dust to float down. A rat. A really big one. They seemed to get bigger down here every year.

"What the hell do you bastards eat?"

Another one ran across.

Stan pulled the crescent wrench out. Dinged and pitted, the silver piece of metal looked like it had gone through a war.

A third rat darted along the beam. This one was bigger than the first two, and slower.

"Oh shit," he said, anticipation building in the pit of his stomach. "This could be the one." He hefted the wrench.

The rat hesitated.

Stan hurled his wrench and a squeal of almost human agony answered. The rat, the wrench jammed in its side, fell with a splat like an overripe apple from a tree. Despite the streaks of red squirting from the animal's nose and the fact that its guts were spilling out like red confetti with every step it took, it still crawled after Stan with bared teeth. The wrench kept dragging the rat off course.

The big track inspector watched the rat move toward him, dragging the wrench. It got close enough to latch onto Stan's size eleven work boot and bite into the leather before its legs gave way and it collapsed into a twitching heap. Stan stepped down. Bones popped.

"Jesus." Stan laughed uneasily, looking down at his bloody boot. He'd never seen one this big before. Or this mean. He prodded the gray monster once more with his foot before reaching down and pulling the wrench out. "Number 331. Nolan Ryan ain't got shit on me and I bet he never had a batter try to bite him, neither."

There were more of them back there in the dark, milling around, squealing, but he didn't have any more time to play. He had track to inspect. Stan wiped off his wrench and walked up the tunnel, checking the rails with almost mechanical intensity until he was satisfied that everything was right.

This job was his life; it was all he had left since his wife Beth had died.

He returned to pick up the dead rat. This one could win this month's pool for the biggest kill. That could be a hundred bucks. That cheating bastard, Manny DeCarlo, had won the last two months, although Stan was certain Manny was killing his rats over at the dump and bringing them in. Stan shook his head sadly at the thought. There was no honor anymore.

His movements were slow as he swung down and hobbled over to where he'd left the rat. Years of rooting around in the cold, damp subway had left him with stiff knees.

He scouted around for the dead animal. Didn't see it.

A sound, distant and ominous, rattled down through the quiet of the tunnel.

Spooked, he straightened up and looked around.

Faint echoes, dying.

His ears must be playing tricks. He went back to searching, but damn it, the rat wasn't there. The thing just plain wasn't there. A whisper of unease nestled between his shoulder blades.

"Christ, I'm getting senile too." He saw the bolt he had tightened earlier. Maybe the other rats had eaten the dead one, except he would have heard them.

He scanned the tunnel to the left.

And saw nothing.

He brushed the sweat from his eyes.

And looked to the right.

Bloodstains from where his rat had died. He looked back to his left.

Two yellowish unwinking eyes were staring back.

This time he knew they didn't belong to a rat, they were the wrong color and much too large. Much too high above the track. He wasn't sure what the hell they *did* belong to. They peered at him from a stretch of darkness in the middle of the rails, just out of the reach of his flashlight, and for the first time Stan realized just how much higher than a man's eyes they were. They were a good nine feet above the ground.

Stan tried to spit, found he had nothing to spit with.

Lots of thoughts raced through his churning mind. He wanted fervently to believe Les over at dispatch had sent someone out on another handcar to check up on him.

He wanted to believe he would find his hundred-dollar rat.

He wanted to believe he would get through this alive.

But he believed that least of all.

The figure was moving now. Coming toward him, its footsteps deliberate and massive, sending the loose gravel bouncing off the tunnel walls.

Someone called out his name. It sounded like Beth's voice.

A furtive scuttling noise followed, then a sound like two pieces of old leather rubbing together floated through the silence, and Stan couldn't identify it. Then he realized the sound was—laughter.

The wind gusted, carrying the high sweet odor of rotting flesh.

Whatever the hell was back there would be in the light in a few seconds and Stan would be able to see it clearly. The thought brought him no comfort.

Stan reached in his coat pocket and pulled out a .32 he'd taken to carrying recently. The rules strictly prohibited carrying a gun and he could lose his job if Les found out, but this was New York.

"If this ain't *America's Funniest Home Videos,*" Stan said, "I'm gonna put my size eleven in somebody's ass!"

The eyes kept coming. The laughter grew louder.

Stan's rat flew out of the dark and landed at his feet. It had been bitten in half.

"This is your last chance," Stan announced without any real hope. "I'm gonna shoot. I swear to God, I'm gonna shoot." He centered the sights a few feet beneath the yellow eyes.

The eyes never hesitated.

Stan shot.

In the flash he caught a glimpse of dead gray, slightly reptilian skin. The thing, whatever it was, wasn't put together right, too many parts that didn't fit together right. And too many teeth. *Way too many teeth.*

Stan fired again and saw where the first slug had struck. The creature was hurt, the skin along its right side was soaked with something dark that welled up from a jagged hole above the ribs. Dazed, Stan fired again. And saw the darkness trail down to splatter softly into the dirt—the only sound he could hear now and it didn't sound real, no more real than the toy pop of the .32.

The creature hestitated, as though puzzled.

"Who's laughing now, you son of a bitch?" Stan asked. "Who's laughing now?"

Somewhere, far removed, Stan thought he heard the thumping of his own heart. Distant. Not real. None of this was real.

Stan measured the distance to the handcar. Way too far. Besides, he'd never get up enough speed to get away from whatever this was. Still, the handcar was the only chance he had. He edged in that direction.

The creature edged in his direction.

He stopped.

It stopped.

They were engaged in a bizarre, silent waltz.

One thing for sure, the creature wasn't going to let him near the handcar.

They were at an impasse. There was no chance of killing it, especially with something as small as his .32. The creature was just too damn huge. The handgun popped again, sounding absurdly like a cap pistol in the vastness of the tunnel. Stan gritted his teeth, held the sight on target, pulled back the hammer and squeezed the trigger again. The bullet struck home and still the damned thing refused to go down.

The creature's high-pitched scream filled his ears as it edged closer and closer to the light.

As it edged closer to him.

At the edge of the darkness, it stopped.

Stan stared into the yellow eyes and felt the first ray of hope since this waking nightmare had started. "You don't like the light, do you?"

There was one shot left in the .32. For all the good that would do. Taking aim, he placed a bullet between the creature's yellow eyes. Another scream of rage and it was coming for him again. Full tilt. Running on its hands as well as its feet. The thing clung to the dark along one wall, making it impossible to get a good look at it.

This was all she wrote, he was going to end up as lunch, light or no light . . . when it missed a step, staggered, missed another step and fell forward. The thing almost recovered for a moment, then faltered and sank to its knees, a penitent kneeling in a dark church, waiting to be blessed. A long red tongue shot from the creature's mouth and touched the bullet hole in its forehead. A black tarry substance was leaking out. The screams came again and, this time they were so piercing, Stan felt blood seep from his ears.

Then voices began pouring from the hole in the creature's head, lonely sad voices filled with a lifetime of guilt, filled with regret, floating away to die in the dark.

The misshapen thing fell forward onto the ground, lay there for a second, righted itself and crawled a few more feet before collapsing again. Then it writhed around like a snake that had been run over on the highway.

It kept on twitching.

But this time it didn't get up.

Stan heard a clicking noise and looked down. He realized he was firing an empty pistol.

Shock began setting in, and Stan slowly let his body uncoil as he sank down next to his toolbox. His legs simply wouldn't hold him up any longer. "Goddamn forty years on the job and I ain't never seen nothing like this. Monsters in the subway." He wiped his forehead with a blood-stained rag, unknowingly using the one he'd used to clean the rat blood off his wrench, and left a red smear.

The .32 dangled from fingers that twitched and jerked with a strange life all their own. He was breathing like he'd just run the hundred-yard dash. "Bit my rat in two. Cost me a hundred dollars." He felt hysteria building inside and fought to hold it down. "Ain't nobody ever gonna believe me." He looked over at the gray hump in the dark that was the creature. It was still there, though he couldn't make out any details. The idea of going over there for a closer look didn't appeal to him.

After a few minutes, his breathing slowed enough so that he felt like he wouldn't pass out if he stood. He picked up his walkie-talkie, thumbed the send button and tried to figure how he was going to explain this to Les when

—a second set of eyes appeared—

A brief precious moment was lost while Stan stood rooted to the spot, watching in disbelief before he stumbled to the handcar and tried to get it moving.

Handcars weren't built for speed.

He wasn't built for speed.

But Stan was no quitter, he was giving it his best shot, grunting with the effort of moving the handcar handle which seemed to be deliberately resisting him. "C'mon, baby," he coaxed. "Come on."

The wheels began moving. Slowly. Too slowly.

The sound of clawed feet sliding over concrete rose above his grunting efforts. Getting closer.

The handcar picked up a little speed.

The clawed feet sounded a lot closer.

Stan wondered just how close the thing was, but he was afraid to look, afraid that if he saw it too clearly he would freeze up. What he'd seen back there in the dark had been bad enough.

Fighting against the agony in his knees, he continued to pump the handle desperately, trying to pick up some more speed. He had to know how close it was. He chanced a look out of the corner of his eye and saw the yellow eyes were nearly into the light. Another high-pitched scream vibrated the tunnel. Farther back, something answered.

Dispatch was over three miles away, most of it through dark stretches of tunnel, some very dark stretches. Even if he got away from this creature, he could run into another one. This was going from bad to worse.

Cursing his stiff joints, he managed at last to get the handcar rolling. Really rolling. As fast as he could make it go, but it wasn't going to be fast enough. The creature was covering the ground in incredibly long lupine strides that would put them face-to-face in just a few seconds.

The handcar entered a dark stretch. The glowing yellow eyes were maybe twenty yards back now.

Stan had one move left.

The timing had to be perfect.

The waiting would be the hard part. He would have to let the thing get a little closer.

That part he didn't like.

It was fifteen yards back now.

Reaching into his toolbox, Stan rummaged around until he found what he was looking for. It weighed three pounds and two ounces and was as familiar to him as his own hand. He picked it up, hefted it. His rat-killing crescent wrench.

The creature wasn't close enough yet.

"Come to Poppa." He held the wrench behind his back.

All Stan could see now were the yellow eyes. They were ten yards back, still coming fast.

The handcar swayed and in the dark Stan fought for balance. He fell to one knee. A flash of unbelievable agony shot up his leg, causing the wrench to slip from his fingers and slide into the dark.

Stan felt around on the floor of the handcar. He looked like a man desperately searching for a lost contact lens.

The creature was very close now. Closer than Stan had planned. Less than ten yards away. The odor of the thing was almost overpowering.

Stan's fingers closed around cold slippery metal. Putting every ounce of his 245-pound body into the effort, Stan threw the wrench.

The huge silver chunk of forged steel rotated end over end and the creature saw it, and tried to veer away. But it was too late. The wrench that had killed 331 rats struck the creature, burying itself in one of the glowing eyes with a wet, squishy sound. The thing was rocked back as though it had run head-first into an invisible brick wall. A scream of pure hatred undulated down the tunnel.

Stan knew he had killed the damned thing and he also knew the wrench was too late to stop the headlong rush.

The creature caved in at the knees.

Began rolling.

The burly track inspector attempted to throw himself from the handcar. He was too slow. All he could do now was watch. The creature slid beneath the wheels and the handcar left the tracks. For some odd reason Stan expected his fall to hurt a lot more than it did, because he heard more than felt something give way in his right arm.

The subway swapped ends a few times and he felt some of his front teeth go. Warm blood filled his mouth, began trickling down the back of his throat. Shit, Beth said she always liked his smile. His hard hat joined the teeth. He quit rolling and began to slow. The thought that he might come out of this okay entered his mind. Just before his head struck something hard. A shower of bright sparks exploded inside his head.

When they died—

Stan was again standing in the tunnel that had no end, watching as the black dot drew closer. It was a train with countless numbers of cars stretching back as far as he could see. The earth began to tremble at its approach as it swept toward him like wildfire before a raging wind, chasing what little light remained from the tunnel.

Engrossed by the magnitude of what he saw, he stood frozen in that dank muddy tunnel watching the train's progress for what seemed forever, and all during that time the train kept moving nearer, growing closer and closer, until finally it drew near enough for Stan to see there was something wrong with the passengers. As he looked at them, he saw they were all dead, their eyes were fixed in terrible gaping stares, and they were all crying, but instead of regular tears, some black

*tarred substance leaked from their eyes. It was the fuel that
powered the train, and the air became filled with its acrid
stench.*

*In a moment Stan would be crushed by the train. He lifted
his hands in an effort to fend off the inevitable, and when his
fingers touched the hard metal of the engine*

—his eyes opened—

and he stared without understanding at the metal clutched
in his hands. After a moment he realized it belonged to the rail
he was lying on. As he lay pinned beneath the handcar, he
could still hear the thunder of that endless train echoing in his
mind.

Finally the sound quieted and he looked around.

The creature was gone.

There were others. He'd heard them. Why hadn't one of
them come after him?

Because the handcar had tipped over in the light?

Maybe.

There was one other explanation that made his insides go
all loose and wet. The creatures had only existed in his mind,
that he'd finally gone off the deep end for good. He'd seen it
happen to guys who spent too much time down here. Old
Stew Hirschfield had come back one day, claiming he'd heard
voices talking to him. Stew was up in Bellevue now in a little
room with a light on all the time and a radio to keep him
company.

No, Stan decided. He hadn't gone crazy like old Stew. He'd
seen them, smelled them. *Killed them.*

Stan inventoried his working parts and decided everything
was okay, except for his right arm, which was now one raw
nerve ending. When he tried to move, he found the handcar
on top of his legs. A smile that wasn't entirely sane touched his
face. He looked at his watch. "This is just fucking great. Not
only am I probably crazy, I'm gonna have my head cut off by
the nine-thirty express."

Stan began crawling from beneath the overturned handcar.

Skin had to sacrificed, but he had incentive—the nine-thirty was less than ten minutes away. He looked at his arm: it would be a while before he tossed any more wrenches at rats. *Or at monsters.* His hand hung at an unnatural angle, and when he eased back his coat sleeve, he could see red-flecked bone poking through the shirt.

Dull waves of agony flowed over him every time he pushed the handle down on the handcar, but there was no choice. He had to get clear of the tracks. The pain became a solid tangible thing. By the time the dispatch office swam into view, he felt like he'd pumped halfway across New York. When he went to climb down, he found he couldn't get his legs to move. His knees were locked into place. "Somebody get Manny DeCarlo's ass out here!"

Several people appeared, none of them Manny, and then hands reached out and gently lowered him to the concrete. "Somebody tell Manny I killed the biggest damn rat he ever saw." Shock was setting in and Stan realized he was babbling. "Tell that bastard I want my hundred dollars right now. Right now!"

A cup of hot black coffee found its way into his left hand and he tipped the cup up, taking a long gulp and burning his tongue. Little pockets of warmth banked themselves in his stomach, and the pain was starting to bank a little too when somebody grabbed his right arm.

Stan tried to scream, but white-hot agony choked him, towed him silently back down into the blackness

—and the train swept right through him—a dark, swiftly flowing leviathan that could be seen but not touched. He realized the train was no more than a mere shadow, yet the earth shook and he heard the tortured cries of the passengers when they swept past. Pain and sorrow were etched in their faces. Their staring eyes were filled with tears of darkness while they stared back at him out of the train windows. Worse than the tears was the loss of hope that Stan saw.

Some things were moving among the passengers and Stan

fought to get a look at whatever they were. He saw there were many of them, they were shadowy and they moved quickly, and they weren't human. As the train rocketed on down the track, he saw one of them coming toward him. Drifting from car to car, the thing reminded him of a kite caught in a strong wind.

As the cars continued flowing through him, he saw this creature was identical to the shadowy creatures he had fought in the tunnel earlier. It had the same gray reptilian skin, the same yellowish eyes that glowed in the dark.

From time to time one of them would stop to torture a passenger, and then it would extend a huge scaly tongue and lick the dark tears from its victim's face.

One paused and stared at him. It was unbelievably foul-looking. When Stan stared into the inhuman face, he saw it smile at him before blowing the train whistle.

The creature approached to within a few feet and sniffed at him as though trying to identify his scent. It seemed puzzled by his presence on the train. Its arm reached out in a snakelike movement to touch him. The hand should have passed right through Stan, but it didn't. He felt the scaly hand touch his wrist and he screamed when his skin began smoldering.

More of them began to gather.

Stan staggered back, trying to free himself, but the creature held him fast. He took a quick look around, and to his horror, he saw he was surrounded by them.

One of the figures smiled and pulled him closer. Stan fought to escape, but his efforts were useless. The figure and he were now scant inches apart. The creature reached out with its long cold tongue and licked something off Stan's face. "We like the taste of sin," it said in an angel's voice. "And regret," another one added. "Especially regret."

"What are you talking about?" Stan asked. "What regret?"

The creature smiled. "Why, your wife, Beth, of course. You let her die, didn't you?"

Stan began to cry and tried to cover his face, but the crea-
tures pulled his hands away and their scaly tongues touched
him again and again until
—his eyes jerked open—
and Stan saw something long and red moving toward his
face. He tried to turn away but he was too weak. Bits and
pieces of the nightmare fled across his mind, chased away by
the light.

Then remembering, he looked over to see his right arm was
in a cast and that he was in a hospital bed. A nurse was wiping
the sweat from his forehead with a damp towel. What she was
doing felt too much like the long, cold tongue of the creature
in his dream. He pushed her hand away.

Throwing back the sheet, he slowly eased his legs around
and set his feet on the floor. Little black dots swarmed around
his head as he fought to remain sitting. After a few seconds,
they flew away and he got a look at the lacerations that
crisscrossed his body. Christ, he was messed up pretty good.
Except for his arm and mouth, nothing felt busted. The arm
began throbbing like an abscessed tooth as he stood and
limped toward the bathroom.

The bright light from the mirror hurt his eyes, and for a
moment he could see nothing except cuts and bruises.

And two red streaks that ran all the way up to his eyes.

As though a scaly tongue had licked away his tears.

Stan was flicking the peas from his lunch at a cockroach
crawling up the wall when Dr. Martin Antonelli materialized
in the hospital room. The doctor was a mystery to Stan and
was more than a little spooky. A lot of guys back at work had
their own ideas why the pale, aristocratic man continued
working in this shithole of a hospital, and they didn't mind
discussing those ideas.

Some said the doctor craved the adrenaline rush of working
in the trauma unit.

Others said he worked there so he could drink the blood of the injured patients.

All called him Count Dracula behind his back.

Nobody really knew what Dr. Martin Antonelli's story was. The doctor just stood at the foot of Stan's bed and made notes on his chart.

"How's it going?" Stan inquired, meaning, am I going to get out of here soon? Hospitals scared the crap out of him.

"Not bad," the doctor finally answered without looking up from his clipboard. "I got three pints of blood from the last patient in this bed and nobody noticed a thing."

Stan glanced up from his plate. "I guess you heard what we been saying, huh?"

"Yes, but you don't have to worry because I only took one pint from you." The doctor's face never changed expression and Stan was glad he didn't play poker with this guy. He had the feeling he might go home broke.

"Your arm is broken in four places," Dr. Antonelli said matter-of-factly. "Not a record by any means. And you have a mild concussion. We also took thirty-one pieces of gravel from various parts of your anatomy." He tossed a clear plastic packet containing red-stained gravel on the bed. "A little souvenir. You're a very lucky man, Mr. Macklin."

"You're right about that. It could've been a lot worse."

The doctor scribbled something down. "I'm going to give you something for the pain."

"When can I—"

"Tomorrow," the doctor finished for him. "You can go home tomorrow. We found some blood in your ears and we're still a little concerned about the concussion."

"Thanks, but you don't hafta worry. Beth always said that concrete didn't stand a chance against my skull." Stan's grin faded. "Is my arm gonna heal up all right, doctor? It really looked like shit the last time I saw it. I like to throw . . . you know . . . things."

"Well," Dr. Antonelli said, putting down the clipboard.

"You're not too young but you appear healthy. We can't make any promises. You should be able to use it, though it'll be stiff, and you can count on not liking cold weather much."

"Hell, I never much liked the cold anyhow." Stan hesitated, working up his courage. "Doctor, anyone talking about anything strange going on in the subway?"

"Like what?" The man in white regarded Stan.

"Oh, nothing in particular, I just wanted to know if anyone saw anything, you know, unusual." Stan couldn't quite meet the doctor's inquisitive stare. "Graffitti artists, stuff like that. I just thought maybe I mighta seen something a little weird down there the last time I was inspecting track."

"Is that why you turned over your handcar, Mr. Macklin?"

"Jesus, no, doctor. That'd be crazy."

"Mr. Macklin, how long have you been working down there in the subway?"

"Forty years, come May."

"This is your fifth visit with us. You seem to be getting a little accident prone. You're thinking about retiring soon, aren't you?"

"No, I'm not thinking about retiring soon. I got a lot of good years left. Still got twenty-twenty vision, too," Stan said defiantly. "You're not going to write down there that I gotta retire, are you?" His voice had taken on a sudden note of desperation.

The doctor studied him and saw the desperation there. His expression softened a little. "No, Mr. Macklin, I'm not going to make you retire."

Stan relaxed a little and a smile crossed his face. "The guys at work been wanting to know something for a long time now, doctor. They asked me to ask you. I know it ain't none of my business and I hope you don't get offended. But where the hell are you from?"

The doctor considered. "The truth?"

Stan nodded.

"Transylvania."

"No shit?" Stan asked, digesting this tidbit. "Just like Dracula?"

"No shit. Just like Dracula."

"The guys at work ain't gonna believe this," Stan said. Then he took a hard look to see if the doctor was pulling his leg.

Doctor Antonelli read the doubt on his face. "Come by my office tomorrow and I'll show you a picture of my father's church." And then, sotto voce, "Bats and all."

After Dr. Antonelli left, Stan let his thoughts turn to the subway and what was down there. God, how he wished Beth were here. She would know what to do, but she'd been dead almost nine years now. He thought about the words of the creature on the train. That thing in his dream had been right— her death *had* been his fault. He should have let her have the baby.

Lately Beth stayed on his mind. He longed to relive that night, to undo what had happened or at least to say the words he had never said enough to her. God, they were hard words to say even though he was all by himself. It seemed like that was all he thought about anymore.

That and dying.

He touched the scabs beneath his eyes and saw blood.

The pain pills kicked in, and when he closed his eyes, he dreamed sad dreams. A tear ran down his face.

And disappeared.

A week later Stan was sitting in Les Jacobs's office and poking a coat hanger into his cast to get at an itch. Sonofabitchin' itch was way back there. He wasn't having any luck, the coat hanger kept missing the right spot. Another day or two and he would be crazy. It seemed like he itched all over lately. He banged the cast on Les's desk in frustration.

Les cleared his throat and examined his desk for scratches, and when he found one, his lips became so thin they disappeared. "I talked to the front office yesterday and they said

you have *got* to start thinking about training a replacement."
He cocked his bald head, waiting for Stan's response.

"Well, Les, you can tell the front office to kiss my ass." Stan
bent the coat hanger into a different angle and attacked his
itch again. Closer, but no cigar.

Les shook his head sadly as though the older man had gone
simple. "You got two years to go, max. I'd think you'd want
to consider taking life a little easier."

"And become a pencil-pushing geek?" Stan asked.

Red-faced, Les touched the pens in his pocket, straightening
them unconsciously. "You either train someone or your ass is
going behind a desk for the next three months. You know I
can do it. Your safety record . . ."

"You're coming on kinda forceful there, Les." Stan laughed.
"You must be taking those management classes again." He
put his feet on Les's desk, the coat hanger forgotten now.

"Just for the sake of argument," Les said, "hear me out."

Stan threw the hanger on the desk. "Who you got in mind?"

"You serious?" Les asked.

"Let's say I am, just for the sake of argument."

"He's one of our new men, a minority, and you know how
the front office is about promoting—"

"Does he have a name or am I supposed to go out there and
pick the first brown guy I see?"

"Manny DeCarlo."

Stan considered this for a moment, feeling a savage glee
building deep inside. "Did Manny specifically ask for me to
train him?"

"No, he thinks he's going with Fredericks."

The itch went away. "Okay, you got a deal, Les. Under one
condition. We start today."

"What about your arm?" Les asked.

"I wouldn't give it a second thought. After all, I'm going to
be taking life a lot easier now."

Les finally nodded. "You want me to tell Manny?"

"No, I'd rather break the good news to him myself."

* * *

The lights in the equipment yard were coming on while Stan
was checking out his toolbox. He sure missed his crescent
wrench. Three hundred thirty-one rats and one monster.

Footsteps approached, but he gave no sign that he noticed.
When his visitor's shadow fell across the toolbox, he looked
up.

Neither said anything as they regarded each other intently.
The younger man broke the silence first. "Oh man, this has
got to be some kind of cruel joke."

Stan looked at Manny DeCarlo evenly and tried hard not to
smile. He didn't quite succeed. "Yeah, I couldn't quite believe
your good fortune myself."

Manny was a kid, not much over twenty-five, and the mustache he was trying to grow wasn't working out. He was small
and wiry. Could probably run real fast. That might come in
handy.

"Manny, why don't you sit down and try not to be a pain
in my neck?"

"Thanks," the younger man said. "I think my pain's gonna
be a whole lot lower." He sat himself on one of the handcars.
"I hear this inspecting track crap is a piece of cake."

Stan let the comments pass. Beyond them, in the yard, the
sounds of the city filled the night. A subway train passed and
the concrete vibrated slightly. "You know, Manny, I don't
believe you ever said if you were born here or Puerto Rico."

"Puerto Rico. Been here seven years."

"How you liking New York?"

"Pretty good, up till about a minute ago."

Stan ignored the barb. "Got any family in Puerto Rico?"

Manny looked like he didn't want to answer. "No. Say Stan,
what's with the twenty questions? Am I gonna get a prize if I
answer 'em all right?"

Stan reached down with his left hand and took hold of the
front of Manny's uniform, and lifted him from the handcar

until they were face-to-face. "I need your attention for a second," Stan said, staring into Manny's suddenly wide eyes. "We've known each other about what? Two years now? And you'd say I'm a guy who shoots straight. Wouldn't you?"

Manny's head bobbed in agreement.

"You wouldn't say I'm a guy given to flights of fancy?"

Manny's head quit bobbing, began going from side to side.

"Manny, what I'm about to say will make you think I've gone off the deep end, I know that, but I've got to say it anyway. I saw something in the subway last time I was down there, something—real bad."

Manny waited, his feet ten inches above the concrete.

Stan couldn't say the words. Lowering the younger man back to the handcar, Stan pulled out a handkerchief and turned away. The big man mopped his face, which started the scabs beneath his eyes to bleeding again.

"You can forget it, Stan, you're not scaring me off my big chance. Les said you might try something like this."

Stan went over and again busied himself with his toolbox, even though everything was in perfect order. "He did, huh? Les doesn't know his ass from a hole in the ground. Do you believe in Hell, Manny?"

"You mean like fire and brimstone, and all that shit?" Manny laughed. "No, man, not since I was about twelve. What're you saying here, Stan, that you saw the boogeyman taking the IRT, that the whole New York subway has become Hell? You'd better tell Dr. Antonelli to take another look at your head. He missed something the first time."

"No, not the whole subway," Stan replied, "just the section under 125th Street and Lenox Avenue."

"You're going to have to do a lot better than that to keep me from going down there." There was definite anger in Manny's eyes when he stood up. "I know you think I can't hold up my end. Well, you don't know shit. I been making my own way ever since I got to New York and I can handle anything you can dish out."

"Is that a fact?" Stan said. "If we run into something down there, we ain't gonna have time to go into a huddle about what to do." He fixed Manny with an unblinking stare. "I call the shots. You hear me?"

Manny didn't look away. "Yeah, I hear you."

"I'm gonna show you a few things. You listen and you might come out of this alive."

"You gonna show me how you leap off the handcar?"

Something about Manny's spunk made Stan warm to the kid. A voice in the back of his head said he was a damn fool for making snap judgments, that the only reason he was doing this was because Manny's wisecracking attitude somehow reminded him of Beth. Before the pregnancy.

Before the . . . accident.

THE SUBWAY, JUST BELOW 125TH STREET AND LENOX AVENUE

Stan and Manny were standing in front of the spray-painted wall. Something about the painting didn't seem right to Stan. Several days has passed since he'd seen it, but he thought he could make out the vague outline of gray reptilian skin and disjointed limbs a little clearer.

"This is what made your underwear ride up?" Manny asked. "You think the painting's changing?"

"I'm telling you it's different today than it was last time. It's changing a little bit every day. You gotta look close to see the changes."

"Could be what you're seeing is not the same picture," Manny suggested. "We spray painted over the thing. The guy who painted it just didn't get everything back the same."

When Stan scrubbed his fingers across the paint, they came back bone dry. "I don't think so. I think we're looking at the same painting and those things in it are getting closer to the light."

"Oh man, don't talk that voodoo shit." Manny peered at the creatures in the painting. "You want me to believe you killed two of these ugly motherfuckers? Not one, but *two?*"

"That's right."

"Then how come nobody's seen the dead bodies?" Manny asked. It was the same question he always asked. "And how come we ain't seen no more of them?"

"I don't know," Stan admitted. After five weeks, the whole thing seemed more and more like a dream. "But I killed them." His voice held no conviction.

An ice storm hit the city at 5:07 A.M. the next morning, taking down power lines, bringing traffic to a standstill, and putting a massive strain on the subway system. Breakdowns kept everyone on twenty-four-hour call for the next three days. Manny and Stan were loaned out to track repair. They slept in their clothes on the floor of the dispatch station, too exhausted to go home.

The temperature dipped below zero, then moved down some more. And if things weren't bad enough, the rails started icing up, so Manny and Stan went back to track inspection. They were over by 131st Street, riding a handcar and spraying deicer on rails at the curves. The glittering frost on the subway walls made everything seem clean.

Sitting hunched over, trying to protect himself from the wind, Stan was jolted when the handcar almost slewed off the tracks. "Jesus, Manny, take it easy!"

The handcar stopped and their labored breathing filled the air with plumes of whiteness. As Manny bent down to have a closer look at the tracks, he started rubbing at eyes that were nearly frozen shut. Exhaustion or his imagination was making him see something that wasn't there.

"What's the holdup," Stan asked, climbing down.

Manny pointed.

Stan's face went white as he plodded over on wooden legs.

On the wall was a duplicate of the painting from 125th Street. Almost. This one was a little different. Farther back, beyond the severed limbs and the gray amorphous shapes in the shadows, was a single black dot. It wasn't very large, but it was large enough for Stan to see what it was.

It was a train.

Manny let the flashlight play over the painting and blew out his breath in disgust. "How come this son of a bitch don't paint nothing else? I gotta tell you, this shit is starting to get real boring. I wouldn't mind seeing some naked girls or something like that, you know what I mean?"

The train in the painting held Stan's attention.

Manny began jogging in place, trying to keep warm. "Come on, Stanley, let's go. We're not supposed to be here. Les finds out, we're gonna be in deep shit."

The tunnel soaked up Manny's voice, and when they walked back to the handcar, their footsteps crunched on the ice. To Stan they sounded like old, brittle bones breaking.

They moved down the line a little farther and saw some dark brown droppings littering the concrete. A couple were still steaming.

"Rats?"

"Yeah," Stan answered. "From the looks of this mess, I'd say they must've found something to eat."

"Like what?"

"Lots of things," Stan answered. The last time he'd seen the creatures, there had been rats around. "Over in Harlem I seen 'em eat a Doberman that wandered into the subway. The cold makes 'em crazy hungry."

"Man, I wish you wouldn't tell me this stuff. You ever had a rat bite you?" Despite the cold, a trickle of sweat ran down the younger man's back.

"No." Stan lied.

"Why don't I believe that?"

They had gone past several spurs that branched off the main line when they came up on another stretch of dark tunnel. Manny kept on pumping the handcar, his voice rising in irritation. "Goddamn punks break out the lights. How we supposed to see what we're doing?"

"Hold up," Stan said, pulling out a flashlight and shining the beam along the wall. Odd, none of the tunnel lights were broken. They just weren't working. The flashlight flickered and dimmed as though something was sucking the juice out of it and, for an instant, the darkness moved in close, reminding them just how isolated they were.

"What are we waiting on now?" Manny asked in a long-suffering voice. "I'm freezing my ass off here."

"I thought I saw something."

"Man, you're always seeing something."

The handcar moved a little farther into the blackness.

"You see that?" Stan asked, pointing at a tall shadow along the left-hand wall.

"I don't see nothing."

A noise whispered, like wind blowing dry leaves across the ground, before quiet again settled on the tunnel.

Stan moved the handcar a little closer.

"This subway-to-Hell routine you been laying on me has been kind of fun," Manny said, "but it's starting to get old. Real old."

As Stan neared the tall shadow, he felt that familiar itchy sensation wash over him.

The handcar creaked closer.

Something was up there.

Something huge.

Stan played his light along the wall, trying to take in what he saw.

He couldn't.

In front of them was a tilted cross made of railroad ties—with a derelict crucified on it. Spike nails held what was left of the man on the heavy wooden frame. Something with lots of teeth had been chewing on him and now the rats were taking their turn. That was where the rustling sound had come from: the rats crawling around what was left of the corpse.

Everything was covered with blood and that accounted for the acrid coppery smell, but beneath that, barely detectable, was another odor. One that Stan was familiar with. It was the odor of the creatures.

Manny was the first to speak, his voice dropping to a whisper. "What kind of sick son of a bitch would do something like this?"

"Someone who's trying to open up some new doors," Stan answered.

Manny raised his voice several notches. "You're talking about doors when we got a psycho running around loose down here killing people?" He reached in his coat pocket and came out with a .357 Magnum Colt Python, prepared to shoot at the first sign of movement.

Stan eyed the huge handgun.

"This is for any *human* assholes we see down here," Manny said. "Don't be laying no more of your crazy shit on me. I ain't in the mood."

Stan started to turn away when something caught his eye. Squinting in the dim light, he tried to see what was on the other side of the tracks.

A painting.

The right-hand tunnel wall had been painted into a mural that stretched out more than a hundred feet, disappearing into the dark.

"Hand me your flashlight," Stan said.

In the dim light they studied the painting, fascinated by the terrible power and beauty of what they saw. The images were so realistic they felt as though they could reach out and touch the passengers of the train. And the creatures who drove it.

There were crude slashes of red, the strange letters that Stan had seen on the first painting. He could make no sense of what they were trying to say. Only this time he knew what the letters were written in.

Blood.

"What do those words mean?" Manny asked.

"I think they mean," Stan said softly, "that we've been invited to the grand opening of a new spur to Hell."

"No no no, man, don't talk like that. Don't go talking that crazy stuff about Hell." His voice sounded desperate. "We just got a psycho who killed a wino, that's all."

"There's more to this mess than a dead wino, and you damn well know it." Stan wearily walked over to the cross. Holding the light above his head, he studied the remains of the figure nailed to the bare wood. Both men steeled themselves at the sight. It was impossible to tell how long the dead man had been there, most of the clothing had been ripped away, along with large chunks of flesh. The death was recent, though: blood was still trickling down the old man's face. The blood almost caused Stan to miss the two raw streaks that ran up to where the dead man's eyes used to be. The same streaks Stan had found under his own eyes.

"Why would anybody do something like this?" Manny asked, his face going the color of ash. "I know this guy. This is my old buddy, Max, the can man. I see him around all the time, pushing his cart. He didn't ever bother nobody."

Stan pulled Manny back to the painting, pointed. One of the creatures had blood on its mouth.

There was something more.

"Tell me I ain't seeing this," Manny begged.

Behind the creature, two familiar faces stared back.

Their own.

Stan threw some more logs in the fireplace and punched them around until they were burning well. Both men were huddled in the family room of Stan's tiny shotgun house, trying to thaw out. Manny's face was still the color of rotten eggs and his hands wouldn't quit shaking. He kept spilling his coffee.

The story about the crucified derelict was all over the TV, the result of the anonymous tip that Manny had phoned in. There was actual footage of the scene. The cameraman lovingly scanned the blood-soaked section of tunnel where the derelict had died, catching enough of the far tunnel wall that Stan and Manny could see that no trace of the painting now remained.

"Did you see that?" Stan asked. "The painting's gone."

"I don't know, man." Manny ceased his pacing. "All I know is our faces were in that painting. Whoever killed that old wino knows what we look like, where you live. We can't stay here."

"We got a bigger problem than that. The painting is gone. It ain't been painted over. The damned thing is *gone.*" Stan lapsed into silence, realizing he was never going to get Manny to see the truth no matter how many times he explained it.

Manny went over to the window and peered out. Snow was falling heavily. "We can't stay here," he repeated.

"You wanna go outside?" Stan asked. "Go ahead. This place only has five ways to get in or out." He held up his left hand and began knocking down fingers as he counted. "We got two doors, both of which have deadbolts. We got three windows, all of which have bars on 'em. This house is a lot safer than some goddamned motel room and I'm not budging."

Manny relented. "All right, all right, give it a rest. You convinced me."

Stan reached under his chair and pulled out his ever-present coat hanger, went to work in his cast. The lines in his face smoothed out in obvious enjoyment.

Manny looked on in disgust. "There ain't no kind of weird sex thing going on with you and that coat hanger, is there?" He listened as Stan grunted in satisfaction. "You were supposed to get that nasty thing off your arm three days ago." He eyed the greasy black plaster with distaste.

"Ain't had time to get to the doctor."

"You don't need no doctor. I can get that off for you."
Manny produced an six-inch switchblade, pressed a button
and the blade appeared with a soft snick.

"You're not coming near me with that thing. I saw you cut
your toenails with it."

"We're not gonna operate. I'm just gonna cut that plaster off
your arm."

"No, you ain't," Stan said. "Hand it over and I'll do it myself." He reached out and took the knife.

"Nice scar you got on your knuckles. Get that punching
your last trainee around?"

"Yeah, but Dr. Antonelli stitches me right back up."

"Weird-shaped scar," Manny commented. "Looks kind of
like a cross." He looked away, hesitated, choosing his words.
"Maybe in the morning we could go down and talk to the
cops. Tell 'em our story. Minus the crazy stuff."

"Maybe." Stan rose to his feet. "We need some more wood
for the fire."

Manny didn't move.

"What's on your mind now?" Stan asked.

Manny's laugh sounded nervous and he looked ashamed,
yet from his voice, Stan could tell he was still frightened. "It's
the way you looked when you first saw that painting. Your
face turned paler than when you saw the dead guy. Right then
I knew you weren't jiving me."

Stan picked up a poker and stabbed at the fire, even though
it was burning just fine.

A look of acceptance crossed Manny's face and he finally
nodded. "Okay, I'm not gonna say anymore about it."

They dumped the wood near the fireplace and prepared to
wait out the night, neither man saying anything. The only
sounds were the crackle of the fireplace and the hiss of the icy
rain pelting the window.

Rolling down in rivulets, endless cold rivulets.

To Stan they looked like tears of regret.

* * *

Beth had wanted the baby.

Stan hadn't.

She was too old and the doctor had advised against her trying to carry the baby to term. He had said it could kill her. Beth had fought, but her wishes were ignored, knocked aside by medical opinion and Stan's stronger will.

The baby was aborted.

Even though Beth was a devout Catholic and believed that what she was doing was a mortal sin.

She never said anything about the dead baby in the months that followed. She never complained. She never cried, at least not where Stan could see.

But something in her died.

One afternoon Beth cooked porkchops, Stan's favorite, and stuck them in the oven, got dressed in her best Sunday dress and wrote a short note that said she was sorry for being so weak. That she hoped God would forgive her.

Then she walked into the subway and jumped in front of the first train that passed.

The authorities couldn't figure out the meaning of the shredded piece of blue cloth that she'd had in her hand.

Stan knew.

It was what was left of their unborn baby's blanket.

Stan looked away from the window and into the fireplace when a log popped. The sparks made him think of the painting on the tunnel wall. A feeling of unease twisted up his guts. Something was familiar about the writing on the painting. He pictured the strange letters.

His hand itched and he looked down at his knuckle. The scar . . . something almost registered.

Stan stared at Manny on the couch and decided to let him sleep. He thought about his own son who had never been born— the doctors had told him it was a boy. Sometimes he wondered how his son would have turned out, what he would have been like. Stan shook his head, trying to push away the painful images that chased him through his empty life. There was no point thinking about the past. It only brought regret.

The itch beneath Stan's cast grew worse.

The hours drifted by. Manny continued sleeping, the huge .357 Magnum lying beside him on the couch, the tip of the barrel poking out from beneath the blanket like the head of some exotic silvered lethal snake standing guard.

Tiptoeing across the wooden floor, Stan grabbed up Manny's switchblade lying on the coffee table and silently headed for the bathroom. The cast had to come off.

He eased open the door, stepped into the dark.

And fell ten feet straight down

. . . into the subway tunnel.

And it was twilight just like he remembered in his dreams, the ground damp, filled with the odor of rot.

Of ancient sin.

Blood dripped from high overhead, falling out of the dark and striking the ground, sounding like odd, random footsteps. A feeling of utter desolation permeated the tunnel, punctuated now and then by streaks of blue lightning that crackled and crawled down the walls in their spidery fashion, leaving behind faint scratches that looked like the words that Stan had seen on the painting. There was a feeling of an impending storm, as though the very air itself was charged with some sort of energy.

The main line track stretched out, arrow straight, into the shimmering distance, shrinking to a bright pinhead of light that was so far away it defied calculation.

The tracks began vibrating as the pinhead of light grew brighter. The light caught the painting on the wall, and in it Stan saw himself. He was a bloody horror. The creatures had been feeding off him.

Stan didn't need to look at the painting to know what was in store for him. The thrumming of the track beneath his feet was unmistakable. The train was coming. The blue lightning grew in intensity, dancing over the rails, bouncing off the ceiling, and an arctic wind began blowing in his face, causing his eyes to tear.

Stan wanted to believe he was dreaming. He knew he wasn't. He looked around for the bathroom door and saw only bare tunnel wall. Overhead, a sign said "WELCOME TO NEW YORK. THANK YOU FOR RIDING THE HELL TRAIN. SUICIDES STRAIGHT AHEAD."

Several spurs branched off the main track, too far away for Stan to reach any of them in time. There wasn't enough room beside the tracks to let the train go by. The wheels would pull him under.

Gauging the distance to the nearest spur, he began limping in that direction.

The tracks were beginning to hum a little now.

He limped on.

The train lights grew steadily brighter and he could hear the metallic rattle of the train itself now, chattering like teeth in a cold mouth. A look down the tracks showed it was only fifty yards to the spur, but the distance might as well have been fifty miles. The train wasn't close enough to make out any faces yet.

The clatter grew louder.

Stan's feet sought out the slick wooden ties beneath the rails. Had to be careful here. A fall now and he would never get up in time. His knees felt like they were coming apart, grating agony each time his weight came down.

The train was almost close enough to see faces now.

A gray reptilian creature was pressed against a window in the train, yellow eyes fastened on the tracks ahead. A clawed hand grabbed one of the passengers and a scream of agony floated down the tunnel when flesh began smoldering. The long scaly tongue snaked out of the creature's mouth and roamed over its teeth, as though in anticipation.

The train whistle sounded a long thin wail.

A voice continued to scream.

Something was different, wrong. The voice was coming from the wrong direction. Stan looked back and in the distance saw Manny hotfooting it down the tracks, arms pumping, legs a blur. Stan watched in awe. He'd been right about that skinny little Puerto Rican—the son of a bitch could *run*.

Manny yelled something that the train drowned out.

Sign language followed.

Manny kept pointing at his right arm and making some kind of ripping motions.

Complete bewilderment crossed Stan's face.

More screaming, more running. Manny stopped and began hopping around on one foot, making cutting motions at his toes.

Understanding settled on Stan. He looked at the switchblade that he still carried and inserted the blade beneath the grimy plaster. He grunted with pain as the heavy knife sliced skin and plaster with equal ease.

The cast began peeling off his arm, like snake shedding its skin, revealing pale bloody flesh beneath.

And something else.

Dotting his arm were stitches. The tiny raised black threads sticking up from his skin spelled words. The words were unknown and yet familiar.

Manny sprinted the rest of the distance and grabbed hold of Stan, hanging on, his breath coming in spurts. "I recognized that scar on your knuckle. Couldn't place it." He gasped for breath. "Fell asleep. That's when it came to me. Where I seen the scar. On the painting . . . same as the words on your arm."

The train was close enough to see faces now.

Dozens of the creatures were gathered at the front of the train watching the two men on the track.

"You got to get rid of those words," Manny said. "There's no other way."

"Those words are on my arm."

"Your arm is gonna be under that train."

"I know that." Stan looked at the knife and then at his arm as he tried to work up his courage. "Damn, why did you have to trim your toenails with this thing?"

"Shit, Stanley, I cleaned it since then." He glanced once at the train. "We got about ten seconds."

Stan grimaced, hefted the switchblade and placed the razor-sharp edge just above the wrist. He sliced. A small patch of bloody skin puckered up. Stan grasped it between his thumb and the knife and jerked up in one swift motion. A strip of his skin peeled away from his wrist to his shoulder, a bright red ribbon stripped from a Christmas package. The pain went off the Richter scale.

Manny's face drained of color when he took the wet flap of skin and pulled out a cigarette lighter, began thumbing it.

Nothing happened.

"Been meanin' to get a new flint." Manny shook the lighter against his leg a couple of times, tried again. This time the flint sparked and the lighter ignited. He held the flap of skin over the flame and the skin began smoking, the sickening odor gagging the two of them.

The roar of the train was deafening. They could see sparks flying up from the wheels.

"Oh Jesus, it ain't gonna burn," Manny said.

But the skin caught fire and went up in a greasy black swirl of smoke, and the train became a shadow that gradually started fading away, the thin wail of its whistle becoming insubstantial, dying. Echoing into nothingness. The streaks of blue lightning traveled along with the train, scratching out their arcane symbols, signposts that marked the way to Hell.

The cold became unbearable. Both men felt like they had been plunged into ice water as the train swept past them. Face after face passed in front of them, too many to see, too many to comprehend. A feeling of sorrow, of regret, united the faces.

Stan stared after the train, watching the shadow dissolve.

But before it vanished completely, Stan saw one of the passengers looking back at him.

Someone he knew.

Beth. Someone was standing beside her, a small boy of about nine or so holding onto her hand, and Stan stared at him without comprehension until he realized the boy had his eyes.

His son had his eyes.

He couldn't be sure but he thought the two figures waved.

A small sad wave of good-bye.

The subway tunnel faded away and both men found themselves standing on a dark street while a snowplow ghosted by. A group of Christmas carolers passed them and someone wished them a merry Christmas.

They were a good five miles from Stan's house.

Manny was bent over, still trying to catch his breath. He finally gave it up, began heaving up his guts. When the spasms passed, he picked up a handful of snow and rubbed it against his sweaty face.

Stan looked at the oozing red strip that decorated his arm and felt his own stomach climb up into his throat. "Thanks, Manny. You did real good for somebody who hasn't believed in Hell since he was twelve."

"You're just lucky I hadda take a piss."

Stan could see beneath Manny's bravado that the younger man was still frightened out of his mind.

Stan felt his injured arm begin to burn and reached down, scooped up some snow. "I've got to get someone to look at this."

Manny straightened up. "Dr. Antonelli?"

Stan nodded. "He's the man who set my broken arm. Bastard works nights at the hospital."

* * *

To Dr. Martin Antonelli's credit, his eyes didn't widen until Stan placed the switchblade against his throat. Manny closed the door of the examining room and the three of them were alone.

"You've got ten seconds to give me one good reason why I shouldn't cut your throat," Stan said.

"I say we cut it anyway," Manny suggested.

Dr. Antonelli gazed at Stan, his pale face serene, and yet sad. He was dressed in a beautifully tailored gray wool suit and an immaculate white shirt. "Because I can do you a favor." He leaned closer, as though confiding a secret. "I know what you really want."

"Yeah, and what might that be?"

The doctor reached in his pocket and pulled out a cigarette. His hand was steady when he lit it. "I can get your wife back. You'd like that, wouldn't you, having Beth off the train?"

Stan felt like someone had kicked him hard in the stomach, leaving him unable to breathe. "Say I believe this," Stan said, "and I let you live." He pricked the doctor below the chin with the point of the knife and a trickle of blood formed roses that slowly unfurled on the white collar. "I gotta know something. Why did you choose me in the first place?"

Martin Antonelli dabbed his throat, looked at the blood on his snowy handkerchief, his calm expression unchanging. "Because the New York subway is a natural magnet for the train. Add to that the fact your wife committed suicide in the subway and you work there." He folded his handkerchief, put it away. "You were the perfect choice."

"The perfect choice for what?" Stan asked, mystified.

"To trade for my father. He was a priest with cancer, and when the pain became too much, he killed himself." For the first time the doctor's face showed emotion. "The creatures— demons, whatever you want to call them—are very hard on him because he was a priest. They torture him constantly. I hear his screams every night."

Manny moved closer, his face filled with anger. "What about Max, the can man? He was just an old wino, so why did you have to kill him?"

Antonelli ignored the question. "Would you hand me some of that antiseptic and a couple of those swabs?" He motioned at a shelf behind Manny. "That knife doesn't look very clean."

"You don't know the half of it," Manny said with a smile. "I cut my toenails with that knife." But he reluctantly tossed the stuff to the doctor.

"Answer his question." Stan pricked the doctor with the switchblade again.

"Simply a matter of speeding things up. The Hell Train has to come a great distance and I was afraid your cast would come off before it arrived." Dr. Antonelli dabbed at his bleeding throat again. "I couldn't have that. You would have recognized what the stitches meant. Besides, Max was already dead, alcohol poisoning."

"Max had teeth marks on him," Stan said. "Like something big had been at him."

"The demons who drive the Hell Train live mostly on the tears of regret. But they like a taste of human flesh now and then."

"And that's why I saw a couple of them in the subway five weeks ago." Understanding spread across Stan's face, leaving rage in its wake. "Because they stopped the train for me. They were supposed to pick me up and let your father go. That's right, isn't it?"

Martin Antonelli nodded. "I would sacrifice anyone, do anything to get my father back. You understand that, don't you, Mr. Macklin?"

Something flickered behind Stan's eyes.

"We saw a sign that said THANK YOU FOR RIDING THE HELL TRAIN," Manny said, his face alternating between fear and anger. "Is there only one of those things?"

"Not exactly," the doctor answered. "Hell is a lot like the New York subway. Lots of trains. Lots of destinations." A slight, sad smile crossed his face. "What you saw is the suicide express on the way back from a ten-year run."

"Oh man, I can't take any more of this," Manny said. "Cut this crazy motherfucker's throat and let's get out of here."

"Hold on." Stan raised his hand. "Why the painting on the subway wall?"

"What you saw isn't really a painting at all, not in the sense you understand it. It's more like a projection into our reality. The painting helps to ease their way, otherwise they would meet too much resistance." The doctor's voice had taken on a lecturing tone. "You see, they can't remain in our world for very long. Just long enough to pick up a passenger before moving on to their next destination."

"Or let a couple off," Stan added. "You said you could get Beth off that—"

"Shit, you're not gonna trust this guy!" Manny grabbed Stan by the arm. "This asshole killed Max and he was gonna trade you to those things for his father. If we leave him alive, he could come around some night and paint some more of that voodoo shit on your house."

"Your friend is right, you know," the doctor said. "The only way you will ever be safe is to kill me."

Stan pressed the point of the knife deeper, but, in the end, he couldn't bring himself to cut Martin Antonelli's throat.

A slight tremor ran through the waiting room.

"What the Christ was that?" Manny asked.

The doctor ground out his cigarette. "Nothing, they're moving some vending machines in the back."

Manny cracked the examining room door and peeked outside.

No waiting room with patients.

The all too familiar tracks stretched out into the distance. The train was on its way. And it had gotten close while the doctor had stalled them.

Very close.

Stan yanked their captive to his feet and forced him to open his clenched fist. Written on the doctor's palm with a bloody swab were the symbols that would bring the Hell Train.

"Grab the alcohol, Manny." Stan said. "Hurry. We've got to clean this stuff off his hand."

"You do," Dr. Antonelli said, "and you'll never see your wife again."

Grasping the blood-stained hand, Stan applied pressure and brought the smaller man to his knees. "Why is that, doctor? Make it the short version."

"Ten-year run . . . finishing up . . ." The pale, serene face lost all composure, twisted up in agony when Stan applied more pressure. "The train has to deliver its passengers every ten years. Today is the last day." Bones popped, sounding like dry twigs breaking. "You don't get her off today, she goes to Hell. No getting her back ever."

"You're lying," Stan said, savagely tightening his grip. Sweat drenched the injured man's face.

Stan released him.

Martin Antonelli tucked his broken hand beneath his armpit. "There's no way you can be sure, is there?"

Manny moved forward and tried to grab the knife away. "Don't believe anything this lying sack of shit says. He's bluffing."

A look of regret crossed Stan's face when he closed the switchblade and backhanded Manny across the face, driving the younger man against the wall. The blow was a powerful one. Manny crumpled into a heap.

"I hate to do this to you, kid, I really do," Stan said, sighing, "but there's no other way." He reached down, picked up Manny and carried him over to the examining table. "Hand me some of that tape, doctor."

Within seconds Manny was bound to the sturdy metal table.

The office was vibrating heavily now. The light fixtures overhead were winking off and on, and plaster was falling from the ceiling like snow. They were showered with broken glass as the fluorescent lights began shattering one after another.

The glare of the train headlights pinned them in the dark.

Manny's mouth was bleeding heavily, and when Stan bent over him, Manny spat the bloody saliva into Stan's face. "You can't do this. You can't give me to those things. I saved your ass, you son of a—"

Stan put tape over Manny's mouth, silencing him. "Sorry, kid. Can't have you trying to talk me out of this. I might listen."

The supplies on the shelf were hopping around now, crashing to the floor.

The train whistle came again.

Manny thrashed frantically back and forth, his eyes bulging with the strain, but his efforts were useless. The tape held.

"Sorry, kid," Stan said. "I don't have a lot of time to explain. I'm not gonna give you to those things, but I can't have you trying to save me again." He reached out with a huge hand and slapped Manny on the shoulder. "I didn't mean to scare the shit out of you. Well, maybe just a little bit." Stan laid the closed switchblade on his bound friend's chest. "You take care of yourself, Manny, and stop going to the dump to get your rats. It's not fair to the other guys."

Manny tried to speak through the tape. Finally he just nodded.

"Come on, doctor," Stan said. "We've got a train to catch."

Grasping Martin Antonelli by the injured hand, Stan forced the small pale man out the door and onto the track.

The door to the examining room began swinging shut behind them, forcing Manny to strain to keep the two men in sight. They were only shadows caught in the light. Moving down the tracks toward the oncoming train. Growing smaller. One limping, one holding a hand close to his side.

Going to salvation or Hell. Manny didn't know.

The examining-room door slowly swung closed and the two men vanished from sight.

All Manny could do was listen.

The vibrations ceased and yet he could still hear the muted thunder of the idling train, and he knew it had stopped.

The long thin wail of a train whistle came, followed by the sound of rising thunder as the train began gathering speed. The sound rose and then gradually faded away.

Then there was only silence.

After a while, Manny managed to cut the tape and free himself from the examining table and walk out of the small room.

No tracks on the other side of the door.

No train.

This was the week before Christmas and it was business as usual for the hospital. The staff was busy trying to save a black hooker who had slashed her wrists because her pimp wouldn't let her buy presents for her kids.

Manny thought maybe they were going to save her. That was good. There were already too many people on the Suicide Express, as Dr. Antonelli referred to it. He walked out the door and nobody paid any attention to the young man with the bloody mouth. This was New York and bloody mouths were a dime a dozen.

Manny DeCarlo walked home in the snow, feeling, in the alien whiteness, as though he had somehow set foot on the far side of the moon. Nothing was real. Somewhere in the distance, barely detectable, a freight train eased through the dark on its way to some faraway place and, when it blew the whistle, the mournful sound made him more lonely than he'd ever been since coming to the city.

Manny made two stops before reaching home.

The first stop was by the river. There he threw the bloody switchblade as far as he could. The knife slid across the ice, made a small splash when it went in.

His last tie with Stan. Gone.

The second stop was at a church. There he lit a solitary candle to Saint Christopher, the patron saint of travelers. Kneeling in the flickering shadows, Manny hoped Stan would find peace in the land of the dead.

Missing persons reports were filed on Stan Macklin and Dr. Martin Antonelli, and that was about the extent of what the police could do, since neither man's body ever showed up.

New York's finest came by Manny's place several times and asked him some questions about Stan, because the two men had worked together, but Manny kept the truth to himself.

Life went on.

So did death.

Pretty soon the cops quit coming.

Manny DeCarlo never saw Stan Macklin again, at least not in this world. Maybe he never saw him again at all.

Still . . .

One day, many years later, while working the stretch of subway beneath 125th and Lenox Avenue, Manny found an old crescent wrench jammed between two railroad ties. He jumped down, walked over. There wasn't much left of it; time and the elements had rusted most of the metal away. Still, he managed to work the wrench loose and take it home with him.

He laid the pitted chunk of metal on a nightstand next to his bed.

That night Manny dreamed he saw Stan standing at the front of a train and Manny could swear the big man was at the engine throttle. The night was cold, filled with stars, and the train was far away from any city. The smell of new-mown hay was in the air. There were no creatures around. The passengers all looked happy. A woman and a young boy were standing close to Stan, smiling, the wind whipping their hair. The boy looked a lot like Stan. They looked like a family.

Stan mouthed two words to Manny: *No regrets.*

Just before the dream ended, Stan winked at Manny and

blew the whistle. Everyone on board smiled and waved, and then the train thundered off into the night.

Maybe it was only a dream.

But if it was, it was a damned good one.